The Healer's Secret

The Healer's Secret

GIVEN HOFFMAN

ISBN: 979-8-9852244-3-6 (print)
ISBN: 979-8-9852244-4-3 (ebook)

To Kate, for believing in Gage's story from the very start and always cheering me on in my writing. You were the first person to officially meet Gage the night you helped me choose names for the characters in my castle story.

Author's Note

THERE IS SOMETHING continually intriguing about the medieval time period. I'm still not sure what exactly draws so many of us to tales of knights and nobility. Perhaps it's the battles, weapons, castles, honor, and bravery. Regardless, when Gage first began to emerge as a character, I knew he belonged in a medieval setting, so I dove into researching what it would have been like to live during that time period.

Accuracy in historical fiction has always mattered a great deal to me, and the fear that I might misrepresent real people and times in history is why I have never attempted to write historical fiction. While creating Gage's story, I allowed myself several concessions, which shifted this novel's genre from historical to simply medieval action/adventure. I wanted readers to feel as if they had truly entered into a medieval setting while still giving myself the freedom to take this story where it was going. Thus…

1. I chose to make the setting medieval but still fictitious.
2. I chose no particular historical dates but rather used details and research from the medieval age as a whole.
3. I took liberties within my fictitious setting, and at times I altered what would have been the typical religious styles, governments, laws, and so on.

These decisions allowed me to write Gage's story without being restricted by the fear of holding perfectly to history while still including many of the fascinating historical factors and elements of the period.

I hope you enjoy the medieval flavor and setting of this story.

Carson
Decoro
Nardell
Iceland
The Nixor River
Indomitas
Arcis
Keric
Cdc
Kolby
Asper
Catorre
Tenebris
Durann
Nikor Falls
Nikor Harbor
Nikor
Ivenyhan
Aro
Ulbin
Dudall
claustrom
Dinslage
Nikledon
Lemar
Lego
delmar
Awngnera
Delipp
Lyster
Legan
Dialcis
Leurt
Blakely
Maneo
The Piena River
Burnd
Ivett
Denbor
Einhart
Clement
Umbra
Delkara
Nissdin
Hallims
Weldon
Asplin
Tallus
Kelmour
Lapidus
Phenes
Koth
Ithera
Pictum
Orrim
Rush
The Apse River
Dail
Murrel
Mallely
Ogden
Platti
Milstrom
warlein
Opes
The Valens River
Salura
Supernus
Salvas
Nauta
S
W
E
N

Glossary of Terms

Barding – Hardened leather or metal armor connected to a horse's tack by laces

Caltrop – Spiked metal device with four or more spines used to cripple mounts and men

Charger – Swift, strong horse trained for battle.

Curtain Wall – Fortified wall surrounding a castle or fortress

Gauntlets – Thick leather or metal gloves

Gorget – Piece of neck armor

Keep – Fortified tower, typically within a castle or fortress

Liege – Feudal superior or sovereign, entitled to the allegiance and service of their vassal(s)

Mayhap – "Perhaps"

Palfrey – Valuable riding horse with a smooth gait

Parapet – Protective wall around the edge of a roof, bridge, balcony, or walkway

Parlour – Room where the monks conducted business with outsiders

Pell Post – Single, fixed post used as a target for practicing swordsmanship and shield work

Pommel – Round knob on the end of the handle of a sword or dagger

Portcullis – Defensive metal grid gate dropped vertically to block an entrance

Prithee – "Please"

Quintain – Post with a swinging arm that holds a shield on one side to strike and a sandbag on the other to avoid and is used in competitions and in lance training

Refectory – Room used for communal meals

Rouncy – Ordinary all-purpose horse

Sext – Midday, approximately 12:00 p.m.

Scythe – Tool with a long curved blade used for cutting grain

Surcoat – Loose, sleeveless robe that bears an insignia and is worn over a knight's armor

Tabard – Similar to a surcoat but often shorter with open sides and made of a rougher material

Tilt – Wooden barrier between jousting competitors; also, to joust

Vambrace – Piece of protective wear for the forearm made of leather or metal

Vassal – Subordinate who is granted land in exchange for service, often a knight or noble

Vespers – Time of day, traditionally at sunset or around 6:00 p.m.

Wasters – Practice sword made of wood and used in sparring

Wimple – Cloth headdress that covers the head, neck, and sides of the face

Character List

King Axel – King of Edelmar

Prince Haaken – Firstborn son of King Axel and Queen Irena

Prince Gage – Second-born son of King Axel and Queen Irena. He goes by Gabe or Gabriel when traveling as a commoner.

    Allard – Deceased son of Baron Roger of Ulbin; Gage's squire who died in the Blue Crow's attack

    Sir Wick – Youngest knight to serve in Gage's retinue, seventh son of the lord of Clement, and previous White Fortress guardsman

    Bardon – Deceased servant from Gage's retinue; died as a result of the Blue Crow's attack

King Bryant – King of Keric

Queen Vivian – Second wife of King Bryant

Princess Rhonalyn – Acting queen of Keric, only child of King Bryant

    Lady Aisley – Young lady-in-waiting to Princess Rhonalyn

    Baron Philip – Commander of Keric's Royal Guard

    Sir Nolan – Second-in-command of Keric's Royal Guard and Rhonalyn's cousin

    Sir Erwyn – (Wyn) a member of Keric's Royal Guard and Rhonalyn's cousin

King Maurice – Deceased king of Delkara

Queen Marjorie – Living Queen Mother of Delkara

King Strephon – Current king of Delkara

Prince Thayer – Deceased son of King Maurice; died in a shipwreck at age twelve

Baroness Murielle – Sister to King Strephon and wife of Baron Rayburn of Deubor

The Blue Crow – Deceased thief who attacked the lords of Edelmar and ambushed Gage

Felix – Deceased agent and thief who worked for the Unavowed

Manton – Gage's traveling companion

Lady Novia – The childhood friend of Gage and Haaken's who drowned

Baron Roger – The baron of Ulbin; the man who trained Gage to be a knight

Lord Henry – Lord of Aro, son of Baron Roger, and Allard's older brother

Lady Natriece – Daughter of Lord Gregory of Veiroot; she tips Gage off to Felix's location

Prior Joseph – Manton's friend, the prior of a monastery in Burnel

Brother Sholan – Monk who tended Gage's wounds after he was almost killed by Felix

Baron Elmon – Baron of Awnquera and Gage's uncle on his mother's side

Baron Selwin – Baron of Nikledon, son of the deceased Lord Terryn

Baron Bertram – Baron of Lyster who takes a heavy hand against rebel commoners

Lord Braxton – Lord of Verfeld, a small manor northwest of Koth

The Healer – The mysterious woman who keeps a shelter in the woods outside of Verfeld

Baron Fitch – Baron of Nissdin, the city southeast of Ithera Castle in Delkara

Baron Hewitt – Baron of Duvall, son of the deceased Baron Lucas a past friend of Baron Elmon of Awnquera

Baron Rayburn – Baron of Deubor and husband to Baroness Murielle

Carys – Untitled "touched" young woman who sits beside King Strephon

Lord Hadrian – Lord of Delipp, the city with the artesian well

Sir Jarret – The knight who marked Gage

Sir Treyson – The knight responsible for the supply entourage in which Gage was being transported as a prisoner

1

THE CLOUDS ABOVE the small clearing split apart, exposing Gage and his four companions in the moonlight. Gage shifted on his feet and gripped Athalos's reins. The remaining clouds shrouded the forest around them in darkness while the night's insects pulsed a shrill objection to his and his companions' recent arrival at the woodsman's hut. Gage's fatigued and anxious mind mulled over why Manton had brought them there.

Split logs, stacked in dark heaps, filled the air around the hut with the smell of freshly cut timber, mildewy bark, and damp moss. Though the place appeared isolated, Gage knew that woodsmen typically lived within hauling distance of whatever manor they supplied.

A manor meant a lord and lord's men. Both were guaranteed enemies to at least three members of the party, considering they had two kidnapped noblewomen with them. The peasant tenants of a manor could go either way. So, why would Manton risk coming to such a spot? Uncertainty prickled Gage's spine. What was Manton's plan?

Athalos sidestepped. A stick cracked under the horse's hoof. The cloak-wrapped noble girl standing with Sir Wick squeaked in response, and in front of Gage, the similarly cloaked noblewoman jumped. Gage's own heart lurched, then settled into a fast thumping. At the hut's door, even Manton paused. Then, leaning back toward the woodsman, Manton resumed their conversation in low, hurried tones.

The longer Gage stood there, unable to discern the two men's words over the drone of insects and the chatter of night animals, the more his limited trust in Manton fractured.

While fleeing the soldiers after the attack in the meadow, Gage had contained his fears by focusing on getting to wherever Manton was leading them. But that was when he had believed Manton would take them someplace with real protection, or at least adequate concealment. This place provided neither.

Gage's mind spun with worry while sweat slid down his sides. If the traitorous soldiers found their trail and caught up with them, the five of them would be killed within moments. Gage glanced over his shoulder. How long did they have before the soldiers tracked them there? He considered his and his companions' swift descent from the game trail and the stinging reminders on his sweaty body of the numerous branches they had broken and bent while fleeing through the forest afterward. In daylight, anyone with eyes would be able to follow their trail. In moonlight, an experienced tracker could do so with equal swiftness.

Swatting at the insects buzzing near his ears, Gage glanced up at the moon. Thankfully, its bright orb was still high in the sky and dimmed by drifting clouds. They had half the night left. If they kept moving—this time with more caution—maybe they could stay ahead of the soldiers and any tracker.

Exhaustion swept through him at the thought, along with a new fear. What if the soldiers used dogs to search for them? The stench of Athalos's horseflesh and the smell of his own hot, unwashed body rankled his nose. No matter how cautious they were, the five of them and their mounts would leave an easy scent trail for hounds. He shuddered at the thought and winced at the pain it caused. His haphazard and unarmored joust in the meadow, the fistfight he'd had with

Manton in the barn before that, and his experiences days prior being dragged along in the custody of the Nikledon soldiers were abuses his body would not soon forget.

The injuries served as a sharp reminder of why they couldn't get caught by the soldiers following them or by loyal lord's men. The consequences either way for him, Sir Wick, and Manton could be fatal, and when it came to the traitorous soldiers after them, he didn't have to speculate. The soldiers would no doubt carry out their original plan—kill the two noblewomen, then blame their murders on Gage and his companions, and likely hang them on the spot.

A new layer of raw fear prickled down Gage's spine. He glanced at the cloak-wrapped noblewoman before him. He had naively thought saving her and the noble girl from the meadow would be the impossible part of their rescue. No thought had he given to what would happen after or of how far either side might go to get the two of them back.

On their ride there, the noblewoman had demanded to be returned to Dinslage where her guard was, but Manton had said if she returned there the soldiers would find her and kill her.

With everything Gage had witnessed earlier that night, he believed Manton about the risk. But now that he was staring at a woodsman's hut, he wasn't so sure Manton's own goal was solely about the women's safety.

The hushed conversation between Manton and the woodsman paused once more. In the flickering flame of the woodsman's candle, Gage watched the man's eyes widen, then shift to take in the noblewoman.

Manton's tone increased in urgency, and this time Gage caught his words. "Decide now, for we've no time to spare."

"I serve the same cause as you," the woodsman replied.

"Then I'll count on you." Relief was evident in Manton's response.

Gage's stomach knotted, and his concerns about Manton's intentions felt all the more justified. Had he and Sir Wick rescued two noblemen's daughters, or had they just helped Manton and his rebel friends finish kidnapping them? The fact that he wasn't sure made more heat rush through him. He wasn't going to be used by the rebels, not again. He eased toward the noblewoman. He didn't have a plan, but he figured whatever happened next would determine his choices.

The moon breached another set of clouds and cast them all in a silver light. Gage glanced over his shoulder at Sir Wick. The knight stood with one hand gripping his horse's bridle and the other resting on his sword's hilt. Gage returned his gaze to the two rebels, hoping that Sir Wick would note the concern in his voice. "What're you doing, Manton?"

Manton turned to face him. "I'm getting us help."

Picturing Manton's rebel friends gathering to ambush the soldiers as they came to the hut, Gage gritted his teeth. "Help for what?"

"To hide, of course. By morning the soldiers will have checked every building in or within reach of this forest, and by midday they'll have searched these woods. Our only hope of not being found is to shelter someplace they won't search. That requires the aid of someone who knows this area better than anyone else."

The noblewoman shifted forward. "Your people promised I'd" —a tremor ran through her voice— "be returned to my guard by morning."

"Yeah, well, if you haven't noticed," Manton replied, "things changed. Those soldiers want us and you dead. Therefore, you're going to follow my friend. And if we're fortunate and very careful, perhaps we'll all still be alive by tomorrow." Manton's tone turned icy with sarcasm. "Unless, of course, you think they'll stay their murderous blades long enough for you to talk them into not killing you. In which case, by all means, take the road back to Dinslage."

"Don't treat her like a fool, Manton," Gage snapped. "After all, you're the ones who put her in this situation."

"Oh, well, forgive me then, Your Royal Highness, for spending my efforts trying to keep us alive rather than leading the way back to Dinslage."

At Manton's use of his royal title, a cold wave of shock swept through Gage and smashed aside his concerns for the noblewomen. How did Manton know who he was? He thought back to anything that could have given him away. Discordant thoughts and a bombardment of emotions spiraled through him. The colliding possibilities led him everywhere and nowhere. His swirling questions dissolved into a pool of fear that rippled with dread. Had Manton known who he was all this time? Was this a trap for *him*?

Whether or not it was, he had only one choice left. He tried to pull the noblewoman away from Manton. "Stay close to me," he said as he reached for his knife.

Her elbow slammed into his stomach, causing his lungs to refuse to inhale. She shoved away from him. "Don't touch me, peasant!"

Gage grunted, struggling to breathe.

Behind him, Sir Wick's sword made a soft *shiiing* as he drew it from its scabbard.

"No!" the noble girl cried out. "Don't hurt her!" The child flew past Gage and flung her small, dark form in front of the noblewoman. "She didn't mean any harm." The girl pleaded, "Please, Princess Rhonalyn, tell them you didn't mean any harm."

"Princess Rhonalyn!" Gage stared at the older of the two cloaked girls. She was a royal? He blinked. Manton hadn't been referring to him. A wash of relief doused his panic, but then the realization of what the woman's royal status meant caused a new flood of alarm to rush through him. He had met King Strephon and Prince Thayer's only sister years ago, and her name had not been Rhonalyn. That meant they were on the run with a kidnapped princess from Keric or some other kingdom. Regardless of where she came from, he was a marked man, and she a kidnapped royal. If discovered by any lord's men, he and Sir Wick would bear the cost of the rebels' crime.

"She's right," Rhonalyn said, her voice shaking. "I didn't mean any harm. Please lower your weapon."

"I wasn't raising it against you, Your Royal Highness," Sir Wick said, anger trailing through his voice.

"Would everyone just calm down, already?" Manton said. "Gabriel, tell your friend to lower his weapon. You and he saved them once. Don't be fools now and risk their lives by trying to flee on your own."

"Fools?" Gage hurled the word at Manton. "You're one to talk. You—"

"Berate me later," Manton interrupted. "Right now, you're gonna have to accept that I know what I'm doing. If you want everyone to be safe, follow the woodsman."

"Gabe, as much as I'm loath to admit it, he's right," Sir Wick said. "We have a common enemy to evade. The rest can wait."

Gage heaved a breath. The next catastrophe always kept him from getting justice. "Fine. For now we go on." He gripped his horse's reins and muttered, "But this isn't over."

☙❧

RHONALYN STOOD THERE with her empty hands turning cold and her pounding heart shaking her body. They were making decisions without her input or her permission, and she didn't trust any of them.

Gabe's pushy, impulsive actions were less than reassuring, and at the moment Manton's power and callousness were threats she didn't dare attempt to navigate.

As much as both men terrified her, though, at least they weren't trying to kill her. A third option had presented itself when she realized they were near a manor, but when she considered running for its door, she was reminded of her position. Even though the two sets of commoners were her saviors and current protectors, they were also her captors. They wouldn't let her seek out a Delkaran lord's help, not when they still wanted something from her. She placed a hand on Aisley's shoulder and forced herself to breathe. There was little she could do but yield to their decisions and wait for a chance to escape back to her guard.

She yearned to know who the rogue soldiers were, why they wanted her dead, what each group of men wanted, and what issues Gabriel and Manton had with each other, but she held her tongue. Having the two men at odds with each other was dangerous enough. She had no wish to turn their combined frustration upon herself.

She smacked at an insect biting her hand, then clawed her fingers into her dress to keep her tension and frustration bottled inside.

Manton, it seemed, had won the delicate balance of power tottering between him and Gabe. Probably because he had a plan, whereas Gabriel clearly did not. She swished at more insects, fear tingling in her stomach as she wondered what would happen when the four men no longer had a common enemy. Would their disagreement escalate to an actual fight? If so, in whose hands would she and Aisley end up? And to what end? Manton clearly had his own goals, and though Gabriel spouted words of honor, would he live up to them?

"It'll take me a moment," the woodsman said, his voice gruff, "to gather what I need, but then we should get moving. The place I have in mind is a good distance from here. Put the women on the same horse. I'll lead their mount. The rest of you can follow." With that, he disappeared inside his hut.

In the moonlight, Manton headed toward Rhonalyn. "I'll help the two of you remount."

She jerked away, pulling Aisley with her. "We can mount on our own, thank you very much."

Manton seized the horse's reins. "Oh, I see. I'm allowed to kill for you, but how dare I help Her Royal Highness climb on her horse?"

Rhonalyn's mind returned her to the meadow and how Manton had smashed his own mount into the soldier's horse, then fought and stabbed the soldier to save her. Her stomach flip-flopped at the reminder, and yet anger caused her cold fingers to curl. Manton had saved her, but if his people hadn't poisoned her guard and stolen her from her inn in Dinslage, she wouldn't have needed his help at all.

"Princess Rhonalyn," Aisley said in the noblemen's tongue in her small voice, "are we to mount or not?"

Trembling, Rhonalyn gathered up her skirt and dark cloak. She wanted to snatch the reins out of Manton's hand. Instead, she swept herself up into the horse's saddle, thankful she was wearing a dress designed for riding astride and not one for the side-seat Vivian often chose. She glared at Manton in the dark while removing her foot from the closest stirrup, so that Aisley could use it to follow her up. Being shorter than Rhonalyn, the child managed to get her foot in the stirrup but couldn't quite stretch far enough to swing herself up behind the saddle.

Having just refused Manton's help, Rhonalyn had no choice but to help the child herself. Grabbing Aisley's arm, she tried to pull her onto the horse. There was a great deal of scrambling on Aisley's part—and more than a little concern on Rhonalyn's part that they'd both end up on the ground—but Aisley managed to squirm her cloak-wrapped form up behind her. Straightening, Rhonalyn exhaled.

"You all ready?" There was amusement in Manton's voice.

Thankful for the darkness, for she was certain her face was red, Rhonalyn forced a syrupy sweetness into her voice. "Yes, we are."

The woodsman emerged from his hut with a lit, shielded lantern, two axes shoved in his belt, and a satchel slung over his shoulders. "You two," he said to Gabe and his companion as they mounted, "stay close and stay quiet." He took Rhonalyn's horse's reins from Manton and tugged the animal into motion.

Insects stirred around them, and twigs snapped under their horses' hooves as the woodsman led them around his hut and toward a gap in the trees. Soon, soft thudding replaced the crack of sticks. The change in ground debris was also accompanied by the absence of any branches within reach of horse height. The limbs appeared to have all been chopped off and taken away, leaving their path unhindered.

Clutching the saddle with one hand and waving away insects with the other, Rhonalyn swayed with her horse's stride. She hated having no control of the animal. She considered the woodsman's heavyset form in front of her. His solid, muscular outline was easy to see against the chevron of lantern light illuminating a swath of forest before him. She pictured him swinging one of his axes at a tree and decided she would not want to dismount and attempt to run from the man.

The woodsman moved confidently and quietly as he led their small company through the woods. The scent of pine overtook the smell of wet moss, and for a moment Rhonalyn could have sworn she smelled woodsmoke in the air. To their left, an owl hooted, and in that same direction, she thought she saw the square forms of buildings. In the shifting shadows of the clouds passing between them and the moon, it was impossible to be sure of anything. She sat straighter and peered harder. What if it was the manor where the woodsman served?

If she screamed, would help come? She considered the question long and hard, and ultimately the idea suffered a slow, depressing death. She had no way of knowing if it was a manor house. And even if screaming did alert someone to her presence, by the time anyone sought the source of the cry, she would have been silenced and dragged away by the woodsman's strong hands. So she let the opportunity pass.

Branches encroached once more on their path, and she had to use both arms to ward off the prickly boughs. She felt Aisley duck and press close against her back. Branch after branch scraped over them. Closing her eyes, Rhonalyn wrapped her arms over her head and was just about to protest the onslaught when the trees receded. She opened her eyes and saw by the woodsman's lantern that they had emerged into a long meadow. He led them along its edge, near the trees but not in them.

Rhonalyn breathed easier at the lack of branches and relaxed. Within moments her weariness and the horse's even stride caused her eyelids to drift closed. Her mind was arguing with her body about the foolishness of letting her exhaustion take over when the splashing of water jerked her awake.

Her horse was standing in the middle of a silvery stream. The woodsman's light shone for a moment across the water to the opposite shore, then the man extinguished the lantern. With only moonlight illuminating the way, the woodsman forsook the forest and tugged her horse upstream.

Rhonalyn gasped as the animal haphazardly splashed after the man. The woodsman walked against the current, water rolling against his boots like it was not at all odd to use a stream like a road. Rhonalyn curled her toes in her leather boots, thankful not to be touching the dark water. Behind her, she heard the splashing of the other horses entering the water, followed by heavy breathing. She wanted to look back, but with her horse stumbling over hidden rocks, she didn't dare.

As they trekked along, the stream widened, its surface broken by jutting rocks and tree limbs that groped outward from the shore. The water gurgled around the obstacles in silvery trails, and in the moonlight, bugs swarmed above the swells in columns.

The woodsman adjusted his course and veered closer to the left shore. The rising water flowed nearer to Rhonalyn's feet, and the woodsman's movements made it clear he was choosing his way carefully. He would reach out a leg, shuffle it about until he seemed satisfied, take a step, then pause, and repeat the process.

"Where's Manton?" Gabe's companion asked, his voice sharp.

Rhonalyn twisted around and felt Aisley do the same. Behind them, two horses with riders stood in the moonlight, water rippling around their legs. There was no sign of anyone else.

Gabriel look behind as well. "I thought he was following us."

"I've not seen him since a little while after we left the woodsman's hut," his companion replied.

Breathing heavily, Gabe urged his horse forward. "Woodsman, where is Manton?"

Rhonalyn turned back to face the man.

With the dark water heaped around his knees, the woodsman answered in his gruff voice, "Once Manton knew Her Royal Highness was safely on her way, he went back."

"Back where?" Gabe asked.

"To the meadow."

"What?" Alarm and what sounded like fury mixed in Gabe's voice. "Why would he do that?"

"That's his concern. Mine's to get Keric's princess somewhere safe."

Gabriel's companion rode forward as Gabe lifted his reins, preparing to turn his horse around. "Gabe, it's too late to go after him. He's long gone."

Even over the stream's gurgling current, Rhonalyn could hear Gabe's angry response. She didn't understand why Manton's absence upset him or why he would want to go after him. Frankly, she was relieved to have Manton gone, but by Gabe's frustration she had a feeling Manton had just made their situation worse.

"Wick, if he gets caught by the soldiers, they'll kill him." Gabe heaved a breath. "And even if he doesn't get caught…"

"I know," Wick replied, "but there's nothing we can do about that now."

"Woodsman," Gabriel said, "why'd you let him go?"

The man shrugged in the moonlight. "Manton makes his own choices." With that the woodsman tugged Rhonalyn's horse around a large rock.

She dug her fingernails into the saddle as the animal twisted to follow him. She wished like Manton she too could slip away, but she had no better option than to let the woodsman take her where the soldiers would not find her. She exhaled an angry, shuddering breath. She was tethered to the man not just by her horse's reins but also by her need of him.

2

WICK KEPT AN eye on Prince Gage long enough to be certain he would stick to their current course. He knew Manton's absence was a major problem, especially considering what Prince Gage needed from him. Much of the information they required to set right Prince Gage's marking was in Manton's possession, but there wasn't any point stewing about that. They had more pressing concerns. He returned his attention to the forest beyond the water's edges. He understood and embraced the woodsman's choice to use the rocky stream. It would mask their hoof prints and carry away their scent. The part Wick did not like was that while traveling the widening expanse of water they were left plainly visible in the moonlight.

Watching for movement in the woods, Wick kept a hand ready to draw his sword but wished he also had a bow and quiver full of arrows that could reach farther.

Gage asked in a low, unsteady tone. "How much longer do you think we'll be traveling in this stream?"

His wavering tone stirred concern in Wick. Was His Highness unwell again? He was about to ask, but a series of loud splashes upstream stopped him. There was no mistaking the sound of a large group entering the water. A surge of panic and reckless determination filled Wick. He closed his fingers around his sword's hilt, and despite a twinge of pain in his arm where earlier that night he'd been cut by a soldier's blade, he prepared to draw his weapon.

The woodsman paused midstream and forcefully gestured at them to stop moving and stay quiet.

Wick frowned. How would staying where they were help? Any moment now whoever was upstream would see them. Though agitated and uneasy, he forced himself to obey the man and wait, hoping that perhaps he had misjudged the distance and somehow the woodsman knew whoever was upstream wouldn't spot them.

Wick flinched. He hadn't misjudged the distance. Dark, bulky forms waded into view. When he saw them, though, Wick understood why the woodsman had urged them to stay still. It wasn't soldiers; it was wild boars. Their stocky bodies—reaching up to a horse's chest—crashed through the water on short legs.

Wick held his breath. The hogs' huge, wiry backs moved up and down as they trotted across the stream toward the opposite shore. Several slowed to drink. As one did so, it lifted its head and looked their way. Water dripped off its curved tusks, which could kill humans and horses alike.

As the youngest of seven sons, Wick had only been brought on a few boar hunts, but he remembered the men who hunted boar regularly saying that the animal's eyesight was far less keen than their sense of smell or hearing. Wick desperately hoped that was true.

It must have been, for the boar lowered its head and continued drinking. Meanwhile, the first few creatures snorted their way out of the stream and smashed back into the foliage on the opposite shore like they had no idea five humans and three horses were staring at them from downstream. Wick exhaled and drew a shallow breath. The moment he did, he recoiled at the stench that hit him. It was worse than a wet dog that had rolled in the city's rubbish heap. One of the girls gagged, but thankfully, none of the boars seemed to notice. Holding his breath, Wick cast a grateful prayer to God that they were the ones smelling the hogs instead of the other way around.

The final boar scrambled onto the shore and disappeared into the woods after the others. It wasn't until all sound of the hogs was gone, that the woodsman continued wading forward. Urging his horse on while swatting at the bugs stirred up by their movement, Wick relaxed his grip on his weapon but remained vigilant to any more unwanted company.

As they continued their trek through the water, the sound of the current began to build. The stream's depth hadn't really changed, but the water was moving faster. It sprayed off the rocks and made the air smell like green slime.

Maneuvering around rocks and roots became increasingly difficult, and their mounts struggled to find footing. Wick's horse tripped twice, and beside him Prince Gage's horse lunged forward on three legs as if it had caught or injured a foot. It landed on all four hooves like a colt trying to find its balance. By its next step the horse looked to have sorted itself out, but instead of moving forward, it twisted its head from side to side as if fighting the reins. Wick frowned but then realized His Highness was restraining the animal. Something was amiss, Wick urged his own horse as close as he dared to His Highness's temperamental and often aggressive mount. He could hear Prince Gage's labored breathing.

"Are you alright?" Wick asked.

Vexation edged Prince Gage's voice. "I'd be a lot better if he'd get us out of this water."

Of course, the water. During his first months with Prince Gage's retinue, Wick remembered Sir Brent informing him that His Highness had a strong dislike for moving water. The information had not surprised Wick, considering most of Edelmar knew their king's second-born son had almost drowned in the Apse River as a boy. With so much else on his mind, Wick had forgotten Prince Gage's history. He tried to sound reassuring. "Your horse will find its way. And even if it were to lose its footing, the water's not deep."

"For now," Prince Gage replied, "but how much farther will we go?"

"I don't know," Wick said, "but the woodsman's on foot. He won't be able to navigate anything much deeper than this."

A good bit later Wick's words remained true, but he too wondered how far upstream the man would take them, especially since the water was beginning to sound less like it was crashing around rocks and more like it was pouring over ledges. With the cascading sound out in front of them, they came to a portion of the watercourse that broadened. On the far left it disappeared into what appeared to be an expansive wetland. Meanwhile, the center of the stream smoothed into low curls, and to the right it rippled through rocks and sand along the base of a steep earthen incline.

"We're almost there," the woodsman said over the rushing water as he kept to the right. "Stay close to the edge. It drops off in the center."

In the moonlight, Wick saw Prince Gage shudder in response to the man's words. His Highness reined his horse as close to the earthen incline as possible.

With his own foot bumping the root-entwined wall and his other foot pointed out at the smooth, fast moving water, Wick was also leery of accidentally venturing into its depths. Lined up nose to tail, their horses splashed along behind the woodsman. Upstream, the glistening whitewater created by a series of short waterfalls became visible just as the woodsman reached the end of the earthen cliff. Turning behind it, the man disappeared from sight. The girls swung around the corner after him.

Prince Gage pulled his horse to a stop but then seemed to muster his courage and turned the corner as well. Wick followed and found that their path wrapped along the back edge of the cliff. From there it led to a long beach tucked within a cavernous-like area eroded from the base of the earthen cliff that rose above it. If one stood above, they would look down at only water, the beach completely hidden below their feet.

The woodsman drew the girls' horse up onto the sand, half of which was lit by the descending moon, and helped the younger girl off the horse. Prince Gage followed them out of the water, and Wick urged his own horse onto the dry ground under the high earthen ceiling. He was surprised to find the sound of the water lessened within the hollow space rather than being amplified by it.

Princess Rhonalyn and Prince Gage both dismounted, and Wick did the same. He landed in the deep, loose sand. The pain in his arm spiked at the impact and then settled to a dull ache. Beside him, Prince Gage exhaled a sigh. Wick shared his relief at being out of the stream and no longer on the move.

"You should be well hidden here," the woodsman said. "This spot can't be seen from above, and no one ventures through the wetland across from here. The only way to discover this spot is to travel up to it the way we just came, and no one journeys this section because of the impassable falls upstream. Even I, who've inhabited these woods all my life and traveled in and across this stream countless times, didn't know this spot was here until a fortunate accident two years ago.

"An accident?" Prince Gage said.

"During a hunt my lord's favorite hat blew off and fell in the stream, which carried it away. I was commanded to retrieve it. It went through the falls and caught in a shrub out there." He pointed toward the edge of the wetland. "To reach it, I had to circle around and come up the stream like we just did, which is when, to my surprise, I came upon this spot. I've shown it to no one else and have never found a trace of anyone being here. If you stay here out of sight, you should be safe. When the way is clear, I'll bring word."

Concern crashed through Wick. "Wait, you're leaving?"

"Of course," the woodsman said. "I must return to my place, or questions will be asked. If suspicion falls upon me, I'll be of no more help to you. It's likely the soldiers will expect local woodsmen to aid them in their search. Best if I'm there to steer them away from this spot rather than my absence causing them to wonder if I had a hand in hiding you."

Wick couldn't argue against the man's reasoning, but as the woodsman splashed back into the water, Wick felt a rush of apprehension. With the woodsman gone, he would be left as the sole guardian of a noble and two royals. As the woodsman waded out of sight, a fear-laced panic and overwhelming weariness crept through Wick. Drawing deep breaths, he forced himself to resist its encroachment and turned instead to His Highness.

"What now?" he asked Prince Gage over the noise of the moving water.

"I supposed we make camp. What other choice do we have?"

Wick shook his head. "None that I can see."

"Then we settle here for the night."

Wick dismounted and untied his saddlebags. "At least this spot's dry and cheap," he joked cheerfully.

"You dare jest at a time like this?" Princess Rhonalyn snapped. "There's nothing amusing about any of this!"

Wick faced her and her little companion. "Forgive me, Your Royal Highness," he replied in the same calm, even tone he had used with Commander Hedrick of the White Fortress. "I wasn't suggesting amusement at the night's events. I was simply appreciating the place being cheap and dry since this isn't exactly the first time we've been in this sort of situation. A fact you may find reassuring."

"Reassuring? Really?" She sounded even angrier as she swatted at insects. "So, you've hidden from soldiers in the forest with a kidnapped princess before, have you?"

Wick had meant the part about camping in the woods, but ironically, her comparison wasn't far off. He kept himself from glancing at Prince Gage. "Well, no. Not exactly."

"Then really," she snapped at him, "there's nothing I'd find reassuring about your words except that you don't typically make a habit of kidnapping princesses. So, perhaps you sh—"

"We weren't the ones who kidnapped you," Prince Gage interrupted with surprising force. "And you had best not forget that." He tugged loose his horse's cinch strap and said over his shoulder, "You'd also do well to mind your tone, for we're not your servants."

There was a long moment filled with only the sound of the moving water, buzzing insects, and distant frogs. "No, clearly you're not," Princess Rhonalyn said, her tone less belligerent but holding the same bite. "Rather, you're acquainted with my kidnappers and willingly do as they say."

Prince Gage's saddle and saddlebags hit the sand with a thud, and his voice jabbed at her like an accusing finger. "We're currently in the same predicament as you *because* we helped you. We could've left you to be killed by those soldiers and gone on our merry way. But we didn't. We came to your aid. Therefore, you might try to show at least a hint of gratitude."

Wick held his breath. He feared what Prince Gage might reveal if Princess Rhonalyn continued to respond as if they were rebel sympathizers. At the same time, he wondered if His Highness declaring their titles might actually help in their current situation.

Considering Prince Gage's mark, though, and the fact that they themselves were wanted by at least two Delkaran lords, the tradeoff may not be worth the possible risk. Better for Prince Gage to remain unidentified and unable to be betrayed by her, intentionally or unintentionally. But did His Highness feel the same way?

"If you think I owe you my gratitude for your aid," Princess Rhonalyn said in a controlled tone, "then tell me, are we your prisoners?"

Wick blinked in surprise.

"Prisoners?" Prince Gage sounded startled but also frustrated. "Is that what you think of us? That you've been traded from one set of kidnappers to another?"

At her silence, Wick cringed. Apparently, that was exactly what she'd thought. Not only had she and her young companion been stolen from her guard by rebels and almost killed by soldiers, the two girls had also been dragged by them to this secluded spot with no idea of what would happen once they got there. Wick felt an abundance of sympathy toward her.

Prince Gage, on the other hand, sounded annoyed. "Really? That's what you thought?"

"What else was she supposed to think, Gabe?" Wick said, coming to her defense. "She doesn't know us. And we didn't exactly disclose our intentions."

His Highness growled, "I'd have thought my opinion on your kidnappings was made clear back in the barn."

Princess Rhonalyn sniffed. "Oh, I heard your disdain for Manton and his companion's actions, but that was before you knew me to be crown princess of Keric."

"Ah, I see," Prince Gage said in a knowing yet angry tone. "You assumed us hearing that you were royalty might've changed our minds. That perhaps we'd consider it worth sacrificing our honor to take you ourselves and trade you for a ransom. Is that it?"

Princess Rhonalyn drew her young companion closer. "So, the thought has crossed your mind."

"Yes,"—frustration tightened Prince Gage's voice—"it crossed my mind that a ransom may've been what the rebels wanted, but that's not my intention, nor is it Wick's. And to answer your question, no, you're not our prisoners. Leave if you wish. We won't stop you. But as much as I'd question Manton's motives, I believe he's correct. If you attempt to return to Dinslage now, you'll likely be killed before reaching your guard. Therefore, I'd suggest staying here for your own well-being, but that's up to you."

Princess Rhonalyn eyed him as if weighing his words. "If you're not seeking a ransom, then why help us?"

Prince Gage turned back to his horse. "Because if we hadn't, you'd be dead."

3

Swallowing hard, Rhonalyn stared at Gabe's back. She wished she could believe that their intentions were honorable, but two random commoners didn't risk their lives to rescue complete strangers. There had to be more to it. "Are you hoping for a reward then?" She slapped at an insect. "Is that why you helped us?"

Gathering his horse's reins, Gabe answered forcefully. "No."

"We helped you," Wick said slowly as if hesitant to expound where Gabriel wouldn't, "because it was the right thing to do. Those soldiers intended to murder the two of you and the rebels. And though Manton and his companions ought to face justice, murder isn't that."

Rhonalyn frowned. "You speak as if you'd stand against Manton and his people, yet clearly, you're both well acquainted with them."

"Yes, I'm acquainted with them," Gabe replied icily. "But now so are you. Does knowing them make you one of them? Do you now agree with their cause simply because you've spent time in their company?"

She crossed her arms. "Of course not."

"Then you have your answer." Clicking to his horse, Gabe led the animal toward the back of the overhanging cliff and tied its reins to protruding tree roots.

Rhonalyn glanced from Gabe's dark form to Wick. She realized she had reached the extent of Gabriel's explanation, and despite Wick's forthrightness a moment before, it seemed he too had reached the conclusion of what he was willing to communicate.

Unfolding her arms, Rhonalyn pressed her right hand into the folds of her skirt. Her fingers found the hard edge of the coin concealed beneath. As she coiled her hand around the gold piece, she thought about her mother's quiet ambition, her father's foolish leadership choices, and the thieves who had brazenly stolen the gold. She recalled the agreement she had made with King Strephon to reopen trade between their people and to root out the criminals plaguing their mutual border. Had that been what led to all of this?

Were the rebels trying to stop her alliance with Strephon to protect themselves from being rooted out? Or had they taken her for some other reason? Who were the soldiers who wanted her dead? And why?

Could it really be that Wick and Gabe were truly just honorable men who had risked their lives to save her? She doubted it, but for the time being it seemed that was the only explanation she would receive.

She had only ever been protected by those who owed her their loyalty because they had sworn to serve her in exchange for what she could give them. To be in a position of having to trust two total strangers who had no loyalty to her and who owed her nothing was not at all comforting.

"Princess Rhonalyn, are we to stay the night here?" Aisley asked timidly in the noblemen's tongue.

Glancing at the sand that stretched to the dark, cavernous embankments beyond, Rhonalyn shuddered.

Gabriel returned and took hold of the horse she and Aisley had ridden. "Well, Your Royal Highness," he questioned in the commoners' tongue, "will you stay or will you go?"

Anger stirred within Rhonalyn. "You know I've no idea where I am or how to get back to Dinslage."

"Neither do the two of us. I wasn't asking if you want to return to Dinslage. I was saying that whether you stay or go, it must be your choice."

Her skin crawling, Rhonalyn tugged the dark commoner's cloak closer about herself. "I'd rather not spend the night outside at all." She instantly regretted her statement, for it made her sound as vulnerable as she felt.

Gabe answered flatly, "I'm afraid in that you've no choice."

"It's already far into the night, Your Royal Highness," Wick said, sounding far more sympathetic than Gabe. "Morning will come quickly. Perhaps in the light of day the four of us can sort out where we are and the best course of action to get you back to your guard."

Rhonalyn swallowed. She appreciated Wick's kindness, but she hated that she needed it. She tried to sound more like a leader as she replied. "Is it safe to stay the night here? What about the woodsman and Manton? What happens when they return?"

For a moment neither man answered, then Gabe began stripping the saddle off the next horse. "I doubt Manton will return at all. The woodsman's another matter, but I'd say our chances of survival are better against him and his kind than the soldiers. For, unlike the soldiers, the commoners at least aren't trying to kill us. So, for now, I believe it's safer here than anywhere else we could go in these woods."

"We're hidden and protected in this spot," Wick added while untacking his own mount, "and the sand will mean fewer rocks jabbing our ribs and, hopefully, a better night's sleep."

Rhonalyn glared at the sand in abhorrence. They were to sleep on the ground?

"You two girls can have my blanket," Wick continued. "It's a warm night. My cloak'll be enough for me."

Rhonalyn knew she should be grateful, but all she wanted to do was scream her indignation at being stuck in such circumstances. She took a breath instead and mustered enough dignity not to act like a petulant, terrified child. "A blanket would be appreciated."

Wick handed her the rolled wool from his belongings while Gabriel led both animals to where he had tied his own mount. When he returned, he picked up the saddle and saddlebags, then trudged toward the cliff's base. Wick gathered his things and followed.

Holding onto Aisley and clutching Wick's blanket, Rhonalyn stayed where she was.

4

"Should I keep watch?"

Gage considered Sir Wick's murmured question as they dumped their bags and tack in the sand. "Why bother?" he said quietly. "If anyone comes, we've nowhere to go and little means by which to fight. We might as well accept the risk and all attempt to get some sleep."

"True enough, but I'll keep my sword at hand regardless."

Grunting in response, Gage settled his cloak around his shoulders and sat with his back against the cliff. Sir Wick sprawled beside him, and within moments the knight was snoring.

Gage watched the two girls in their dark cloaks move about, silhouetted by the moonlit. After a fair bit of tromping around, Princess Rhonalyn picked a section of sand a stone's throw away and spread out Sir Wick's blanket. The younger girl curled up on one side of it. Rhonalyn sat toward its center and pulled her legs under her cloak, as if determined not to sleep or let anything touch her.

Gage gritted his teeth. Because of the distraction of trying to make sure she was safe, Manton had been able to slip away. The one chance he had to prove the injustice of the brand seared into his wrist was gone. He had done what God asked and risked his safety to prevent the soldiers from murdering the girls, but instead of getting closer to regaining his own freedom, he was entangled in yet one more of the rebels' crimes. And this time, Manton hadn't just left him with stolen goods but stolen people.

Gage clenched his fingers over his right vambrace that covered the flail and crossbow seared into his skin, all because of Manton. Raw heat ignited in his chest. Even if they managed to escape the soldiers and get the girls back to Rhonalyn's guard in Dinslage, what then? Without Manton's testimony, there was no way home for him.

He'd had a plan. Find Manton. Use him to track down and detain those who had actually stolen the gold. Locate the lord who had owned the gold and whose mark he bore. Deliver Manton, Manton's testimony, and the actual thieves to the lord and gain a freedom brand from the lord and a brand of pardon from King Strephon. But without Manton, his plan was hopeless.

He knew blaming Rhonalyn for Manton's disappearance was unfair. After all, she had become entangled with the rebels just as unwillingly as he had. But that was just it. He had helped her, but it was Manton whom he needed.

For a candle's nub of time, he had believed he could redeem his identity from the title of rebel thief. Now he was burdened with yet another of the rebels' crimes, an offense that could get him and Sir Wick hanged. That is, if they weren't murdered for interfering.

Gage's stomach twisted at the thought, and sweat pooled on his skin. He glared at the two forms out on the blanket. Why did they have to be his problem? He had enough trouble to deal with already. Couldn't God have sent someone else? With Rhonalyn's title and his brand, she and he were the worst possible combination. And why did God have to dangle Manton and freedom from his mark before him, only to let both slip away the moment he was irrevocably committed to helping the girls?

A question stirred through him, demanding an honest response: what if the means to regain his freedom hadn't been a part of helping the girls?

Gage considered his indecision outside the barn. Tendrils of doubt about his full motivation crept through him. Yes, he had wanted to help the girls, but in choosing to risk his life, he had been after more than that.

The question reformed, taking an even deeper stab at him. What if rescuing the girls had been in the *opposite* direction of getting his hands on Manton? Would he have ignored Sir Wick's compulsion to ride to the girls' aid?

A tingling chill crawled over Gage. Haaken's challenge from their conversation at Awnquera surfaced in his mind. *"You doubt God's trustworthiness, but are you sure you can trust yourself?"*

The question was joined by some of Allard's last words, which twisted like a knife in Gage's chest. *"Prince Gage of Edelmar is a good man, worth following into the mud."* Gage bit his cheek until it bled. He wasn't a good man. He was selfish and apparently so intent upon solving his own problems that he had to be manipulated into fulfilling his sworn duty as a knight.

Gage squirmed at his own dishonorableness. When had he stopped being an honorable and protective knight? He pressed his fingers to his temples and closed his eyes. Had he ever really been one?

Inside him, the question cracked apart the barriers he had built around the day of Allard's death. Bitter pain poured into all the raw, unhealed places within him. Gage tried to re-contain the shame, but it was no use. Agony tightened around his lungs, rose in his throat, and pressed at the back of his eyes.

He clenched his jaw and tried to force back the sting of angry tears. But no matter how he tried, he couldn't stop the memories. Waves of shame and pain coursed through his body. He could hear again the accusations of Henry, Allard's older brother. *"He should have been protected! You should never have been allowed to train him."*

If only he *hadn't* been allowed to train Allard. Pressing a hand across his mouth, Gage coiled forward, his shoulders trembling. He had failed Allard in every possible way—as a prince, as a knight, and as a friend.

Growing up, Gage had been surrounded by either instructors, who were always pushing him to meet their grand expectations for him, or those nearer his own age who resented, revered, or feared him. Making friends under such circumstances was nearly impossible. But that had never been an issue with Allard. The day Gage had arrived to train under Baron Roger, Allard—who was barely four at the time— had for whatever reason claimed Gage as *his* friend. Having always wished for a younger brother, Gage had accepted Allard's declaration, which was fortunate since he learned later it was useless to argue with the four-year-old.

Over the years, Allard's faithful friendship and stubborn determination were traits Gage had come to appreciate most about the boy, particularly after Novia's death.

Upon recovering after nearly drowning along with Novia, Gage had been delivered back to Baron Roger's manor to continue his training. He did everything that was asked of him, but the moment he was finished each day, he would retreat to the horse field and sit alone on a stump and wait for the day to end.

Everyone else left him alone in his emptiness. But after a fortnight, five-year-old Allard took matters into his own hands. Tromping out to where Gage sat, Allard commanded him in the noblemen's tongue, "Get up. I have a list of things we are going to do."

Gage shook his head. "Mayhap some other time."

Huffing, Allard marched over and, with a mighty shove, pushed him off his stump.

Shocked by the unexpected and unacceptable action, Gage looked up at the boy and shouted angrily, "What do you think you are doing?"

Allard planted his small fists on his hips. "Getting determined. Because, I want you back."

The anger drained out of Gage, and he sighed. "I want me back too, Allard. But I have no idea how to get back."

"Well, I know how. By doing the things you used to do." Allard thrust out his small hand. "Come on. I shall show you."

Gage scoffed at the younger boy, but he took his hand anyway and allowed Allard to tug him along to participate in a list of Allard's favorite things.

Thus began the way he spent his time after training. Allard would find him on his stump, shove him off it, then they would embark on whatever plan Allard had for the last hours of the day.

Eventually, the intensity of Gage's grief faded, and his numbness disappeared as he began to feel again—the rush of jumping from barn beams into the hay pile, the downy softness of the baby hawks in Roger's mew, the shocking embrace of the cold water that Allard *accidentally* dumped on him instead of into the watering trough, the warm evening wind as they ran in the fields, arriving late for the evening meal after pretending they were errant knights on a quest, and the satisfying vibrations of a lance's shaft when he landed a perfect hit to the quintain.

It was Allard who had reminded him again and again that he was more than just the wearisomeness of his title, and it was Allard who cheered him on most in his jousting endeavors. It had felt as if Allard had always been and would always be a part of his world, kin to him by everything but blood.

But now Allard was gone. No longer there to push him out of his anger and sadness, spout words of insight, tease him, or exhort him to become a better person. Gage pressed his stinging eyes shut.

Despite all Allard's faithfulness and protection, he had failed to do the same for the boy.

Tears escaped down his cheeks. Gage swiped a hand at his face and dragged air into his lungs. Heat rushed through his body, and his stomach twisted hard. Allard shouldn't have died. Gage looked up and silently hurled his words at the cliff's underbelly. "Allard was a better person than I am, God! Why didn't You help him? Haaken, the monks, they all say You can be trusted, that You are good. But I don't see it."

Haaken's statement at Awnquera about Novia's death seeped into Gage's grief-riddled question. *"With her gone, my life was devoid of joy. I was in agony, and I had no idea how to find my way out of it. She had something that I did not have and had never had. Thus, I wanted—nay, I needed—to understand God. Because if He was why she had been able to have joy despite loss, then I needed Him too."*

Gage frowned into the darkness. How *had* Novia found peace and known joy toward God, even after her brother's death? He scrubbed his wet face against his cloak and brushed a hand under his nose. What had she known about God that he didn't?

Ever since he had acknowledged God's existence again, all Gage had felt toward Him was anger. But never had he seen Novia angry at God. She had delighted in God and had possessed such an irresistible joy for life that always filled her face with the brightest smile.

Gage's eyes burned afresh at the memory, and he blinked hard. Could understanding God better really hold answers to what had given Novia joy?

Curiosity trailed through his stomach as he flip-flopped between trepidation and vexation. Could he truly find peace in knowing God?

Agitation raced through him in response to the question, and he had to take a moment to breathe through it. He clenched his fingers and recalled Sir Wick's words during their debate about rescuing Rhonalyn and her young companion. *"It's like there's a hand pressing me forward and a compulsion inside me from God that we're supposed to go after them."*

Gage dug the heels of his boots into the sand. He understood pressure and compulsion from God, particularly amid his own losses and God's laws, but not peace and not joy. In his experience, he was a pawn kept alive to be moved and used for whatever purpose God deemed necessary. He didn't get joy from God. God was a master, demanding his obedience and compliance; that was all.

Brother Sholan's statements from their conversation on the abbey's lawn contradicted that thought, though. *"That's not God's nature. He's not underhanded, vindictive, or cruel. He is good and honorable."*

Shaking his head, Gage screamed soundlessly at the earthen ceiling. "You expect me to believe that?"

Chest aching, Gage drew a shuddering breath. He didn't believe it, and yet deep down he felt a pain-filled longing that he couldn't shake. Could he have missed something? Could God yet be the person who Haaken, Novia, and Brother Sholan said He was?

In a desperate act, he sent a plea into the darkness. "If You do care, God, if You are good, if You really do bring joy and peace, then help me know You."

He waited with a strange sort of expectancy.

Nothing came in response. Not a voice, not a thought, not even an impression. Nothing.

Every wounded place inside Gage pulsed with the loud, lonely silence of it. Angry all over again, he grabbed a handful of sand and threw it across the beach.

Instantly regretting the action, he glanced at Rhonalyn. From what he could tell, her back was to him. Exhaling in relief, Gage used his cloak to wipe the grit from between his fingers, but the sand clung to his skin. He heaved an angry breath and silently spat. "So that's it then? You don't answer my questions but demand my obedience?" His eyes stinging, he drew his cloak in around himself.

"Fine then." He glared into the dark. "I'll be your slave to repay the debt I owe. But that's all You and I are then, a master and a slave." Gage gritted his teeth and felt a fool for having hoped for anything more.

5

Gage slept fitfully and woke to the moonlight still glowing through the trees. Rhonalyn had succumbed to sleep at some point and was now lying beside Aisley. The moving water out past the sand rippled in a consistent sound that left Gage wishing he could just listen to it and drift back to sleep.

Exhausted and weary, he stared out at the night and found his mind contemplating the night's events involving the rebel commoners and traitorous soldiers.

It seemed so obvious to him now that the Blue Crow and Felix were not commoners fighting contrived injustices by taking on the nobles of Edelmar. Their weapons, their skills, even their stated agenda had all contradicted who they had pretended to be.

But since everyone except Felix from the Blue Crow's group had been defeated and hanged, there hadn't been a reason to question their identities. And at the point he had learned of others taking similar actions, an explanation had been readily available. Commoners in Delkara were attacking lords and justifying their actions by the same claims expressed by the Blue Crow. So, clearly, the Blue Crow had been one of them and Felix as well.

Gage had assumed that Felix, as a commoner, would live in hiding to avoid facing the justice he deserved. To learn instead from Lady Natriece that Felix was by no means hiding and, in fact, actively gathering a group of men whom he intended to bring back to Edelmar had been so startling that Gage had thought only of stopping him, not of how a commoner could have manipulated Lord Gregory into serving as his own private protector and host.

Felix had boasted that those he had gathered would bring Edelmar to her knees. Gage had seen for himself the truth of Manton's statement that the rebel commoners of Delkara were ill-equipped to match the lords of Delkara, which made Felix's boast toward Edelmar impossible. Unless it wasn't the rebel commoners Felix spoke of but another force, perhaps one like the company in which Gage had last encountered Felix and that which had attempted to assassinate Princess Rhonalyn.

While chained in the midst of such soldiers, Gage had believed those present had chosen not to display any coat-of-arms in order to protect themselves from being targeted by the rebel commoners, but now he wondered if the real reason was to prevent anyone from pointing back at them for their own treasonous actions.

He recalled how the soldiers' commander, Sir Treyson, had looked angry and then laughed at Gage's warning that Felix was a traitor and murderer of lords' men. Felix hadn't been a rebel commoner, helping ambush and murder the soldiers. He was a murderer for and with the soldiers.

Felix and the Blue Crow had masqueraded in Edelmar as commoners. That explained Felix's surprise and amusement when Gage threatened to expose him to a Delkaran lord as a commoner. No doubt Felix could have had dozens of Delkaran soldiers and even knights testify that he was by no means a commoner, demanding restitution from the lords as recompense for some list of injustices.

Fear twisted up Gage's spine. If he was right that the two groups of soldiers were connected, it was the soldiers responsible for those acts of treason, and by one means or another they were covering up their involvement by implicating commoners. It had been working too, until now.

Gage wondered about the three Dinslage guards who had been with the soldiers outside the barn. When sent back to report to their lord about Princess Rhonalyn being taken by the rebel commoners, had they known that the soldiers intended to murder Her Royal Highness? Or were the guardsmen of Dinslage as oblivious to the soldiers' intentions and true allegiances as Gage had been the first two times he had encountered them?

Gage scrubbed his hands down his face. Sweat dampened his grimy skin. If not for his encounter with Lady Natriece, no one else would have known about Felix's connection to Lord Gregory in Edelmar. The soldiers were willing to commit murder and treason, and at least some of them spoke the noblemen's tongue. Whoever they served could be located in any of the three kingdoms or beyond, and whatever their goal, they were far from finished.

Gage's stomach rolled. The situation wasn't about a dozen thieves or a hundred disgruntled commoners. It wasn't one treasonous lord abusing his power or one group of armed, traitorous soldiers. It was a nightmarish combination of all of it. And if there was one thing his nightmares had taught him, it was that he always lost.

His slick hands began to tremble. Surviving the Blue Crow's ambush in Edelmar had cost him Allard and Bardon, and now he and Sir Wick had stolen the soldiers' latest target right out from before their lances.

The soldiers had intended to leave no witnesses and hide their actions by blaming the rebel commoners. Now not only were he and Sir Wick witnesses, Princess Rhonalyn was still alive to tell the tale herself. The soldiers would be highly motivated to silence her and anyone who could point back to them. Gage pressed his fingers to his temples. None of them would be safe, not until the traitorous soldiers were caught.

6

A GIRL'S TERRIFIED scream jerked Gage from sleep into bright daylight. He scrambled to his feet, throwing off his cloak. Disoriented by the sandy ground, earthen ceiling, and cacophony of water around him, he stumbled over a chunk of driftwood, then oriented himself to the source of the cry.

He headed past Sir Wick. The knight was kneeling in his own cloak, blinking with sword in hand. Sir Wick's gaze scanned the beach, as if trying hard to figure out what and where the threat was.

On the girls' blanket, Rhonalyn sat arrow straight and breathing hard. A smaller, cloak-wrapped form lay sprawled beside her. No one else was in sight. Squinting in the sunlight, Gage strode toward Rhonalyn, suspecting there was no actual threat to fight.

Rhonalyn flinched at his approach, then lifted her gaze. Seeing her in full daylight with her head uncovered and the dark commoner's cloak falling off her shoulders made Gage catch his breath. She was far younger than he had realized. Her royal dress, with its conspicuous lack of jewelry, emphasized her youthful face, which was marred by fresh scrapes, and her mass of chestnut-brown hair displayed the semblance of what was once an elaborate hairstyle. When he met her turbulent gaze, he found remnants of terror and confusion.

"Are you alright?" he asked.

The lines in her forehead deepened, and then in the next second she seemed to understand why he was asking. Her shoulders rolled straight, and every bit of alarm traipsing across her face vanished. She drew her cloak back over her shoulders, lifted her chin, and answered stiffly, "I'm fine."

Sympathizing with her embarrassment at being a victim of her own mind, Gage directed his attention to Aisley. "She's a sound sleeper."

Rhonalyn's gaze fell to the child. "She's usually up before anyone else."

He shrugged. "It was a long night."

Rhonalyn's fingers grasping her cloak turned white. "Yes, it was." She glanced out toward the stream. "And now it's morning."

Gage followed her gaze. By the angle of the sun glinting off the current, it was almost past morning. His stomach growled, reminding him that he needed food.

He cringed. They all needed food. That reality dumped a cold bucket of concern over him. He and Sir Wick had some food supplies in their saddlebags, but neither of them had planned on camping again so soon. Nor had they expected to need to feed extra people. He glanced at the horses and groaned. Their guests weren't the only stomachs he had forgotten.

They had no fodder for the horses. He had tied them up the night before without any thought to hay. Their hiding spot offered plenty of water but nothing else edible for the animals. The horses needed to graze, but hobbling them in the woods beyond their refuge would be foolish with the soldiers searching for them.

Thinking about the soldiers, he sent a hurried glance at the earthen ceiling and hoped that he and Sir Wick were the only ones to hear Rhonalyn's cry.

Heaving a breath, he focused on the one part of the problem he could somewhat solve. "Are you hungry?"

Rhonalyn nodded.

"We'll share what food we have."

Reaching forward, Rhonalyn shook her young companion's shoulder. "Aisley."

The blonde-haired child groaned and rolled onto her back.

Rhonalyn gasped. "Aisley! What in heaven's name?"

Gage stiffened. "What is it? What's the matter?"

"She's covered in blood!" Rhonalyn pushed back the child's cloak, exposing to him smears of blood covering Aisley's dress and left arm.

Wide-eyed, Aisley sat up and looked down at herself. "I didn't know I was bleeding."

Rhonalyn quickly examined the child's arm and side. She glanced up at Gage, her voice tight with concern and pleading. "I can't find the wound."

Relating all too well to her panic, Gage knelt beside her and searched Aisley's arm and side. He found no cuts or puncture wounds either. He looked into Aisley's frightened gaze. "Do you hurt anywhere?"

The girl shook her head.

Using Aisley's cloak, Gage wiped away the dried blood on her arm but still found no wounds. He straightened. "I don't think it's her blood."

"Then how is she covered in it?" Rhonalyn asked.

"Um, I think riding with me," Sir Wick said in an apologetic tone. He set aside the cloak he had just folded and lifted his left arm. "I must have bled on her while she and I rode together."

At the sight of the thick trails of blood dried down Sir Wick's arm, Gage's own fear spiked. "You were injured! Why didn't you say something?"

"Well, if you recall, we were in a bit of a hurry at the time." Sir Wick twisted his arm around, trying to evaluate the injury. "Besides, it's not that bad. Just a graze."

Coming to him, Gage took hold of the knight's blood-covered arm to inspect the scabbed over cut. It appeared to be a smooth slice, not deep but definitely more than a graze. He frowned. "When did this happen?"

"In the meadow, of course." Sir Wick shrugged and said with a smile. "A parting gift to remember a night well-spent snatching innocents away from evil."

Gage was not amused. "You should have told me you were injured."

Sir Wick's eyebrows rose. "*I* should have? What about you? You're not exactly unscathed yourself. Atop your previous scrapes, bruises, and abrasions you've got a bloody lip, a grazed eyebrow, and a cut under your chin."

The instant Gage turned his attention to his own body, he could feel pain in just about every part of him. He licked his split lip, then lifted a hand to feel his chin. He winced. The cut was barely more than a scratch, but the bruising that accompanied it went up into his teeth.

"Not unscathed, but at least we're all alive," Sir Wick said with a grim expression yet thankful tone.

"Yes, but for how long, and to what end?" Gage added in an intentionally low tone to keep the girls from hearing. "Wick, a company of murderous soldiers is looking for those two and us. We don't know where we are. We have limited food and no idea how long the soldiers will search for us. And we have no way of knowing when the woodsman will return or how many of his rebel companions he'll bring with him when he does—no doubt to retake those two and rid themselves of us. So, yes, we're alive, but we have no allies and more enemies than we can count."

Sir Wick glanced at the two girls, then back at him. "Princess Rhonalyn's royal guard is still out there," he said with a tone of hopefulness that didn't match his worried expression. "Having a common enemy might suffice for gaining us an alliance with at least them."

"That is," Gage replied, "if somehow they manage to find us or we survive to get to them. Even then, an alliance to fight what and whom? Wick, they intended to murder the crown princess of Keric. They wore no colors or coat-of-arms, exactly like the entourage I witnessed outside Legan, the one in which Felix rode as second in command. And the same type of traitorous force Felix boasted about bringing back to Edelmar."

Sir Wick's eyebrows shot up in surprise. "Then you believe Manton, that his people aren't to blame for the attacks in Edelmar?"

"I didn't until I heard those soldiers give orders and saw their actions. But Manton's rebel friends not being responsible for Allard and Bardon's deaths doesn't change much. Felix is already dead. Manton is still a rebel smuggler of stolen goods and my only witness. Meanwhile, we're trapped here, facing a force whose identity and reach is beyond us. We have no idea how long it'll be safe to stay here or when it'll be safe to leave. No matter what we do, we're gambling with our lives." He nodded toward the girls. "As well as theirs."

"Well, at least we all still have lives to gamble with."

Gage frowned at Sir Wick. He needed advice, not gratitude. "Yes, but which do we risk, staying or fleeing?"

"God led us into this." Sir Wick said with conviction, "I think we need to trust that He'll show us what to do next and when to do it."

Gage grunted his annoyance but couldn't help acknowledging

that Sir Wick might be right. God had provided the means to rescue Rhonalyn and Aisley, so perhaps God's provision for the girls and communication with Sir Wick would continue. "Fine then," he muttered, "when God tells you what we should do next, let me know."

7

Rhonalyn rose to her feet and eyed Wick and Gabe. Their voices were too quiet for her to overhear, but their faces told her whatever they were discussing was a far cry from the casualness Wick had just expressed about his injury.

She fretted that perhaps they were discussing sharing their food. Her stomach knotted in hunger, then fear. She had never been in a situation where inadequate provisions were an issue of survival and not just a temporary inconvenience.

"Princess Rhonalyn," Aisley questioned in the noblemen's tongue, "do you think mayhap we will be able to return to Dinslage today?"

Rhonalyn glanced at the child. "I do not know." She wished she could order it to be so.

Aisley frowned. "If they will not convey us to Dinslage, Baron Philip will come seeking us, will he not?"

Rhonalyn thought of the commander of her guard and the rest of her faithful men-at-arms, including her two cousins, Sir Nolan and Sir Erwyn. "Aye, they will seek us, of that I am certain."

She kept to herself her thought that hidden as they were from the treacherous soldiers would mean her royal guard would be hindered from finding them—and that assumed the soldiers didn't find them first. The knot in her stomach tightened as she recalled her nightmare earlier that morning of the soldiers slaughtering everyone around her before killing her too. A shudder passed through her body, and cold fear coursed through her veins.

"Food, anyone?" The cheerfulness in Wick's voice sounded forced.

Rhonalyn wasn't sure if he had observed her expression or if she had missed something in Wick and Gabe's exchange, but she was too hungry to care and relieved to have the distraction.

Wick strapped on his sword, then crouched and unlaced his saddlebags. Gabe joined him, and they continued murmuring to each other. Rhonalyn caught something about the horses but couldn't make out anything else. Tired of their secrecy and the additional unease it stirred within her, she snapped at them in the commoners' tongue. "Enough with the secrets. What's the issue?"

They both looked surprised.

"Well?" she demanded. "Talk!"

Gabe muttered something to Wick, who shrugged and smirked.

Infuriated, she stormed toward them. "I said, tell me what's going on!"

Gabe eyed her before answering flatly, "We're discussing the need to feed the horses."

"Oh." Trying to ignore the warmth that crept up her neck, Rhonalyn lifted her chin and swept her hands down her skirt in a manner that would normally brush away the rumples in her dress and give her a sense of control and confidence. But the wrinkles in her skirt weren't going anywhere, and the moment she lifted her chin, her previously well-pinned hair slid farther down her neck.

She curled her toes to keep her mortification in check, but that caused the sand that she'd inadvertently stomped into her boots to grate against her ankles. The air in her chest caught, and she fought a wave of unwanted emotions. She blinked hard and stiffened her body against a tremor in her chest.

Seemingly oblivious to her sudden struggle, Gabe turned to Wick. "I say we feed two thirds of the barley to the horses. That will give us a third to eat later, and even though it won't sustain them long, it's better than leaving them with nothing."

"True," Wick said. "And right now we can eat the nuts and cheese that I have and the bread you have. Then we can build a fire and cook the remaining third of the barley for another meal." He pointed down the beach. "There's enough dry driftwood. We should be able to make a safe fire."

Gabriel nodded. "There might also be fish in the stream."

Wick glanced that way. "Good thought. We may be able to rig a hook and line and catch something."

"Right," Gabe said. "I'll tend to the horses. You divide up the food. Rhonalyn, you can take the cooking pot and get water."

Rhonalyn blinked. "Excuse me? That's 'Princess Rhonalyn' to you or 'Your Royal Highness,' and I don't fetch water."

Standing, Gabe shoved a cooking pot into her hands. It clinked against the two rings on her fingers. "You do now."

Her mouth fell open, and she stared at him in stunned outrage.

"I'll fetch it for you, Princess Rhonalyn." Aisley took the pot and ran toward the water's edge.

Exhaling in a huff, Rhonalyn straightened her posture. "Well, at least *someone* understands that just because I've been forced to flee soldiers and hide on a beach doesn't mean I should be treated with any less respect."

"Respect. Really?" Gabe said, his tone sounding vexed.

Rhonalyn stiffened. "Yes."

"And what about the respect due to her?" He jutted his chin after Aisley. "Doesn't she have a title too? Because, if I'm not mistaken, the sleeves and gold embroidery on her dress make her a lady-in-waiting, not your maidservant, though I'm sure you're used to having several of those."

Rhonalyn shifted in discomfort and felt a twinge of guilt at the accuracy of his words. She hadn't given any thought to Aisley's title, though she wasn't about to admit that to him. She swiftly composed a justification for her actions. "Lady Aisley serves me just as all the people of Keric serve Keric's crown. As I'm sure you serve Delkara's crown."

"We're not Delkaran," Gabriel growled.

Confused and feeling even more unsettled by his tone, she glanced from him to Wick. "You're not?"

"No," Wick answered, glancing at Gabe, who seized a small, bulging linen bag from his pack and headed toward their horses. "We're Edelmarian." Aisley returned then with the water and set the pot in front of Wick. He thanked her, then dug into the saddlebags.

While watching him shuffle through the bags and Gabriel feed the horses handfuls of the barley, Rhonalyn wondered why it felt like she'd stepped into something that made both men uncomfortable. "If you're both Edelmarian," she said, "why are you here in Delkara?"

Wick unfolded a cloth from around a hunk of cheese. "That depends on which one of us you ask."

"Then you're not traveling companions?"

"Oh we're traveling companions." Wick yanked a knife from a sheath at his belt and hacked the cheese into chunks.

Hugely curious about what he wasn't saying, Rhonalyn risked digging further. "In the barn, Manton said something about Gabriel being an old traveling companion of his. Did you all used to travel together?"

Wick sheathed his knife with a snap. "No. Gabe traveled with Manton—before he knew who Manton was."

"And before you and he traveled together?"

"Not exactly." Wick's gaze flicked toward Gabe, but he said

nothing more. Pulling out a loaf of bread, he tore it into four pieces, then placed each piece with the chunks of cheese on the linen cloth. Next, he sorted nuts into the four piles. Rhonalyn's stomach growled as she watched.

"I think a more relevant question, Your Royal Highness," Gabriel said as he came back toward them, wiping his hands on his tunic, "is what is Keric's crown princess doing in Delkara?"

She opened her mouth but hesitated to give an answer. It seemed like a lifetime ago that she had stood with Strephon absorbing the view from the tower at Nikledon's manor and discussing their mutual difficulties with a group of thieving commoners. At that point she had known nothing of treacherous soldiers, and those seditious common-ers they discussed had seemed like a distant problem. She shuddered. Now, dealing with them was highly relevant and far more complicated, for the only person beyond the four of them who knew her location was one of those seditious commoners. The last thing she needed their group knowing, if they didn't already, was that she and Strephon had agreed to unite against them.

Her paying the harbor toll, however, was a matter of public busi-ness between Keric and Delkara. Not that "paying the toll" is what her father would call her agreement with Strephon to reinstate trade between their two kingdoms, particularly not at a guaranteed profit to Strephon. Regardless, though, she was still proud of having bought them a year's reprieve. Irritation and fear stirred inside her. Not that her success did her any good now.

"Well?" Gabe asked, arching an eyebrow at her. "Will you answer or not? Why are *you* here in Delkara?"

She swished her hands down her dress again and responded. "I came to deliver the yearly toll that Keric pays to Delkara for use of Nikor Harbor."

Gabe looked dismayed. "So the rebels attacked you to steal that toll?"

"No. The toll had already been paid." Saying it aloud and seeing his surprise made her reflect on how strange it was that they hadn't come for the toll a second time. She frowned and continued, "They snatched me from the inn where I was staying with my guard and said they sought an audience with me."

"Why?" Gabe asked.

She shook head. "I don't know. They were about to tell me in the meadow when the soldiers arrived. Then everyone"—she swallowed—"everyone tried to flee."

"Those soldiers wanted you dead. Why?"

"I don't know," she replied, feeling lightheaded. "I came to Delkara to pay a toll. That's all. I have no idea what either of these groups wants with me."

Gabe frowned. "So you're of no help then?"

She glared at him. "You say that as if I'm intentionally being unhelpful."

"Are you?" he asked.

She huffed. "No. I'm just—

"Food." Wick interrupted. "Why don't we eat some food?" He motioned to the bread, cheese, and nuts. "You both might also want to keep your voices down." He jutted his chin upward. "Best not to reveal ourselves to anyone who might be venturing overhead."

8

Wick cringed at the cold annoyance his reminder elicited from both royals. It had been bad enough managing Prince Gage when he'd been disgruntled. Now he had two of them to appease or exhort. If he could keep them busy enough with relevant tasks, perhaps they wouldn't spew their frustration on each other or him and Lady Aisley.

The moment their meager meal was finished, Wick dove into his efforts.

It was easy to delegate Gage to fire making and barley cooking, but it took all Wick's patience and his best negotiating skills to get Princess Rhonalyn to help Lady Aisley bind together a horsehair fishing line. She agreed only after he had pointed out that her supervision of Lady Aisley's efforts would no doubt be paramount to the task's success.

He supplied them with horsehair cut from his mount's tail while also warning them to stay away from the horses themselves to spare them from any hazardous encounter with Prince Gage's unpredictable beast. Then he sharpened a stick into a hook and searched for bait. The latter task proved more difficult than he would have thought, but a rotting log yielded several white grubs that he collected into the empty barley bag.

With the girls still working on the fishing line, he tipped his sword's hilt and crouched beside Prince Gage, who was laying a fire. The two girls were talking in the noblemen's tongue as they sat working on his blanket.

"Do you think they wilt truly catch fish with this?" Lady Aisley asked.

"I hope so," Princess Rhonalyn replied, "for the food served so far was not particularly satisfying."

"I agree," Aisley said, rubbing her midsection. "My stomach had but just stopped growling when I ate the last of my cheese, and Gabe said the barley would not be cooked until later." She looked out at the stream. "I wish we could catch a fish right now."

"Let not your hands wander with your thoughts," Princess Rhonalyn chided. "Keep a tight hold of the hair, so the binding stays strong, or any fish that is caught will break your work and get away."

"Aye, Your Royal Highness," Lady Aisley replied, lowering her eyes.

Wick flicked his gaze back to the fire.

Beside him Prince Gage murmured, "Hopefully, she's as good at following her own orders as she is at giving them."

Wick smirked and said, "I'm just happy she's helping."

"Even if we manage to catch fish and feed ourselves, the horses still need food." Prince Gage jabbed a stick into the sand. "Tonight after dark, you and I are going to have to risk taking them back down the stream to graze."

Anxiety twisted inside Wick. He knew Prince Gage was right, but he couldn't help thinking about the boars. Encountering *them* in the dark would be just as dangerous as running into the soldiers. The only advantage was that the swine weren't looking for them. "What about the girls? I doubt Her Royal Highness will be very happy being left here."

"Probably not," Prince Gage said, "but it's not like she'd be any safer or happier coming along."

"Good point. Though in the meantime, we'd better pray we catch some fish to feed those two."

Prince Gage nodded. "True. For if we don't, we're likely to be criminalized by Rhonalyn for starving the two of them long before we're killed for protecting them or arrested for supposedly kidnapping them."

Wick snorted. "Exactly."

☙❧

While feeding wood to the fire snapping beneath the pot of barley, Gage twisted a stick in his hands. Out beyond their refuge, the sun had descended more than halfway to the horizon. He wasn't sure whether to feel relieved or stressed by the passing time, but he knew restlessness and hunger were a bad combination.

Aisley rose from the blanket the two girls shared and flipped off her shoes to traipse barefoot along the beach. She missed seeing the disapproving frown Rhonalyn sent after her, and Gage smirked at the child's innocent disregard for propriety. Allard came to mind along with a surge of grief. Gage pushed the emotion away. She wasn't Allard.

Aisley ran to a high spot in the sand, above where Sir Wick stood at the sand's edge throwing the horsehair-fishing line out into the stream. She raced down to stand beside the knight as he drew in the line. Aisley bounced on her toes next to him. Wick pulled the empty hook from the water, then swung the line out again.

Fishing was not a task for the impatient. Gage glanced down at the pot and frowned. Neither was cooking barley. He stirred the pot's contents to feel the grain's consistency. It was still too firm.

Trying to ignore his growling stomach, he returned his attention to the others just as Rhonalyn pulled several pins loose from her upswept hair. The brown twists uncoiled and cascaded down her back in waves that almost reached the blanket. She combed her fingers through her dark tresses, picking out twigs and pine needles and working out snarls. It reminded Gage of a day at Ulbin Manor when he had been about fourteen. Sophia, Allard's older sister, had been seated outside, watching her nieces and nephews playing. One of the little boys had run up to her and dumped a handful of dirt on her head. Being the forbearing soul that she was, Sophia had gently reprimanded the child and then undone her hair to shake out the dirt. Her hair had fallen all the way to her knees, and he had stared open-mouthed. Allard had caught him gawking and teased him to no end.

Gage blinked hard and gripped the spoon he held. Why was everything reminding him of Allard?

A loud splash jerked his attention back to Aisley and Sir Wick. Spotting ripples spreading out from whatever was thrown into the water, he rose to his feet. It was one thing to risk fishing. It was another to throw rocks, which would scare off fish, make unnecessary noise, and be visible from above.

He opened his mouth but then noted the look on Sir Wick's face. Something was wrong. Dropping his fishing line, Sir Wick clamped a hand over Aisley's mouth and, scooping her off her feet, retreated with her away from the water's edge. Just then another rock slammed into the water, causing a second splash and ripples that raced across the moving water toward their hiding spot. Only then did Gage realize what was happening.

Someone was directly above them, and the smoke of his fire was winding its way straight to them.

Dropping to his knees, Gage shoveled sand over the fire. He kept shoveling until its flames were fully smothered. Then he sat back on his knees and held his breath. The sound of voices drifted down to them over the babbling water. Gage strained to hear what was being said but could only make out bits and pieces. Maybe it was just travelers.

"…the falls…not passable."

"Our orders…search everywhere…"

Gage clenched his fingers. Definitely not travelers.

"…he's determined…you should have…find them."

"…check below…"

"…another long trek."

Gage's blood ran cold. They had nowhere to go to escape the soldiers if they checked below. He looked to Sir Wick who slowly released Aisley. The girl stood like a statue across from Rhonalyn, who sat frozen with her fingers entwined in her hair. Wick eased across the sand and planted himself behind the ceiling's edge in the spot where they had ridden out of the water the night before. The knight's hands rested upon his sword, but he did not draw it.

His heart pounding, Gage gripped his own short weapon, not that it would do much good. With his hand locked about the knife's hilt, he waited, listening.

The moving water in front of him remained undisturbed, and the voices above faded away. Gage glanced at the earthen ceiling, trying to envision what might be taking place up there. Did "check below" mean they intended to search directly below or simply that they would check downstream? He looked around the area. The beach had several sections to it with jutting walls that concealed small portions of it but nowhere big enough to hide them all, and if they tried to run, the only path they could take was straight at anyone coming upstream.

Agonizing moments went by.

Gage's heart thudded in rhythm with his anxiety, and his hand sweated on his knife's hilt. He felt like the fear of being discovered might itself suffocate him. Struggling to draw air, he sent up a silent prayer. "Please, God, if You care at all, let them move on."

The only noise he could hear coming from the stream was the endless cascading, gurgling clamor of its constant movement. Meanwhile, all four of them remained still and silent. The air on the beach felt like it had thickened with the relentless possibility of impending doom. Gage's lungs felt incapable of inhaling enough air to sustain him, and his heart hammered.

His body began to tremble. He maintained his position on his knees, enduring the cramping of his joints as one moment after another came and went.

Eventually, Rhonalyn lowered her hand from her hair, and Aisley crawled across the blanket to sit beside her. Unable to maintain his crouched position any longer, Gage sank sideways onto the sand.

Time dragged on.

Beyond the flowing water was the chatter of flitting birds and the croaking of frogs in the wetland opposite them. No new sounds came from above, nor was there any indication anyone was coming upstream toward them.

Ever so slowly, the tension in the air began to fade, and Gage's heart eased back to a normal pace. If the soldiers had intended to come up the stream, surely they would have reached them by now. They must have simply meant that they would check downstream. Gage released his knife's hilt and breathed a sigh.

A moment later, Sir Wick trooped back toward them, looking like a massive weight had rolled off his shoulders. "I think they've moved on."

9

RHONALYN COULD NOT understand how Wick and Gabe could so calmly return to their tasks. Her head ached from the panic that had poured through her and kept her perfectly still. Now that it was past, her body was trembling so badly she could hardly comb through her hair.

She wanted real walls and actual protection. It felt insane to stay put, hoping they wouldn't be found and killed. But neither of the men seemed to think as she did.

Having unburied the fire, Gabe coaxed the flames back to life, and Wick collected his fishing line and tossed the hook back into the water.

"I recognize none of their voices," Aisley said in the noblemen's tongue.

Drawn from her thoughts, Rhonalyn blinked. "What?"

"I hoped that mayhap it was Baron Philip and your guard and not the bad soldiers. But I did not recognize their voices." The child's voice trembled. "So I stayed quiet, just like Wick said."

Biting her lip to contain the rush of appreciation and apprehension that Aisley's words unleashed inside her, Rhonalyn squeezed the girl's arm. Realizing Aisley's hair was as disheveled as hers and needing something to do, she motioned to the girl. "Sit. I shall help you plait your hair, then mayhap you can do mine, hmm?"

Aisley nodded and sat in front of her. When Rhonalyn was done braiding her hair and Aisley began working on hers, Rhonalyn watched Wick once more toss and retrieve his fishing line. The endless repetition of his actions was suddenly interrupted when he gave the line a swift tug and pulled it from the water. There, flopping at the end of it, was a fish. It was a pathetically small fish, but by the look on Wick's face one would have thought he'd hooked an arm's-length trout rather than a chub the length of his hand.

He unhooked the fish and tossed it onto the sand.

He caught two more fish over the next hour, and not long after that, Gabe brought Rhonalyn a half-full bowl of barley combined with plumped dried apples and instructed her to share the portion with Aisley. She opened her mouth to object, then noted that the bowl he and Wick shared held just as little.

She bit back her complaint and forced herself to swallow her list of grievances as she ate the measly amount of food and watched the sun set.

The barley was not as bland as she had expected. Gabe must have added spices with the apples, which surprised her since she had not thought they would have spices. But then again, what did she really know of Edelmarian commoners or how they traveled? She glanced at Gabe as she handed the remaining barley to Aisley. "As Edelmarians, do you often travel in Delkara?"

Gabe shook his head. "No."

She frowned. "Yet you're here in Delkara now. Why?"

He passed his bowl to Wick. "There was a fair. It was a good place to buy and sell mounts."

"Then your trade is in animals?"

"More or less." She sensed annoyance in Gabe's voice.

"Are you freemen or servants sent to the fair by your lord?"

"Sent or free, what difference does it make?" There was no mistaking his anger now.

She folded her arms. "I was just wondering if perhaps an Edelmarian lord might notice the absence of two of his men and come looking."

"If so, it'd do little good. Our absence isn't going to bring anyone here to this spot. Not any more than your absence will guide your men here to you."

"Yes, but now that the soldiers have searched this area and gone, anyone else who—"

"You think those soldiers are just going to make one pass and move on?" Gabe scoffed and shook his head.

Rhonalyn gripped her skirt. "Well, they can't search the area forever."

"No, but I suspect they might spend longer than a day."

She frowned. "How much longer?"

He held her gaze. "I don't know. How long would you spend trying to fix something that could get you hanged if you failed to finish dealing with it?"

An expanse of cold dread opened around Rhonalyn. He was right. The soldiers weren't likely to stop searching anytime soon.

Wick's optimistic voice broke through the bone-chilling silence created by her and Gabe's exchange. "Anyone interested in a two-course meal? Fish will be next. Just need to catch a few more." He stood up. "Anyone coming?"

"Me." Aisley crept away from Rhonalyn and rose to her feet. She and Wick headed off to the water while Gabe turned back to the fire.

Rhonalyn stayed where she was on the blanket as dusk crept in around them. She hated the loathsome dismay the encroaching darkness brought along with the sense of hopelessness that spread through her even as she wished her guard would come sweeping in to rescue her.

Swatting at the evening's insects that were beginning to buzz around her ears, she bit down a shriek of exasperation and turned her fingers into talons. She dug them into the blanket, picturing herself sinking her nails instead into the necks of the treacherous soldiers and the commoners who had taken her from her inn.

Something small and dark swooped down from the earthen ceiling. She gasped and ducked as the winged creature swept overhead and out across the water. Revulsion seized her. A bat! Now there were bats! She was the princess of Keric. She shouldn't have to put up with any of this.

Grabbing her cloak, Rhonalyn yanked it around her shoulders and thrust herself to her feet. "That's it!" she declared. "I'm not staying here any longer."

"Where do you plan to go, hm?" Gabe shook his head at her as if she were just a buzzing insect. "You're just…" His attention shifted to one of the horses. The dark animal had been digging in the sand, but now it had twisted around on its lead to stare out at the water.

"I'm just what?" Rhonalyn snarled.

Gabe glanced back at her. "You're just hungry and restless. Like someone else."

Anger made her heart beat faster. "Are you comparing me to a horse?"

"Well, I wasn't talking about Si—" He flinched. "Someone else."

She squinted at him, wondering what he had been about to say.

Gabe stood up. "I think I'll help Wick with the fishing." He headed away from her.

Remembering her reasons for standing there, she huffed, then hurriedly trekked through the sand after him. "I'm not thr—" A loud whinny burst from the dark horse. Rhonalyn jumped, then clenched her fists. Stupid creature.

Gabe altered his course toward the animal. "I know you're hungry, Athalos, but you've got to stay—"

Dropping his fishing line, Wick drew his sword. "Gabe, company!"

Gabe drew his knife, and Rhonalyn froze and searched the direction they both stared.

Out in the water, a dark figure tarried at the corner of the earthen cliff.

10

Wick clenched his sword's hilt and squinted at the back of the lanky figure who tugged something around the cliff's corner. A pack mule with a large, prickly bundle and several smaller bags waded into view. The man turned, and Wick recognized his face, long hair, and scraggly beard just as Manton addressed them in his gratingly familiar, lazy-sounding voice. "Really? I look like a soldier?"

Wick grunted in response. Considering what he knew of Manton, he wasn't happy to see him, but since Manton possessed information and a testimony that Prince Gage needed, seeing him was a relief. But had he come alone?

Wick eyed the watery path behind Manton. He couldn't see or hear anyone else, but considering how close Manton had come before he had noticed him, that wasn't much of a reassurance. Keeping his sword in hand and motioning for Lady Aisley to retreat toward the fire, Wick eased backward to allow Manton to wade out of the water and onto the beach.

The mule followed Manton onto the sand, blocking Wick's view of Prince Gage.

Manton patted the mule's shoulder, then gestured toward Wick's sword. "You can put that away."

Movement out of the corner of his eye caught Wick's attention. Princess Rhonalyn rushed at Manton, her fingers curled like claws. Swapping his sword to his other hand, Wick caught her around the waist to keep her out of Manton's reach. The forward motion of her weight hit his arm hard. He had to dig his feet into the sand to stay upright.

Since he would have liked to have seen her shred Manton, he briefly considered letting her go, but he didn't dare compromise her safety. So, instead of Manton's face, her fingernails dug into his arm as she spit at Manton. "You! You and your people are responsible for all of this!" Wick re-braced himself to keep her from knocking him over while she continued to spew her anger at Manton. "You ought to hang! You wretched sc—"

"You're angry," Manton cut her off. "I understand. I even sympathize." Annoyance contorted his face and tone as he gestured to the beach. "But surely you realize this isn't the result my people wanted either. A meeting with you was all we were after. Soldiers coming after us. We figured that would happen, but them coming at *you* wasn't something we anticipated. We didn't intend to put you in danger. And if you haven't noticed, we're attempting to set things right."

Scoffing, Princess Rhonalyn struggled to break free of Wick's hold. "I don't believe you."

Wick grunted as her claws again bit into his arm. He glared at Manton, wishing he could at the very least have his own hands free, so he could punch Manton himself.

"Well, believe it or not, I came back to help." Manton motioned over his shoulder to his mule. "I brought food for you all and hay for your horses." His eyes darted to Wick, then back to Princess Rhonalyn. "Consider it a peace offering."

Wick raised his eyebrows as he felt Princess Rhonalyn's body stiffen. He feared she might make another lunge at Manton. But it wasn't Her Royal Highness who made the next move.

Prince Gage ducked around Manton's mule, drew a knife, and came at Manton from behind.

Seizing Manton's left arm while kicking him in the back of his knees, His Highness yanked Manton backward and brought his knife to the man's throat. "A peace offering, really?"

With his body arched at an odd angle due to their height difference, Manton tried to shift in Prince Gage's grasp.

"Don't." His Highness slid the blade.

Manton flinched and became motionless as dark droplets of blood trailed down his neck.

Princess Rhonalyn stilled, no longer attempting to close the distance between herself and Manton. Wick eased his arm away from her waist. The moment he did, she retreated up the beach toward Lady Aisley. Glad to have her out of harm's way, Wick shifted his weapon back to his dominant hand. He stepped forward and nodded to Prince Gage, ready to aid His Highness if necessary.

"Disarm yourself," Prince Gage instructed, keeping his knife against Manton's throat.

Growling, Manton used his free left hand to tug his two knives from his belt and tossed them onto the sand between himself and Wick. "There," he said. "Happy now?"

Wick retrieved both knives.

"Far from it," Prince Gage replied. "Tell your friends to show themselves."

"I came alone."

Prince Gage scoffed. "Right, so this isn't like the barn where you distract us while your companions sneak in to ambush and apprehend us?"

"No, it isn't." A note of reprimand entered Manton's voice. "And, as I recall, back at the barn, it was you who arrived uninvited and ambushed us."

Prince Gage's expression darkened. "Oh, I see, so you're the victims of this situation?"

"No. I'm simply saying we had a mission to complete, and I did what I had to in the barn."

"A mission? Is that what you call kidnapping two people?" With a look of disgust, Prince Gage kicked again at the back of Manton's knees. Manton lurched, his knees buckling, but he maintained his footing.

"Kneel!" Prince Gage ordered, twisting his hold on Manton's arm and using the knife as an added incentive.

Manton dropped to his knees.

"You don't get it." Prince Gage's voice was rigid with anger. "When you lie to people and mess with their lives, there's a cost. And this time you're going to answer for what you've done."

Manton tipped his head to the side. "Look, I'm not sure why you're so mad at me considering what happened, but regardless you need to set aside your anger and let—"

"This isn't a negotiation!"

Manton rolled his eyes and sighed. "Would you just listen to me?"

"No! You forfeited the right to ask me to listen when you lied to me. Now, shut your mouth until I tell you otherwise."

A look of angry determination flashed across Manton's face. "This is ridiculous. Just hear me out." He lifted his hand as if to seize Prince Gage's knife arm.

Wick started forward, but Prince Gage was faster. He pulled away his hand, twisting his wrist as he did so, and swung down, striking Manton's face with the knife's hilt. Manton reeled at the blow, and His Highness used his body weight to slam Manton forward into the sand.

Manton recovered quickly and tried to shove back up, but Prince

Gage, still holding Manton's left arm, dropped a knee onto his back. Manton hissed air, and Prince Gage ordered him to be still.

"Alright already!" Manton stopped struggling and heaved an angry breath. "You win. I'll follow your rules. Now, will you get off?"

"Not a chance," Prince Gage replied. "Wick, some rope, please."

"My pleasure." Wick headed for Manton's mule. He untied the animal's lead line and brought it. Prince Gage yanked Manton's arms behind his back and bound the man's wrists together.

With his forehead in the sand and long hair falling about his face, Manton sighed. "Come on, Gabriel. Think. This isn't necessary. You really believe I'd have come here on my own like this if I wanted to cause any of you harm?"

"I have no idea." Prince Gage drew tight the knot on the rope. "That's why this time I'm not taking any chances." Using what remained of the rope, His Highness secured Manton's ankles together as well, making it impossible for him to stand, let alone run.

Manton endured Prince Gage's actions without further resistance but with plenty of verbal objections. "This is foolishness, Gabe. I'm not your enemy. I brought you all food, I protected Her Royal Highness during the attack, and I helped you all escape and hide."

Wick snorted in response to Manton's list of laurels and commented. "Of course you helped. If Princess Rhonalyn was killed after being kidnapped by your band of rebels, the full wrath of all three kingdoms would have come down on you all. You said yourself your cause didn't need new enemies."

Manton craned his neck to look up at him. "We don't. We want her safe and alive."

"For what purpose?" Prince Gage grabbed Manton's bound arms and pulled him to his knees.

With sand clinging to the side of his face, Manton glanced at

Princess Rhonalyn, who now stood a good twelve paces away. His voice implored her with more humility than Wick had yet heard him express. "To ask for her help, or at the very least to ask her not to aid King Strephon or his lords."

"Aid them how?" Prince Gage demanded.

Behind strands of his long, dirty hair, Manton's gaze shifted between Prince Gage and Princess Rhonalyn before he replied. "By not uniting with them against us."

Princess Rhonalyn scoffed. "Considering your actions against me and my people, I'd be hard pressed to consider uniting with Strephon against the lot of you a bad thing."

Manton swallowed, then spoke with calm conviction. "That's because you don't know who King Strephon truly is. And without that knowledge, you won't understand who we are either. So, please let me explain."

Manton glanced at Prince Gage, then continued without waiting for permission. "In the past, when King Maurice ruled Delkara, the common people willingly worked to provide for themselves and those who ruled over them. Rarely did that result in an abundance on any commoner's table, but there was enough. Then Strephon became king. Initially, he was lenient, more so than his father. We thought we'd been blessed with a generous ruler. Taxes were lowered, and on many manors anyone with debts could have them forgiven if they joined the service of their lord's garrison, which paid generously.

"But then things began to change. Taxes in the kingdom were increased and have continued to go up. Even now, at many manors almost forty percent of what is harvested is carted away in what is claimed to be lawful taxation. People aren't just going hungry; they're beginning to starve. Yet the demands on the purses and resources of the common people continue. Those who resist are met with harsh force. And none of the barons will acknowledge these abuses of power as unjust. People have tried to bring the matter before their lords, but they are disregarded or punished for speaking out. Stricter and stricter laws have been made, and there is no lenience for the sick or unable. A few brave souls sought to appeal to King Strephon, but nothing changed, and they never returned.

"With no recourse left, commoners armed themselves with whatever weapons they still had and arose to take back their grain and goods. It was then the same lords who'd ignored the legitimate grievances of the people began arresting all who had previously spoken out against the taxes and abuses. The lords called them traitors, saying they were like flames that needed to be stamped out. But as one of our leaders said in response, 'A fire that's burned long in a tree's roots is not so easily extinguished.'"

"That is your justification?" Prince Gage said. Shaking his head, he paced away from Manton, his expression stormy.

"It is, for the lords are the cause of this," Manton said, his words pursuing Prince Gage across the sand. "We did what we had to do to protect ourselves and to demand that King Strephon see to the needs of his people."

Manton turned his gaze to Princess Rhonalyn. "Hear me in this. If you help King Strephon come after us, you'll not be stopping an unjust rebellion but silencing the last voices in Delkara willing to speak and fight for justice. Don't ally yourself with Strephon. He's the one destroying Delkara."

Were it not for flashbacks to the Blue Crow, Wick might have been swayed to consider Manton's plea and admired his zeal. But as it was, his cynicism toward Manton's cause ran high, and fear of believing fervent words twisted by unseen lies left him uneasy. Statements without proof meant little, and back at the barn, Prince Gage had dismissed the proof that Manton had claimed existed about the lords' abuse of power. For was it not just as possible the lords were responding to attacks the rebel commoners had made against them?

Still, that supposition had come before they themselves had fled soldiers who were willing to murder commoners, nobles, and royalty alike. So, was there truth in Manton's words? Were injustices happening? Were people actually starving? Or was Manton lying? Were the rebel commoners the victims of abuse in Delkara, or were they the perpetrators of it?

"If you hoped," Princess Rhonalyn said coldly, "that I'd believe the tale you have just spun and the accusations you've spouted against King Strephon, you'll be sorely disappointed." Her Royal Highness's voice and bearing was no longer that of someone on the run but of a royal stating her judgment of Manton's spoken petition. "I've heard your story before, but it is a far different tale when relayed from the lips of the one you accuse. What you view as abuses can also be viewed as tough choices made to implement changes to prevent destruction in Delkara.

"Strephon told me himself that he has worked hard over the past four years to improve the lives of his people but that his efforts are continually being hindered by those who cannot see what he's trying to accomplish. You think you're aiding your people, but you ought to put down your weapons, for it is you who are causing your people harm."

Manton looked taken aback, but then he drew a breath and responded. "Tell that to those in Delkara who have been killed, are missing, or are starving because of King Strephon's commands."

Princess Rhonalyn shook her head and answered disdainfully, "You don't know all the pieces. Commoners see problems from an individualistic point of view, but royals see the world for what it is as a whole. It's that view from above that enables an accurate perspective and allows us to find the best solutions to difficult problems."

"Is it?" Manton asked, his voice tinged with anger. "Or does that high and lofty view leave royalty blind or indifferent to the plight of the common man?"

Bristling, Princess Rhonalyn pressed her lips together. Prince Gage, on the other hand, looked unsettled by Manton's words. Wick wondered about His Highness's position in the debate. How aware was Prince Gage of such shortcomings in leadership?

Wick knew both sides. As a baron's son he knew the complicated and difficult decisions faced by leaders. But he had also spent enough time serving as a bottom-rung knight to be intimately acquainted with the many problems leaders didn't see and the consequences that resulted from their blindness, like a cook being expected to provide the exact same service despite lacking two scullions.

Princess Rhonalyn seemed to have had no such experiences. She paused for a mere moment before continuing with undaunted condescension. "As a commoner, you cannot possibly understand the complexities of ruling, and you're wrong to take actions against your king. It's treason."

Manton leaned forward and strained against his bonds, his voice rising. "It's not treason if you're trying to save your kingdom."

"You're disloyal to your sovereign. That is treason." Rhonalyn's declaration seemed to suck the air from Manton's lungs.

Manton sat back on his heels and shook his head.

"But is it disloyalty?" Prince Gage stepped into the conversation. "If a leader wants the truth and wishes to care well for the people they rule, then that leader should not consider a person's willingness to voice concerns over mistreatment an act of disloyalty."

Manton's face filled with surprise and appreciation. Wick felt instantly annoyed, for it wasn't as if Manton had won Prince Gage to his side or changed his mind. Such was the mindset Prince Gage had always had.

"Sometimes those in authority abuse their power and should be stopped," His Highness continued, his gaze fixed on Princess Rhonalyn, "and sometimes events cause harm to one side or another and ought to be resolved."

A look of solidarity filled Manton's face, and Wick yearned to smack it off him. Thankfully, Prince Gage's next words did the task for him.

"For instance, it's possible the abuses taking place in Delkara, currently being blamed upon King Strephon, may not be Strephon's actions or intentions at all but rather the work of someone else—someone issuing to soldiers orders designed to undermine King Strephon."

"You mean like whoever's commanding the soldiers who're after us?" Lady Aisley asked in her young voice.

Wick glanced at the child sitting by the fire. Despite her innocent gaze and indifferent expression, she was clearly quite astute.

Prince Gage nodded. "Exactly."

"You're speaking of whoever commands the Unavowed." Manton's comment resulted in confused looks. He grunted and added. "The soldiers who bear no colors or coat-of-arms. We call them the Unavowed, because their lack of identification makes them deniable by their master. You may wish to believe someone else commands them, but it's King Strephon."

"King Strephon isn't behind this," Princess Rhonalyn replied. "I'm confident of that. If he wanted me dead, he could've accomplished that far easier at Nikledon. And why spend two days negotiating with me first? For that matter, why waste his time seeking my support against the likes of you if he were simply planning to murder me on my way home?"

Manton frowned. "I agree with you that it seems illogical, but—"

"It may be an illogical choice for King Strephon," Prince Gage interrupted, "but it wouldn't be for someone who wants to destroy the people's confidence in King Strephon's leadership. Strephon was young when he assumed the Delkaran throne. People didn't believe he was ready to be king. Perhaps someone is taking advantage of those doubts. If, under King Strephon's name, someone abuses the common people to the point that they rise up against the crown, then it would create an opportunity for that person to put themselves forward as a new leader. Making a move for Delkara's throne would definitely be enough motivation for treason. And whoever's taking such actions can conveniently conceal their hand in it by blaming such events upon rebel commoners. That blame—like what the soldiers intended to do with Princess Rhonalyn's death—would be a precise way to motivate King Strephon's harsh punishments toward the rebels and his inattention toward the common people's complaints about actions that King Strephon knows he hasn't taken. The common people would see him as heartless, and he would perceive them as liars."

Easily seeing the scenario Prince Gage presented, Wick nodded. "Such would indeed be possible. Furthermore, it would explain why a man like Lord Gregory might fear that person and find their offer tempting enough to risk his own neck to align with them."

"Exactly," Prince Gage continued, "and considering all the stolen wealth they've acquired in their attacks, whoever it is could provide plenty of incentive to their allies and clearly has adequate protection in power and deception."

"Deception indeed," Manton muttered angrily. He heaved a breath and said to them all, "Listen, regardless of who you believe issues the Unavowed's orders, it doesn't change the fact that Princess Rhonalyn isn't safe in Delkara. She needs to be delivered safely back to her royal guard, so they can see her back to Keric. That is of utmost importance." Manton's gaze traveled to Prince Gage. "Wouldn't you agree, Gabe?"

Manton waited with an expectant look, but His Highness's response was slow in coming. Princess Rhonalyn's lips pressed together and her face became a blank expression of stiff control. Unsure what was about to happen, Wick watched the three of them and held his breath.

11

In the deepening dusk, heat pulsed through Rhonalyn's body. Between Manton and Gabriel, Gabe was the person she had thought she could trust to help, and yet he was hesitant to take her back to her guard. Her insides trembled, and she wished with every bit of her being that she didn't need any of them.

When Gabe finally answered Manton, his voice and features held the same anger she had seen him express back at the barn. "Let me guess. The best way to get her to her guard is to untie you and let you lead us."

The tension in Rhonalyn's body shifted as she realized Gabe wasn't hesitant about returning her to her guard but about working with Manton to do so.

Manton shrugged. "That would be your best choice."

"Of course it would." Gabe's voice emanated resentment. "Because you're the only one of us who knows the way back to Dinslage."

Manton shrugged again. "So it would seem."

Rhonalyn's stomach twisted. Manton's tone wasn't pleading anymore. He had power, and he knew it.

Gabriel glared. "That's why you figured it was safe to come here alone because you knew we needed you as a guide."

"I knew you'd see it eventually," Manton replied.

Growling, Gabe raised a fist and stepped toward him.

Manton flinched. "You'd strike me while I'm bound?"

To Rhonalyn's relief and frustration, Gabe lowered his fist, then marched off toward the mule Manton had brought.

"I'm not your enemy, Gabriel," Manton called after him.

"No one unties him!" Gabe said. "Is that clear?"

Rhonalyn's heart pounded. She didn't trust Manton either, and didn't want him free, but what did that mean for her return to Dinslage?

Gabe stripped the bundles from the mule's packsaddle. He carried the hay to the horses, and then helped Wick deposit the other bags near the fire.

Aisley pressed close to Rhonalyn and asked in the noblemen's tongue, "Princess Rhonalyn, prithee, what is to happen now? Will they or will they not take us back to Dinslage?"

Gabe glanced over at them.

Rhonalyn met his gaze with a glare. "I do not know."

Aisley sighed. "I wish they would make up their minds."

"As do I." Rhonalyn stated sharply as she continued to stare down Gabe.

He questioned her in the commoners' tongue, "What?"

Rhonalyn allowed her anger to flow into her voice as she spoke to him in his own language. "She wants to know the same thing I do. Are you going to help us get back to my guard or not?"

Gabe's gaze flicked to where Manton knelt. His jaw flexed, and his left hand rose to grip his right vambrace. He stood there, clearly debating something in his own head. There was obviously far more to his and Manton's past disagreements than either man had expressed aloud, but she didn't care. She needed Manton to get her home, and Gabe was in the way of that.

She stepped toward him. "Well?"

Gabriel heaved a breath. "Fine. Manton, what's your plan?"

A smug smile crept onto Manton's face. "It's fairly simple, but I don't think you're going to like it."

Gabe rolled his eyes and growled. "Why's that?"

"Because, the best option is to bring her guard to her, not her to her guard. One of you two will stay here with Her Royal Highness while the other two of us will return to Dinslage."

Wick shook his head. "I don't think splitting up is a good idea."

"I'd be willing to return to Dinslage alone," Manton said, "but I assume that would be unacceptable to some if not all of you."

Wick scoffed. "You think."

"Will her guard still even be in Dinslage?" Gabe asked. "Isn't it more likely they'll be out looking for her?"

Rhonalyn shifted. He was right. Her guardsmen would likely be out looking for her. So how were they to make contact with them?

"Most of them, yes," Wick answered, "but likely they'll have left at least one guardsman in Dinslage at the inn to relay messages and help coordinate their search."

"He's correct," Manton said, "and the plan would be to get there early enough in the morning to catch her whole guard before they go back out. The only problem I see is that they aren't likely to trust us when we tell them their princess is hidden away in the woods and that they should follow us to her."

"As a member of her royal guard dealing with the likes of you," Wick said, "I'd definitely want proof that she was safe and in agreement with the plan. And even then I'd still be concerned you were leading me into the woods to some nefarious end."

"I can provide what is needed to allay their concerns," Rhonalyn said.

Gabe's eyebrows rose in surprise. "You can?"

"Of course I can. I've had code words established with my guard since I was old enough to talk. All royals do."

Gabe blinked, looking impressed and taken back.

Wick smirked. "Yeah, Gabe, all royals do."

Rhonalyn thought for a moment he was teasing her, but his gaze stayed on Gabe.

Gabriel rolled his eyes, then looked to Manton. "What about Delkaran soldiers? Will they be a problem when it comes to getting inside the city?"

"Local soldiers will likely have been tasked with searching Dinslage and the surrounding area for Her Royal Highness," Manton said. "No doubt as a show of support to Keric. They'll question us, but if we stick to a reliable story that shouldn't be a problem. The Unavowed'll be wherever they believe they'll find Princess Rhonalyn and focused on looking for women. In either case, as two men, we should be able to make our way to her guard without too much trouble."

12

Dawn had yet to break as Wick steered his horse close behind Manton's mount and held his lantern above his shoulder to navigate the rutted road. His saddle creaked, and he absorbed the sound and smell of the layers of pine needles being crushed under their horses' hooves.

Him being the one to accompany Manton to Dinslage had never been a question in his mind. His orders from Prince Haaken had been to see to Prince Gage's safety and to make sure His Highness received justice. The best way Wick saw to do that was having Prince Gage remain at the beach while he accompanied Manton to Dinslage to oversee making contact with Princess Rhonalyn's guard and making sure Manton didn't slip away after. As far as he was concerned, no matter what it took or what was in their way, Manton would serve as a witness to His Highness's innocence over the stolen gold.

A squirrel chittered to Wick's right. He jerked, causing his horse to sidestep. Exhaling, he loosened his reins. Usually, being a knight with orders provided him a sense of security, but not this time. His orders wouldn't matter to the soldiers Manton called the Unavowed. Meanwhile, his distrust for Manton ran rampant.

The man ambled along on the girls' mount as if completely at ease, swaying with its stride and even humming a few notes. Wick was more than a little tempted to silence him with some choice words, but he held his tongue.

Before leaving the beach, to differ their appearance and look more like locals, they had changed their tunics, shaved, and left their packs on the beach. When Wick had gone to strap on his sword, Manton shook his head. "You can't bring that. I don't know how you've gotten this far with it, but it isn't legal for commoners to carry such a weapon in Delkara. If any guardsman sees it, at best they'll confiscate it and fine you for carrying it. At worst, they'll arrest us."

"As of when?" Prince Gage asked.

"Over a year ago," Manton said. "It was announced as law in Delkara. No commoner may carry a bladed weapon longer than a dagger's length." He shrugged. "Not that many people still had any. Almost every commoner in Delkara who once owned such weapons surrendered them as a means to pay their taxes."

It crossed Wick's mind that Manton could be lying about the law to manipulate him into disarming himself, but that seemed unlikely since a sword would have protected them both. In the end he concluded that Manton could be speaking the truth. The possibility bothered him since it meant King Strephon of Delkara had issued such a law. However, having lived through an attack in Edelmar that he'd once thought perpetrated by rebel commoners, Wick couldn't fault King Strephon for forbidding commoners from carrying such weapons.

But it meant that now he had at hand naught but a knife and his wits while traveling with a rebel smuggler into the heart of a city that was doubtless crawling with loyal and disloyal soldiers in hopes of convincing Keric's royal guard that they too wanted Keric's princess returned safely to her kingdom. What could possibly go wrong?

Wick had expected he and Manton would cross paths with soldiers in some form once they reached a road, but so far they had seen none. They had overtaken a cart man who seemed half asleep, passed merchants' wagons camped by the side of the road, and met a huntsman with two dogs.

Dawn began to lighten the road, and they encountered a group of barefoot children. The oldest, a boy of probably twelve, carried a basket with a spattering of gooseberries in it while a girl, who looked a few years younger, held a lantern and a collection of hazelnuts caught up in her skirt. One of the five younger children held a fistful of dandelions. Most likely they had come from the city to search for wild flowers, fruits, nuts, roots, and mushrooms to sell or eat. Such foraging wasn't unusual among the common, but the children's silence was. They didn't talk or joke as Edelmarian children would have, and most of them were as skinny as a weapon trainer's pell post. That made Wick wonder anew about Manton's claims. Could conditions in Delkara be as bad as Manton had implied?

Wick studied Manton's back, finding it difficult to reconcile assisting and even sympathizing with someone whom he would have been much happier to have locked in a cell.

Manton must have felt his gaze for he twisted around and looked back at him. "You're an even quieter companion than Gabe."

"I'll take that as a compliment," Wick muttered.

"You know, not so long ago, Gabe and I were friends," Manton said, his voice carrying a trace of remorse.

Wick scoffed. "Friends? Yeah, right up until you left stolen goods in his saddlebag."

"Four of us were sharing that tent," Manton said. "His saddlebag just happened to be closest. My intent was only to store the goods there until I could load them where they were meant to go, and I was in the middle of doing exactly that when he returned. It was he who left unexpectedly without giving me a chance to remove them. So, other than perhaps feeling lied to about my allegiances, which considering our previous conversations shouldn't have been a shock to him, I don't see why he's so angry. It was I who answered to my people for the loss of the coins and he who walked away with them. Clearly, Gabe wasn't caught with them. He wouldn't be a free man if he had been. So why does he act like I ruined his life?"

Wick swallowed the outraged response that rose on his tongue. He shouldn't even have been having this conversation. He clenched his jaw and shifted his gaze to the road ahead. "How much farther to Dinslage?"

Manton grunted. "It's just up ahead."

Silence stretched between them.

"How do *you* and Gabriel know each other?" Manton asked.

Wick was hesitant to reply, but he feared refusing to answer might fuel Manton's curiosity. "We met a couple of years back. He and I had similar interests, and Gabe asked me to travel with him."

"But you didn't keep traveling with him. Why?"

Wick's mind filled with memories from Aro. He had known that day that something was terribly wrong and that His Highness shouldn't be left alone, yet Prince Gage had used his power to silence and control him. He'd been so certain Prince Gage had some alternative plan and wouldn't return with Sir Reid and Sir Brent, but to accuse him aloud of such a deception or break his orders had seemed unthinkable. Wick wondered now what would have happened had he defied his orders that day. He shoved the thought aside along with the resentment and anger it stirred. "Gabriel and I had a difference of opinion about the direction we should go. I went one way; he went another. After that we didn't cross paths again, until recently."

"Recently," Manton questioned, "as in you decided to travel with him again and, what, help him track me down?"

"He was upset about what you had done. I simply offered to help."

"But from what you've both seen and learned, you know now that I have good reasons for what I do."

Wick clenched his jaw. He wanted to say, "Do I?" But he bit

back the words. Better to let Manton assume he had convinced them, than to make it clear they were still seeking justice. As they rode on in silence, Wick's thoughts returned to their current task. "I'd have thought we'd have encountered at least one patrol by now."

Manton nodded with a frown. "Me too."

Wick peered through the shadowy trees, wondering what the lack of soldiers meant. He didn't have long to consider the question before the forest ended and sunlit fields came into view surrounding the disorderly sprawl of Dinslage. Renewed tension rose in him.

The sun was barely an orange slice on the horizon, and yet it was bright enough to make Wick squint. They turned onto a dirt lane between crops high enough on either side of them that they could have trailed their hands through the grain heads. In another field of shorter, bushier plants, serfs carrying baskets were harvesting broad beans. Other serfs moved among a strip of grapevines, using hoes to cut away weeds from the plants' bases. A few fallow fields left dark, empty tracks in the rock-strewn land while in front of them more grain fields wrestled produce from the soil even up to the very edge of the dwellings that hunkered outside the closest jagged piece of Dinslage's city wall.

As they approached the city's outer edge, entering a squalor of buildings, Wick kept a wary eye. This portion of the city was unfamiliar to him. It wasn't the way he and Prince Gage had entered Dinslage, and it certainly wasn't the direction they had taken when they left. Manton led the way past the hovels on the city's fringe into a twisting maze of homes and dingy shops that looked as haggard as the people bustling among them.

Stagnant, reeking puddles filled the rutted street. Beggars were hunched in doorways, and shopkeepers kept watchful gazes while opening their windows and straightening their wares for the day's business.

Those managing livestock drove the animals around those entering the city and out toward wasteland grazing. The bleating sheep and goats, barking dogs, creaking wood, squawking birds, and muttering voices mingled together in the narrow, convoluted lanes, putting Wick even more on edge. Normally, the clamor of city life would have made him feel at home, but after so much quiet, it felt like the rising wind of a coming storm.

Seemingly unaffected by the noise, Manton maintained an appearance of ease, navigating the squalor like someone with every confidence he would be left to his own business.

Several turns and a narrow alley later, Manton slid off his horse in front of what Wick identified as a stable only because of the creaky, rusted sign hanging on iron loops outside the building's large doors. "What are you doing?" Wick asked.

Manton flipped the reins over his horse's head. "Going the rest of the way on foot. It'll allow us more maneuverability"

Wick took that to mean it would allow them to slip out of sight faster if anything went wrong. "Fine." He slid off his mount.

Once they had stabled their horses, they trekked onward, wading through a flock of honking geese herded by a boy with a stick. Not long after, Manton turned down a crooked, rubbish-filled alley scattered with chickens and ripe with the stench of decaying produce. Wick held his breath as he avoided the worst piles and kept an eye on the chickens pecking at the produce, ready to kick any that might rush at him. Many of the birds clucked at them, while others puffed their dirty feathers and beat their wings in annoyance. A rooster eyed them but kept to itself.

The alley came out on a busy, straight-ish street that Wick recognized from his and Prince Gage's previous wanderings in Dinslage. He glanced down the street to where he recalled a guard tower was located. The tower was there, but it appeared empty.

Thankful for that but feeling even more unsettled by it, he followed Manton, who turned away from what Wick was pretty sure was the direction of Murk Tavern and toward what seemed to be the city's center.

As he caught up with Manton, he became aware of Manton's easy pace in contrast to his own marching stride. Slowing, Wick loosened his form from a soldier on a mission to a yielding stride that blended more effectively with the townspeople.

After traveling three more streets and taking an arched passage through a building, they exited onto a broad street with nicer shops and minimal activity. The few people moving about felt like a blessing, as they provided cover, but then Wick caught sight of two soldiers in bright yellow tabards heading their way.

His insides lurched. He had to remind himself twice that even if the Dinslage soldiers stopped and searched them, they would be fine. Neither of them were marked. They weren't carrying anything suspicious. And no one would recognize them because no Dinslage soldiers had been at the meadow. Or would they? He thought of Prince Gage being identified by Radnor, a Nikledon guard who had been at the same manor as the Unavowed soldiers. Sweat beaded on Wick's palms, and his heart beat quickened.

The Dinslage soldiers drew closer. Wick knew that fleeing would only draw suspicion, and yet everything in him wanted to bolt. Through sheer willpower he forced his feet to keep moving forward at the same pace.

Manton grasped his arm and tugged him toward a shop. "That's the one. Come look!"

Confused and yet relieved to have his path diverted, Wick followed Manton into a shop. He wasn't sure if they were heading toward the inn or doing something else entirely, but he didn't care as long as it meant putting distance between himself and the soldiers.

Manton picked up a clay pitcher and turned it in his hands. "Do you think this will do for her?"

Standing beside him, Wick glanced in confusion at the pitcher, then looked back toward the street to see if the soldiers had taken note of them.

"Hey!" Manton said. "I need your eyes on this."

Wick jerked his gaze back to the pitcher. "Right." Manton's reprimand wasn't necessary. Wick was already kicking himself. How much stupider and more obvious could he be? He eyed the pitcher as if truly evaluating it, sensing the shop owner coming their way. "If you want my opinion," Wick said, forcing his racing mind to play his role, "I think she'd hate it. You should buy her something more personal."

Manton set the pitcher back on the shelf. "You're probably right. So, I should look elsewhere?"

"Yeah."

"Right." Manton pointed toward the shop's back door. "I know another spot we can try."

With a new appreciation for Manton's skill at evasion, Wick moved with him out the back door onto a cobblestone lane. Cleaner than other streets they'd been on, it had several people wandering it and two townspeople purchasing firewood from a seller with a handcart. Keeping an eye out for yellow tabards, Wick's gaze was roving the street ahead when a hand clapped down on his shoulder. His heart leapt in his chest.

"You know," Manton said, leaning in close, "you're not half bad at this."

Taking a breath and trying to ease his racing heartbeat, Wick shook off Manton's grip in annoyance. "Where to next?"

Manton nodded to their right. "Our destination is one street over."

"Great. Lead the way." Wick fell in behind Manton and prayed that Princess Rhonalyn's guard would actually be at the inn.

13

SHADOWS CLOSED INTO darkness around Wick and Manton as they moved through a curving, tunnel-like passage created between a cobbler's and tanner's shops. Wick felt his way along the stone walls that reminded him of being in the bowels of the White Fortress. He was thinking about Osbert's cooking when something squished beneath his boot. The stench of animal dung assaulted him. Gagging and dragging his foot to scrape it off, he breathed through his mouth and hurried after Manton.

They emerged into open air at the end of an alley between the side door of a clothier and the window of an apothecary. Wick happily inhaled the smell of sheep's wool mixed with the sharp scent of medicinal herbs.

They crossed the street together and headed toward a three-story building that wrapped around a large yard and open-sided stable. Three saddle horses and a matched team were stabled there, and parked on the opposite side of the yard was a carriage. Intricately carved and painted in bold colors and rich gold leaf, there was no question that it belonged to Princess Rhonalyn of Keric. Wick exchanged a look with Manton as they passed the carriage and headed for the inn's front door.

Considering how few horses there were outside, Wick wasn't surprised to find that the inn's common room wasn't bustling with Princess Rhonalyn's guard, as they had hoped. Instead, it held a gathering of random travelers. At the far back of the room, though, seated across a table from each other were two guardsmen whose armor and colors matched that of the carriage outside. Like many of the inn's occupants, the guardsmen glanced up when Wick and Manton entered. They then returned their attention to their food and a parchment spread between them.

Wick took a breath and rehearsed the plan in his head.

"Welcome, travelers," the innkeeper said as he approached. "Looking for a night's stay?"

Manton shook his head. "We're here to speak with guests of yours."

"Ah, are you to meet them here, or shall I show you to their room?"

"No need," Manton said. "We see them."

"Very good then." The innkeeper moved off.

Wick glanced across the room to where the royal guardsmen sat, then turned to Manton. "Shall we?"

Manton gestured for him to go first.

Wick frowned. Of course Manton would throw the responsibility of the approach on him. "Fine," he said, rolling his eyes. He strolled toward the guardsmen, trying to look as non-threatening as possible.

When he drew even with the guards' table, he leaned over it. "We, um, came across an eagle you might wish to take into your charge. Its name is Vanquisher. We— "

Before he could say another word, the closest guardsman seized the front of Wick's tunic and, leaping to his feet, drove Wick backward against the edge of an empty table. Wick's upper body tipped backward, and his feet slid out from under him. He seized the guard's arm to keep himself from crashing onto the boards. His tunic dug into his damp armpits, and his heart thudded in his chest.

As he teetered there, Wick realized too late that he'd failed to consider the fear and anger in Princess Rhonalyn's retinue. His eyes wavered between the guardsman's livid gaze and the tip of a dagger that was a hand's breadth from his throat.

The guardsman's knuckles were white on the dagger. "Vanquisher. Who told you to come here and mention Vanquisher?"

Wick blinked. He'd expected the man to demand to know where Princess Rhonalyn was, not question the source of his information, particularly since the source should have been obvious.

"Answer him! Or forfeit *his* life!" The other guard ordered. Wick flicked his gaze toward the other guard who had Manton backed against a wall with a sword pointed at his chest. Every eye in the room was on the four of them.

Wishing he had attempted diplomacy rather than subtlety, Wick tried to make his voice sound calmer than he felt. "Vanquisher's owner did."

"She also said that Vanquisher flies untethered and enjoys the skies," Manton added in a casual tone as if telling someone they'd wrongly identified the meat in a pottage as chicken when it was actually mutton.

Both soldiers seemed to breathe for the first time since Wick had spoken, but the first guard's grip on Wick's tunic remained and neither the sword nor the dagger moved. Wick recalled the next phrase Princess Rhonalyn had said to use and hoped it produced better results. "And she said to tell you that the horse you picked for her is one she would recommend."

The guard's hostility morphed into uncertainty. Clearing his throat, the guard lowered his dagger. "Perhaps I've been a bit hasty." He backed off a step, allowing Wick to regain his footing, and released his tunic. "I'd like to hear what you have to say."

Wick tugged straight his tunic and sent a reproachful glance at their audience. Most of those present stirred back to life and began murmuring to each other over their food, but one traveler toward the front of the common room continued to watch them.

The Keric guard pointed toward a nearby passageway. "In private might be best."

Wick couldn't have agreed more. He wanted to step aside and compel the man to go down the passage first, but he knew the same reason he wanted the guardsman in his sight was probably why the guard had directed him to go first. One of them had to choose to trust the other, and Wick figured he'd have to risk it.

He strode into the passage on unsteady legs. Considering the knife that had been at his throat and that he had no protection against whatever came next, he was just glad his legs were supporting him at all. As he walked down the passage, he glanced over his shoulder. The first guard trailed him while the second guard followed, the edge of his sword still threatening Manton.

Wick noted the annoyance on Manton's face, but he felt no pity for him. In fact, considering that Manton had insisted Wick be their spokesperson, Wick found it rather fitting that Manton was the one being treated as leverage.

"Upstairs," the guard directed.

Wick climbed the stairs, then followed each consecutive order the guard gave, which led to him standing in the middle of the room where the guardsmen were staying. Their cloaks were hanging by a fireplace, and bedrolls and saddlebags lined one wall. The second guard followed them inside with Manton, kicking the door closed.

"You've clearly spoken with Princess Rhonalyn," the first guard said, addressing Wick. "Where is she?"

"She and Lady Aisley are safe and hidden in the woods," Wick replied. "We would've brought them to you, but the risk to Her Royal Highness's safety was too great. The group of commoners who took her wanted to petition her. But there are others—soldiers, well armed and displaying no identification—that answer to someone who desires Her Royal Highness dead. They followed her when she was taken from here." Wick saw confusion and doubt flicker through the man's eyes, but he kept going. "We rescued her from these soldiers, but they are still hunting her. She needs the protection of her royal guard. We—" Wick paused at the look of trepidation that passed over the man's face. A chill ran up his back. "What's wrong?"

The guard shifted on his feet, angst filling his features. "The rest of her guard…" He glanced at the other guardsman.

The man shook his head at his fellow guardsman and spoke in the noblemen's tongue. "Nay. Do not tell him. We do not even know who they are."

"She sent them," the first guardsman replied in the noblemen's tongue. "And she has indicated we can trust them. Besides, if she is with them and not our people, then the rest of the guard did not tarry overnight because of finding her. We said it ourselves, Tristan; we art running out of options. These two may be the only aid we have."

At their exchange, apprehension coiled around Wick's chest. If the guardsmen were hoping to find help in him and Manton, they were all in serious trouble.

"I told you," Tristan said in the noblemen's tongue, "we need only to wait a bit longer. The rest of the guard will return."

"How much longer? You know as well as I do that if the commander changed his plans, he would have sent someone to inform us." The first guard pointed at Wick. "And now he is saying a group of soldiers is seeking to kill Princess Rhonalyn. What if—" He pressed his lips together as if afraid to say it aloud.

"Nay, do not borrow trouble!" Tristan snapped. "They wilt return. They must!"

Wick finished the first guard's thought in his own head. What if the rest of Princess Rhonalyn's guard had been attacked and weren't coming back? Needing Manton to know what they were saying but also needing to conceal his knowledge of their language, Wick addressed the guards in the commoners' tongue, hoping they would assume he had interpreted their tone rather than their words. "You don't know where the rest of her guard is, do you?"

The two men exchanged looks. The first guard switched back to the commoners' tongue as well. "We've been waiting for them to return."

"Waiting?" Manton exclaimed with a stir of concern. "You mean the rest of her guard is late coming back? By how long?"

Tristan frowned at his companion before replying himself. "They were supposed to return at sundown last night."

"We assumed," the first guard added, "that we'd see them this morning or at the very least that our commander would send word. But we've heard nothing, and none of the local soldiers have been forthcoming with information, even though they were supposedly helping our men search."

Manton cursed. "We need to get out of here."

Tristan shook his head, keeping his sword on Manton. "Neither of you are going anywhere."

"You don't understand," Manton said. His tone turned commanding. "We all need to get out of here. Right now! Your princess knows it was soldiers who tried to kill her, which means those soldiers don't just want her dead; they need her dead. They can't find her, but if they can eliminate her guard before any of you find her or learn the truth about the attempt on her life, they will have a better chance of containing and silencing Princess Rhonalyn and her young lady-in-waiting."

Wick shuddered at Manton's assessment. An unguarded princess would indeed be easier to kill and an unsuspecting royal guard spread out searching would be far easier for the soldiers to target than a guard on full alert rallied around those they had pledged their lives to protect.

"If that's true," Tristan said, "why wouldn't the soldiers also come for me and Cayden?"

"Because you're the bait to lure her here," Manton replied. "This is a trap, and all four of us are going to get caught in it if we don't leave right now!"

His heart racing in response to the urgency in Manton's voice, Wick turned to the first guard. "Cayden, I really think you should listen to him."

Cayden, who had moved to the window to look through its slats, cursed. "It's already too late." He turned back to them, fear etched across his features. "There's a group of soldiers entering the yard below."

14

FEELING LIKE HE'D just fallen off a cliff, Wick rushed to the window. Sure enough, heavily armed soldiers wearing armor but no colors or coat-of-arms were dispersing around the inn's yard. A handful of them headed for the inn's front door. They must have had a spy in the inn's common room who had tipped them off to his and Manton's arrival. Wick gripped the window's ledge. "Is there another way out of here?"

"Several," Cayden replied. "The best way is the servants' stairs. Leads to a passage with a door out the back of the inn."

Tristan grabbed a set of saddlebags and seized the door's bolt. "Follow me, and stay close." He drew open the door, checked the passage, then hurried out. Manton followed, and Wick sprinted after them with Cayden close behind.

They heard a commotion from the common room below. "What's the meaning of this?" the innkeeper shouted.

If someone replied, Wick didn't hear it as he dodged past the guests' stairs and fled with the others around a corner.

Halfway along the passage, Tristan turned toward a narrow stairway and was about to launch down the steps when he caught himself and turned back with a look of consternation. "Cayden, her maids, Kendra and Tess?"

Cayden looked toward the steps leading upward. "I'll get them. Go! We'll meet you at the water." Cayden dashed up the stairs.

With a grim look of determination, Tristan raced down the stairs,

Manton close behind him. Wick flew after them. At the bottom, Tristan and Manton turned left. Wick was about to follow when they came scrambling back toward him.

"Run!" Manton bellowed.

Wick didn't need to see what was behind them. Tristan's uniform must have given them away. Wick raced down the passage the opposite way, only to realize it was a dead end.

Dismay filled him, and his mind grasped for options. They needed a way out. A window, maybe? Better to exit at the back of the inn away from the soldiers in the yard. He angled toward the next door to his right, praying it was unlocked.

Wick heaved the handle upward and smashed his body into the door. It flew open, slamming against something behind it. Someone screamed. Wick flinched, but he kept moving. He spotted a wooden-slatted window and dashed toward it. Turning sideways at the last moment, he leapt into the air, curled his arms around his head, and smashed through the slats. The wood burst around him with the snap of cracking timber.

He landed with a jolt outside the room. For a moment, he couldn't draw air. Another cry came from inside the room. Metal clanged on metal.

"Get out of the way!" someone bellowed.

Gasping, Wick struggled to his feet, clutching his right elbow. People stared and pointed at him, and shopkeepers leaned out their windows, trying to see what the ruckus was about. Wick's fingers tingled, his elbow throbbed, and his shoulder screamed in pain. But he didn't have time to assess if he'd done any lasting damage. Instead, he glanced around, trying to figure out where to go.

Another yell came from his left. He turned. Two Unavowed soldiers were shoving people aside as they ran toward him.

"Over here!" another soldier shouted from the opposite end of the street, weaving through the crowd toward him.

Wick glanced back in the inn's smashed window. Manton and Tristan seemed to be engaged within, trying to pin the door closed. Wick knew if he didn't do something, they would all be surrounded in a matter of moments. He bolted, hoping the Unavowed soldiers would follow him and give Manton and Tristan a chance to get out.

He sprinted for the only alley he could see that went through to another street. The soldiers veered after him. Dodging around people, Wick slid into the narrow lane and put on a burst of speed. He reached its end, turned left, and crashed into a woman carrying a basket of produce. She screamed, and her basket and everything in it went flying. Grabbing her, Wick managed to shove her back upright while maintaining his momentum. "Sorry!" he shouted over his shoulder as he ran onward.

More cries came from behind him, followed by the clatter of metal as the soldiers raced after him. Feeling exposed without any armor of his own but also thankful not to be weighed down, Wick leapt over a street vendor's wares and darted into the closest shop that had daylight coming through its open back door.

The moment he made it to the shop's rear door, however, he regretted his decision. It didn't open to a street but to an enclosure of small gardens fully surrounded by shops. The owner of the shop he had just come through yelled at him to stop, but it was too late for that. Wick dashed across the first garden, trying to avoid the vines and bigger produce, and hurdled a small fence as he launched himself into the next garden. Landing in a row of chives, he fled between rows of strawberry plants and redcurrant bushes and up the steps of another shop.

As he grabbed the door's latch, a knife slammed into the wood beside his shoulder. His heart lurched. He yanked the door open and fled through it.

"Halt!" Someone shouted after him. "Or the next one'll be in your back!"

Wick kept moving. Weaving through small barrels and sacks of flour, he passed a startled lad at a board, kneading dough. Wick then barely dodged a baker's wooden paddle.

"What are you doing in my supplies?" the baker roared. "Get out of my bakery!"

Happy to oblige, Wick lunged out the shop's front door. He skidded on wet cobblestones and burst into a sprint. He could hear the baker bellow behind him. "Soldiers! What is this? He went out the front!"

With a burst of speed, Wick dodged into a crowd. He didn't dare run through another shop for fear of being trapped. The people around him, oblivious to his situation or the dire importance of his escape, commented on him zigzagging through their midst as if he were a curiosity. That is, until the soldiers came after him. Then their murmurs turned into cries of surprise, outrage, and pain.

Breathing hard, Wick burst from the group, swerved around a merchant's cart and, with a running leap, cleared a craftsman's display of wooden benches. He landed hard and banked left down a rocky dirt lane that ran beside two shops and a portion of the city wall.

There were few people in the lane, which allowed him to move faster, but it also left him exposed. The thought of a knife impaling his back inspired a new level of speed. He tore headlong down the lane, searching for somewhere to go.

Ahead, he saw to his left a street and to his right an arched opening in the city wall. He opted for the opening. Not slowing to make the turn, he caught himself as he slammed into the far side of the arch and shoved off, sending himself rebounding through the opening to his right. His choice proved to be a mistake. The opening was at the top of a flight of stairs. He half-leapt, half-fell down the steps and landed in a painful jumble just shy of a muddy trench.

The muddy trench occupied a space between the wall and a discordant sprawl of dwellings. A few paces from where he had dented the sloppy ground, a gnarled old woman in a worn dress and with a hard gaze eyed him as she emptied the contents of a wooden bucket into the ditch with a splat. The reek reached Wick's nose at the same moment as the jangle of armor assaulted his ears. He shoved himself to his feet and ran past the woman.

The moment he could, he dove out of sight behind a hovel. Wick leaned against the building's cracked and crumbling wattle-and-daub wall, fighting to catch his breath. His mind was so occupied with whether or not he'd been spotted by his pursuers that it took a moment before he realized he had an audience. A young girl with a toddler on her hip and four chickens pecking the ground around her stood at the next hut over, staring at him with wide eyes as if he were some sort of wild creature.

Gasping for breath, he didn't care what she thought of him. He lurched back into a run. Trying to keep the city wall in sight as he raced deeper into the dwellings, he swerved around one hut and then the next. Nothing in Dinslage seemed to continue in a straight line for long, which gave him cover but also made it nearly impossible to stay oriented.

Pausing between two huts to gulp air, he glanced back the way he had come. There was no sign or sound of the soldiers, only the peasants who were either too young or two old to work the fields. Relief flooded him. He had lost those pursing him. Now he just needed to get somewhere he could blend in, then he could figure out what to do next. He moved to the end of the huts, checked both ways, and strolled across to the opposite set of homes. Hurrying between these huts, he stepped out into the next lane. Out of the corner of his eye, Wick caught a flash of movement. Something thick and hard slammed into his chest, knocking him over backwards. He hit the ground so hard his head bounced and his vision blurred.

15

Wick groaned. Pain pulsed in his head, and black spots danced in his blurred vision. He blinked, trying to regain his sight. Someone yanked the knife from his belt. He tried to fend the person off but couldn't see well enough to do so. Gauntleted fingers clamped around his arms. With rapid blinking, Wick's eyesight cleared, and he found himself staring into the callous, victorious gaze of an Unavowed soldier. The soldier yanked Wick's wrists together and pinned them in one gloved fist.

A dizzying urge to fight him filled Wick, but his stunned body wouldn't respond. The soldier drew a strip of cord from his belt, looped it multiple times around Wick's wrists, then tied it in a tight knot. With a secure one-handed grip on Wick's arm, the soldier dragged him upright and out into the center of the lane.

Wick stumbled over his own feet and was just regaining a sense of stability when the soldier jerked him off balance. He landed in a heap in the dirt, his head pulsing. The soldier lifted his gauntleted hand over his head as if signaling someone. Wick followed his captor's gaze to where another soldier stood high on the city wall. The lookout signaled back, then turned away.

Wick's stomach rolled. The soldier's position on the wall had no doubt provided a bird's-eye view of the dwellings he'd been running through, which explained how he'd been intercepted.

His captor wrenched Wick back to his feet and sneered. "That's right, the scattered walls of Dinslage aren't as useless as you stupid commoners think. Now move." He tried to muscle Wick forward.

Wick dug in his heels and twisted his arms. The man's grip on his arm slipped, but the soldier twisted, slamming his opposite metal-gloved hand into Wick's stomach. The impact doubled Wick and made his eyes water. Blinking back tears, he gasped for air, but his lungs wouldn't work. He crumpled to his knees. His insides spasmed and then finally released. He dragged in air. Relief and nausea flooded him. Swallowing, he inhaled breath after breath.

"Get up." A sharp tug on his bound arms forced him to acknowl-edge his captor. At the man's second insistent yank, Wick struggled to his feet to avoid the soldier dislocating his arm. The moment he was on his feet, something stabbed his side with a biting pain. He looked down. A small circle of blood saturated his tunic where the blade of his own knife had pierced him. "Resist again," the soldier warned withdrawing the blade, "and you'll find out just how deep your own weapon can go. Now, move."

Wick choked back another bout of nausea and this time allowed the soldier to steer him forward. As Wick walked, icy dread traveled into every fiber of his being. He'd been in rough spots before but never anything like this. Once the Unavowed had him off the street, they would demand he tell them everything he knew about Princess Rhonalyn. And he had no doubt they would use whatever means necessary to get that information from him. Cold sweat pooled on his damp skin. It wasn't a question of if he would break but when.

Panic wrapped around his chest. The only chance he had of not betraying the royalty of two kingdoms would be if he escaped or with-held the truth long enough for the others to flee.

At some point, Prince Gage would have to realize their plan had gone awry and they should leave their sandy refuge. But how long would that take? Wick swallowed hard. And how long could he keep silent while being questioned by the Unavowed?

Prodding him with the knife, Wick's captor directed him around a half-dozen huts and toward the city wall. The peasants they passed averted their gazes, the message clear. Wick would get no help from them.

A prickling dread traveled up and down his spine. He was alone, and he was running out of time. Out in the open with only one captor, he still had a chance, but once the soldier brought him to the others, escape would become impossible.

They approached the city wall, and the soldier turned him to follow the edge of another section of the same trench Wick had encountered earlier. The ground was higher there, and the mud dry. The trench narrowed as it passed under an earthen ramp that led through a large gate. Built of vertical timbers, the gate looked as if it had been breached by a battering ram at some point. Chunks of wood were missing from the timbers, and its rusted hinges were buckled inward.

An oxcart driver was just coming through the opening. With one look at the soldier and Wick, the driver veered his cart as far to the side of the ramp as he could and rolled past them without a second glance. It was the same with everyone they encountered. As the soldier forced Wick along a street bustling with people, everyone observed them, but no one stopped what they were doing or made eye contact. Instead, they gave the captor and captive a wide berth.

For the first time that morning, Wick wished to encounter Dinslage soldiers, but none were to be seen in any direction.

His insides churned, and his heart pounded. He wanted to scream at the people to help him, but he knew no one would risk their own neck for him. And even if they did, he would likely end up stabbed by his own blade before they could succeed. The more he thought, though, the more he realized being killed trying to escape would be preferable to the fate that likely awaited him.

"This way." The soldier jerked him around a corner and along a broad street lined with shops. Wick walked past the first couple of windows and their wares half oblivious. Then he saw pottery that he recognized. It was the same shop he and Manton had stood in that morning. Hope rushed through him. For the first time since entering the city, he knew exactly where he was and where he could go.

He glanced around, spotted what he needed, and prayed it would work. Veering toward a parked wagon, he planned out his steps to the pounding beat of his heart. He needed height and distance from the blade to avoid serious injury. When they drew even with the wagon's front wheel, Wick clenched his jaw and looked to the middle of the wagon's high side.

The moment it was within reach, Wick clamped his fingers onto the wagon's edge and drove his feet back into the soldier.

Wick expected to feel the sting of the blade. Instead, his spine jarred with the impact of slamming his feet into the soldier's armored hip, and his arm screamed with the pinching pain of the man's gauntleted fingers tearing loose. The soldier stumbled backward. It was now or never. Free of his grasp, Wick bolted around the wagon and back the way they'd come.

He was through the pottery shop and into the next street, racing around the firewood seller's handcart before he thought about the fact that his hands were still bound. Hoping the townspeople would be even less inclined to aid the soldier than they were him, he dodged into the tunnel-like passage beside the cobbler's shop. Slowing as the darkness closed in around him, he worked to quiet his frantic breathing and thundering heartbeat.

The rank odor of animal dung filled his nose once again. He glanced back at the opening behind him. He'd taken a chance that the tunnel would hide him, but the gamble left him trapped between the soldiers ahead of him at the inn and his captor behind him. He would need to be ready if anyone entered the tunnel. Lifting his hands, he used his chin to feel the cord binding his wrists. Once he found the knot, he bit the leather cord and tried to work it loose with his teeth.

Suddenly a wave of frantic relief washed over him, and his entire body began to shake. He leaned against the wall and stopped working on his wrists. His throat burned from dragging in air, and his chest felt bruised from his battering heartbeat. He forced himself to slow his breathing and lower his head to counter the lightheadedness that threatened to topple him. As his mind raced on, he returned to working on the cord with his teeth. He needed to get free and figure out what had happened to Manton and Princess Rhonalyn's two knights.

16

GAGE SHOVED TO his feet and paced through the deep sand along the back edge of the cliff. It had been too long. Manton and Sir Wick should have returned with Princess Rhonalyn's guard hours ago. Concern clenched in his stomach. He pivoted in the sand and slogged away from his saddlebags, then turned back toward them. Each step just increased his anxiety.

He had managed to keep calm all morning, waiting with the girls and listening to the monotonous noise of the cascading falls, gurgling water, droning insects, and trilling frogs. But now the sun was descending.

He glanced at the watery path along the cliff's edge. Where were they? Had they just been delayed or had something else happened? His mind reran the gauntlet of what their absence might mean. He could no longer deny that something had gone wrong.

Panic coursed through him, threatening to consume him. He needed to figure out what to do next. But how? None of their plans had accounted for any of them staying in that spot past midday. They had no food left, and their mounts hadn't eaten since the night before.

As if hearing his thoughts, Athalos nickered at him and then turned and bit Nigel. The poor mule brayed in complaint. Gage gritted his teeth to keep from screaming at the both of them.

He should have already been able to hand off the girls to Keric's royal guard and be on his way with Sir Wick and Manton to solve his own problems. But any hope he'd had of that had walked off the beach that morning.

He glanced at Rhonalyn. Unlike Aisley, who was building sand structures near the water, Rhonalyn sat with pompous composure on Sir Wick's blanket, staring out at the water.

No matter how Gage looked at it, Rhonalyn was at the center of all his current problems, and he suddenly wanted to release on her all his pent-up words and anger. His heart pounded, and his body hurt from containing the strain of his emotions.

He knew Rhonalyn was also a victim, but his control over his tongue wavered on a knife's edge. His mind provided words he could justify throwing at her, and he opened his mouth. Immediately Baron Roger's frequently bellowed rebuke during Gage's early days of training filled his head. *"Master yourself! You're letting your feelings conquer you. Implement self-control, and evaluate your situation logically. Only then will you stop reacting out of fickle feelings and start thinking and responding with your rational head."*

Gage swallowed what he'd intended to hurl at Rhonalyn. The action redirected his emotions to his own fears. His insides trembled. The situation was too big. And what could he do to solve it? Every resource and recourse he'd ever had was gone. His title was useless. His authority as a knight was null. His last friend, and the only person he could count on in Delkara was missing. And his mark condemned him to being bound and dismissed by anyone with the power to help them—if any help could even be found or trusted.

He could see no safe way forward. The more he thought about it, the more the cliff's walls felt like they were closing in on him. He wanted nothing more than to escape it all. He needed space to think, to breathe. If he could just get space, maybe he could clear his head and find a way through.

Athalos nickered at him again. Gage glanced at the animals and had an idea. Feeding them was the perfect excuse to leave the beach and the girls. Turning, he scooped up his saddle and headed toward the mounts.

Aisley straightened and pinned him with a sharp, inquiring look. With her long sleeves tucked up and her embroidered gold skirt knotted at her waist, she stood barefoot in the watery moat of her latest sand creation—a four-tower castle. The child's earlier happy humming had given way hours ago to silent determination as she smashed sand into the curtain walls and poked holes for arrow loops. And now her gaze pierced him.

Even Rhonalyn, who had sat in what appeared enduring patience, showed the cracks of someone who knew control was a fading illusion. Her hands flexed in agitation, then flattened and smoothed down her skirt. But her sharp, unsteady tone revealed the truth. "What are you doing?"

Gage's insides jumped. They'd said almost nothing to each other since Manton and Sir Wick's departure, and he had thought she'd maintain her stony silence. "The animals are hungry," he snapped. "I'm taking them to graze."

Rhonalyn squinted at him with a mixture of doubt and suspicion.

Gage continued toward the mounts anyway, anticipating further objections and all too ready to shred her verbally if she tried to stop him.

As he approached Athalos, the horse's ears angled backward. Gripping his saddle with its blanket, Gage kept a careful eye as he came in range of the animal's teeth and hooves. "Easy, fella."

Athalos flicked his ears forward and snorted at him.

"That's right. We're getting food." Gage ran his left hand down

Athalos's side and used his other hand to heave the saddle onto the horse's back.

Flattening his ears, Athalos tucked his tail and bucked hard. The saddle flew into the air and landed behind Nigel. The mule jumped sideways and brayed at Gage as if the assault were his fault.

Gage glared at Athalos. "Really?"

Athalos tossed his head, then bit at the lead line.

"Yeah, I know," Gage muttered. "You want me to feed you, not put you to work. But this is the only way you're getting food because, with or without a saddle, I'm riding you out of here." He wasn't about to lead the two mounts downstream, wading its rocky depths.

"Do you need someone to ride the mule?" Aisley asked from behind him. "I can help."

"You're not going with him!" Rhonalyn commanded before Gage could respond.

Out of spite, Gage considered countering Rhonalyn's order, but he didn't want Aisley with him. He faced the two girls. "I can manage on my own."

Furrows knit Rhonalyn's forehead, and her fingers clenched in her lap. "How long will you be gone?"

"An hour, or two. Maybe longer."

Rhonalyn glanced at the stream, then rose to her feet. "Then perhaps all three of us should go."

Gage's stomach lurched. "No! It's safer if you wait here."

Turmoil and apprehension filled Rhonalyn's gaze, reflecting Gage's own feelings, though he wasn't about to acknowledge his concerns to her.

The decision appeared to be mutual, for Rhonalyn's expression hardened as she straightened her shoulders and sat down on the blanket. "Of course, you're correct. It's best if the two of us stay, so that someone's here when my men arrive."

Her words and her gaze carried a threat and accusation, but Gage didn't care. He needed to breathe freely, and feeding the mounts was at least one problem he could solve.

<h1 style="text-align:center">17</h1>

Having picked edible plants while Athalos and Nigel tore up meadow grass but failing to snare any game, Gage headed back up the shadowy stream, riding Athalos bareback. He waved off insects as he steered Athalos beside the base of the cliff. Behind them, Nigel splashed through the rippling current. Gage tugged the mule closer and tried to listen ahead over the sloshing of hooves and chirping frogs.

He hoped he would round the corner and find only Sir Wick and Manton awaiting him on the beach, Princess Rhonalyn's royal guard having already departed with Her Royal Highness and Lady Aisley. Then, even if his stomach was mostly empty, he'd rest easier, knowing the morrow would have fewer problems in it.

With the last rays of the sun shimmering on the curves of the water ahead, he twisted Athalos around the tip of the embankment and looked toward the beach. The hope rising in him plummeted back into his gnawing stomach. Nothing had changed. The two girls were still waiting there.

A heavy weariness crept over him as he slid off Athalos's back, and his knees almost buckled as he landed in the sand. The fact that he'd gathered firewood to roast meat that he hadn't returned with, just made his failure to provide adequate food that much more glaring.

As he tethered the two animals, he felt Rhonalyn watching him from where she sat on Sir Wick's blanket. When he looked her way, she swung her gaze back to the water and took a breath as if grasping support from the disappearing sun.

Aisley said mournfully, "I'm guessing you didn't come across any sign of Manton or Wick or Princess Rhonalyn's guard?"

Gage shook his head. He hadn't even been able to find where Manton and Wick exited the stream on their way to Dinslage. He swallowed. "I think we're on our own."

He noted Rhonalyn's jaw clench and her hands knot in her lap around what looked like a book. Gage glanced about the beach, wondering where she'd gotten anything book-shaped. He realized then that not everything was the same as it had been. Manton's pack had been relocated to the far side of the dead fire, and the top of one of Sir Wick's bags lay open. His heartbeat sped up, and anger stirred inside him. "What have you been doing?"

"What have *we* been doing?" Pressing the book-shaped item into the folds of her skirt, Rhonalyn rose to her feet. "What have *you* been doing?"

Gage grabbed the saddle Athalos had refused to carry and glanced at its underside. The hidden leather compartment that his uncle's saddler had added to his replacement tack appeared undisturbed. Relieved his signet ring was still hidden but by no means appeased, he turned to Rhonalyn. "I said I was going to feed the mounts."

"Yes and that you'd be back in an hour or two."

"Or longer," he growled. With his hands balling, he trudged toward their bags. The straps on his own saddlebags were tied in neat, little bows. Anger ripped through him. He opened his mouth to demand an explanation, but Rhonalyn wasn't finished.

"Longer?" She pointed out at the water. "It's almost dark."

Gage yanked up his saddlebags and swung them toward her.

"It wasn't dark when you decided to dig through our things. You had no right!"

She crossed her arms, tucking the book-shaped item under her elbow. "We were hungry."

At her disdain-filled explanation, he dropped his saddlebags and marched toward her. "I told you there wasn't anything left to eat in our packs. Did you think I lied?"

He expected her to pull back, but Rhonalyn gave him a look like he was making a mountain out of a molehill. "We were looking for Wick's fishing line."

"We thought we could use it to help catch some fish," Aisley added, her tone placating.

The tantalizing hope of food shifted Gage's focus. "Did you? Catch any fish?"

Aisley shook her head.

"We never found the line," Rhonalyn said sharply and gestured across the sand. "And with all the mounts gone we couldn't exactly make another."

Her tone reignited Gage's outrage. "But you went through our bags anyway, just in case it was in one of them. You had no right!"

She stood her ground. "Well, had you been here, I'd have asked."

"You would have asked what, exactly? To rummage through our belongings?"

"No. I would have asked where Wick put the fishing line. But to your point, had I known one of you possessed an item that could make hours of waiting less mind-numbingly dull, yes, I'd have asked for it too. However, since you seem to think it outrageous of me to have made use of it, by all means put it back." Unfolding her arms, she thrust into his hands an actual book.

Since books were rare and usually owned only by the wealthy, it took him a moment to accept the truth of what he was holding. The book had a beautifully tooled leather cover and gilded clasps to keep its pages compressed. Fear coursed through Gage, swiftly outdistancing his anger. "In whose bag did you find this?"

"That one." Rhonalyn pointed to Sir Wick's saddlebags.

Gage wasn't sure whether to be relieved or even more frightened. "You're sure?"

"Yes," she answered. "It was with another book at the bag's bottom. They were wrapped together in a cut of leather. I borrowed this one but left the other for it appeared to be a journal. A journal is private, but books like that—" she tipped her head— "they're meant to be read."

Gage turned the book over in his hands. The edges of its leather cover showed signs of wear, a few pages were dented, and the ends of the clasps were shiny. Clearly, it had been well used, which seemed strange since he'd never seen Sir Wick reading it. With questions stacking in his mind, he unlatched the book's cover and ruffled through its soft pages. The script was flowing and precise. Every few pages the first line had an illuminated letter, and he recognized the titles and text.

"It's Scripture," Rhonalyn explained.

A flicker of annoyance passed through Gage that she just assumed he wouldn't know that. But then he remembered, she thought him a commoner and illiterate. Not to mention, though the book's tooling and illuminations were beautifully done, neither were particularly ornate, making it that much more unlikely that someone who couldn't read would be able to identify it as Scripture.

He closed and latched its cover, but his curiosity was not so easily shut. He glanced past her. "You said there was a journal with it?"

"Aisley." Rhonalyn gestured, clearly meaning for the girl to get the book.

"No, don't retrieve it," Gage said. He thrust the book of Scripture back into Rhonalyn's grasp. "Put them together and return them to where you got them. Neither should have been disturbed."

"You left us here hungry," Rhonalyn said. "An empty stomach needs a distraction."

With only a few wilted leaves of daisies and shepherd's purse to offer her, Gage couldn't exactly throw the comment back at her. But that didn't stop his anger. "I said, put it back! And from now on, stay out of our saddlebags." He held her gaze long enough to make his point, then marched toward Athalos.

"I'm not staying here another night," Rhonalyn declared.

Gage pivoted to face her. Her expression held resolve, but as she pressed the book against her skirt, he noticed her hand tremble. "Really?" he said. "Then what do you plan on doing?"

She looked out at the stream, then toward Athalos and Nigel. She lifted her chin. "Aisley and I are going to ride Manton's mule out of here and find our own way back to Dinslage."

"Manton's mule, huh?"

She glared. "Yes, and if you ever see Manton again, you can tell him I'll repay him for the animal the day he surrenders himself to Keric."

Gage scoffed and yet shook his head at her plan. Despite how much he would welcome being free of her and Aisley, the two of them departing to get lost in Delkara, killed by boars, or murdered by the Unavowed wasn't something he wanted on his conscience. "Delay until morning and I'll help you find a manor. You can seek help there to return to Keric."

Rhonalyn's expression wavered. "In the morning?" Her eyes

narrowed as she scrutinized his face. "Do I have your word on that?"

"I'm aiding you of my own free will. Don't you dare insult my honor as if I've been disloyal to you." He gestured toward the watery path leading to the surrounding forest. "Do you even realize the cost I've paid for helping you? Manton and Wick could be dead. Do you even understand that? Or were you too busy going through our belongings to care that *my* friend has disappeared while trying to help *you*?"

Rhonalyn sputtered at his words, and her expression turned into such a stormy mix that Gage wasn't sure whether she was about to respond in anger or tears. Instead, he got reprimanded from a direction he didn't expect.

"You shouldn't talk to her like that," Aisley said, planting both hands on her hips.

"Why not?" Gage snarled at the child. "Because I'm beneath her?"

"No," Aisley replied, looking like a vexed woodland nymph with her fingers forked into her embroidered gown and wisps of her blonde hair floating about her face. "You shouldn't treat her like that because she's a woman, and you're a man. You're supposed to protect her, regardless of her being a princess."

Jarred from his annoyance, Gage took a step back and for the first time considered Princess Rhonalyn in light of her womanhood and not in the context of her being a stolen valuable that he was now responsible to return. He pictured her as if she were Allard's sister, Sophia, and realized if a commoner were in his place, he would hope to God the man would respond honorably and with every bit of protection he could offer.

He swallowed, heat rising in his cheeks. "You're right," he murmured. Then he nodded to Rhonalyn. "I'm sorry."

"I accept your apology," she replied with stuffy arrogance.

Gage waited, but she said nothing else. Anger boiled again inside him. Really? She was going to act like she was being magnanimous and that out of the two of them *he* was the one who should apologize? He shook his head in disgust. She was hungry, bored, and homesick. He was grappling with the fact that his friend along with the only witness he had to prove his innocence and restore the life he'd once had might both be dead. Or if they were alive, they were likely captured by soldiers and being held.

The Unavowed! If the Unavowed had recognized and caught Manton and Sir Wick, killing them wouldn't be the soldiers' first action. They would want to known where Rhonalyn was. Icy panic raced through Gage, and he cursed his stupidity for not realizing the possibility sooner.

"We need to leave here. Now!"

Rhonalyn blinked. "What? You said we'd go to a manor in the morning."

"Listen to me!" Gage scooped up his saddle. "If the Unavowed got their hands on Manton or Wick, by now they could've learned where you are."

Rhonalyn's confusion was replaced by a look of alarm. She turned toward Aisley. "Grab the blanket. I'll get the other saddlebags."

The three of them scrambled around the beach in the growing darkness, grabbing the few items not already packed. After two tries, Gage managed to saddle Athalos. Next, he dumped the wood off Nigel and was in the process of swinging the saddlebags onto the mule when he heard the unmistakable splashing of someone coming up the stream.

18

Gage dropped the saddlebags and ran for Sir Wick's sword. The weapon would likely do him little good, but he wasn't about to be taken without a fight.

"If you're leaving on our account," a voice called out of the darkness, "you may want to reconsider."

"Manton? Wick!" Gage exclaimed, making out the knight's silhouette in the darkness. "Oh, thank God! I thought the two of you were either dead or captured."

The two men sloshed out of the water, trailing Sir Wick's horse, burdened with lumpy sacks.

"We came close to both," Manton said.

Wick nodded, sounding exhausted. "More than close."

Rhonalyn's gaze searched the water behind them. For a moment confusion and disbelief filled her face, then her expression became a hard mask.

"Princess Rhonalyn," Aisley questioned in the noblemen's tongue, "why are Baron Philip and the guard not with them?"

Rhonalyn shook her head and made no reply.

Gage swallowed. The rescue they had all hoped to gain in her guard clearly wasn't coming.

❧

Wick propped his wet boots at an angle in the sand next to the snapping fire and watched miserably as Manton told Prince Gage and Princess Rhonalyn about Dinslage.

Having packed food, purchased with money from the mount they'd sold, Wick had suggested starting a fire and eating while they talked. Prince Gage and Lady Aisley had accepted food, but Princess Rhonalyn had refused to eat anything. That was probably a good thing since the moment she'd heard Manton's theory about her missing guard, her face had turned even more ashen.

Wick had feared she would have a hundred questions, but instead she sat in silence. All too well Wick remembered Prince Gage's similar response after Allard's death. Cringing, he wished Manton would wrap up his retelling of the day's events. For at the moment, what good would more information do Princess Rhonalyn? People she cared about were missing and possibly dead, and now her path home was even more fraught.

"That," Manton said, "was when Wick smashed through the window and took off down the street with soldiers chasing him. Tristan and I drove back those attempting to breach the door and bolted it closed before we also dove out the window. But by then four more soldiers had reached the rear of the inn. I had Tristan's dagger, and he had his sword. Even so, I thought we'd be cut down immediately.

"It became clear in their first attack, though, that the soldiers wanted us alive. Multiple times they held back from strikes that could have ended one or both of us. Tristan became emboldened by this and went at them then with a vengeance. Together, he and I disabled two of them. The other soldiers learned from their fellow soldiers' mistakes and changed their tactics. Instead of trying to rout us, they kept their distance, engaging us just enough to prevent us from escaping.

"We knew it was only a matter of time before more soldiers arrived. Tristan created an opening and told me to take it. I did, only to round the corner and come face to face with three more of the Unavowed. I sprinted through an alley and used every bit of knowledge I had of the city to avoid getting caught. Thanks to a barrel at the top of some narrow stairs that I sent rolling down on top of two soldiers and a wall with enough cracks to scale, I finally lost them.

"After I was well clear of them, I trekked all over Dinslage trying to find Cayden and Tristan. But there was no sign of them or any women who looked like royal maidservants. When I could think of nowhere else to look, I made my way back to the livery where Wick and I left our horses and found him there."

"You never saw Sir Tristan again?" Rhonalyn asked, her voice a pained murmur.

Manton shook his head.

Wick winced as her gaze landed on him. He too shook his head. "Once I evaded the soldiers, I snuck back to where I could see the inn's yard but didn't find Sir Tristan. The Unavowed and every trace of your guard's presence, your carriage, your horses, all of it was gone. I'm sorry." He swallowed and added, "Sir Tristan knew you were with us but didn't know your location. If he escaped, he's probably searching for you. And if he was taken, no matter what, his loyalty and protection cannot be tarnished." Hearing her intake of breath, Wick continued despite a growing tightness in his chest. "As for the rest of your guard, it's impossible to know whether they're free, dead, or detained."

Princess Rhonalyn exhaled a slow, shuddering breath like she was struggling to hold herself together. Aisley, however, burst into tears and cried unashamedly.

None of them said anything. For a long stretch of time, the only sounds within their somber circle were Aisley's sniffling and the fire crackling and snapping as it consumed what had once been living trees.

Wick stared into the twisting flames, wishing there was anything he could say or do to fix what felt so broken. Back in the tunnel by the cobbler's shop, he had shifted his belt to cover the bloody hole in his tunic, but the pain in his side and the lingering ache in his head reminded him how close he'd come to becoming a captive of the Unavowed. The threat of the Unavowed, the need for a new plan, and the unpredictable nature of Princess Rhonalyn's grief left him struggling to know how to proceed.

He and Manton had discussed a plan back in Dinslage while waiting for a safe time to depart the city. They had even taken the first steps to implement that plan, but it depended greatly upon Princess Rhonalyn's willingness to accept something he was certain she would hate.

19

GAGE POKED THE end of a short stick he held into the fire, causing sparks to burst forth into the smoke. Hearing that the Unavowed had laid such a trap in the middle of Dinslage using Keric's royal guard deepened his fear. The Unavowed daring such a thing suggested either Dinslage's baron was complicit in the Unavowed's plot or that the Unavowed had known the Dinslage guards would be unable to respond, perhaps occupied elsewhere by the Unavowed's own doing.

At the thought, Gage shivered despite the heat of the fire. He had feared the damage Manton's rebel commoners could do. But the more he saw and heard of the Unavowed, the more he realized Manton's rebels were nothing in comparison. Manton's motives were different from his, but as for keeping Rhonalyn alive and preventing the Unavowed from destabilizing peace between Delkara and Keric, he found himself more than aligned with Manton's goal. But their options for getting Rhonalyn back to Keric were dwindling fast.

When he spoke, his voice sounded strained even to his own ears. "I agree we need to get her back to Keric. But, without her royal guard, is there even a safe way to do so?"

Manton shifted in the sand. "The Unavowed will no doubt have put a watch on the two bridges to Keric's border. And though there are paths through the cliffs of Nikor, the routes are complicated and perilous. Such a journey requires a guide, and the one person I knew with knowledge of those paths was killed two days ago. However, fortunately for all of you, you're traveling with a smuggler who knows people with ways to circumnavigate such issues as bridges. We'll still need to travel to meet up with my person, though." Manton tipped his head. "Which means, as Wick suggested back in Dinslage, the best protection for Princess Rhonalyn and Lady Aisley is for them to disappear in plain sight. In commoners' dresses, the two of you will become just two more women among the thousands in Delkara. Soldiers won't recognize you."

Gage glanced sharply at Sir Wick.

Responding with a shrug, Sir Wick gave him a look that said he really couldn't argue against the plan.

Gage stabbed his stick deeper into the fire. Sure, it was a great idea if all they were trying to do was conceal the girls' identities, but considering the results of his own journey while masquerading as a commoner, he wasn't convinced it would keep the girls safe. He also doubted Rhonalyn could pull it off. Even now she held her chin high, and her eyes flashed with the authority she so arrogantly wielded.

"There'll be no need to smuggle me over Keric's border." Rhonalyn's statement caused them all to look to her. She continued, "I'm not returning to Keric. At least not yet. I'm going to King Strephon." Steel edged her tone. "He needs to be made aware of what's happening in his kingdom, and he will help me find my guard. He and I will get answers together and deal with these traitorous soldiers."

Taken aback by her words, Gage remained too long with his stick stuck deep in the fire. The heat of the flames singed his skin. He yanked his hand back, leaving the stick behind. He flexed his fingers and turned Rhonalyn's words over in his mind. Despite the risk involved, her plan made sense to him.

A new and tantalizing idea entered his mind. He touched the vambrace on his right wrist as hope stirred through him. Perhaps

God had had a helpful reason after all for causing his and Rhonalyn's paths to cross.

Rhonalyn had just met with King Strephon, so there would be no question as to her identity as Princess of Keric, nor would anyone question her right to bring forward the issue of the Unavowed and the rebel commoners. And Strephon could scarcely refuse her request for aid.

To track down and deal with those who had attempted to assassinate her and who had made her royal guard disappear, she would need witnesses who could attest to the actions of the rebel commoners and the unidentifiable soldiers, and he, Sir Wick, and Manton were in the perfect position to do so. Among the five of them, they could testify to all of it—the treachery of the Unavowed soldiers, the reality of the rebel commoners, and the rash actions or inactions taken by the Delkaran lords.

The prospect of restoring justice within all three kingdoms and regaining his freedom stirred to life inside Gage. Providing such proof would also give him the perfect opportunity to petition for absolution from his mark. He took a deep breath. If successful, Rhonalyn's plan could help solve all his problems, not to mention get justice for Allard and Bardon.

"You can't go to King Strephon," Manton said.

"Why not?" Rhonalyn asked, her tone rising angrily.

"Because you'll be handing yourself to your enemy."

She huffed. "We've had this discussion. He's your enemy because you have made him so. He's not mine. Someone is undermining him, and he deserves to know. He also owes me the help to find my guard. I will not return to Keric without them."

"You aren't listening to me. If you take on this fight without an army to back you…" Manton shook his head. "You won't survive. Return to Keric first, for your sake as well as all of ours. Because the moment Strephon convinces your father it was rebel commoners who murdered you, it will go badly for us all.”

Rhonalyn’s lips curled into a frighteningly convincing smile. “Well then, the solution is simple. You need me alive, so that your people aren’t blamed for my death, and I need to get to King Strephon. So, you’ll take me to him and provide me protection along the way, so I can return alive to Keric.”

“No, you need to return to Keric now while you still can!” Manton’s gaze swung to Gage. “Gabriel, please. Tell her that she’s being a fool to challenge King Strephon about the Unavowed without having an army with her.”

Gage glanced between the two of them. If anything it sounded as if Manton wanted Keric to incite a war against King Strephon by marching an army into Delkara. He shook his head. “It seems to me she’s making more sense than you are. Her speaking straight to King Strephon sounds like the best way to deal with all of this. She wants to take down the Unavowed and whoever’s behind them, and I agree with her. I want the Unavowed brought to justice.”

“I’m with Gabe.” Sir Wick nodded at the girls. “And going to King Strephon, it’ll be all the more important for Her Royal Highness and Lady Aisley to travel under the guise of commoners.”

“I met with Strephon at Baron Selwin’s manor in Nikledon,” Rhonalyn said. “I suggest we return there. His Majesty may yet be there, and even if he’s not, Baron Selwin may know where he journeyed to next.”

At the mention of Nikledon, fear shot through Gage. “No!” The response popped from his mouth before he realized he and Sir Wick were both shaking their heads. “We should, um…” Gage tried to find a way to justify his outburst without explaining why neither he nor Sir Wick could return to Nikledon.

Sir Wick came to his rescue. "We should go to King Strephon's castle in Ithera. It will be safer to approach His Majesty somewhere the Unavowed won't expect you to travel. Besides, there's no way for us to know for certain which lords and soldiers in any given place are safe. There may be some in Nikledon who spy for or are part of the Unavowed. Thus, the best and safest choice is to go to King Strephon directly."

Rhonalyn's brow furrowed. "You may be right." Nodding, she lifted her head. "It's decided then. We head for Ithera."

With eyebrows raised, Sir Wick glanced at Gage. Realizing the knight was seeking his final approval, Gage felt a tremor run up his spine. Sir Wick was making it his choice, but what if he chose wrong? His heartbeat quickened, and his chest tightened. He couldn't. He couldn't be the one to launch them on this endeavor. At the thought, he battled to draw air. Every bit of him wanted to back away from the decision. He heard Haaken's voice in his head. *It is not honor or protectiveness driving you but fear. You are running scared.*

Gage held himself still even as panic ravaged his body. He longed indeed to run. To leave behind all the responsibility, the needs, the fears, the pain, and the losses. But he had tried that before; escape was impossible. The weight of it all simply found some other way to settle over him. His insides trembled. He had to find a means to carry it all, but how, and on what path?

He saw the hope there was in bringing Rhonalyn to Strephon. With King Strephon of Delkara and Keric's crown princess working together, there would be enough influence and power to restore order and justice in their kingdoms and help end the incursions into Edelmar as well. And he might gain his own freedom.

His grasp on that hope faltered. What if Strephon couldn't or wouldn't help? Or what if the Unavowed found them before they got to Strephon? Feeling as if he were drowning in indecision, he met Sir Wick's gaze.

Understanding flickering in the knight's eyes, Sir Wick spoke. "You asked me earlier to tell you if there was a *when* to knowing what we should do next." The knight nodded. "I believe this is it."

At Sir Wick's words, the pressure squeezing Gage's chest eased. "Right," Gage said. "Then we go."

20

In the early light of dawn, Gage packed his bags. He was filled with hope and unease. He comforted himself with the knowledge that Ithera was in the opposite direction from where the Unavowed were likely seeking them.

He glanced at the others. They'd eaten a swift meal, then the girls had gone down the beach to change behind one of the folds in the cliff.

The night before, Manton and Sir Wick had retrieved from the packs the commoner dresses they'd procured for the girls in Dinslage. The frock for Rhonalyn, a linen woad-blue, was much closer to the right size than the gray-brown dress they'd gotten for Aisley.

Sir Wick had explained they'd opted for larger rather than smaller with Aisley's dress since they hadn't remembered the girl's exact size. When Aisley held the frock up, it was clear their estimation had gone awry. The girl completely disappeared behind the dress.

Cringing, Sir Wick glanced at Manton. "Guess it's a good thing we also bought that needle and shears."

"Yeah, but that means someone's got to do the sewing." Manton eyed the gray-brown frock.

Sir Wick shrugged. "I'll give it a go. How hard can it be? Just cut it to size, then sew up the edges, right?" He reached for the dress, but Princess Rhonalyn snatched it away.

"Oh, no you don't! It's ugly enough as it is. Aisley and I will fix it." She snapped her fingers at Sir Wick, and held out her hand.

As Sir Wick dug the needle and shears out of his saddlebags, Gage noted a smile playing on his lips. Realizing then that the knight had gotten Rhonalyn to volunteer to do a task she never would have agreed to do if asked, Gage stifled a chuckle.

Looking at Aisley now in the morning light, he nodded in approval of the girls' work. Aisley looked very much the part of a commoner. Barefoot with a single blonde braid trailing down her back, grit under her nails, and her downcast eyes all combined into a fitting image.

Rhonalyn, not so much.

Despite the plain, loose-fitting blue dress she wore and the undyed cloth tied over her hair, she trekked across the sand with a commanding stride and annoyance on her face. She held her and Aisley's previous dresses as she used her free hand to pluck at her commoner skirt. "How am I supposed to ride in this? It is hardly a proper cut for a riding dress."

Gage coughed on a laugh as he grabbed his saddle.

"Well," Sir Wick explained, "most common women don't ride much, so there weren't many options. And since we don't have enough mounts, you may end up walking some of the time anyway."

"Excuse me?"

The knight lifted a hand. "Of course, you and Lady Aisley will start off riding. You'll ride double on my horse, and I'll walk. Gabe will have his mount, the mule will carry the supplies, and Manton will lead us on foot."

Rhonalyn huffed as she lifted her full arms. "And in which bag do I put our dresses?"

Having just settled his saddle on Athalos, Gage glanced over at her.

"Leave them," Manton said. "If we're searched, they'll cause trouble no matter who finds them."

Rhonalyn stiffened as she sought out Gage and Sir Wick's gazes. "I'm to seek an audience with King Strephon. I'm not"—she gestured at herself—"about to do so looking like this."

"It's not ideal," Sir Wick admitted, "but Manton's right. Those dresses are too identifiable as items that would never belong to commoners. We can't carry them with us."

"Exactly," Manton said. "Nor can any soldiers find that." He pointed to Sir Wick's sword.

Sir Wick's fingers turned white on the sword's sheath, but then he sighed. He gestured to Rhonalyn to hand over the dresses. She relinquished them to him. Sir Wick trudged to the back of the cliff and hung the sword and the dresses over a tree root.

Trying not to dwell on the loss of the weapon, Gage cinched Athalos's saddle, then evaluated the rest of Rhonalyn's appearance to make sure she looked the part of a commoner. The cuts and scrapes she'd acquired on her arms and face as they fled the soldiers were actually a blessing, for they created the illusion of someone who had worked in a rough outdoor environment. Her boots were somewhat questionable, but once they'd been dirtied up on the trail, they could pass for a commoner's. Besides, her flinching along barefoot would be far more noticeable than her expensive boots.

He searched her hands, for previously, there had been two rings on her fingers. They were gone. "Where are your rings?" he asked, wondering in whose saddlebags they'd ended up.

She folded her arms. "Hidden."

"I gathered that. Where?"

"On me," she replied, scowling at him.

Gage swept his gaze down her form and for a moment wondered what else she could have concealed beneath her skirt. Did she have a weapon? He doubted it, considering what had transpired with the rebels, but the possibility made him realize he shouldn't underestimate her. "Fine. Just make sure they stay hidden. And, going forward," he said, "you must behave like a commoner. Especially when it comes to keeping your gaze down and your royal tongue silent."

"And if in front of anyone"—Manton gestured around the group—"an assertion is made by any one of us about you, accept what's said and don't contradict it, no matter how distasteful or ridiculous it might be to you."

Gage nodded. "Like if one of us claims Aisley is Wick's cousin, Amy, and you're my sister, Rose."

Her eyes flashing, Rhonalyn pressed her lips together. The muscles in her jawline flexed, but she remained silent.

"Not bad," Gage said. "Now, if you can curb your facial expressions too, we might all survive this trip."

"My facial expressions?" A flutter of confusion filled Rhonalyn's face. "You think I can't control my expressions?" She flashed a smile as if offering him a plate of sweets. "Do think before making such an assertion." Her face and tone transformed again, this time into extreme sadness. "Or you'll never be sure of anything I say again." Her voice turned flat and derisive. "Now, do you have any more suggestions for me?"

Unnerved, Gage shook his head. "It seems you have things well in hand."

Her reply held cold determination, "I'll manage whatever I must to find my men."

Gage had a feeling this time she wasn't trying to make a point but rather stating a fact, one with which he sympathized.

"Now," Rhonalyn snapped, "why is everyone just standing around?"

The other three, who were paused watching their exchange, launched back into motion.

Manton threw the last supply pack onto Nigel. Aisley headed for the horse she was to share with Rhonalyn, and Sir Wick approached Gage.

"Before we depart," the knight said quietly, "I have something I was supposed to give you. Forgive me for not doing so earlier. I'd forgotten about it until this morning when I came across it again in my pack. I don't know what it contains, but your brother gave it to me to give to you." Sir Wick handed him the leather-wrapped books.

Gage's breath caught. "These came from my brother?" That they had belonged to Haaken made sense. Gage had often seen Haaken during a quiet moment, jotting notes in a journal, and he wondered what he wrote on those pages. He had assumed his curiosity would go unanswered, for he would never have dared trespass upon Haaken's privacy to read it. But now Haaken had given it to him. Why?

Sir Wick cleared his throat. "He also told me to tell you that, um, 'her prayer for you is his prayer for you.' Or, wait…" Sir Wick frowned and shook his head. "No, maybe it was, 'his prayer for you was her prayer,' I think." He cringed. "I'm sorry. It was when I was leaving Awnquera to come after you. I should remember, but I—"

Flinching at the bombardment of memories Sir Wick's words brought, Gage raised his hand. "It's alright, Wick." Between the Scripture and the words, Gage had a feeling Haaken's message was that Novia's prayer had become his brother's prayer for him. He gripped the leather-wrapped books. If Novia's hope for Haaken to know God the way she had was why Haaken had passed along the two books, what would he find within their pages?

"Are we departing or not?" Rhonalyn asked with commanding annoyance from where she sat in front of Aisley.

Clenching his teeth, Gage exchanged a look with Sir Wick and murmured, "Tell me, how does one interact with those above the salt and manage to remain civil?"

Sir Wick blinked. "You're asking me?"

"Well, you seem to have mastered the skill of it."

"Have I?" A flicker of something passed through Sir Wick's gaze before the knight smirked. "I supposed the secret is quite simple, really. Patience and the ability to bite one's tongue."

Gage rolled his eyes. "Ah, I see, quite simple."

21

WICK'S BOOTS SQUISHED with water as he trudged through leafy underbrush just ahead of the girls' horse and two steps behind the mule Manton was leading. According to the plan, Manton was to take them halfway to Lyster to a location they could shelter for the night.

By all appearances, Manton had accepted his role as their guide, but Wick wasn't convinced Manton wouldn't betray them and abandon that plan the moment it suited him.

Since leaving the beach, they had traveled downstream, then north into a dense forest filled with the chatter of wildlife. Wick could only catch glimpses of the rising sun through the trees' heavy canopy, but it appeared they were heading in the right direction.

At first, breaking trail through tangled branches and tall undergrowth, especially with the horses and mule, was hot, buggy work. Then the tree trunks became bigger, their canopy thicker, and the ground cover below sparser and easier to navigate. Walking in the trees' deep shade, Wick shivered and found himself wishing back the sunlight.

They wound among huge, gnarly oaks, the branches of the behemoths spreading far over their heads. Wick marveled at their scope but then noted the bases of several trees were scored and rubbed raw. Large sections of ground between the oaks was also turned up, like someone had plowed the area but not planted it.

Quickening his pace, he caught up with Manton and murmured, "We're in boar territory."

Manton smiled at him. "Guess it's a good thing then that they tend to sleep during the day."

Wick clenched his fists. "Boars are nothing to joke about."

"True," Manton said. "Which is why soldiers aren't likely to come this way. So doesn't that make this a safer route?"

Speechless, Wick stopped keeping stride with Manton. The mule passed him by, then so did the girls. He stepped sideways to avoid Prince Gage's horse coming too close and glanced up at His Highness. It took him a moment before he could find his voice. "I'm not sure how long I can handle having Manton as our guide."

"He's definitely no guardsman," Prince Gage replied, "but isn't that the point?"

Wick eyed another tree scored by the rubbing of boars tusks and swallowed. "I suppose. But that won't help us much if we—"

A shriek rent the air behind them. Wick jumped, and Prince Gage jerked in his saddle.

"What was that?" Lady Aisley asked.

"Bird, probably," Manton said as he tugged his mule back into motion.

Wick muttered, "More like a rabbit getting hit by a bird." He eased his hand away from his hip. The shriek had ended abruptly, which meant the sound had most likely come from a prey, not a predator.

Wick's concern about their route lessened only once all evidence of the wild hogs had been left behind, but then not long after through the trees ahead he caught sight of a pasture of shorn sheep and beyond that serfs at work around a barn and several outbuildings.

He caught up to Manton once again. Manton was angling them toward the manor's pasture as if he had not the least intention of avoiding the place. "What are you doing? Shouldn't we be keeping away from manors?" Wick asked.

"Has he always been like this?" Manton tossed the words over his shoulder, presumably at Prince Gage. Tsking, Manton then pointed ahead. "Off the pasture is a path. It departs this manor and heads north to another manor. You know," his tone turned sarcastic, "the way local peasants travel between manors and villages? We could take the roads, but since we don't have a cart, we don't need to circumvent steep inclines and lowlands. These footpaths aren't ideal for horseback, but since we'd prefer to avoid roads for more reasons than efficiency, I assume you won't object to us taking that path."

Wick grunted. "No."

"Oh, good," Manton replied with more sarcasm.

Wick glared at Manton's back even as the mule's pack-laden rump swayed between them. He hated Manton's flippancy toward safety. But since Manton's life hung in the balance too, he had to assume the commoner was accurately weighing the risks.

Angling his mule away from the manor, Manton cut through a line of underbrush. Wick wrestled through the bushes after him and found himself on a footpath just as Manton had said. Loud braying erupted from the direction of the manor's flock of sheep, and it was coming their direction. Wick swung around and spotted a gray donkey galloping through the manor's pasture toward them, braying loudly as it came.

Despite the leafy foliage, Wick could see serfs across the manor pasture pause in their task and look their way. Wishing the donkey would shut up, Wick could only hope the trees hid their group better than it obscured his view of those on the manor.

As the donkey charged the head of the trail, Wick's concern shifted to what it would do. He grabbed a downed branch in case he needed to fend off the animal.

"It's alright, buddy," Manton called out. "We're not here to bother you or your flock. You can stop yelling at us."

Rolling his eyes, since he had for a moment thought Manton was talking to him, Wick held his ground, gripping the branch.

The donkey halted and brayed once more, its long ears pointing straight at them.

Keeping his eyes on the creature, Wick gestured for the girls to ride past him. They did so, and the donkey started down the trail after them. Wick raised the branch and was about to run at the animal when Prince Gage's horse plowed through the underbrush between them. His Highness's dark brown beast turned its hind end toward the donkey and, with its ears pinned back, lashed out at the smaller creature with both back legs.

The donkey slid to a stop. They cautiously moved away from it, and finally it returned to its pasture. Wick sighed and tossed the branch aside as he faced forward on the path.

No wider than a game trail, the footpath was a well-traveled route. It cut up hills, over rocks, and through lowlands. The remnants of boot prints and footprints were evident in muddy patches, under and over which were the tracks of deer, fox, rabbit, wolf, and other woodland creatures.

More than once the trail divided, and each time it did, Manton would check the trees. Signs and shapes, which Wick assumed represented different manors, were carved in tree trunks at each division. Upon locating them, Manton would choose their direction.

They encountered a number of peasants on their way. Most concerning were a careworn woman with two wary-eyed children that had clearly been out foraging and a long line of men and youth transporting baskets of produce. Both groups took significant note of them.

With the five of them, two horses, and a pack mule, Wick knew their group was unique enough to those they passed that they could end up a topic of conversation later that night. He just hoped none of them were friends or relatives of any Unavowed soldiers.

Before midday they reached the next manor that Manton had spoken of. Wick found himself holding his breath as their party traveled between fields in full sight of serfs harvesting flax. The line of men and women were hard at work pulling up the narrow, thigh-high stocks that had turned yellow and seeded brown.

The serfs shook loose the dirt clinging to the plants' roots, then laid the crop in rows to dry. Wick had watched flax be processed every year throughout his boyhood, either riding from his family's manor beside his father or at his mother's side when she went to check on the workers' progress. After being gathered and drawn through coarse combs to remove the seeds, the flax stocks were retted in water to loosen the inner fibers from the outer stock. The plants were then dried and the stocks crushed in a hinged, jaw-like, wooden brake.

In his mind, Wick could still hear the chewing sound the brake made. The two peasant women, Joan and Essie, would then take turns holding the plant fibers against a board and swishing the edge of a wooden knife down them. This scutching removed chunks of stock clinging to the inner flax fibers. The women would then pull the fibers through a hackling comb to finish separating all the inner plant fibers from the straw. Only then could the hair-like flax be twisted into linen thread on a distaff or spinning wheel. But that wasn't the end of it. The thread had to be stretched and boiled after that and, if desired, dyed before being woven or kitted into anything from sacks to surcoats.

Out in the Delkaran flax field, a serf straightened and pulled his sweat-drenched, undyed tunic free from his thin body. As he wiped his brow with a dark arm, the man's eyes met Wick's. The weariness on the serf's lean face made Wick consider again Manton's comments about Delkara's commoners.

The man nudged a shorter, equally gaunt fellow next to him and pointed at them. Both men watched them while exchanging words. Wick glanced at Manton, who had his eyes on the trail and seemed not to notice the attention they were garnering.

Wick flicked his gaze back to the two serfs. The men continued to observe them with curious expressions, then the shorter fellow shrugged, said something, and the two of them bent back to work.

Wick's heartbeat reverberated. He hated having no way of knowing who was friend or foe in Delkara, and he resented having to hope people wouldn't recognize the royalty of two kingdoms. Prince Gage and Princess Rhonalyn should have been riding the main roads accompanied by prestigious entourages able to provide adequate protection, not skulking through the woods guided by a rebel commoner and accompanied by a single knight.

With that thought, Wick considered Rhonalyn's royal guard and the Unavowed. Who gave the Unavowed their orders? They were definitely present in Delkara and had crossed into Edelmar. But what about Keric? Were Rhonalyn's people faithful to her? Had her men been killed or captured, or had they disappeared for some other reason?

Judging from Princess Rhonalyn's response to their loss and Sir Tristan's seemingly genuine distress over her safety, it seemed her people were loyal. But after so recently navigating Prince Gage's secrets and learning about Lord Gregory of Veiroot's connection to Felix, Wick was reminded that everything wasn't always what it seemed.

He passed under a cracked tree trunk hanging at an angle over their path and took the opportunity to look back at Princess Rhonalyn, who was three horse lengths behind him. He searched her face. What kind of person was she, really?

Her eyes met his, and her gaze narrowed.

Heat spread up Wick's neck.

Rhonalyn opened her mouth but at that moment had to duck, so that she and Lady Aisley wouldn't be wiped off their mount by the angled tree trunk.

Hoping to avoid being questioned by her, Wick shifted his gaze forward. He jerked to a stop to keep from crashing full stride into the rump of Manton's mule, which had for some reason stopped in front of him. Someone giggled behind him. He glanced over his shoulder. Lady Aisley pulled back behind Princess Rhonalyn. Her Royal Highness's own lips twisted in an equally amused smirk. "You know, you really should watch where you're going."

Lady Aisley giggled again.

Wick suppressed a smile and replied formally, "I'll keep that in mind."

Manton tugged his mule around. "What're you keeping in mind?"

"Nothing." Wick gestured forward. "Why'd you stop?"

"I figured this was a decent place to eat and trade up the mounts." Manton grunted. "Unless, of course, you find that unacceptable."

At the mention of food, Wick's stomach clenched hungrily. He brushed past Manton to reach the food packs on the mule. "You could have stopped an hour ago."

22

RHONALYN BIT INTO the hunk of dark rye bread that Wick had handed her. The five of them were sitting beneath a giant beech tree, their mounts grazing nearby. The rye bread was coarser than any Rhonalyn had ever eaten, and its hard crust was nearly unchewable. She would have complained about its poor quality, but her mind was occupied with weightier matters—as it had been since the night before.

She had little choice but to seek King Strephon and demand redress for her missing guard. For if she returned to Keric now without her men and without amends from King Strephon, her nobles would despise her. She'd violated her kingdom's pride by risking reopening negotiation and trade with Delkara. And as a result, she had been attacked and her men lost.

Every bit of respect she had ever worked to gain among her own lords hung in the balance, all because she had come to Delkara. The Unavowed's treachery now bound her and Strephon together as either each other's deliverers or each other's downfall. She raised the waterskin Wick had given her and washed down the dry chunks of bread in her mouth.

Wick divided cuts of cheese among them next, while Manton handed a small, lumpy bag to Gabriel. "Back in Dinslage, Wick and I could have purchased dried plums. But I knew you'd prefer these."

With a frown, Gabe withdrew from the bag a small, oddly shaped brown fruit. A smile spread across his face. "Figs. You bought figs."

Manton smirked. "I paid a reasonable price for them too."

A laugh burst from Gabe, making his features come alive in a way Rhonalyn hadn't seen since meeting him. He bit into the fig and murmured. "So good."

Wick's voice smashed through the moment. "How're we trading up who's riding?"

Manton's smile disappeared, as did Gabe's.

Rhonalyn watched the three of them. Whatever the men's troubled history, the imbalance it created among them was unsettling. At the same time she understood how relating to Manton could create a strange kind of paradox of feeling as if he were both ally and enemy.

Gabe fished another fig out of the bag. "I can walk for a while. Someone else can ride."

Manton nodded. "We'll need to swap packs then from Nigel to Athalos."

"Why?" Rhonalyn asked. "Just put someone else on Gabe's horse."

Wick shook his head and raised his hands, and Manton laughed and said, "Clearly, you've not actually been introduced to Gabe's horse."

"I've seen that it's temperamental about tacking, but it rides fine," Rhonalyn replied.

"Uh, no." Manton gestured at the horse with his cheese. "Athalos rides fine for Gabe only. Anyone else, not a chance. And the attitude he shows Gabe on the ground is nothing compared to how that animal behaves when anyone else tries to mount him. It isn't about patience either. Gabe and I attempted for months to train him to take a different rider, but Athalos won't have it. He'll tolerate being led and occasionally untacked by someone else, but even then, getting bit and kicked remains a definite possibility."

Rhonalyn blinked. She hadn't believed Wick's warning to stay away from the horse, but was glad now she'd not gotten close to the animal. She frowned at Gabe. "Why would you keep such a creature?"

"Why?" Gabe sounded offended. "Because it's not Athalos's fault his previous owner was cruel." He stood up and walked toward his grazing mount, whistling softly. The dark horse lifted its head and stretched out its neck, its ears pricked inquisitively. Gabe ran a hand down its nose. "I mean, sure, he gets scared and protective at times, but he's not intentionally mean." The horse tossed its head, knocking off Gabe's hand, and returned to grazing. "Besides, his temperament has been…helpful at times. I don't have to worry about anyone stealing my mount or taking anything of mine off him." Gabe finished his fig and ran his hand down the horse's shoulder.

Rhonalyn observed with new understanding the thin, crisscrossing lines in the animal's fur, and wondered again at the odd connection between Gabriel and Manton.

☙❧

After the hassle of transitioning the packs and packsaddle to Athalos, Gage settled into stride at the back of their group, trailing Athalos. Sir Wick walked with him, allowing Manton to ride Nigel. Gage suspected the knight did so not out of regard for Manton but out of deference to Gage walking.

Aisley had also joined them on foot, explaining to Rhonalyn that she would prefer to stretch her legs. Even though she was barefoot, the young girl would one moment halt beside the path to view something and the next run ahead to climb a large rock or race along the spine of a downed tree.

She appeared amazingly carefree, which bewildered Gage, considering that what she knew of their current circumstances was enough to terrify most adults, let alone a child. Her peacefulness reminded him of Novia and the way she had alway embraced life with an ease and joy that one couldn't help feel too. He smiled as he pictured her running ahead of him across the fields of Kelmour. Another image flashed into his mind—her disappearing in front of him as the ground beside the river gave way beneath her. The feelings and emotions of that day swept back over him. The panic. The rush of river water. His desperation. Trying to hold onto her and the branch. His body going numb from the cold. It consumed him a moment before the wall of grief hit. He drew in a shuddering breath.

"Are you alright?" Sir Wick's question pulled Gage out of the memories.

He exhaled. "I'm fine."

Sir Wick eyed him. "Are you truly? If it's your previous injuries, we can slow down, or you can return to riding."

Gage steadied his voice and said again, "I'm fine."

Sir Wick feel silent.

Over the next couple of hours, they trekked up and down hills, through mucky patches, around rocks, over roots, across meadows, and along what seemed like an endless path amid nothing but tree trunks and underbrush. Gage glanced to his left but couldn't see the descending sun through the trees.

He thought about asking Manton how much farther but instead just forced his tired legs to keep moving.

Sometime later, Rhonalyn spoke up. "Are we going to eat again anytime soon?"

Gage wasn't sure who was meant to answer her question. It had seemed Manton, as their guide, would make the call of when they would stop again to eat, like he had with their midday meal. But with their current leadership structure being what it was, they hadn't formally established who would make such decisions.

"We can stop to cook a meal now," Manton replied, "but it will mean arriving at our destination after dark. Or we can keep going and get there in the light. Which do you prefer?"

Rhonalyn swung off her horse and landed beside it with a groan. She walked forward and grasped the horse's reins. "We keep going."

Surprised, since her actions had seemed to indicate the opposite decision, Gage felt his body waver in response. He eyed the empty saddle of the mount Rhonalyn was leading, but just then Aisley circled back, saying she'd like to ride again. She mounted the horse, and Gage pinned his gaze to the trail, pushing his weary body onward.

23

Wick shifted his belt and pressed against the discomfort emanating from where he'd been pricked by his own blade. His mind was reliving that encounter when sounds of people ahead stirred his vigilance back to the present. Distant calls and the cadence of voices became distinguishable from the sounds of the forest, along with the repetitive clang of a blacksmith's hammer and the noise of animals.

Their path ended at the back of a barn that sat at the edge of a bustling village lane. Manton entered the lane, embracing the assault of activity as if joining those hurrying to finish their day's tasks was not at all a risk.

Princess Rhonalyn apparently felt the same concern as Wick for she slowed while leading the horse Lady Aisley rode.

Wick quickened his pace and, coming alongside her, seized the horse's bridle just below her hand. "Just keep walking," he urged.

"But there're so many people." Agitation filled her voice as she whispered, "What if one of them reveals our presence to the Unavowed?"

Wick spoke with forced confidence. "What would they tell them? That five commoners visited their village?"

"Right," she said. "To them we're just travelers."

"Exactly. So, lower your gaze, and keep it that way." Wick clicked to the horse to get it moving and glanced at Lady Aisley. Her body drifted with the horse's stride while her curious gaze took in the village. Wick didn't curb her visual exploration, for there was no way she would be suspected of being a noble, not with her muddy feet, sweat-stained dress, and inquisitive expression. Also, the village wasn't likely to have heard yet that a Keric royal was missing in Delkara, but they were still capable of speculating about five strangers, which could be just as dangerous.

The village—colored a gold and red hue by the setting sun—wasn't grand in comparison to many places Wick had been, but it was pretty. Throughout the sloping area, the homes, barns, and buildings were situated in an organized fashion, all of them constructed of russet-colored clay, dark-brown cruck frames, and roofs thatched with straw. The exceptions were the church, the windmill, and the blacksmith shop, which were built of red bricks and had red-tiled roofs.

The homes' high-peaks suggested a loft in each for storing goods. Meanwhile nearby large barns had their doors thrown wide to facilitate crops being brought in by oxcart. Drivers were using such carts currently to transport sheaves of wheat and rye from the fields out in the farmland beyond the village. Other commoners with handcarts and baskets came from different fields, conveying into the village loganberries, melons, cherries, and cucumbers.

A steady wind turned the mill's cloth sails and blew the dust kicked up by the field work toward the church's bell tower, over its tithe barn, and out into its cemetery beyond the village green. Closer to Wick and the others, at the center of the village, the blacksmith shop sat in a wide patch in the lane. The squat, little shop rang with hammer strikes. Outside the shop a large horse pawed the ground as people and carts flowed around the building.

Rather than join the village flow, their small group turned off the lane before the smithy and followed a rutted, shrub-lined path just wide enough for a single cart. The path cut beside a home behind which a shushing sound could be heard. Wick glanced past Princess Rhonalyn and spotted a child standing, dripping water over a grindstone, and turning its crank while a man held the bladed edge of a scythe against the stone's moving circle. Two more curved scythe blades leaned against the house's back wall alongside several axes and a plow.

Wick glanced back at Manton's mule as they traveled up a sharp incline and between two bluffs that took them out of sight of the village. The sounds of human activity faded as well, replaced by the chirping of birds and the jangle of bells in a meadow. A handful of cows, several goats, and a large flock of sheep came into view. The herd's young shepherdess reclined on a pile of rocks near their rutted path. She glanced up at them. Chewing on a grass stem, she shooed away a fly and nodded to them as they passed.

Manton nodded back and led their group through a grove of fruit trees and toward a tall bluff behind which rose three columns of smoke.

Their path circled the bluff and ended facing a large horseshoe-shaped bowl of land cast half in shadow and half in the bronze light of the setting sun. The spot contained a large open-air structure and two cottages, thatched and plastered with the same russet material as the village.

As Wick viewed the spot, he realized that russet clay formed the edge of the bluff. It also made up the ground beneath their feet and turned brown the sloppy patch of mud beyond the cottages where two small children—a girl and a boy—tread the ground with their feet. Streaks and splotches of the clay stuck to the children's arms and made their clothing hang heavy about their legs.

"Sebastian, family's still hard at work for the day I see!" Manton called out.

"It's Manton!" a youth exclaimed from inside the shaded structure.

The building held dozens of shelves bearing numerous pots, bowls, and other pottery. Under these shelves were stacks of bricks and tiles. And at one end of the structure a maybe eight-year-old boy stood beside a tall, muscular man who was bent over a pottery wheel, his hands wrapped around a huge, spinning hunk of clay. The man removed his hands from the half-molded jar shape. The boy inserted a stick between the spokes of the wheel and began to spin the wheel faster. The man wiped his hands on a cloth and waved the boy off. "Let it stop, Ezra. We've company to greet." Rising, the man walked stiffly from the building. His deep blue eyes looked troubled even though his features held a welcoming smile. "Manton."

Dismounting, Manton met the man near the shelter. "Sebastian."

While the two spoke, Wick noted the other people around the place. A second man outside the back of the shelter wrestled a barrel from a collection of barrels. He emptied its silty brown contents into a wide trough-like container. Beyond the trough, a woman fed wood into fires under two large kilns, one built of brick and the other of plaster.

To the north of the kilns, another woman and three youths worked in a line at a raised board.

The first boy in line scooped clay onto the board from a pile—supplied, it seemed, from the mud hole trodden by the two youngest children. The boy picked impurities out of the clay and worked it with his hands. Next, the woman kneaded the lump into a loaf shape. Then the second boy slapped the clay loaf into a wooden mold, forced the clay down, and used a tool to strike off the excess material before he handed the full mold to a girl.

The girl carried the mold to a large, sand-covered section of ground where several chickens roamed. She shook the soft brick out, shifted it into line with the other bricks that were already drying there, then returned and dropped the empty mold into a bucket of liquid. Each person worked with a mesmerizing efficiency, even while their eyes flicked toward the five of them.

"As always, it's good to see you, Manton," Sebastian said. "Though it's a bit surprising to have you back in these parts so soon. Are you in need of a pot?"

Manton shook his head. "Not this time."

Knowing Manton's history involving hidden compartments in chess pieces and barrels, Wick wondered, did these people also provide containers capable of concealing items Manton was smuggling?

Ezra came to stand beside Sebastian. The man placed his arm upon the boy's shoulders and asked Manton, "Then what brings you here?"

"We need lodging for the night, and I'm wondering if you'd provide it." Manton tipped his head toward his mule. "We have food of our own."

Sebastian's troubled gaze swept over their group. "You don't normally travel with company."

"No, but believe me, it's important." Manton hesitated, and Wick held his breath, fearing Manton might be about to reveal Princess Rhonalyn's identity, but Manton simply added. "Just shelter for one night. That's all I ask, then we'll be on our way."

With the shadow of a smile, Sebastian shook his head. "With you and Hugh, it's always 'just one more thing.' And it's always important." Sebastian motioned to the cottages. "We're not as full as we usually are. If you don't mind being a little snug, I think we can find places to fit you all."

Princess Rhonalyn stirred. Concern over what she might say coursed through Wick. But instead of speaking to Manton or

Sebastian, she leaned toward him and whispered, "We're staying *here?*"

Not thrilled with the arrangement himself but well aware they didn't have a lot of options, Wick murmured back, "So it seems."

Prince Gage led his horse forward and nodded to Sebastian. "Thank you for your hospitality. Please tell us where to unload our things where they won't be in the way."

"Hang 'em inside the first cottage on the beam behind the door," Sebastian replied. "As for your animals, there's a meadow not far from here where they can graze."

Prince Gage began stripping packs off his mount. Taking that as a cue to do the same, Wick circled around Princess Rhonalyn to reach the horse's cinch and looked up at Lady Aisley. "Time to dismount, little one."

Leaning forward, Aisley placed her hands on his shoulders and slid toward him. Startled by her actions but familiar with them, Wick grasped her waist and swung her to the ground. She gave him an appreciative smile. "Thank you."

Wick froze. She'd spoken the words in the noblemen's tongue.

Mortification filled the girl's young face, and she shrank back. "I'm sorry," she whispered in the commoners' tongue. "I forgot."

Wick looked around. No one else seemed to have noticed, not even Princess Rhonalyn who was closest to them but apparently focused on something Manton was saying. Wick heaved a breath. "It's alright. Just don't do it again. And remember: you're Amy, and she's Rose."

With a frightened nod, Aisley moved toward Princess Rhonalyn.

Wick pulled off the horse's saddle and carried it to where Prince Gage was depositing the rest of their packs.

"Hugh isn't here then?" Manton asked, a frown in his voice.

"He's delivering bricks to Delipp," Ezra replied.

"Ah. Well, pass along my greeting when he returns, yeah?"

The boy nodded.

"Claudia," Sebastian called loudly.

A diminutive woman in a stained dress with a bronzed face and partially covered steel-colored hair emerged from one of the cottages. A toddler in a formless tunic wobbled out after her. The woman placed a fist on her hip atop a belt holding a ring of two keys, a pouch, and a sheathed knife. She raised her other hand to block the glare of the setting sun and squinted at the new arrivals.

"Manton's come visiting," Sebastian called. "He and his companions will be staying the night."

"Is that so?" Claudia said.

Manton scooped up one of their food packs, unlaced it, and dug inside it. He drew out a sack that Wick knew contained a large portion of their smoked meat and took it to the woman. Claudia accepted the bag, glanced inside, and nodded with a look of approval.

Anger surged through Wick. What was Manton doing? That was the majority of their meat.

Prince Gage caught his arm. "It's alright," he whispered. "She'll cook what he just gave her with whatever they have and serve it to everyone, including us. Sharing benefits us and them and will alleviate the burden of our presence."

Seeing the logic but still not liking it, Wick scooped up as many packs as he could carry and said, "I'll put these inside."

Prince Gage nodded. "I'll take care of the animals."

24

Rhonalyn was never so relieved to leave a place as she was the following morning when they departed the brickmakers' and potters' cottages.

The evening before, Manton had offered to help around the place. Sebastian had suggested that some of them could aid in brick making. Rhonalyn had assumed that meant the men would work, but Gabe had blithely volunteered her to assist in kneading clay while he slung the stuff onto the board and picked rocks out of it. She could still smell the stench of the wet, clingy soil. It had grated her skin, and despite her best efforts, it remained under her fingernails.

As for Aisley, the girl had taken to her assignment of placing bricks to dry like it was the first of the twelve days of Christmas. Rhonalyn could scarcely look at the girl now without feeling indignation over the child's disregard toward her title and willingness to adapt to all things common. Nor could she stomach the sight of Gabriel who, unlike the other two men, had no qualms about forcing her into humiliating situations.

The same had been the case with their sleeping arrangements. She and Aisley had been forced to share space with three girls and two younger boys on the floor of the smaller of the two cottages. Straw was strewn across the floor in the pretense of making the ground comfortable. Meanwhile, a goat was tied in the corner, chickens slept among the children, and the husband and wife, who tended to the kilns and pottery clay, occupied a narrow bed in the corner with their toddler.

Still hungry despite eating the same amount as everyone else and unable to get comfortable, Rhonalyn had lain awake most of the night between Aisley and one of the other girls. However, she had been thankful to be under a roof since it rained hard during the night.

Now on the move again, she feared she might drift off and fall from the horse she and Aisley were riding.

With his mule carrying their packs, Manton led them through the village and onto a route full of watery potholes. "This road joins with another route that will take us toward Lyster," he explained. "Three fourths of the way there, we'll split off onto a less traveled road to an abbey where we can stay the night. The following day we'll head toward Lyster and bypass the city by means of a commoners' footpath."

Rhonalyn didn't know anything about Lyster or where they were in Delkara, so she could only assume from Gabriel and Wick's agreement with his plan, that Manton was leading them toward Ithera.

Having survived an entire evening with commoners without giving herself away, she felt less frightened of the peasants, merchants, herdsmen, and pilgrims they encountered on the road. But she still breathed a sigh of relief when what felt like an endless day concluded just as Manton had said—with them arriving at the gate of a small abbey.

The monks there received them with quiet dignity, and she and Aisley were given their own chamber for the night. Furnished for guests, it had a decent bed with, wonder of wonders, an actual mattress. They were also supplied with a generous amount of water, which allowed her to feel at least somewhat herself again.

The meal the monks provided was a simple fare, but as hungry and exhausted as she was, Rhonalyn was just happy it was food. After eating, she fell asleep almost the moment she climbed into the bed.

❧

Lying awake in the abbey's refectory, Gage rolled to his side on a layer of straw. His foot thudded into a table support. He stilled and listened to the others. Sir Wick rustled around an arm's length behind him. Manton, occupying his own heap of straw on the other side of Sir Wick, hadn't moved in awhile.

Gage's mind traveled to his saddlebags by his knees. He had yet to open Haaken's journal. As the abbey's sole guests, they alone occupied the refectory. Gage waited until he heard Manton's quiet snoring, then pushed aside his blanket and sat up. He dug in his bag for a candle. With the wax stub in hand, he crept to the lamp the monks had left burning by the door.

He lit his candle, then tiptoed back to his saddlebags, and withdrew the leather-wrapped books. Setting his candle aside, he uncovered the journal and cracked it open. Gage stared at Haaken's flowing script.

Despite the curiosity tugging at him, he hesitated to read the words. Doing so still felt like violating Haaken's privacy. However, since Haaken had given him the journal, he must have intended for it to be read. Taking a breath, Gage absorbed Haaken's words.

I scarce know how to take on this endeavor, but I know I must. It hath been nearly a fortnight since I received Novia's letter from her mother. No longer can I bear to carry Novia's words without at least attempting to do as she asked.

Honoring her request is all I have left to give to her, and it is mayhap my only hope of finding anything to live for beyond the pain and grief that is consuming me.

My beloved Novia, without you it hurts even to breathe. You were my everything. My delight. My joy. My future. It was you who was to be crowned Queen of Edelmar beside me when Edelmar's throne became mine. But alas, you are gone, and where my heart once beat fully for you, there is now but only an empty, aching hole.

I cling to your final words, penned the day before your death, and mourn all the more. For your words reveal what you wished of me and what you knew I was not. You desired for me to know God the way you did. To delight in Him the way you did. To serve Him with all my heart, as you did.

But this I grieve too, for I do not even know if it is possible for me to have what you had with God. I fear that it is not, yet in years past I watched you trust in God to help you bear your own hardships and how you knew such joy in Him despite your own pain and losses. So, mayhap if you could, so can I.

But how does one even come to know God in such a way? He and I are little more than strangers. Always, He hath felt to me like a distant God and I a future ruler with gratitude for the wisdom in His Scripture, but beyond that, no further relationship hath He and I had. No such intimate communication with Him have I ever attempted, nor have I ever wanted. Novia, you were all I needed. With you I was content. Happy. Whole.

I cannot help now but remember how you spoke of the LORD with such familiarity and regard, like you and He were friends. You truly talked with Him about His plans and your hopes and fears, and those interactions brought you such joy and peace. I *never understood it, and I am ashamed to admit I resented it. I wanted you to be fully mine, not partially His.*

But now you are fully His and not even a little bit mine. I am angry with Him for that and yet also desperately hoping that He might share with me what He shared with you. For I am in dire need of someone to show me a way through this endless pain.

So, here I am, wretchedly attempting to discover who God is and how to connect with Him. But where do I start?

LORD God, it seems strange to write such a request, but talking aloud to You feels even more odd. Therefore, forgive me if this is not the proper way to go about this.

I know I have not the right to ask this of You, especially since I have certainly shown very little regard for knowing You, but will You help me now know You? For Novia's sake?

Mayhap my reasons for seeking You are selfish. I admit I wish to pacify my own grief by trying to do as Novia asked, but also, LORD God, I know hers was not a false joy. And if that came from You, if her ability to embrace life again after losses and bring with her light and hope everywhere she went, if You gave her that, then it is You now that I want and You that I need.

Gage paused, unable to breathe. His own pain at losing Novia throbbed in concert with Haaken's words, while the vulnerability that Haaken expressed mortified him. It was like coming upon someone he'd been confident was undefeatable and finding them devastated. He didn't want to see it, but he couldn't look away either.

For the sake of his own questions, he needed to understand

what Haaken had learned. Because, in the years since Novia's death, though not without grief, Haaken had seemed to have found peace again. But how?

Had God actually answered him?

Gage longed and feared to investigate Haaken's words further. Biting his lip, he read on.

> It hath been over two months since I wrote the above. Unsure exactly how to proceed, I went where I knew I could find more about God.
>
> I opened the Scriptures and started reading in Genesis. And this time, words of passages I have read countless times struck me in new ways.
>
> God is Creator
>
> Before now, this seemed like such a simple thing to know and acknowledge-God created the heavens and the earth and formed and breathed life into mankind.
>
> Yet, I stayed myself in that thought longer and truly considered what it means, ex nihilo "out of nothing" God created everything. Verily, that is such an astonishing and overwhelming knowledge.
>
> God is THE Creator. He made me and absolutely everything and everyone that exists.
>
> King David says it well in his thirty-third and ninety-fifth psalms.
>
> "By the word of the LORD the heavens were made, and all the host of them by the breath of His mouth. He gathers the waters of

the sea together as a heap; He lays up the deep in storehouses. Let all the earth fear the LORD; let all the inhabitants of the world stand in awe of Him. For He spoke, and it was done; He commanded, and it stood fast."

"In His hand are the deep places of the earth; the heights of the hills are His also. The sea is His, for He made it; and His hands formed the dry land. Oh come, let us worship and bow down; let us kneel before the LORD our Maker."

There was a spot of ink below this passage, then further down, two lines had been dashed across the page, the rest of which was empty. Gage flipped the page and found Haaken's writing continued on its other side.

God is All-powerful

The LORD God created and owns all that is. Thus, he holds all power. He spoke everything into existence. His supremacy is absolute. By His doing and plan, the sun rises and sets. The rains come, the seasons change, the seeds of the crops grow–all due to Him.

Humanity's very existence is owed exclusively to God crafting our forms in His own image and deeming us vessels into which He desired to breathe life.

Never before have I slowed enough to grasp that truth, nor have I felt so humbled by it. Always, I have considered having a soul and body as my right, but it is not a right. It is a gift, which is both exorbitant and astonishing. We are creatures of God's making, and yet He bequeathed us life and dominance over the earth–the same way earthly kings even now grant subservient lords authority to rule over parts of their kingdoms.

God is our King

Commissioner, Designer, and Creator of all, God made the world for Himself. He is the pre-eminent owner of everything. King of Kings, He holds the absolute knowledge, authority, and right to direct the ways in which all in His domain should live.

Trying not to recoil from Haaken's words, Gage flipped the page.

As their King, God gave Adam and Eve clear instructions as to what they could do in Eden. He told them which trees they could eat from, including fruit from the tree of life, and warned them not to eat from the tree of the knowledge of good and evil.

While following His instructions, they lived peacefully and in a perfect relationship with their Maker. God walked and talked with them, and they enjoyed life with their Creator.

What would that have been like? To have a face-to face relationship with God?

That perfect relationship broke though when Adam and Eve disobeyed their Creator. They rejected God's authority and acted contrary to His direct command.

They defied their God and King.

God is the Righteous Judge

Those whom—

"Gabe?"

Gage jerked, which tipped Haaken's journal out of his hands. His flailing fingers snagged hold of the book just before it hit the stone floor. He exhaled and shook his head at Sir Wick. "I thought you were Manton."

"Thankfully not," the knight replied.

"Why do you think I waited to take it out?" Gage nodded toward Manton. "His snoring has a specific sound when he's actually sleeping."

"Right," Sir Wick said, "which is why you responded with perfect calmness when I addressed you."

"Well, it's not like I'm used to you calling me Gabe."

Sir Wick scoffed. "Yeah, well, try getting used to it from my position."

Gage cringed at the reminder of why the knight was beside him.

Glancing sideways at him, Sir Wick settled back in the straw. "I can only imagine how well 'Rose' is coping."

"Surprisingly, she's managed so far to stifle her annoyance." Gage smirked. "But I'm pretty sure every time she does, her fingernails are making holes in her dress."

Wick chuckled and shook his head.

Gage's own laugh cracked into a yawn.

Wick spoke. "You should get some sleep."

"I know. We both should." Gage tucked the journal back into his bag, then blew out his candle. Drawing up his blanket, he settled on his back in the straw.

He listened to Manton's snoring and Sir Wick's steady breathing while his thoughts traveled back to Haaken's journal.

Haaken had written that he was humbled by God giving bodies and souls to humans, but why had God created people at all? Why not skip creating beings capable of causing so many problems? Or why hadn't God kept the tree of the knowledge of good and evil out of Adam's and Eve's reach, so that they couldn't disobey Him by eating from it?

Gage supposed if it wasn't them eating from the tree it would have been some other act of defiance against God's authority. People questioned and pushed boundaries. Such were the traits that enable people to take dominance over the earth as God directed and at the same time sourced humanity's resistance to God.

Gage turned that thought over in his mind. Before Novia's death, he had had such confidence in God's actions and wisdom, but watching the ways God had done things or not done things that day had destroyed that assurance. His childish acceptance and adoration for God had turned into questioning. After all, why trust and follow God when to him another way seemed better and more logical? He wasn't alone in stepping back from his faith either. Manton and many others shrugged off God's authority, just as Adam and Eve had done.

Gage stared at the dark ceiling of the refectory. Disregarding God and seeking independence from Him was apparently as old as time. And yet God was the one who gave humanity the freedom to reject Him. Why? Why had God given people liberty and the type of abilities they could just as easily use against Him as for Him?

If God's goal was to have servants to do His bidding, how He'd made humanity didn't make any sense.

There seemed to be only two options. Either God had seriously misjudged what He had given humans while breathing life into them, or His goal in creating humanity wasn't simply that of making compliant servants.

Though if the first was true, as the Creator, God could have easily fixed such a mistake. But God hadn't changed what He made.

Therefore, God's ultimate goal in creating humanity had to be something more than mere compliance.

What did God actually want then from humanity?

Pondering that question kept Gage awake long into the night.

25

WALKING UNDER THE late-morning sun and trying to ignore the persistent pain in his side, Wick observed Lady Aisley skipping down the road toward Lyster. She paused behind Manton's mule and plucked a handful of clover. Making a bouquet of the pink blossoms, the child tarried at the roadside. Wick walked passed her, then glanced over his shoulder to keep an eye on her. They had already shared the road with several travelers and merchants that morning, and though no one was currently around, he wanted to be sure she didn't fall behind.

When Princess Rhonalyn's horse came even with her, Aisley fell into step beside it and offered the animal her fistful of blossoms. Stretching out its neck, the horse lipped the plants into its mouth. Aisley giggled.

Wick considered telling her that she shouldn't be feeding the horse while it was working, but he couldn't bring himself to ruin her enjoyment.

"Aisley, stop that!" Princess Rhonalyn reprimanded. "You'll teach it to graze while it's walking."

Lady Aisley lowered her head. "Yes, Princess Rhonalyn."

Wick winced and anticipated someone adding to Princess Rhonalyn's reproof by admonishing Lady Aisley for her use of Her Royal Highness's title, but Manton seemed not to have heard it from where he rode at the head of their group, and Prince Gage, walking his horse at their tail end, looked lost in thought. Wick debated whether he should take on the responsibility.

"Speaking of your behavior of late," Princess Rhonalyn added, "where were you early this morning?"

Lady Aisley's gaze stayed fixed on the ground. "I, um, I went to the barn to visit the…the horses and to see if—"

"Speak up! I've told you countless times it's impossible to understand you when you mumble at the dirt like some common waif."

Wick stiffened. Someone needed to say something. He glanced at Prince Gage, but His Highness still appeared distracted.

Lady Aisley lifted her chin but kept her eyes down. "I was in the barn."

Princess Rhonalyn shook her head. "Of course you were. I swear, if you paid as much attention to people and your appearance as you do to animals, more than half my job would already be done. A lady should never be found tramping about a barn."

"But I like being with animals."

Princess Rhonalyn switched to the noblemen's tongue. "How do you not understand? You art a lady with the potential of possessing actual power. When we reach King Strephon, who do you think he wilt give an audience to, hmm? These peasants? Nay. They are insignificant nobodies with no real voice or power. But you and I—"

"Enough!" Prince Gage snapped in the commoners' tongue. "You're…putting us all at risk. Now, be quiet."

Princess Rhonalyn closed her mouth and rode on without another word.

Wick wished he himself had silenced her sooner, for her words held a painful edge of truth. He scowled at Manton—the very person who had caused Prince Gage's loss of power.

It was bad enough they were stuck traveling as commoners. Having to do so with Manton, of all people, was infuriating. It took constant self-control for Wick to not pummel Manton, especially every time the man made himself out to be Prince Gage's friend. And no matter how empty the road or how quiet the night, the possibility of Manton betraying them caused an ever present need for vigilance. Wick hated it all, but he kept his mouth shut.

Prince Gage's comment back at the beach about his skill of keeping a civil tongue popped into Wick's head. A cold uneven edge cracked across his knightly resolve. He would never abandon his duty, but the growing pressure of his position made him wish he could. He swallowed hard. "God, help me. I hate this. I am so incredibly ill-equipped to keep the three of them safe. Yet it falls upon me. Prithee, do not let me fail. I ask You, keep our path clear of—"

The jangling of metal and thudding of hoofbeats coming along behind them interrupted Wick's plea as if in direct affront to his prayer. His heart drummed double time. He looked back, knowing by the swiftly approaching sound that there wasn't time to scatter and hide.

Four soldiers rode into view. They wore tabards over their armor—uniforms of red with a chevron of blue above an insignia of a dog holding a ring of keys in its mouth. Wick didn't know to which lord the coat-of-arms belonged, but the mere fact the soldiers displayed colors decreased his concern.

Prince Gage, on the other hand, spoke stiffly. "Manton, they're Lyster soldiers."

"I see them," Manton said, an edge to his voice. He slowed his mule, causing the rest of them to slow as well. "Just keep your heads down," Manton instructed, "and don't get in their way."

Following Manton's instructions, it was obvious to Wick that Prince Gage and Manton's concerns had something to do with the past they shared. But he had no way to know whether it was a general concern or if it involved a specific crime.

The clinking of plate armor against chainmail and the thudding of hooves drew up on them. Without conscious thought, Wick reached his left hand to grip his sword. His fingers found only air. As his heart flip-flopped, Lady Aisley's arm brushed against his empty hand.

Wick looked down at her. She shuffled beside him, biting her lip and looking as if she might bolt into the woods. Wick squeezed her arm reassuringly and kept space for her tucked next to him and between Princess Rhonalyn's mount and Prince Gage. Saplings branches scraped against them all as they vacated the road for the soldiers to pass.

Leaves shuddered against Wick's side. He stared at the ground. He could feel the eyes of the soldiers on him and considered what would happen if the riders recognized any of them. The air in Wick's lungs stuck there. Then the Lyster soldiers were past them and on their way. Wick's pulse continued to throb. He stepped back onto the road with the others, but it wasn't until the soldiers were fully out of sight that he was able to breathe normally.

26

Overwhelmingly relieved the soldiers hadn't taken any interest in them, Gage kept stride at the back of their group and wondered how much longer until they could leave the road behind.

Two turns later, Manton twisted around on Nigel and spoke with quiet force. "Change of plans. We're not taking the footpath around Lyster."

"Why not?" Sir Wick asked, marching forward. "That footpath's the best option we—oh."

"What is it?" Gage pulled Athalos forward toward the two of them. Sir Wick stepped aside giving him a view ahead. The mounted Lyster soldiers, who had just passed them, were stopped on the road, speaking with several foot soldiers. Three of the soldiers were at the roadside while two others dragged a male traveler from a footpath that led off into the woods. Another foot soldier stood at attention at the start of the path as if posted there as a guard.

Memories surged through Gage of riding into a similar patrol outside the fair in Nikledon. The recollections of the fair mixed with reminders of the swift and brutal actions of Lyster's soldiers in Delipp. Fear twisted around Gage's spine and squeezed the air from his lungs.

"We have two options. We can risk going through Lyster," Manton said over his shoulder, "or backtrack to a different route."

"It's too late to backtrack," Sir Wick replied. "We're in their sight. If we turn back now, any soldier worth his salt would chase us down and demand to know why. Better we continue on and give them no reason to wonder about us."

Manton dipped his head. "You make a good point." He pushed Nigel's reins forward.

Gage opened his mouth to object to the plan, but what could he say? Sir Wick's reasoning was valid. Yet what if the soldiers weren't just there to detain those taking the footpath?

The pleas of the traveler held by the soldiers reached Gage's ears. "Please, using the trail hasn't been against the law before. I beg you, let me go. I meant no offense to my lord. I'll pay the city toll."

The soldiers ignored the man.

Gage felt lightheaded as he walked close behind the others as Manton led them forward toward the soldiers. Gage tightened his grip on Athalos's reins, attempting to anchor himself to something in order to keep the ground from tipping out from under him. Athalos snorted and sidestepped, jerking on the reins.

Knowing Athalos was probably reacting to his fear, Gage inhaled a painful breath and focused on trying to calm himself. The reins pulled once more as Gage shuffled forward, keeping his gaze down.

Manton led the way around the rumps of the soldiers' horses and on down the road.

All Gage's fears pounded inside him. He pinned his eyes to the road and kept his feet moving. He could no longer feel Athalos's reins in his hand or the ground beneath his feet. He waited for boots to step in his way, a hand to seize his arm, or a voice to call for them to halt, but the soldiers did nothing to prevent them passing. The mounted soldiers simply continued their discussion with the foot soldiers about guarding the path, and the five of them slipped on down the road.

A sense of buoyant relief filled Gage the moment they were

out of sight. But then he thought of the city ahead. A new wave of trepidation swept over him. What if entering the walled city of Lyster wasn't safe? What if there were lord's men there who could identify Princess Rhonalyn and Lady Aisley or him as Gabe or him as Prince Gage? Or what if he or Wick were recognized by someone who knew they had illegally fled Nikledon or someone who knew he was marked?

And what about Manton? The last time he and Manton were in Lyster, a reeve had ordered Manton to leave the city, believing his chess game might stir rebellious ideas in the locals. Ironically, the reeve's concern hadn't been far off considering Manton's use of chess pieces.

Athalos jerked the reins, making Gage realize he was gripping the leather straps so hard they were denting his hand. Gage relaxed his grip. They couldn't turn around right now, but what if they found a place to tarry long enough to legitimize their return past the soldiers, they could wait and then backtrack and take another route to avoid entering Lyster.

Gage was composing in his mind how to convince the others of his plan when he heard the plodding of hooves behind them.

He glanced over his shoulder, and his heartbeat skipped back into a run that he wished his feet could match. The mounted soldiers were on the move again. How many times were they going to have to deal with the same patrol? Gage braced himself for the soldiers approach, but this time the four riders settled in behind them, keeping pace with them.

Was trailing them happenstance or were the soldiers intentionally following them? At the thought, Gage fought a new round of battering panic while forcing his feet to maintain a steady pace.

There was no choice now. They had to continue on to Lyster.

❧

Wick watched Princess Rhonalyn glance over her shoulder at the soldiers trailing them. Her chin lifted, and her eyes flashed, as if she'd suddenly had a thought. For a moment her expression held something akin to a debate. Fear spread through Wick. Would she betray them? All it would take was her calling out to the soldiers and telling them she was Keric's kidnapped princess.

In doing so she would be risking her safety on the assumption that the Lyster soldiers weren't corrupt or connected to the Unavowed. Wick calculated that she had sense enough not to take that chance and hoped more than believed that she would continue to trust them to be the ones to get her safely to King Strephon. But at the same time, Princess Rhonalyn's arrogance made her vulnerable to the belief that her title would protect her, and Wick feared her disregard for those she considered her lessers could mean she'd ignore Manton and Prince Gage's opinions about the soldiers.

She must have felt his concentrated gaze, for she glanced down at him. Their eyes met, and Wick saw a flash of something he couldn't identify. Choosing to believe the best of her, he spoke quietly. "We'll get you where you need to go."

She dipped her head in a nod that carried more than an acknowledgment of his words. But whether it was gratitude or capitulation, Wick couldn't tell. And before he could make up his mind about it, Lyster was spread across the horizon.

Its nearside gate, with sentinel towers, lay beyond a mix of isolated trees and trails that crisscrossed through fields and pasture land, dotted with dwellings and barns that required more space than the city could provide. Crops, peasant laborers, grazing livestock, ox drivers, plowmen, and mixed herders populated the outer land. Meanwhile, occupying the road cutting through the land was a string of people—merchants driving wagons, sellers walking with goods in handcarts and baskets, and peasants leading animals or standing empty-handed. They all moved in a meandering line leading to Lyster's gate.

Squinting, Wick noted the sun's position and did a swift evaluation. It was almost midday, an odd time for delays in entering a city. Usually, such only happened in the early morning when city gates were first opened or at night when merchants tried to make it into a city before the gates closed. A line at midday did not bode well for them making a quick and quiet entrance.

In the hot sun, Manton stopped behind the last wagon in line. Princess Rhonalyn's mount came to a standstill nose to tail with Manton's mule. The rest of them halted with them. With Lady Aisley in front of him, Wick shifted sideways to see up and down the line. He swept his gaze past Prince Gage and swished at the flies that had immediately swarmed them.

The soldiers drew their mounts to a stop a good five horse lengths behind their group. Wick had expected them to ignore the line and ride to the gate, but the soldiers tarried. It didn't make sense to Wick. Then a female peasant with a goat abandoned the line and started across one of the fields. Instantly, there was a jangle of metal, and two of the soldiers galloped after her.

They cut in front of her and pointed back at the line. The woman gestured forward. The soldiers again pointed at the line. After another brief exchange, the peasant woman retreated from them and hauled her goat back to the line. The two riders returned then to their companions, whose mounts stood flicking their tails at the flies.

Wick's skin turned clammy. If soldiers had orders to make sure no one left the line, what awaited them all at the city gate?

Princess Rhonalyn must have been asking herself the same

question, for she dismounted to face him and Prince Gage. "Why're they keeping people from leaving?" she asked, swishing fiercely at a fly that had dared land on her arm.

Wick wasn't sure how to answer her.

Dropping off his mule, Manton circled back to them and said to Princess Rhonalyn in a hushed tone, "You're drawing attention with your prattling."

"Prattling?" Anger and fear were evident in Rhonalyn's controlled response. "They're herding people back to this line like cattle."

"Yes," Manton said, "so they can collect a toll from every last person here. They're asserting their power and garnering as many tolls as they can. That's all."

Princess Rhonalyn looked somewhat reassured, but then her expression faltered. "Do you have enough to pay such a toll?"

"Wick?"

Since he had insisted on being the one to carry what was left of the money he and Manton had acquired in Dinslage, Wick wasn't surprised that Manton would throw the question his way. He answered Princess Rhonalyn, "We'll have enough."

She looked content with his answer, but Wick glanced at Prince Gage. What if Manton was wrong, and a toll wasn't the only reason for the line at the gate?

27

After waiting so long in the sun, Gage shivered as he and the others shuffled forward into the cool darkness of Lyster's thick gate. While unobserved in the confines of the gate's tunnel, Gage carefully slid off his vambraces and shoved them into his saddlebag.

While approaching the gate, Sir Wick had urged him to remove the leather and simply keep his mark out of sight. The knight's thought was that the guards were more likely to pay attention to someone wearing vambraces due to wondering if they concealed something. Better to take the leather off and give the guards no reason to focus on him.

With his right wrist vulnerably bare, Gage gripped Athalos's reins and closed his left hand over his mark. He shivered again and hoped his stance looked more natural than it felt. Upon reaching the gate, he had spotted heavily armored soldiers posted outside it and had feared he was too late removing the vambraces, but the line had simply rolled past into the tunnel.

The crowdedness of the line and narrowness of the gate had made it safe for him to remove his vambraces once inside, but it also made it impossible for him to see what was taking place ahead in the noisy city. The further they got in the cool darkness the more the tunnel stank of sweat and manure, but at least it gave them a reprieve from the relentless flies.

Ahead of him, Aisley gagged.

"Breathe through your mouth not your nose," Rhonalyn instructed.

The line crawled forward, and eventually the others shuffled ahead of him out of the gate. Gage emerged from the tunnel into a ruckus of noise and activity. Squinting in the sunlight but unable to lift a hand to shade his eyes, he cringed at the sight that met him.

Travelers who had been in front of them were digging out coins to pay their tolls or watching as the soldiers dumped out their bags and sacks and went through them. These soldiers wore kettle hat helmets and minimal armor under their Lyster tabards. The screech of nails and boards being pried loose from crates and barrels bled into the voices of both soldiers and commoners. The loud protests of one particular tradesman rose above them all, but despite the man's objections, the soldiers continued kicking his wares out of his cart in a clatter of metal. Other sellers were unloading their baskets and sacks, so that the soldiers could go through them. Screeching gulls and pigeons flew in and out of the mess, grabbing bits of grain and smashed produce.

People who had been much farther ahead in line were reloading their bags and baskets or putting their sacks and barrels of goods back in their carts and wagons. Many shooed away birds while trying to salvage whatever they could of their goods.

The air was filled with dust and stank of manure and a dozen other smells that Gage couldn't identify. The rising voices from commanding to pleading, the jangle of armor and coins, the snorting and squawking of animals and birds, and the scuffle of all the people spun around Gage. His heartbeat and breathing quickened. A buzzing in his ears joined the noise.

A soldier elbowed past Gage, knocking him sideways. Gage stumbled a step but managed to stay upright without removing his hand from his wrist. The passing soldier barked instructions at another soldier who was approaching a merchant's wagon that had entered just ahead of their group. "Rothberg, inform him, we're accepting no one's word, and he'd better hurry up and unload his goods, else we'll do it for him. And if he refuses to pay the toll or can't pay it, we'll seize his goods instead."

Rothberg gestured to the merchant. "You heard him. Hurry up."

A flash of anger crossed the merchant's face before vanishing beneath a look of resignation. As the merchant climbed down from his wagon, Gage saw beyond the wagon a set of pillories in front of a building extending from the left gate tower. In the first of the wooden frames, with his wrists and neck locked through the wood was a thin, older peasant clothed in little more than rags. In the other pillory was a muscular fellow about Gage's own age, stripped to his waist and with a cloth gag tied through his mouth.

Recalling the gag shoved in his own mouth at his branding, Gage's body flushed with heat. He could taste the soot again in his mind. Then the memory of the pain hit. He squeezed his wrist tighter, trying to silence the sensation.

"You there!"

Jerking, Gage snapped his head up.

☙❧

Rhonalyn ground her teeth to keep herself from rebuking the soldier for his manner of address. The soldier demanded of Manton at the head of their group, "You selling, buying, or passing through?"

"Wish we were selling," Manton replied in a calm, lazy voice, "but we've brought nothing to sell and have no time for it anyway. Gotta get on our way to Koth. Going to a wedding there for Rose's cousin." Manton gestured at Rhonalyn, who flicked her gaze to the ground. Manton's feet shuffled nearer the soldier, and he lowered his voice. "If ya ask me, I'd've been a lot happier not having to bring her other cousins along. The little one's constantly com-plaining, and that one eats more than his fair share, if you know what I mean."

The soldier harrumphed and stepped away from Manton. "Your toll is four pence each."

Staring at the ground, Rhonalyn blinked in disbelief. Four pence? It should have been half that for a rider and mount.

"I said we weren't selling," Manton replied.

"Did I say that was the toll for sellers?" the soldier asked.

"No," Manton replied. "Four pence it is. And the price of those on foot?"

The soldier's tone held mirthless amusement. "Four pence."

Rhonalyn knew well the soldier's tone. Used by those with power, it was that of partial warning and partial anticipation of the lower person daring to further question their authority. If the lower person was foolish enough to continue, what followed usually made a thor-ough example of them.

One of Rhonalyn's earliest childhood memories was her father using such a tone on a disrespectful servant. The servant failed to heed the warning and was whipped for it. Her father had later used the same tone on a lord who was hesitating to follow an order. The lord had wisely reconsidered his stance.

Such was the way of power. Those who were beneath it either learned to respect it or else to bear the consequences of disregarding it. As a leader, she knew that taking a strong response against opposi-tion was needed, but when such judgment turned violent, it always made her feel ill. She had never taken pleasure in making an example of someone through pain the way that some people did, and she had a feeling the soldier opposite Manton was one of those who enjoyed mistreating others.

Thankfully, Manton heeded the warning. "Right. Four pence each." He turned to Wick.

"You'll also unload your packs," the soldier ordered over the din of activity around them, "to prove that you haven't come here to sell. If you've lied, you'll pay double and forfeit your goods. And you, girl. Show me your hands."

Before Rhonalyn had the chance to realize he meant her, the soldier seized her palms and drew her arms out in front of her. His rough fingers gripped her hands hard enough to hurt. She bit back an angry retort and steeled herself against the affront. At the very least she wanted to yank her hands away and drive her gaze into his, but she stayed still and left her eyes aimed at the ground.

The guard twisted her hands over, then grunted and shoved her arms away. "You can move on."

She rubbed the spots where his fingers had dug in and told herself, as soon as she reached King Strephon, she would never again put up with such treatment.

The man checked Aisley's hands as well, then marched toward Gabriel. "You!"

Gabe's eyes flashed with fear.

"Get moving unloading those packs."

"Yes,…of course. Right away." Gabe turned to his horse and began untying the packs, but using only one hand.

Wick paid the toll, then headed toward Gabe. Saying something to Gabe, Wick took the pack Gabe had just worked loose. Gabriel's hand shook as he reached back up to release the next bag, but he nodded in response to Wick.

Rhonalyn frowned. What was going on? Why was Gabe so frightened? She and Aisley had both been seen and treated like commoners, so the soldiers obviously had no idea who she was. No one seemed particularly interested in them, and they had the coins to pay for the toll. So, what was the problem?

While Wick emptied the packs for the soldier to inspect, Gabriel slid his saddlebags off his horse. His gaze stayed on the soldier until the man was distracted with Wick. Gabe then swiftly withdrew the leather-wrapped books. He tucked them under his arm.

Was that the issue? The book of Scripture. Were they not supposed to have it? Rhonalyn's mind spun. She recalled how on the beach Gabe had been disturbed when she showed it to him. But if it could get them in trouble, why hadn't they left it behind?

"You! Hurry it up!" The soldier kicked through the items Wick had emptied from their bags and marched toward Gabe. Rhonalyn stiffened.

The soldier reached for Gabe's right arm. "What're you—"

"Watch out!" Wick yelled while hurling a set of saddlebags toward the soldier. The bags flew through the air and slammed into the soldier's legs, knocking him off balance. Gabriel jerked away and bolted into the crowd as the soldier stumbled into Gabe's horse. The animal squealed and kicked at him. The soldier took a hoof to his leg and landed on his knees. Red-faced he pointed after Gabe. "Stop him!"

Soldiers sprinted from several directions toward Gabe.

Fleeing around wagons and carts, Gabriel dodged the soldiers like a rabbit avoiding hawks. The guard who had instigated the chase charged after them, hollering for them to catch him.

Rhonalyn could see the books still clutched in Gabe's hand as he leapt over a pile of goods a trader was reloading and took off down the closest bustling city street. Three soldiers tore after him, shoving people out of their way.

A commotion behind Rhonalyn yanked her attention back to the others. Wick stumbled forward as if he too was about to join the chase. Manton grabbed his arm. "What do you think you're doing?"

"I've got to help him!" Desperation filled Wick's voice.

Manton glanced at the remaining soldiers. All of them were invested in their own searches and had not yet taken any interest in the four of them. Manton grunted and turned back to Wick. "Leave Gabe to me. Get the girls to the city's north gate. I'll meet you there." Manton thrust his mule's reins into Rhonalyn's hand, and before either she or Wick could object, he slipped away through the crowd.

Looking mortified, Wick stared after Manton.

More than a little angry at all three men, Rhonalyn pulled Aisley close and glared at Wick. "Well, a fine mess this is. If he's not at the north gate when we get there, what then?"

28

His lungs burning, Gage raced through Lyster's streets. He narrowly avoided multiple collisions with traders and shoppers as he tried desperately to stay ahead of the soldiers. His fingers cramped around the books he held while his mind spun with the stupidity of what he had just done.

He didn't have time to focus on criticizing himself for his panicked response. The clamor of armor and the pounding of boots were too close behind him.

A wagon turned into the street ahead, pushing people together and blocking his route. To his left, Gage spotted an alley half-hidden by baskets and a stack of crated vegetables. He veered toward it at full speed only to find as he entered the alley that five horse lengths in was a wall closing off its end. Skidding on the wet, uneven ground, he attempted to reverse course. His feet slid out from under him. He threw open his hands and crashed to the ground. The leather-wrapped books flew across the alley, bounced twice, and landed under a pile of empty crates. With no time to retrieve them, Gage scrambled to his feet and flung himself toward the street. He reached it and aimed himself for a small gap beside the wagon.

The back of Gage's tunic caught on something, jerking him backward. He spun around and found himself face to face with a Lyster soldier. The guard grabbed hold of Gage's left arm. Gasping, Gage tried to fight him off, but bare fists weren't much good against armor. The soldier blocked the punches Gage sent at his face and seized Gage's right wrist. Caught in the man's clutches, Gage twisted his body around, intending to use his weight as leverage to dislodge the soldier's hold. Before he could do so, a second soldier grabbed his upper arm and shoulder in a solid grip. Together, the two soldiers wrestled his hands behind his back and pinned him between them.

Gage knew he was fighting a losing battle, but still he twisted and fought trying to break free of their hold. It was no use.

A third guardsman ran up, and the soldier on Gage's right spoke to him. "Nivard and I have him. You can return to the gate."

"Yes, sir." The guard ushered two more arriving soldiers back the way they'd come.

Nivard commented from Gage's left. "It's been a while since one's run like this. Makes me wonder what he didn't want us finding. Shall we locate whatever it was he ditched?" Adjusting his grip, Nivard twisted Gage's arm and shoved him into the alley.

Pain streaked through Gage's elbow and up into his shoulder. He hissed in a sharp breath.

"Where'd you put what you were carrying, huh?" Nivard asked in his ear.

Gage gritted his teeth. He had tried reasoning with the likes of them before, better to keep his mouth shut.

"Fine," Nivard said. "We'll do this the hard way then."

Before Gage could speculate about what that meant, a foot swept his legs out from under him. He crashed to the uneven ground and grunted as his face hit the wet, putrid dirt. His arms were thrust against his back and pinned there. Then a sharp weight—most likely a knee—dug into his lower back. Gage grunted against the pain.

Nivard spoke to his companion. "Look around. The item must be here somewhere. He had it in his hand when he entered the alley."

Gage's whole body pulsed with his heartbeat. They were search-ing for the books, but he knew it'd be only a matter of time before they discovered his mark. Clenching his teeth, he tried to twist up a knee in hopes of pushing Nivard off his back.

"What? You think you're goin' somewhere?" Nivard snorted. "Think again." He dug his knee in even harder and pried Gage's left wrist into a position it was never meant to take.

Crying out, Gage hissed in air and lay still. With his chest heav-ing, his face pressed into the dirt, and pain radiating through his arm and shoulder, he couldn't motivate himself to attempt any further resistance. Instead, he silently pleaded for the man to ease the pressure on his wrist.

Dread consumed Gage. If he didn't escape now, how much more pain might he have to endure? He had barely survived a day in the custody of Nikledon's soldiers, and he had watched Lyster soldiers in Delipp beat Jack until he couldn't rise. And if this was how they treated someone they thought was simply evading a toll, what would they do to him once they realized he was a marked man?

"Found it!" the first soldier called out. "He threw it under these crates." He kicked the crates aside with a splintering crash. "What do we have here?"

Gage lifted his head to see. As the soldier scooped up the books and unwrapped the leather, a new concern flooded Gage's mind. Could anything in Haaken's journal identify who wrote it? If so, how much worse might it make his situation if it was discovered that he, a marked man, was carrying a private journal belonging to the crown prince of Edelmar?

Nivard grunted, and his weight on Gage's back shifted. The soldier's hand released Gage's right arm, then his knee dug down even harder into Gage's lower ribs. A muffled growl followed. Gage hesitated to move, trying to decide if he dared take advantage of his free arm or if Nivard was just tempting him to try something. He heard a low gurgling noise. Nivard's grip on his left wrist also went slack, and the guard's weight slid off Gage's back.

As Nivard fell to the ground beside him, a set of boots stepped over Gage's shoulder. The newcomer moved toward the other soldier, who was engrossed with what he'd found.

"Books is definitely not what I expected," the guard said over his shoulder.

A knife flashed, and the newcomer sunk his blade up under the soldier's armor.

The guard grunted, then he, too, crumpled to the ground.

Scrambling backward, Gage shoved to his feet and stared mortified at his rescuer. "Manton! What did you just do?"

Manton bent to wiped his blade on Nivard's uniform. "What did I just do?" he murmured angrily. "I just saved you and made sure they didn't find out about Rose. Now, come on."

Gage stared at the soldiers' bodies, his mind spinning.

"Now!" Manton headed for the street.

Shaken back into motion by the urgency of the situation, Gage snatched up the leather and books and dashed after Manton. Manton caught his arm and yanked him to a stroll beside him. Gage tried to shake him off to run.

"No." Manton held onto him. "Move at a normal speed, and don't attract attention."

"You think what you just did isn't going to do that?" Gage asked, his voice tight with accusation and panic.

"One advantage to the harshness of Lyster's soldiers," Manton answered with a detached calmness, "is that everyone here fears and hates them. So, anyone who may have just seen what happened down that alley isn't going to report it, because rather than be rewarded, they'd more likely be blamed for failing to prevent it or accused of having a hand in it. But make no mistake: once other soldiers find those bodies and an incentive is offered for information, hunger will overcome people's hatred. This way." Manton turned into an alley that cut between buildings and led to another street.

They traversed the street to an intersecting lane, then turned right, following that lane until it ended at a guild hall. Manton turned again and directed him into a nearby alehouse.

Inside the busy establishment's shadowy interior, Manton led the way to the bar. A thin, middle-aged alewife with her sleeves rolled up past her bony elbows and her hair pulled back in a severe knot nodded to the two of them. "What can I get you?"

"Phina," Manton said. "I'm in need of your specific type of ale."

The alewife squinted at Manton. "For one or two?"

Gage couldn't wrap his mind around Manton's words. As he stood beside him, the smells of alcohol, woodsmoke, stale air, and unwashed bodies hit his overwrought and panic-riddled senses, making his stomach somersault. He fought the abrupt impulse to retch on the woman's counter.

Swallowing hard and breathing deeply, he managed to conquer the sensation, only to feel weak in the knees and hot, way too hot. Still holding the books in his left hand, he gripped the counter with his right hand trying to keep himself upright. As his vision narrowed into a dark tunnel, Gage could hear Manton saying, "And, Phina, perhaps a tour of your cellar?"

Phina responded stiffly. "It appears you need more than my ale and cellar."

Her words were followed by a curse from Manton and a hand closing over Gage's marked wrist.

At the touch, a visceral fear snapped Gage's vision out of its tunnel. He tried to jerk away, only to realize it was Manton's hand covering his mark.

"Don't fight me," Manton growled in a low tone. Then he looked at the woman. "Can you get word to Stiles or Thom?"

"I'll see what I can do." She pressed her lips together. "And I suggest you take that cellar tour."

"I couldn't agree with you more." Manton steered Gage around the counter after the woman.

She led them to her kitchen. Grabbing a candle, she lit it at the fire, then walked across the floor to a wooden trapdoor. She pulled it up and preceded them down into a cool earthen cellar. Released by Manton, Gage stumbled down the steps. The small space held corked casks on a rack running along its side wall, and against its back wall were two shelves, holding a variety of supplies. A narrow earthen ramp on the empty side of the cellar led up toward slits of sunlight. Gage surmised it led to street level behind the alehouse.

Phina gave Manton the candle, then headed back up the steps. Even before the trapdoor closed behind her, Gage sank to the hard-packed floor. Setting the books in his lap, he dropped his head into his hands and exhaled. A million questions spun through his mind, but he couldn't articulate any of them.

Manton, on the other hand, had no trouble finding words. "You're marked! I can't believe that you're marked!" The candle's light paced with Manton along the rack of casks. "I didn't understand how you could be so stupid as to bolt, but now I find the answer staring me in the face. When? How?"

Gage lifted his head, anger restoring strength to his limbs and punctuating his words. "A patrol was searching everyone leaving Nikledon's fair."

He heard the air leave Manton's lungs. "The gold coins I left in your saddlebags."

"Yes," Gage replied, "and of course they didn't believe me when I told them I had no hand in them being there."

"But you didn't give me up?" Manton sounded amazed.

"Oh, I tried. They just assumed I was lying about that too. After all, why believe a rebel thief and a smuggler?"

Manton's gaze broke from his in the candlelight.

Fury spiked Gage's temperature and sharpened his voice. "They branded me the next morning without giving me a chance to speak first to a lord or prove my innocence."

"You were caught with the gold." A sharp questioning edge stirred in Manton's voice. "How were you able then to come find me outside Dinslage?"

Realizing Manton was now concerned that he was perhaps a lord's spy, Gage snorted at the irony. "The entourage in which I was being transported was attacked, presumably by your rebel friends. In the chaos of the fighting, I escaped. I've been on the run ever since, all because of you."

Manton's posture relaxed even as his voice tightened. "I never meant you to even see those coins, let alone leave the fair with them."

Gage angrily shoved himself to his feet, the books falling to the floor. "Don't make excuses for what you did! You lied to me from the very beginning and involved me in your rebel crimes! And now look where you've gotten us both!" Images of the two soldiers Manton had killed filled Gage's mind, and his body quaked. He shook his head. "You murdered those men."

Manton glared at him, his eyes glittering in the candlelight. "You still don't get it. This is a war. We're fighting to save the common people of Delkara from the injustices and abuses committed by those in power over us. The same sort of injustice that did that to you." Manton took a breath. "And as much as I wish I could stay and convince you of that truth, I haven't the time."

Gage's thoughts jumped to Sir Wick and the girls. "The others! What happened to the others?"

"I don't know," Manton answered. "I left them at the gate to come after you."

"You did what? You have to go back! You have to make sure they're alright."

"No, I don't."

Fury filled Gage. "What do you mean no?"

"I mean, that neither you nor I can go back to that gate. Their best hope is if Wick does what I told him and takes the girls to the north gate. I should be able to find them there, unless there are other surprises you've failed to mention."

Feeling as if he were being reprimanded for the trouble caused by something Manton was responsible for, Gage gritted his teeth. The books came to mind, and he was grateful he had taken them with him. "No," he answered. "There's nothing else."

"Good. Then they should be fine." Manton moved to face the left shelf at the back of the cellar. He grabbed its center board and tugged. The three middle boards and back opened together as a door that concealed a hidden passage. The tunnel was just tall enough for a man bent over, and its length was indistinguishable since its end disappeared into blackness. Two baskets sat just inside the passage's door. "Close yourself in," Manton instructed, "and wait at this end until either Stiles or Thom comes for you. There's food and water in the smallest basket. In the meantime, I've got other arrangements to make." Manton riffled through the large basket, which appeared to be full of clothing. Manton removed a hat with a feather, a tunic of fine material, and a sash. He slipped the merchant's attire over his own clothes, tied the sash, and tucked his long hair under the feathered cap. "How do I look?"

Gage stared at him, not sure what to say.

Manton rolled his eyes. "Never mind. Just do us all a favor and wait here. Whoever comes for you, tell them to bring you to the ash tree by the dump pile. If all goes as hoped, the others and I will find you there."

Gage wanted so badly to seize hold of Manton and demand restitution and answers for everything. But since Manton was helping him, he controlled his anger and decided not to delay or alienate him.

"Take this." Manton thrust the candle into Gage's hands, then hurried up the earthen ramp to the trapdoor that led to the street. Sunlight flashed before the door thudded closed, and Gage was left standing alone in the cellar, wondering if he'd ever be free of the mess Manton had made of his life.

29

As the crowd churned the hot, rank air around them, Rhonalyn clenched the mule's reins and warned Wick. "A soldier's coming this way."

Wick slowed but did not halt his hurried efforts to repack the contents of their saddlebags.

Rhonalyn glanced at the soldier to confirm he was indeed approaching, then dropped her gaze.

The soldier's voice pierced through the din. "You been searched yet?"

"Not exactly," Wick replied. "The soldier who was searching us ran off after someone."

"I see, and he left you here to walk away?" The soldier muttered something about discipline in the ranks, then gestured at Wick. "Show me your bags."

Wick complied and once more spread out the contents of their packs.

When the soldier was done rummaging through them, he nodded. "Your toll's ten pence."

Expecting Wick to inform the soldier they had already paid—in fact, overpaid, it would seem—Rhonalyn was surprised when Wick instead simply dug out the money. She supposed he was more concerned with departing than debating the additional cost.

The guardsman weighed the coins in his hand and nodded. "You may repack now and be on your way." Strolling past Rhonalyn, the soldier shoved her from behind. "Don't just stand there, woman. Get moving and help him."

Her face flushed with heat and words that definitely would have delayed their parting rose on her tongue. She bit them back, reminding herself that for the sake of finding her men and getting out of Delkara, she could endure the humiliation. Walking toward Wick, who was shoving items into the bags as fast as he could grab them, she crouched beside him. "It seems I must help."

He thrust a pair of full saddlebags into her hands. "Then put these on Manton's mule."

She frowned. "But they came off Gabe's horse."

"Yes, but I'm not about to have either of us attempt to put them back on his horse." Wick lowered his voice. "Nor will connecting ourselves to Gabe benefit us. So, do as I said, and help me get us out of here."

Grasping his point, Rhonalyn nodded. "Very well." She took the saddlebags to Manton's mule and gestured for Aisley to help.

With things shoved into random bags, they would have a mess to sort through later, but in short order everything was repacked and on Manton's mule or behind the saddle of their horse.

Wick paused beside her. "We'll leave Gabe's horse?"

Unsure why it sounded like a question since he had already convinced her of the wisdom of doing so, Rhonalyn glanced back at the animal, wondering if the horse would be the last they saw of Gabe and Manton.

Wick grabbed the mule's reins and motioned for her to do likewise with the other horse. "Follow me, and stay close." He headed in the direction of the street Gabe had taken.

Rhonalyn gestured for Aisley to come. The child drew near to her but then pointed back at Gabe's horse. "Should I—"

Grabbing her arm, Rhonalyn pulled her close. "No. Now hush. We're leaving it behind." She looked around. All the soldiers were focused on other people.

Aisley stirred beside her a moment later and tipped her head. "Athalos is coming anyway."

Rhonalyn glanced back. Gabriel's dark horse was indeed following them. A soldier reached for the riderless animal's bridle. The horse pinned its ears flat, opened its mouth, and stretched its neck out. Cursing, the soldier lurched backward, then angrily looked around, no doubt searching for the horse's owner.

Rhonalyn jerked Aisley forward. "Act like it's not ours."

Aisley walked on, her face stoic.

Fearing the soldier would connect the horse's missing rider with the three of them, Rhonalyn quickly considered her options.

She glanced at Wick's back. Out of the three men, he had been the kindest and most respectful toward her. So, to call him one of her abductors and throw him in with Manton and whatever was going on with Gabe felt reprehensible, but if it came down to it, she would do whatever was necessary to save herself and her mission.

30

CONCEALED BEHIND THE alewife's shelf, Gage sat with his elbows on his knees and the candle burning beside him. Every now and then he felt air swirl along the passage from wherever it led and watched the flame waver. Restless and on edge, he considered rummaging through the basket of food just for something to do, but he wasn't really hungry.

For the hundredth time he wondered how long it would take Stiles or Thom to come, or if Manton had simply told him one more lie to keep him there.

He shoved out a foot in anger, and the toe of his boot jammed on the opposite wall. He bit back a cry of pain and frustration. Exhaling, he reminded himself that at least he was better off there than in the custody of soldiers. But that thought brought images from the alley to his mind. Heat flushed his body, and guilt gripped him. Those soldiers had just been doing their job. Their harshness while detaining him wasn't warranted, but it was hardly a justification for Manton to murder them.

Manton had claimed he was rescuing Gage and keeping Rhonalyn safe by preventing the Lyster soldiers from learning about her, but was that true? Were Lyster's soldiers actually dangerous to Rhonalyn's mission or just to Manton's? Who was Manton actually trying to help by keeping Gage from speaking to the Lyster soldiers? Could it be that Manton's real motive in killing the soldiers was about protecting himself from being revealed and arrested for his part in Rhonalyn's kidnapping? What if the Lyster soldiers might have aided

Rhonalyn, but Manton didn't want to lose his control over her?

Gage's skin crawled. He knew Manton was capable of lying about anything, but had he? The behavior of Baron Bertram and his Lyster soldiers was, Gage granted, dishonorable and presented a significant risk to their safety. And yet, was that enough to proclaim a death sentence on the baron and every Lyster soldier?

Gage gripped his bare right wrist. And as for determining if a response was acceptable based on what was legal and just, where did that leave him? Were not his own current deeds in direct violation of Delkaran law? Hadn't he just witnessed two men be murdered, and yet, instead of turning in their killer, he was accepting the murderer's help to avoid facing the injustice of his own situation? Was he being stupid not to speak out against Manton? Or was he protecting Princess Rhonalyn and Lady Aisley by staying silent?

Groaning, Gage pressed his fingers to his temples. It was all so complicated and confusing. More than ever, he felt like a criminal. His gaze slid to the books beside him. The last words he had read in Haaken's journal prodded him. *God is the Righteous Judge*

A knot formed in his stomach, and a compelling yet frightening desire crept over him to understand exactly what that meant for him and where it left him.

Gage reached for the two books and unwrapped them. Leaning toward the candlelight, he paged through Haaken's journal until he found the spot where he had stopped.

God is the Righteous Judge

Those whom God Himself created, those He had every right to command, ignored their Maker and disobeyed His instructions, eating from the tree of the knowledge of good and evil. In response,

God justly brought upon them the consequence that He had warned them would happen if they did so.

"in the day that you eat of it you shall surely die."

At first I did not understand this judgment since it seemed to me that Eve and Adam's disobedience did not bring imminent death. But then it occurred to me that, unlike Adam and Eve, we have always known death. Spiritual death, relational death, and physical death have forever and always been part of our lives, but not so for them.

Before Adam and Eve's treason, the world and all living creatures had only ever experienced a perfect and continuous existence. Not one had come to an undesired end.

And verily, had Adam and Eve not defied God's warning and brought evil into the world, they could have continued living in perpetual harmony with God and their world without ever experiencing death. They could have eaten from the tree of life and lived on forever in paradise.

Adam and Eve's treason ended their perfect relationship with God and corrupted their souls with evil. Fearfully aware they would stand exposed in their wickedness before God, they hid.

And God, the Righteous Judge, brought them and their treason straight into the light. "Have you eaten from the tree of which I commanded you that you should not eat?"

At first I thought it strange God would ask Adam and Eve this question since God obviously knew what they had done. But after reading this several times, I think God did so for two reasons.

First, to ask them to own their treasonous actions. What a horribly painful conversation that must have been.

And, second, I think as an invitation for them to seek His help to address the damage they had done to the world.

Humanity had entwined themselves with evil—an evil that God, in His goodness and righteousness, had to put to death. "For dust you are, and to dust you shall return."

Astonishingly, though, death is not where God concluded His judgment, nor His help.

God is Merciful

Adam and Eve listened to the serpent's lies and, in defiance of their Creator, chose to try to become equal to their Creator. Their desire to be in control rather than under God's control led to them being trapped and corrupted by evil.

What strikes me most about God's response to them, is that despite what Adam and Eve did, God did not simply destroy them and start over. He certainly had every ability and right to do so. And I wonder if mayhap that was what Adam and Eve feared, that God would use His power against them. But He did not.

Why? Why not purify His creation right then and there by destroying Adam and Eve? Why not start over with new, obedient humans untainted by evil?

I have turned the above question over in my mind so many times. Then the other day, I looked at my knights, men whom I have chosen to walk beside me, and I asked myself, if one of them defied and betrayed me, what would I do? Would I sentence that man to death and simply move on?

Nay, because I care about each one of them. They are my friends and companions. To have such a situation unfold would be devastating most of all due to the loss of the loyalty and connection between us.

I realized then that God's response to Adam and Eve was a revelation of His value and regard for them. They were not just some passing novelty to Him.

He chose to walk and talk with His creation. He was their companion, mentor, and friend. He could certainly have destroyed them and made new people, but He did not want to do so. He wanted them, and their sin and act of defiance did not change that. It corrupted and defiled their relationship with Him, but it did not change that God loved them as unique and specific human beings. Human beings to whom He chose to provide a costly forgiveness and help.

God is Patient

Gage closed the journal. His stomach was knotted, and he couldn't bring himself to read more. Yes, God had wanted and valued Adam and Eve enough to forgive their treason. But how was he or anyone else to know if God valued and wanted them enough to offer them the same?

He swallowed. It wasn't as if he and God had ever walked and talked face to face, nor were they friends. He felt no love for God, and he certainly wasn't convinced God felt any specific fondness for him.

So, what was the point of hoping that God actually cared about him?

He already owed God for keeping him alive after Felix's attack and for sending the monks to find and aid him. He didn't want to add any more debt to his tally.

Though perhaps if he tried harder to be what God wanted him to be, maybe God would see him as more than just a sometimes useful slave. Trying to please God, though, felt impossible and overwhelming. And, being deep in messes that his own decisions had caused and having hated God for so long, it felt dishonorable at this point to ask God for His forgiveness and help.

Gage scrubbed his hands down his face, then checked the candle beside him. The decreased candle's wax suggested it had been less than two hours since Manton had left, but it felt like he had already spent half a day in the cramped space.

He thudded his head back against the wall. Dirt came loose and fell into his tunic. Grunting, Gage shifted forward and twisted his arm around to shake out the dirt, but as he did so pain shot through his shoulder. He hissed and eased his arm into his lap. He flexed his fingers, trying to work away the discomfort.

Anger rose within him at Nivard for causing the injury. But then Gage remembered Nivard was dead, and he felt a rush of guilt. The guilt vexed him though, too, because it wasn't as if he'd killed Nivard. But how could he be angry when it was the soldier who was dead?

Too overwhelmed and overwrought to sort out how he should feel and why, Gage closed his eyes and wished he could just erase it all.

A low creaking sound came from beyond the shelf. Gage snapped his eyes open. Someone was in the cellar, but was the person friend or foe? The candle's flame beside him whipped around its wick as the shelf that concealed him was yanked open.

31

THE CANDLE'S FLAME re-grasped its cord, brightening enough for Gage to catch sight of the person standing in the cellar. Recognizing the man's pockmarked face and blocky frame, Gage gasped and scrambled backward, attempting to flee down the tunnel away from the very reeve who had ordered Manton out of Lyster.

The man grabbed his ankle. "Whoa! Don't rabbit on me."

His heart ramming his ribcage, Gage thrashed against the man's grip. Flipping onto his stomach and ignoring the pain in his shoulder, Gage clawed at the tunnel's floor, trying to yank free. His knee hit the candle and plunged the space into darkness.

"Would you calm down already? I'm Stiles. I've come to help you."

Gage's mind received the man's words, but it failed to make sense of them. He ceased his struggle, less because he believed the man and more because he wasn't making any headway. He remained tensed, expecting to be yanked out of the tunnel and onto the cellar's floor. When that didn't happen, he slowed his breathing. "You're Stiles?"

"I am." The man's hand lifted off Gage's ankle. "I take it I wasn't who you were expecting?"

Gage drew himself away and into a crouched position. "I've met you before, at a tavern here in Lyster."

"Ah," Stiles said. "Judging by your response, I presume you were introduced to my loyalties as being opposite those of Phina and Manton's?"

Still not sure he believed any different, Gage used his hands to search the tunnel's floor for the books he had lost in his haste to escape. "You could say that." When he found the books, he swiftly folded them back into the leather. "You told Manton his chess game was a dangerous thing and ordered him to pack it up and get out of Lyster."

"That was the day we met? Well, that explains things. There was no time for subtlety that day. Grain was being moved, and certain people in certain places needed information, among other things. No one else could get to the tavern in time. It was up to me to send Manton where he was needed and warn him to keep his head down. Speaking of keeping his head down, Phina said that Manton had with him someone marked. I take it that's you?"

Gage swallowed, his mind spinning with the new perspective of his last encounter with the man. He forced his lungs to expand and hoped he wasn't being a fool. "Yes, and Manton told me to ask you to bring me to the ash tree by the dump pile. Can you, and will you?" Staring into the darkness, he waited for Stiles's reply.

"Are you marked on one or both wrists?" The way Stiles asked the question, it sounded as if they were discussing something no more shocking than what clothes he was wearing.

Gage breathed easier but also shifted uncomfortably. "On my right wrist only."

"Good," Stiles said. "That will be fairly simple then. Come. We'll depart out the cellar's backdoor and avoid the eyes in the alehouse."

Gage stayed crouched in the tunnel. If Stiles was who he claimed to be, the man was his best chance for getting out of Lyster and back to the others, but trusting him? That wasn't so easy. Gage gripped the books and, making up his mind, climbed out over the shelf. His shoulder brushed Stiles's arm as he rose to his feet, which reminded him the man was a good head and shoulders taller than him.

"Since you're already aware of my reputation in Lyster, the role I'll take and the part you'll play will require less explaining. And since only one of your wrists is marked, there'll be no need to bind you."

Gage stiffened. "Excuse me?"

"Don't panic on me. What I meant is, my plan'll be easier to execute with only one mark to conceal." Gage frowned at Stiles's use of the word "execute," but in the darkness Stiles continued on, oblivious. "The fastest, safest way to get you out of the city isn't waitin' till dark to sneak you out but rather takin' you now in a way no one looking on'll think to question."

Gage's heart beat harder at Stiles's words, and he wondered anew if his fears weren't for good reason. "What do you have in mind?"

"My reputation of loyalty to my lord and my method of service to him as reeve is something no one challenges. As such, I'm going to take hold of your marked wrist so your brand is concealed and haul you across the city to a small side gate. I'll drag you out of it as if I'm taking you to flail your hide for being here instead of off in a field laboring where you belong. You'll play your part and look scared."

Gage swallowed hard. He wouldn't need to play at that.

"Now, I need your marked wrist."

Gage hesitated. "But what you'll really do is take me through the gate to the ash tree by the dump pile, right?" He didn't know why he thought hearing Stiles say it would make him feel any better. After all, if the man was already lying, why wouldn't he lie about that too? Still, he sought the reassurance.

"That I will," Stiles replied.

Hopeful rather than confident that he was telling the truth, Gage asked one more question, "I have an item with me that I cannot lose. What should I do—"

"Give it to me. I'll carry it."

Biting his lip, Gage handed the books and then himself over to the man.

32

By the time Stiles slowed to approach two guards manning a small side gate, Gage was short of breath and drenched in sweat. His wrist was bruised under Stiles's fingers since the man had indeed dragged him a few times, once when he had stumbled, another time when he had slowed in panic upon seeing soldiers coming, and a third time when he had hesitated to turn onto a particularly busy street.

Stiles had been correct though. No one had stopped them or questioned the reeve's actions. In fact, everyone's eyes flicked away from Stiles. Everyone's except the two soldiers' gazes. They watched. And chuckled as Stiles pulled Gage up to them.

"Ah, caught by your reeve, were you?" the stockier of the two guards said. "Should have known better than to try to escape your field work and make a run for it in the city."

"Remind him thoroughly who he answers to, yeah?" the other soldier said to Stiles.

Gage's stomach twisted.

"Oh, I intend to," Stiles replied, sounding fully willing to carry out the threat. In the next moment, with his hand still clenched atop Gage's mark, Stiles hauled him between the two guards and out beyond the city's wall. Even then, Gage's stomach did one more flip.

Stiles pulled him along a descending trail and toward an expanse of forest fringed by saplings.

"How often do you catch serfs trying to use the city to escape their owed field labor?" Gage asked as he struggled to match Stiles's longer stride and wondered once more if the man would actually let him go.

"These days, about every week," Stiles replied. "And I do put the fear of God into them. Because if I don't and the lord's men catch them instead, they're returned more dead than alive."

Gage flinched at the image and realized fear of the reeve was warranted, though it would seem not for the reasons he had thought. "You care about those serving in the fields."

"Of course I do," Stiles said. His tone softened. "We're all people, who ought to be valued equally." He drew Gage off the trail and into the trees until they were well concealed. Then he stopped and, releasing Gage, turned to face him. "We each must care about our fellow man. For without compassion, we're no better than monsters. And I've seen enough monsters to know my hand of punishment is a kindness in comparison. Few see it that way, and some will never know what I've saved them from, but even thankless tasks must be done in such a time as this to spare terrified fools from their own folly." Stiles eyed him. "But then there's the likes of you. Being mark and associated with Manton, I've a feeling you're no fool but rather one of us."

Gage opened his mouth to contest being called one of them but realized doing so would land him in the camp of terrified fools, and he would rather not be that either, so he let the statement stand.

Stiles handed the books back to him. "Do you know where you're going from here?"

Relieved to be free but suddenly unsure of being alone, Gage shook his head.

Stiles pointed. "If you travel along the city wall that way for five towers, you'll reach the refuse pile. The ash tree you're seeking is southwest of it. The tree's got a broken top, a thick trunk, and a split down its side big enough for a man to stand inside."

Gage nodded at Stiles. "Thank you for your help."

Stiles motioned to his exposed mark. "You're very fortunate to have escaped. Once taken and marked by the Unavowed, most people are never seen or heard from again."

Gage stiffened. "What do you mean marked by the Unavowed? Are you telling me this isn't a Delkaran lord's mark?"

"If it's a lord's mark, it's none I know," Stiles replied. "As for the Unavowed, I can't say for certain it belongs to them, but I know they mark their prisoners with it. They also reward any lord's men who deliver anyone bearing that mark to them." Stiles frowned. "Did you not receive it at the hands of the Unavowed?"

Even though Gage had realized days before that Felix, Sir Jarret, and likely part if not all of those with them had been Unavowed, he had not considered his mark in that context. "I thought they were called the Unavowed because they had no insignia."

"It's true they display no identification, least of all a coat-of-arms."

Gage held up his wrist, panic tightening his voice. "Then what is this?"

"All I can tell you is what I've seen. The Unavowed's prisoners either already bear that flail and crossbow or are branded with it. Any prisoner with that mark is kept isolated from others, and once taken by the Unavowed, they're usually never seen again."

A chill ran down Gage's spine. "How do you know all of this?"

"Because the Unavowed come and go from Baron Bertram's manor."

Gage recoiled. "Is Baron Bertram then their master?" He inhaled a breath. "Or does he just host them?"

Stiles shook his head. "He's not their master. Believe me, if anyone around here thought Baron Bertram commanded the Unavowed, an arrow would have taken him out long ago. None of us know for certain where the Unavowed come from or whom they serve, but it is not

Lyster's lord. Some of us do think the Unavowed's master is a Delkaran lord. Others speculate it's a merchant or a powerful individual outside Delkara. A few believe King Strephon is the Unavowed's master, but if you ask me, it makes little sense for a king, who can do whatever he likes in his own kingdom, to disguise his actions. Regardless of whom they serve, the Unavowed travel far and appear always to be on an assignment. They pay well for what they need, and they travel in large, well-armed groups So, I suppose most people consider it safer and more profitable to appease the Unavowed rather than oppose them."

Stiles's pockmarked face filled with a weariness that bent his shoulders. "Meanwhile, the common people bear the abuses of them and of our own lords. For what safety or recourse do we have when even those meant to protect us let wolves in among us?" Stiles sighed. "And words are to no avail. Even action is often futile. Our ability to bring change is fleeting at best. We can only resist from the shadows and dream about accomplishing more."

"There are those with the power to do more." Gage surprised himself by voicing his thought aloud. Princess Rhonalyn's confidence was rubbing off on him. She was so certain she could approach King Strephon, acquire his support, and do something about the Unavowed. And why not? For if not royalty, then who? Was not that royalty's intended role? Weren't they to unite those who could not unite themselves into a force capable of opposing oppression, mandating change, and fighting evil?

Stiles scoffed. "It's true, there are those with power, but do we actually matter enough to any of them for them to lift a finger to help us? No."

Heat rose in Gage's face. "Sometimes people are blind to others' needs until those needs become their own."

Stiles chuckled. "Right, if only we could take control of all food in Delkara and show those who rule over us what it's like to go hungry, perhaps then they'd take note of our troubles." The man shook his head. "But who're we fooling? It'd change nothing, and we'd be hanged for it." Stiles shifted backward and dipped his head. "As we both could merely for having this conversation. Take care, friend, and live to fight on."

"You as well." The words departed Gage's lips before he considered to whom he spoke. He drew a sharp breath and watched Stiles disappear through the trees.

Gage frowned after him. How could he identify with and even endorse so much of what Stiles and Manton believed while being completely unable to reconcile those opinions with their actions? They stole gold, attacked lords, kidnapped people, and murdered Delkaran soldiers. So how were they any different from the Unavowed?

His mind filled with Wes's fierce young voice declaring how he, Prince Gage of Edelmar, should pay restitution to the common people for stealing from them. Knowing now that the Blue Crow and Felix were members of the Unavowed, Gage had no doubt they had lied to Wes and manipulated the boy for their own purposes. But still, the words served a vile reminder that the Unavowed's deception had corrupted even the way common people of his own kingdom saw those in authority over them. But how could such lies be believed, especially in Edelmar where the people had access to their king's help?

Gage had watched his father ride off into the night enough times to know that his father always made himself available to the people.

Listening to and heeding grievances, King Axel of Edelmar did not cringe away from protecting those who needed help nor hesitate to listen to offenses and put an end to what needed stopping. His father cared deeply about justice, and when it came to those in need, his father faithfully applied the Scripture he so often quoted about being eyes to the blind, feet to the lame, a father to the poor, and one who searched out the case he did not know.

King Axel lived to serve his people. And for once no twinge of jealousy or anger rose inside Gage at the acknowledgement. Instead, it filled him with pride and reassurance. But those feelings were chased away by the reminder that his current existence was bound to Delkara and the principles of *its* king.

33

As Gage made his way along the city wall, the smell of the dump pile was the first thing to hit his senses. He wrinkled his nose. Why did Manton have to pick a tree near Lyster's refuse heap, of all places?

Gage wrapped his arm over his nose as he trekked alongside the mound of human waste, rotting food, animal bones, pottery shards, old leather, broken wood, worn fabric, moldy straw, used feathers, rusted metal, and anything else the city of Lyster had thrown out. Buzzing flies infested the pile, and scavenger birds flew in and out of it. Their screeching cries and drifting shadows made Gage shudder. Past the heap, he spotted the ash tree Stiles had described. Thankfully, it was upwind of the dump pile.

When he reached the tree, there was no one anywhere in sight. He noted recent footprints in the ground nearby but no evidence of any horses having been there. Figuring he had gotten to the spot ahead of the others, Gage paced, wearing off his nervous energy.

As he moved, he listened to the chatter of squirrels, the twitter of several birds, and the frequent rustle of life in the undergrowth. Eventually, he slowed, then leaned against the tree. The instant he did, though, impatience and concern gripped him. He pushed off the ash and resumed his pacing. Manton and the others should have arrived not long after him if not ahead of him. Unless Manton had been unable to find the others, or they had gotten in trouble.

Gage fretted over the myriad of possibilities. What if Manton had lied to the others about what had happened to him? What if they were traveling on without him?

He glanced at the sun. It was already on a western dip but still hours above the horizon, so it was past midday but not yet vespers. His stomach clenched, then growled. The last time he had eaten had been early that morning. Gage berated himself for not making use of the food in the cellar. At the very least he should have drunk something. The thought of liquid made his tongue feel even dryer.

Clenching his fists, Gage quickened his pace. His boots churned up the ground among the trees as he trekked back and forth, while hunger, unease, and frustration grappled in his stomach. If something was wrong, how would he know? How much longer should he wait? He grunted in frustration. Why had Manton not given him any further directions?

What if the others needed help? Or what if night came? Was he to stay there? He had no supplies other than a knife, the books, and a few coins in his purse. Not that he would dare re-enter Lyster to purchase anything. Even his cloak was with his saddlebags. He huffed in exasperation and continued to trudge back and forth.

Off to his right, the snap of a stick halted him. He stared in that direction. More twigs cracked, and undergrowth rustled as something big moved his way. Suddenly realizing it may not be the others but rather a dangerous wild animal or worse, soldiers, Gage glanced around for a place of concealment or protection.

He was about to squeeze into the crack in the ash tree when he caught sight of the little spiked buck making all the ruckus. The creature froze in place, staring at Gage, then sprang away and disappeared into the forest.

Heaving a breath, Gage sank to the ground at the base of the ash tree and stared at the books in his hands. Figuring he was going to go crazy if he didn't distract himself, he unwrapped the leather and opened Haaken's journal. He turned the pages looking for where he'd left off reading. He found the spot.

God is Patient

Noah's story is one I have read many times. Never before though have I noted the ark in light of God's patience, but it struck me so deeply as I read it.

In Noah's time, there arose such a great wickedness and violence caused by humanity's rejection of God and their ceaseless desire for evil. Grieved by this, God determines to intervene and destroy humanity in righteous judgment. But before doing so, God instructs Noah—who walked in God's ways—to build an ark so that anyone, who chose, amid such evil, to enter the ark could be rescued from the results of their evil.

Years of warnings were given, and yet despite God's incredible patience, Noah and his family were the only ones saved. Because, unlike everyone else in their time, they listened to and believed God. In facing His judgment against the evil on the earth, they acknowledged God's right, His authority, and His power to destroy them in their evil, recognized their need for His mercy and help, and entered His provision of grace and rescue.

There was a pool of ink and a trail from it across the page. Then lower down, words were scrawled.

None of which have I done

It is sobering and humbling for me to acknowledge this, but it is the truth.

Before this day, I would have said it was Noah's goodness that resulted in Noah being rescued by God and that I too would be found by God good enough to be saved by Him. Verily, I staked my life upon it.

But now, I recognize it is not, and was not, Noah's goodness that rescued him. Despite walking in God's ways, Noah faced the same judgment as all of humanity. The only difference was that he and his family accepted and entered God's grace while others did not.

Until now, I believed that though I sometimes sinned, I always fully made up for it with the good that I did. I did not see myself as a wicked person facing God's judgment. Even though I have at times definitely defied God's authority and walked in my own ways, I never thought of myself as listening to that same serpent from the garden and choosing as Adam and Eve did to reject God's commands, ignore His kingship, and attempt to take His position. But those are the choices I have at times made.

I, too, have committed treason against my God and my King.

I, too, deserve death.

Even writing these words sends shame through my being.

My soul wishes to scratch them out and deny them still. But it would make them no less true.

I believed I was enough on my own. And, though I would never have said that I desired to become God, my goal was to not need Him, which I realize now was, and is, me trying to be God in my own life.

And if I am honest, considering my position, to be God in the lives of others as well.

This realization set me to wondering, how many of those who drowned in Noah's time thought the same? That they did not need their God. That their own choices and power were enough. That they could somehow provide for and protect themselves even while facing the Creator of the world's judgment of their evil.

In obedience to God, Noah built an ark, spending years doing what made no sense from what he could see, and yet, when the floodwaters came, how grateful must Noah have been that he heeded God's instructions and walked in God's ways?

I can stand and proclaim that I am in control of my destiny and that I have the right to choose my own way, but when the Creator's judgment comes upon all sin, what a fool I would be to not be standing within His grace.

We have no ability to rescue ourselves. We are at God's mercy. And for His mercy, patience, and grace I have come to be humbly and profoundly gratef–

Gage's attention snapped from the journal to a loud rustling noise coming his way. He scrambled to his feet and was about to slip within the ash tree when he caught sight of a feathered merchant's cap and Manton's lanky form. Gage's concern folded into relief, but then he noted that only Nigel and Athalos trailed Manton. His heartbeat quickened and he called out. "Where are the others?"

"Relax," Manton said in his infuriatingly laid-back tone. "They're coming."

Exasperated, Gage growled. "They'd better be."

Rolling his eyes, Manton pulled something from Nigel's packs and tossed it toward him. What looked like one leather item divided into two in midair. Gage caught the first of his vambraces but missed the second. It hit the ground in front of him.

Manton looped Nigel's reins around a nearby tree branch. "Wick thought you might want those back before meeting up with Rose."

"You mean, I might want them to conceal the evidence of yet another of your crimes?"

Manton retrieved the second vambrace from the ground and shrugged. "Rose knows who I am." Holding out the curled leather, he nodded to Gage's mark. "It's not me she'll look at differently if she sees that."

Gage snatched the vambrace from Manton's grasp. "Maybe not. But she'd definitely look at you differently if she knew you'd just murdered two lord's men." Gage shoved both vambraces on and laced them tight.

"Murdered? No, you mean the two guardsmen who abandoned their posts and disappeared from Lyster." Manton folded his arms. "No one will find their bodies. It took some doing and some help, but I made sure of that."

"You did what?" The ramifications of Manton's actions made Gage both queasy and furious. "What about those soldiers' families? The kin of those soldiers will think their loved ones broke their oath to their lord and abandoned not only their posts but them too. Men doing their duty, who you murdered, will be viewed as traitors, and their families will never escape that reproach!"

"They already were traitors." Manton replied. "By joining Baron Bertram's garrison, they chose their side. I told you. This is war."

Gage stood there, his pulse pounding. He wondered suddenly on which side Manton would place him and Sir Wick if he knew who they really were. He met Manton's gaze, fury and fear churning inside him. "You think you have the right to just deci—

"Gabe! Thank God you're here!" Sir Wick's voice sliced between him and Manton.

Gage faced Sir Wick and the girls, all three of whom approached on foot with their laden mount trailing behind Sir Wick.

Annoyance rolled off Rhonalyn. Her left elbow was scuffed, and her peasant dress was flecked with mud. Aisley, similarly soiled, stared from behind Rhonalyn, her young gaze wary but inquisitive.

Passing by the girls, Sir Wick looked exhausted and yet sounded full of relief. "When Manton found us and said you'd managed to evade the soldiers and would meet us here, I barely believed it. Thank God you're safe and sound. Had you not been here…" The furrows on the knight's brow deepened, and he shook his head. "Well, never mind that. You're here, and so are we." Sir Wick's lips thinned into a tight smile. "The incident is behind us. Yes?" The knight searched Gage's face, then Manton's, clearly seeking confirmation that all was indeed well.

Gage couldn't breathe. Manton had told them that he'd evaded the soldiers. He swallowed hard. Manton's ability to conceal a crime that no one should have been able to simply sweep away made him feel all the more complicit in it. Gage's insides quivered as two contrary desires warred within him. He could pretend, like Manton, that the encounter and murders had never happened, or he could spout out the truth and…what? Seek some kind of absolution for his part in it?

He tried to speak, but his tongue stuck to the roof of his mouth. Considering what Stiles had said, perhaps there was some legitimacy to Manton's concerns about Lyster's soldiers, but the callousness of Manton's cold disregard for the two lives he'd snuffed out chilled Gage to the bone.

And if Manton could lie so easily about something so significant and could carry so much disdain for any he deemed on the wrong side, what did that mean for their undertaking? Was Manton really taking them and Princess Rhonalyn to King Strephon, or was he plotting something else entirely? What *had* the rebel commoners' true aim been in kidnapping and protecting Keric's princess? Clearly, they wanted Rhonalyn alive, but was Manton being honest about why?

Gage glanced at Rhonalyn. Arms folded, she frowned first at him and then at Manton. "Well, answer Wick," she said. "Is this mess over or not?" Her disgruntled tone seemed to imply that she doubted that it was. Unfolding her arms, she gestured forcefully at Gage. "He still has the books, so what about the next time we're stopped and searched? Won't this just happen again?"

"Books?" Manton asked. "What books?"

Groaning, Sir Wick dragged a hand across his face.

"Oh, don't you groan at me!" Rhonalyn snapped. "You led Aisley and I all over the city before reaching the north gate. Had you listened to me at all, we could've arrived there far sooner." She held out her dress. "And certainly without twice navigating the same muddy street. So, don't test my patience. You all owe me answers and a plan for the future. Because this stupidity isn't happening again."

Gage might have found her ridiculous tirade against Sir Wick amusing, except it occurred to him that the knight's serpentine route to the gate was by no means due to a lack of directional awareness on Sir Wick's part. Which meant, the knight had probably been searching for him. Sir Wick avoided his gaze and offered no reply to Rhonalyn's accusation.

Gage glanced at Her Royal Highness. Whether or not Rhonalyn was aware of the knight's intentions was unclear, though if she was, she showed no compunction for her objections.

"Someone answer me!" she demanded.

Manton opened his mouth.

Unwilling to endure any more lies, Gage spoke. "The books won't be a problem again." He sent a withering look Manton's direction. "For I'm sure Manton can come up with some way to conceal them, what with his extensive experience as a smuggler."

Manton gave him a questioning look. "Books?"

"Yes, books," Gage said in a tone that he hoped conveyed that he wasn't about to answer any questions on the subject. "You have your secrets. I have mine."

Manton snorted. "Careful, raise your moral head too high, Gabe, and your own blade might cut it off. The Unavowed intend to murder her. Everything I've done has been to protect her. My loyalty is to getting her safely back to Keric. When it comes to you and him, though"—Manton nodded at Wick—"how am I to know that, if cornered, you won't give her up to save your own skin?"

Gage coiled his fingers. "Our intentions are without a doubt far more honorable than yours."

Rhonalyn stepped between them. "Excuse me? Give *her* up!" She sounded like she was teetering between outrage and alarm.

"Let's be very clear," Sir Wick said, his gaze on Manton and his voice like chiseled rock, "She has nothing to fear from either of us."

Manton scoffed. "Really? I'd beg to differ." He nodded toward Gage's wrist.

Gage resisted the urge to close his hand over his vambrace.

Sir Wick's tone held steady. "We each carry an element of risk in this endeavor, and if you think Gabe is going to step away and entrust the Princess of Keric to the likes of you, then you don't really know him at all."

Gage felt grateful to Sir Wick for the reminder of his position as well as Manton's. "Wick's right," he said forcefully. "This endeavor is as much ours as it is hers—or yours." He eyed Manton daring him to object. "We're getting her to Ithera to stop the Unavowed, and you're going to take us there."

Manton stared back at him. Then with a laugh that twisted Gage's stomach, Manton shrugged. "Fine. Onward to Ithera it is."

34

Rhonalyn tightened her hand around the coin and rings concealed beneath her skirt. Under different circumstances, she might have considered it impressive—Manton's ability to maintain and exert his power no matter the situation. But with her own authority diminished and feeling horribly unsure of Manton's goals, she found his outmaneuvering of Gabriel's attempts at dominance infuriating and disconcerting. It left her stuck with two men continually jostling over power, and she despised them both for it.

"Which way from here?" She sent the inquiry toward Gabe and wanted to strangle him when he looked to Manton for an answer.

Manton smiled. "That depends. If—"

"Shh." Wick held up a hand.

Manton snorted. "Really, you're gonna—"

"Be quiet!" Wick's sharp concern actually silenced Manton.

Rhonalyn tensed, listening for whatever Wick had heard. A cry of distress reached her ears. She frowned. The sound grew louder and more persistent until it was a rising and falling wail.

"Is that a baby?" Aisley asked.

Manton answered swiftly, "Probably just a family passing through. Not our problem."

Rhonalyn agreed. But the crying continued at the same persistent volume, and no voices rose to quiet it.

"It isn't moving away." Gabe's forehead furrowed. "Either we have company close at hand, or someone left a baby behind. But surely, that isn't possible."

"Oh, yes it is." The sudden cold fury in Wick's voice and his fierce expression startled Rhonalyn. He set off toward the sound.

She stared after him. "What's he doing?"

Looking confused, Gabe shrugged and followed Wick.

"Just leave it alone," Manton called after them. "It's not our concern."

"Isn't it?" Wick said over his shoulder.

Wick's outrage and clear determination stirred Rhonalyn's curiosity. She trailed after him and Gabe. Manton growled, then fell in beside her, muttering to himself. Aisley ran ahead and was two steps behind Wick when they reached the edge of a dump pile and located the source of the wailing cry.

Recoiling from the sight, Rhonalyn covered her mouth and pressed her fingers to her nose. On a blood-smeared cloth deposited among fly-covered bones and moldy straw was the flailing form of a newborn baby boy. His umbilical cord had been tied and cut, but the slime and residue of blood and birth was still on its body. She could see instantly why it had been left so. On its lower stomach, a V shaped patch of darker purplish skin stood out starkly against its pink flesh. Manton's attempts to warn them away now made sense.

The newborn's face was screwed up in a hearty wail, and Rhonalyn was tempted to cover her ears to block out the sound. "We should go," she said.

Wick reached down and scooped up the baby.

Rhonalyn gasped. "What are you doing?"

"You're just going to pick it up?" Manton sounded just as shocked.

"Why shouldn't he?" Aisley asked, her face furrowed with confusion.

Cradling the baby in his hands, Wick spoke over its cries. "They're worried that touching it might spread its evil to me or curse me." He nodded to the purplish mark on the baby's stomach. "There's a superstition that those born with such marks have them because they've been touched or claimed by Satan. Or even more outrageous that they have been swapped out for little devils and aren't human at all."

"But that's foolish and a horrid thing to believe." Aisley turned to Rhonalyn with a questioning look. "Why would anyone believe that?"

Glaring at Wick, Rhonalyn watched appalled as he tucked the baby's tiny, squirming form against his chest. Its incessant wailing subsided to sputtered cries, and it nestled against him. Grateful for the reprieve from the noise but horrified by Wick's actions, Rhonalyn shuddered. Regardless of whether or not it was a foolish superstition, she couldn't understand why Wick would risk touching it. She answered Aisley, "There are many reasons people hold such beliefs. For instance, it could be that the superstition exists because such babies carry disease or worse." She directed her next comment at Wick. "And I don't think it's wise to ignore what many people take quite seriously."

Too busy snatching up the filthy cloth that had been under the baby, Wick didn't seem to hear her comment.

"What do you think you're going to do with it?" Manton asked in frustration. "You can't help it. It needs to be fed. Even if you could find a wet nurse, none will care for the likes of it."

Gabe stepped forward. "What're you saying?" he asked, anger rising in his voice. "Are you suggesting we should just leave it here to die? Well, we're not doing that."

"It's either that or watch it slowly starve to death." Manton's rigid tone faltered. "Don't you see? You can't save it. It was cursed to be rejected before it was even born."

"I've helped rescue babies like this before," Wick said. "Just because their families reject them doesn't mean no one is willing to accept them. Is there a monastery anywhere nearby?"

Manton's eyebrows lifted. "You think monks might take it in?"

The baby boy's cry rose once more to a loud wail.

With a sympathetic frown, Aisley reached out and stroked one of the baby's legs that churned with its cries. Rhonalyn opened her mouth to snap at the girl but then shook her head in defeat. It was already too late. She gritted her teeth against the baby's wailing. "Whatever you plan to do with it, do it quickly."

"The nearest monastery," Manton answered, "is on the edge of Burnel, a day's walk from here. But it needs to be fed now, along the way, and for months to come. And, like I said, no wet nurse will help with the likes of it."

"I know another way to keep it alive." Wick glanced at Gabe. "It won't take me long in Lyster to find what's needed. We can save its life."

Gabe nodded. "Go, get what's needed."

Rhonalyn held back an exasperated scream. Why did they have to come across the baby at all?

ꙮ

Even from a distance, Gage could feel Rhonalyn's disapproval. He couldn't really blame her either. His own heart had lurched in panic when Wick had attempted to hand him the baby. He had sputtered, trying to find some excuse the knight might not ridicule him for, but before he could put voice to his objections, Sir Wick had met his gaze with a look that could not be denied. "Someone's got to look after him till I return."

Gage had then reluctantly allowed Sir Wick to place the squalling infant in his awkward grasp. Now as he held its tiny body in his hands, he wished he could plug his ears to block out its cries. The little one's smeared face was scrunched up in distress, and his tongue quivered in his tiny mouth as he screamed.

Gage wanted to pass the baby to someone better capable of holding, comforting, and quieting it, but Rhonalyn had made it clear she had absolutely no maternal instinct toward it. And though Manton's acceptance of them helping the infant was a vast improvement from his outright dismissal, it was a far cry from any sort of tangible help. Aisley hung nearer to Gage and the baby than the other two, but she looked just as uncertain about what to do for it as Gage was.

Having never felt so inadequate for a task in his life, Gage glanced toward Lyster and silently implored Sir Wick to return with a solution to the little one's cries. He was starting already to share Manton's apprehension that regardless of the efforts they made, there would be nothing they could do for the baby but watch it die.

Gage's insides clenched at the thought. The baby's tiny, grasping hands, kicking feet, and bellowing lungs shook him to his core. Life pulsed through every bit of the little body in his hands, while at the same time the stench of death from the refuse pile clung to the infant. The baby's little stomach rose and fell with every rapid breath it took. Gage traced with his eyes the dark V shape on the infant's skin. He couldn't help but feel a depth of significance in the fact that he and this little one were both marked and facing judgment for it.

He had known such superstitions existed about discolorations on a baby's skin at birth, but he had never experienced or considered the ramifications of such beliefs.

Sir Wick had, though. Gage swallowed hard and wondered how many babies the White Fortress's guards had found on Clement's dump pile. How many had been saved, and how many hadn't been?

Gage's stomach twisted. How often were babies abandoned to die all because of a mark on their skin?

Staring at the crying infant in his hands, he thought of how much his little sister, who had died at birth, had been wanted and loved, yet she had lived for only a few hours despite so much effort made to keep her alive. Then there was Allard. There were so many years the youth should yet have had, years which had been snatched away in an instant. Meanwhile, this little one, who was so full of life, had been left to die. Grief and pain swirled through Gage, and he silently cried out in anger, "God, why would You create this baby knowing he would be rejected and abandoned the moment he was born?"

All his previous questions and doubts about God's goodness and regard for humanity felt suddenly justified. The sorrows of his previous losses, his uncertainty about God's character, and his hopes for what could be, and yet wasn't, crashed together within him, drowning his soul in anguish. "God, why? Why do this, when You're supposed to be good?"

Aisley brushed her fingers against the baby's forehead and spoke, her tone holding sorrow. "How can people be so wicked as to abandon a baby all because of something on its skin?"

Gage blinked. She was right. It wasn't God who had abandoned this little one or caused it to be rejected. Humans had done that, because of a lie, a belief that Satan was more powerful than God and that they knew better than their Creator about this little one's life.

Flinching at the truth, Gage silently acknowledged. "God, it is humanity that has chosen evil and brought all of this about. I have blamed You for it, but it is our fault. We have ignored You and are the cause of all of this. *I* have chosen to ignore You and to believe like Adam and Eve that I knew better than You, my Creator." Gage swallowed hard. "Humanity deserves to die. I deserve to die." Pain tightened in his chest, and he stared at the tiny human life in his hands. Grief flooded Gage. "But, LORD God, what about this little one? Will You care about and help him? Will You save him?"

35

Rhonalyn eyed with revulsion the horned, shaggy-haired goat that Wick had brought back with him. "A nanny goat? That's your plan?" She cast her disgust as well over the two baby goats exuberantly hopping around their mother.

"It is." Wick scooped up one of the baby goats and handed it to Aisley. "Hold this one for me, will you?" After a moment of dodging about, he got hold of the second kid. Rhonalyn stepped back, ready to refuse to take it, but Wick thrust it into Manton's hands instead. Manton grunted but held onto the flailing four-legged creature. Wick then traded Gabe the nanny goat's rope for the squalling newborn and sat down beside the goat with the baby in his hands.

Rhonalyn couldn't help but acknowledge the success of his idea when, a moment later, the newborn's hungry crying was replaced by the blissful quiet of contented suckling. Rhonalyn sighed in relief and the tension in her body eased.

"Whoa. Oh goodness!" Aisley cried out as the baby goat attempted to launch itself over her shoulder. It head-butted her instead, knocking the girl off balance. Aisley landed on her back, the goat still in her grasp.

Rhonalyn opened her mouth to rebuke Wick for putting an animal into the girl's arms, but before she could, Aisley burst into a fit of giggles. Elbowing herself to a seated position, Aisley wrestled the kid back into her lap with a determination that made Rhonalyn blink in surprise and mortification. The child looked very much like a manor milkmaid.

"Aisley, let it go," she commanded. "One of them can see to it."

Aisley shook her head, still giggling. "No, I've got it. Really."

"Ug!" Rhonalyn recoiled. "It's eating your hair!" Feeling herself gag at the sight, she covered her mouth.

"Oh, calm down already. It's just a little slobber." Manton tucked the kid he was holding under one arm and, reaching out, swept Aisley's braid out of the goat's mouth. Rhonalyn huffed in indignation. She had thought he was going to take the second kid, not touch a noble girl's hair.

"Thanks," Aisley said, then laughed as the goat nudged her chin. "They're so cute."

Rhonalyn pinched the bridge of her nose. So much for training up a lady. Catching sight then of her own dirty fingers, Rhonalyn instantly withdrew her hand from her face. She grimaced and wondered what the rest of her looked like. Shuddering at the image her mind conjured, she heaved a breath. There was no way she was presenting herself to King Strephon like this.

She cast a critical eye at the others. Nor would she do so in the sundry companionship of such a misbegotten retinue. She would have to advocate for a means of restoring herself to a presentable state. As for the others, she wasn't sure what she would do with them, but that could wait since her greater concern was reaching Strephon.

"Well?" she said, crossing her arms. "Are we going to get a move on?"

"We have only half a day of light left," Manton said, "and Burnel's monastery is a day's journey from here. We'll have to travel as far as we can, then find somewhere to shelter for the night."

"A spot with water available would be helpful," Wick said.

Rhonalyn sent a cold glare at Gabe. "It's too bad someone caused such a ruckus at Lyster's gate, or we could have stayed here at an inn."

"Never mind that," Manton said. "Better that we cover more ground."

⁂

That night Gage received the baby from Aisley and eased into the grass to sit with his back to the rocky outcropping they were camped beside. He shifted his arms to settle the stirring infant into the crook of his elbow like Sir Wick had shown him. Then he tipped from side to side until the little one's eyes drifted closed.

He, Sir Wick, and Aisley had traded off carrying the baby throughout the day as they walked or rode. And though it wasn't currently his turn, he'd taken him so Aisley could rescue Rhonalyn from the smaller of the two kid goats, which Aisley had named Hungry.

Aisley tugged at the goat's hindquarters, trying to pull it away from Rhonalyn's skirt. "Come on, Hungry, eating clothes isn't good for you. This way, back to your mum. Yep, come on!" She let go and skipped ahead of the goat around the fire. "Come on, Hungry!"

Joining in her playful jaunt, Hungry bounded after the girl. The kid passed Aisley and crashed head first into its mother's legs, knocking itself over. Leaping back up, it looked around, then ran forward and butted into its sibling. Gage shook his head and chuckled at the creature's ridiculous antics.

"I can't believe they don't crack their skulls open doing that," Sir Wick muttered as he stood over a pot of fire-heated water. With a whoosh of water he pulled from the pot the cloth that had been left with the newborn on the refuse pile. He wrung it out and then flapped it until it hung straight.

"If you intend to hang that somewhere to dry, you'd best put it high enough that Hungry and Bouncy can't reach it," Manton said as he dumped an armload of dead wood beside their crackling fire.

"I'm well aware," Sir Wick replied, an edge in his voice.

Since Sir Wick was usually a peacemaker, Gage couldn't help noticing the pattern of the knight's irritation toward Manton.

Manton crouched on the opposite side of the fire from the rest of them and added wood to the blaze, then held his hands over the flames while eyeing the forest's edge. Gage followed Manton's gaze to where darkness filled the space beneath the trees beyond their fire's light.

The rocky outcropping they'd chosen left a lot to be desired as a shelter. But the spot was far enough off the road to provide concealment, the trees blocked wind, and the steep outcropping at their backs protected them from at least one side. It was also close enough to a brook that water was easy to acquire. And the rocks themselves absorbed the fire's heat and reflected it back upon them, making the area almost too warm. But that warmth would be well appreciated later in the night.

Leaning against the closest rock face, Gage glanced down at the sleeping little one. The baby had been fed and then bathed in warm water by Sir Wick. Despite squirming after being transferred into Gage's arms, the tiny fellow had fallen fast asleep again almost instantly. His little body breathed in a steady rhythm that caused the V shape on his stomach to rise and fall. Meanwhile, one of his little hands rested on the moss-lined nappy Sir Wick had made from one of their food bags.

The baby's hair, cleaned of blood and the mess of birth, was the color of acorns, and his eyelashes were the same hue, though they were so fine it was hard to tell they were even there. His tiny lips were pursed and his legs were pulled in close. His toenails and fingernails were so small and perfect.

Gage threaded one of his fingers into the baby's grasp, marveling at the little person asleep in his arms.

Sir Wick sat down next to him, making Gage startle. The knight laughed. "He had you enthralled, didn't he?" Reaching over, Sir Wick brushed his finger against the baby's arm. "They have a way of doing that."

Shifting, Gage spoke quietly. "Wick, what if the monks in Brunel won't take him?"

Sir Wick's brow furrowed. "If they can't or won't, then we'll try whatever next place makes sense."

The doubt trailing his words stirred the pain in Gage's chest. If devoted servants of God rejected this little one, what then? What if there was no grace to be had and no place of rescue and safety for him?

Sir Wick cleared his throat. "It may not be at a monastery, but God will provide for this little one. You'll see. It's—"

Aisley approached, and Sir Wick fell silent. The girl crouched in front of Gage and stroked the baby's head. "He needs a name."

Gage shook his head. "Not a good idea."

Aisley frowned. "Why not?"

"Because he's not ours. And he's not a pet whose name can be changed when he's handed to someone else. Whoever he ends up with should name him."

Undaunted, Aisley met his gaze. "Exactly, he's not a pet. He's a person. And every person needs a name. He shouldn't have to wait to get a name simply because his parents didn't want him."

Gage opened and then closed his mouth. He had no will to argue with her on that point. It didn't take long, though, before he wished he had. Aisley's name ideas fit animals better than people.

He groaned in exasperation as she tried out yet another name on the sleeping baby she now held. "What about Ar—"

"No," Gage said. "No more attempts at naming him. He may need a name, but he can wait for one that's reasonable."

Aisley sank back, a dejected look on her face. "I was going to say Archibald." Her face lit up and she looked down at the little one. "Or how about—"

"What did I just say?" Gage asked.

Aisley cringed, then slipped the name out anyway. "Eliab?"

Sir Wick laughed as Gage threw up his hands in exasperation. Gage shook his head at the knight. "You're laughing? What if she was naming you?"

Sir Wick shrugged. "I don't know, I kind of like the name Eliab."

Gage eyed the knight as if he had just announced he was cheering for the opposite side of a tournament. He squinted at the baby and tried out the name himself. "Eliab." Gage tipped his head from side to side. "He does kind of feel like he could be an Eliab."

Aisley said happily, "Eliab it is then. Eli for short."

36

Chuckling at Prince Gage's interactions with Lady Aisley, Wick rose to add more wood to the fire. He picked up a heavy branch and inhaled a swift breath when a streak of pain through his side reminded him of the wound there that refused to heal. He'd cleaned the puncture the best he could the night after it happened, but it wasn't the surface that was the problem. Wick clenched his jaw and, ignoring the discomfort, set the branch into the blaze.

Sparks burst up. Snapping and popping accompanied the fire consuming the new fuel. Wick straightened and stared into the twisting flames before glancing at Princess Rhonalyn and the others. He heaved a breath. He might as well make his confession sooner rather than later. He cleared his throat. "We're going to need to refill our supplies in Burnel."

"Shouldn't be a problem," Manton said, leaning back on his arms a few paces away. "There's a large market in Burnel. We should find whatever we need there."

"Good," Wick said, then forced himself to continue, "because to pay for supplies, we may need to sell the horse the girls are riding."

"What?" Princess Rhonalyn's voice sliced across the fire.

Manton sat forward. "No, there should still be enough from the sale we made in Dinslage for us to resupply at least once more."

"Well, there were the tolls in Lyster…and other expenses." Refusing to cringe, Wick nodded toward the goats. "I acquired them at a bit of a steep price, considering there was little time to scour the city for a better deal."

Manton scrubbed a hand over his mouth, clearly suppressing frustration, which surprised Wick since he had assumed Manton wouldn't hesitate to ridicule him.

"Well, I'm not walking to Ithera," Princess Rhonalyn declared.

Having already considered solutions, Wick was quick to reply. "You won't have to. The packs can be put on Gabe's horse, allowing you to ride Manton's mule."

Manton's eyebrows rose. "She'll ride Nigel? Bareback?"

Wick glared at him before returning his gaze to Princess Rhonalyn. "We'll purchase a saddle for it."

"Why not sell the mule and keep the horse instead?" Princess Rhonalyn questioned.

"Because," Prince Gage said, rising to his feet, "there's more money to be made selling the horse, and a mule lets us blend in better. When there are no royal coffers to gather from, sacrifices must be made to pay for travel expenses. Though, if you'd prefer, we could all work to earn the coin another way. Reeves are often looking for extra field hands. If we all put in a few days' work, we could purchase supplies that way."

With a huff, Princess Rhonalyn rose to her feet. Glaring at Prince Gage, she lifted her chin, then turned her back on them. Wick wasn't sure whether to cringe in sympathy or brace himself for what might come next.

Her Royal Highness's shoulders remained stiff, but her arms wrestled with her skirt as if she were trying to find a clean corner to cry or scream into. Her calm, forceful voice cast over her shoulder a moment later took him by surprise.

"There will be no need for either option." She turned around and marched to Prince Gage. "I'm not working in some field. I am a royal of Keric. I can pay my own way." She thrust out her balled fist.

Prince Gage opened his hand to accept what she had to offer him, and she dropped the item into his palm. Wick assumed it was one of her rings, which would be more problematic than helpful to sell.

Prince Gage glanced down, and with a cry, he hurled the item away from him as if it had burnt him. Whatever it was glinted as it flew over the fire and hit the ground near Manton.

"What are you doing?" Princess Rhonalyn shrieked. She rushed after the item, but Manton beat her to it.

"What am I doing?" Prince Gage yelled. His voice was so high pitched it made the skin on Wick's arms prickle. "Where did you get—"

The frightened wail of Eliab drowned out his words.

"You're scaring Eli!" Aisley said, trying to calm the little one.

"Shut it up!" Princess Rhonalyn yelled at the girl.

Wick scooped the crying Eliab out of Aisley's lap and moved away from Rhonalyn. Cuddling the little fella against his chest, he bounced on his toes to quiet him. His haste was unnecessary, though, since Her Royal Highness's attention was already focused elsewhere.

She snapped her fingers at Manton. "Give me it back!"

Looking startled, Manton held whatever it was out to her, and she snatched it back.

Prince Gage questioned her forcefully, "Where did you get that?"

"Where did *I* get it?" Princess Rhonalyn's voice surged with anger. "I've had it since before leaving Keric."

"Keric!" Fear filled Prince Gage's voice. "Where and how did you get it in Keric?"

Princess Rhonalyn's gaze narrowed, and her voice took on a hard edge. "It came from a batch of coins minted for my mother, all of which, up until a few months ago, were stored in a chest in the royal treasury of Arcis Castle." Princess Rhonalyn's fingers clenched around the gold. "My father sent a portion of them in payment to Delkara for a toll. But before they reached their destination, the coins were stolen by a group of commoners." She turned an accusing gaze on Manton.

Gold coins stolen by commoners. Swallowing, Wick shifted Eliab up his chest and glanced at Prince Gage.

Appearing uncertain but also determined, His Highness snatched a half-burnt branch out of the fire and strode back to the outcropping. Using the branch's charred end, he began to draw something on the rock face. When he was finished, Prince Gage stepped back and pointed at a roughly sketched flail and crossbow with their handles crossed. "Do you know this mark?" he asked.

Bouncing on his toes to keep Eliab quiet, Wick looked at Princess Rhonalyn, his skin prickling. Surely, the mark Prince Gage bore wasn't hers. But what if it belonged to one of her lords?

Princess Rhonalyn shook her head. "I don't understand. Why're you ask—"

"Just answer my question!"

"No! I've never seen that mark before." Her lips pressed together, and her voice turned hard. "But you've obviously seen my mother's gold before. You, who claim to have honor and no association with Manton's rebels, yet you recognize stolen gold that no commoner beyond a goldsmith would have any lawful reason to know or handle."

"It wasn't by his choice." Manton's voice drew everyone's gaze. "Gabe's involvement with the gold was my doing."

Wick blinked, surprised Manton would admit that so freely.

Princess Rhonalyn folded her arms. "So, it *was* your people who stole my mother's gold."

"I admit," Manton answered calmly, "that my people unlawfully acquired a collection of gold coins, like that one, but they were not stolen in Keric or from anyone from Keric. The coins my people took were seized in a raid upon Delkaran soldiers. Those soldiers were returning from Lamar after selling grain that was taken in unjust taxation."

Princess Rhonalyn scoffed. "Why should I believe you?"

"Normally, you shouldn't," Prince Gage said, "but there's proof that backs his claim. His people didn't steal that gold from you. If they had, no one else would be laying claim to it. But someone else is."

"What are you talking about?" Princess Rhonalyn asked.

"The Unavowed claim that that gold, your gold, belongs to whoever's mark this is. Prince Gage pointed at the flail and crossbow. "And the owner of this mark commands the Unavowed, who wants you dead. We all have the same enemy."

With Eliab's little body making his chest damp with sweat, Wick watched as a parade of emotions traveled across Princess Rhonalyn's face. When she spoke, a new form of anger simmered below the surface of her calm tone. "It would seem then that Strephon and I have reason to reconsider who we have blamed for some of the attacks and thefts that have taken place in our kingdoms." She nodded at Manton. "A matter I'll certainly address with King Strephon, along with tracking down the Unavowed and finding my men. And whoever has dared to deceive and manipulate the sovereigns of two nations, I'll see they pay with their life."

37

Rhonalyn bit back a cry of frustration. They were stopping to feed the baby—again. She was pretty sure none of them had slept much the night before. She certainly had not, on the ground, in the open, and listening repeatedly to the baby's wailing cries. Even now its cries rose and fell in a persistent cadence that set her teeth on edge.

Exhausted, stiff, and jealous of the merchants passing them by who were free of goats and infants, Rhonalyn wished for the hundredth time that morning for a retinue that could get her where she wanted to go.

She knew she wasn't the only one exasperated by the noise and the delays. Manton's normally laidback tone had disappeared somewhere in the night. Gabriel grumbled to himself whenever the baby started crying, and Wick was testy with the animals and highly controlled with everyone else.

Aisley was the only one who seemed unaffected.

Rhonalyn eyed the girl with irritation. How the child could sleep anywhere and through anything and skip along with goats like it was all just some grand adventure was beyond her. Rhonalyn was tempted to inform Aisley just how bad their situation was, but the realization that she wanted to smash the girl's carefree spirit to garner companionship in her own misery sobered her enough to keep her tongue in check, if only to prevent the others from realizing how out of control she felt.

As they pressed onward, she clung to the hope that the monastery at Burnel would provide the tranquility and slumber she craved and needed to regather her thoughts and decide how best to approach King Strephon.

❧❧

With the nanny goat and Athalos in tow, Gage took in the changes in the industrious city of Burnel. When he and Manton had been there last, Manton had commented how different it looked, and there had been changes even since then. Newly built shops, warehouses, and cottages encircled the city's outer edge.

With no walls or gate, the blue-clothed soldiers of Burnel—with a coat-of-arms consisting of a wheat sheaf and a waterwheel—roamed the city's streets. Having taken precautions for the possibility of being searched, Rhonalyn's gold coin was back in her skirt, and the two books were concealed end to end within the lower circumference of the back girth strap of Nigel's packsaddle. It had been Sir Wick who had come up with the idea. He had cautioned them, though, to make sure the strap wouldn't cause injury to the mule but was tight enough to definitely hold the books in place.

They traveled through the outer edge of the city to get to the monastery on Burnel's northwest side. It was slow going with their animals, but they finally arrived as the sun was setting. Foot-sore and travel-weary, Gage had his hands full with Athalos and the nanny goat. Sir Wick carried Eliab. Aisley trailed Nigel. Rhonalyn rode, and Manton had a kid goat tucked under either arm because they had kept getting underfoot or running off.

The sight of the familiar monastery's gate with its sunlit cross, bell, and Latin words brought a wave of relief to Gage. But the feeling vanished when they rang the bell and the gate opened. Rather than a monk, they were met by a soldier in a tabard bearing Burnel's coat-of-arms.

"What's your business here?" the soldier asked.

Even Manton looked taken aback. "We…um…we're here to speak with the monastery's abbot and to request a night's stay."

Just then the monastery's previous porter, Brother Barnabas, with his weathered features and pale robe, stepped forward through the gate. He greeted them with a smile, though tension clung to the edges of it. "Welcome, travelers. You may indeed find lodging for the night with us. As for speaking with our abbot, he is…" The hesitation in his voice was accompanied by a glance at the soldier. "Not currently available. But you are welcome to speak with our prior."

"Prior Joseph?" Gage asked, wanting very much to know if the monk, whom he'd strangely come to respect, was there.

Brother Barnabas nodded stiffly, then gestured for them to enter. "If you will follow me, you may leave your animals in the care of our brothers and speak with our prior." His tone expressed reassurance, but the monk's body was still tense.

Manton walked through the gate, but Gage hesitated. His emotions ricocheted between confidence that the soldier had no interest in them and fear that he and the others might be stepping into an ambush of some kind.

He walked through the gate after Manton, his senses screaming and his body wanting to flee in four different directions. His heart pounding, he searched the area. He spotted only the pale robes of monks going about their normal tasks. Nowhere were there other soldiers.

It was only after they had settled their animals in the barn and their mismatched party was heading for the monastery's parlor that he spotted another of Burnel's blue livery.

An older soldier stepped out of the building ahead of them,

speaking over his shoulder in a commanding tone to Prior Joseph, who was trailing him. "As it is, I trust this time you and your monks will heed the order." The warning in the soldier's words was unmistakable.

"We are well aware of it and will certainly keep it in mind," Prior Joseph replied.

The soldier snorted. "I see, but as to keeping it?"

Prior Joseph smiled stiffly. "We answer to God, not man."

The soldier shook his head. "My advice to you, don't push my lord's lenience. He'll take this as far as he must."

"Good advice for yourself as well," Prior Joseph said, "for God is not mocked."

The soldier scoffed, and as he walked past Gage and his party, he called back. "You're fools, the lot of you."

Prior Joseph's shoulder's rose and fell before his gaze met Gage's. The prior's eyes flickered with recognition, and a smile wreathed his features. "Manton's friend! And Manton! It's so good to see you both. And who have you with you? Three others and a little one?"

"This little fella is the reason we've come to you," Sir Wick said.

"Oh? Is that so?" The prior sounded surprised and curious.

The knight shifted Eliab in his arms. "He's a refuse-pile baby."

"Ah, I see." There was a deep sadness in Prior Joseph's voice. "And you're wondering if we'll take him. I assume he carries a mark on him somewhere?"

Gage flinched at the question.

"He does." Sir Wick unwrapped Eliab's little body and held him before the monk.

Gage couldn't breathe. All he wanted to do was cover Eliab back up and scream, "What does it matter? Why can't you help him anyway?"

Prior Joseph's gaze lowered to the purplish V. Then with a look of such regard and compassion, the monk reached out and placed his hand on Eliab's little body. "It's alright little one," he murmured. "All are welcome here."

38

AT THE CUSP of dawn, Wick yawned and scrubbed his face as he and Manton crossed the monastery grounds. He had stayed up late the night before, sorting through what was left in their food packs, a task he ended up doing twice because he kept thinking about Eliab. He was grateful to be free of being responsible for the little fella and happy to have both his hands empty again, but he was also grieved to say goodbye. He shook away the thought. He did not need to dwell mournfully on a completed mission. The monks had willingly taken Eliab and graciously bought the goats from them, which meant he and Manton could purchase supplies without selling the girls' horse or trying to figure out how to use Rhonalyn's gold.

Wick shifted the strap of the empty food packs slung over his shoulder and trailed Manton toward the barn.

"We can take Nigel," Manton said, "and pack everything back on him."

Wick stifled another yawn. "Agreed."

They entered the barn's open door and stopped short. A lantern hanging at the end of a stall illuminated a small figure standing between Prince Gage's horse and Manton's mule.

Wick stiffened at the sight of the girl. "What're you doing in here?"

Lady Aisley jerked, which sent the brush she was using on Manton's mule flying out of her hand. It hit the flank of Prince Gage's horse, and the animal lashed out a hind foot.

The horse's hoof missed the girl by plenty of space, but Wick's heart still skipped a beat. "You shouldn't be in here." He hurried forward and gestured for Lady Aisley to come out away from the horse. "And you definitely shouldn't be near that animal."

Huffing, Aisley came. "It was *you* who scared us. Athalos was fine until you started yelling."

"Wick's right," Manton replied with equal frustration. "You should stay away from Athalos. You'll only get yourself hurt."

She rolled her eyes at them. Wick opened his mouth to reprimand her but then remembered she was no peasant child or disrespectful stable hand. She was a lady. Not that she was acting like one. He heaved a breath and tried a different approach. "Regardless of our opinions, I believe Rose already expressed her disapproval of your mornings spent in the barn." He raised his eyebrows.

Aisley's expression was a mixture of hurt and determination. "But I love the animals. And she never objects as long as I get back before she wakes."

"In other words, the times when she doesn't know?"

Aisley pressed together her lips and stayed silent.

Wick sighed and dropped the empty packs he was carrying. "Look, it's not safe for you to be in here in the barn alone anyway, especially when you don't know the other people and animals that are around."

Lady Aisley scuffed her bare toes in the dirt and tipped her head toward the packs. "Where you goin'?"

Watching her, Wick thought she made a much better peasant girl than a lady. "To refill our supplies."

She looked up, her eyes brightening. "I wanna come."

"No."

"But Pr—" She caught herself. "Rose is still asleep, and if you leave me here, I'll just stay in the barn. So, really wouldn't I be safer coming with you?"

Wick narrowed his gaze. "We're just getting supplies. That's all."

She bounced on her heels. "And I wanna come. Please let me?"

Unable to divert her and unwilling to leave her in the barn, Wick gave in. "Fine, but we'll leave word for Rose with the monks, and you're to stay right beside me."

After handing Manton enough coin to pay for half the goods they needed, Wick headed off with Lady Aisley toward the shops and stalls where Manton had assured Wick they could find the other half of what they sought.

Assuming Lady Aisley would trail at his elbow just as silently as she normally traveled, Wick was surprised when she spoke in the middle of him trying to mentally tally the price and quantities of the items they needed. "Why do you let Gabe make all the decisions?"

Wick frowned. "Do I?"

"Yeah, you do. Is he older than you?"

"No. I'm older." Wick settled on how much and determined the starting prices he would begin at when bargaining with the seller.

"Then is Gabe above you in some way?"

Lady Aisley's question caught Wick off guard. Realizing the girl's curiosity might not be as naïve or innocent as he supposed, he put more focus into the conversation. "I let Gabe make the decisions because I'm here as his friend to help him, not to make choices for him."

He waited, wondering what she would ask next, but instead of a question she went a different direction with the conversation. "I don't have many friends. I once had three friends my own age." She launched into a story about those three friends and their adventures. Then her happy tone shifted. "But as soon as my papa learned about me spending time with them, he said it was improper for me to have such friends and forbid them from playing with me." She sighed. "That's why I like animals. No one can tell them not to be my friend. And they don't mind if I only see them here and there."

Feeling for her and also curious, Wick delayed approaching the next seller. "Your father, why did he consider your previous friends improper?"

"They were from the village and inferior to me in rank."

"Oh."

"My papa wants for me to make acceptable friends and acquaintances, which is why he sent me to stay with P…with Rose. I'm meant to become more like her, you see."

Wick was tempted to comment that she wasn't much like Princess Rhonalyn and should perhaps refrain from becoming so, but he had no idea who Lady Aisley was in Keric. Perhaps she was the daughter of an important lord, and her becoming a proper lady in Princess Rhonalyn's court was the desired outcome regardless of Lady Aisley's disposition or Her Royal Highness's shortcomings.

"You don't like Rose, do you?" Lady Aisley said as they walked.

Wick stiffened and told himself he really needed to do a better job of keeping his thoughts off his face. "I just think she and you are quite different, is all."

Lady Aisley's forehead furrowed, and she nodded. "That's true." Her eyes rose to his, full of eagerness. "But you've not really seen her for who she is. When she's allowed to be herself, she's bold and fierce, and it's magnificent."

Wick had observed the edge of these traits in Princess Rhonalyn, but he wasn't convinced they made her admirable. He much preferred Lady Aisley's character traits. "Yes, but is she also kind and compassionate? Because those qualities are equally important in a leader."

Lady Aisley stopped in her tracks, surprise and concern filling her voice. "You think her unkind?"

Wick cringed. His intention had been to help the girl see her own kindness and compassion as qualities to be valued and maintained, not as further criticism of Her Royal Highness. Princess Rhonalyn wasn't his royal, but still he felt he had tread onto dangerous ground, especially if the girl chose to repeat his words to Her Royal Highness. He attempted to find a diplomatic way out of the conversation. "I'm sure Rose can be kind. And perhaps you're right; I simply haven't seen enough of her to know who she really is."

Lady Aisley gave him a thoughtful look. "You're not like any other commoner I've ever known."

"No, I'd guess not." Wick shifted and pointed ahead. "I think that's the shop we want."

Lady Aisley quickened her steps to keep up with him. "How'd you and Gabe become friends?"

A moment Wick held his breath. He then brightened his tone. "You know what? I think perhaps we should focus on shopping. It'll go faster if we do."

She huffed. "You're just saying that so that you don't have to answer me."

He silently groaned. Why did she have to be so perceptive? He swallowed and scrambled through ideas. He figured straightforwardness may be the best option. "Very well, you're clearly very smart and quite observant. So, let's make a deal. You use your skills to help me get this job done, and I'll answer your question on the way back. Deal?" It would give him time to come up with a response that hopefully wouldn't lead her to ask even more questions.

Lady Aisley smiled. "Deal." She skipped ahead, and Wick scrubbed a hand down his face.

39

"WATCH OUT!" WICK pulled Lady Aisley out of the way of a cart. Wagons and carts traveled a circular route in the market square, transporting goods and making deliveries to shops and stalls. The square, located west of the towers and Burnel's large keep, was as busy as Manton had predicted.

Lady Aisley pointed. "There! I can see the nut seller."

Wick juggled his armload of supplies and waited with her as a stream of people emptying from a guildhall crossed their path. Utilizing a gap in the flow, he and Lady Aisley hurried though and toward the stall they wanted.

After a good bit of haggling, they acquired the last of what they needed, then found Manton in the square where he said he'd be waiting for them.

Manton opened the top of one of his mule's packs. "Here."

Nodding his thanks, Wick unloaded what he and Lady Aisley had in their arms, including bread, cabbage, beans, smoked meat, nuts, milled grain, and a collection of other food supplies. "I think we're ready to head back."

"Good," Manton said, "because if we—"

With a cry that sounded like dismay, Lady Aisley ran from Wick's side and cut into the midst of the moving crowd.

"What in the…Amy!" Trying to see through the crowd, Wick rose on his toes to follow the girl with his gaze and resisted the urge to call out her real name. The girl was weaving through the crowd, intent upon getting somewhere.

"Where's she going?" Manton asked.

"How should I know?" Wick replied angrily.

"Well, you'd best get after her." Manton took up his mule's reins. "I'll meet you back at the monastery."

"Great. Thanks." It would take longer for Manton to get through the crowd with the mule, but still. With a growl, Wick ran after Lady Aisley.

It wasn't until he was about ten strides into chasing after her that it occurred to him that he had just entrusted all their supplies to Manton. But since it was too late to reverse course now, he kept after Lady Aisley, wishing he hadn't been so stupid as to allow her to come with them. He cut around a group of sellers, ducked past a packhorse, and ran between chatting guild members. What was she thinking? And where was she going?

With his gaze fixed on her back, he closed the distance between them and was two strides from reaching her when the girl burst out of the crowd into a vacant stretch of ground. Wick jerked to a stop. He realized then where Lady Aisley was headed, and his skin turned cold.

A set of pillories stood in front of a gallows in an area the people in the square avoided as if the ground itself might sully them with the unpleasantness of its judicial existence. Or perhaps they feared they would be sullied by the often disreputable occupants of the pillory, a fact that made Lady Aisley's course—headed straight for a prisoner locked in one of the pillories—both disturbing and concerning.

The man's head hung low, too low for Wick to see his face or tell his age. The man was barefoot and wore a dirty, ill-fitting tunic. And yet, despite no doubt starving now, the pillory's prisoner had in the past clearly eaten well, for the man's body carried enough weight and muscle to indicate that he was by no means a beggar or a frequent occupant of the pillory.

The prisoner had not yet noticed Lady Aisley's approach. Determined to intervene before then, Wick breached the expanse of empty ground. Feeling like he had just entered a dungeon, he shuddered. The area was definitely no place for a lady.

Stopping in front of the pillory, Lady Aisley lifted a shaking hand as if about to reach out and touch the man. Wick was only three strides from getting to her, and Lady Aisley spoke, her voice like a gust of wind. "Sir Nolan?"

The prisoner lifted his head, and above a gag, the man's eyes—dulled with pain and fatigue—widened.

Lady Aisley let out another cry and stepped close to the pillory. She grasped the boards as if determined to free the man herself, but a lock prevented that.

The man twisted his bruised wrist in the boards and tried hard to say something, but the grimy cloth binding his mouth made his words indistinguishable.

Changing the focus of her efforts, Lady Aisley seized the gag and attempted to pry it from his mouth. The man shook his head, his surprise had been replaced by a look of such visceral fear it made the hair on Wick's arms rise. Wick grasped Lady Aisley's shoulder. "I think we should go." The man's gaze gripped his as if begging him to do more. Alarm rising within him, Wick pulled at Lady Aisley. "We need to go."

"I'm not leaving him." The girl wrenched free and twisted the gag out of the man's mouth.

"No! Run!" The word burst from the man's cracked lips. "Flee!" His next words confirmed Wick's fears. "It's a trap!"

The clanking of armor across the square and the sound of

authoritative voices yelling for people to get out of the way kicked Wick past any hesitation.

Seizing Lady Aisley's wrist, he yanked her away from the pillory, across the void of ground, and away from the approaching soldiers. He elbowed through a throng of buyers and sprinted between sellers' carts and stalls, pulling Lady Aisley with him. They passed wagons and merchants and wove in and out of shoppers, disgruntled and vocal about being jostled.

Aware that the soldiers probably had a lookout in the towers above, Wick didn't attempt to hide in the square. Instead, he fled with Lady Aisley toward the area's west side where he had earlier spotted an opening between the buildings. He prayed it led to a passable street. Twisting through the crowd, he threaded his way as fast as he could toward it.

They were twenty paces from the gap when Wick spotted two Burnel guardsmen standing at the other end of it. Their gazes searching the crowd. Wick jerked Lady Aisley to a stop behind three people paused together talking. He turned sideways so he could keep an eye on the guards but not face them. One of the guards marched off, heading wide of their position. The other remained where he was, still searching the crowd.

Wick turned to Lady Aisley. "When I say, 'go,' I want you to run for the street ahead. Do you understand?"

Her eyes wide, she nodded.

Wick waited until the guard turned away, then he pointed for Lady Aisley. "That way, now! Go!"

The girl bolted away from him.

The soldier's gaze locked on Lady Aisley the moment she burst into sight. Rushing toward the girl, he was nearly on top of her when Wick crossed paths with him from behind.

"Hey! I've got the gir—" The soldier's call was cut off as Wick's foot hooked around his right leg, sending the soldiers crashing onto his stomach in a clatter of metal and curses.

Stepping upon his armored back and smashing the guard into the ground a second time, Wick launched off the soldier's body and bolted after Lady Aisley. The girl was already fleeing down the street, her skirt flapping behind her and her braid flying.

"Halt!

"You two, stop!"

"Stay where you are!"

The bellowed commands, coming from multiple directions, made Wick's heart lurch as he ran. But no hands laid hold of him, and he flew onward. Five strides behind Lady Aisley, then four, he sprinted in her wake. People expressed their surprise and outrage at their hazardous passing, but Wick didn't care.

"Whatever happens," he yelled, "keep going!"

The street angled to the left. They raced around the curve and found the street ahead ended in an expanse of moving water. The river. Wick remembered Prince Gage mentioning Burnel had two watermills. "Go right!" he yelled. He hoped he was correct that the mills were further downstream.

With her arms cartwheeling and her feet sliding, Lady Aisley lunged toward the next available opening. She narrowly avoided crashing into a peasant coming along the lane with a bulging sack on his shoulder. The man jerked to a stop to avoid her, which threw his load off balance. Aisley escaped past him, but the man and sack tumbled forward, directly into Wick's path.

Wick tripped over the sack and stumbled into the man. They crashed to the ground together, Wick's hands stinging and his heart thundering. Scrambling to his feet and away from the man, he broke back into a run.

"You, come back here!" a voice called out angrily behind him.

Ignoring the command, Wick tore after Lady Aisley. She was approaching a line of people and wagons in front of the first mill.

Wick glanced back. No soldiers were yet visible behind him, only an angry man with a sack. Putting on a burst of speed, he snagged Lady Aisley's arm and dragged her between two wagons. He slowed them to a normal speed and drew her to a walk along the line of people, then split off from them. He led her to the side of the first mill. The second mill was less than a bow's shot away.

The rhythmic rumble of the gears of both stone structures blended with the shushing of the water and the creaking of the paddles and buckets being pushed and filled by the river's flow.

Logs and milled lumber were stacked between the two buildings and gave decent cover, but the stacks would be too easy for the soldiers to search.

Running from one stack to the next through thick grass that tangled around their legs, Wick drew Lady Aisley along the river to the second mill. At the back of this mill he saw a narrow ledge of ground. Created by a wall that helped sluice the water into the mill's wheel, the ledge ran the full length of the back of the building. Wick directed Lady Aisley along it and behind the building.

With the wheel turning within arm's reach of them and the sounds of the water and the rumble of the axle in front of them, Wick couldn't hear anything behind or ahead. He checked both directions as they shuffled along the strip of ground. The wheel's movement kicked up water, sprinkling his legs and boots and splotching Lady Aisley's gray-brown dress. The churning water filled his nose with the scent of green slime.

Wick gestured for Lady Aisley to pass under the waterwheel's axle. Her eyes still wide, the girl ducked under the turning shaft.

Dropping to his knees, Wick crawled after her. He carefully stood up on the other side and eased along behind her to the building's far corner. He laid a hand on her shoulder to stop her from going farther.

He leaned over her to glance toward the street. Beyond a heap of boards, three soldiers were making their way through the second mill's line of people. Pulling back out of sight, Wick gestured for Aisley to stay where she was. With their backs pressed against the building and their feet pointed toward the river, Wick wondered how thoroughly the soldiers would search the area. Were they safe where they were or not?

Taking quick breaths, he leaned forward and glanced down. They were past the mill's wheel and about the height of two horses above where water churned out from its underside.

Inhaling the river's stench, he considered the water below, wondering how deep it was and if there was any part of the wall to hold onto down there. Could they drop in and flee downstream? He'd been trained how to swim and could manage decently well in the water, but he had no idea how Lady Aisley would fare.

A voice yelled from the opposite end of the building. "They're back there!"

40

"YET YOU LEFT them!" Gage felt like strangling Manton. They had been arguing about Sir Wick and Lady Aisley's absence for the better part of an hour. Upon Manton's return, they had all assumed the two would be along shortly. Thus, they had packed and were now waiting on the road outside the monastery, but Sir Wick and Aisley hadn't arrived.

"I still don't understand," Rhonalyn said, her voice holding fear and blame. "Why would she just take off?"

Manton threw his hands up. "I told you, I have no idea."

Gage empathized with Rhonalyn's concern and angst over the situation.

"She shouldn't have even been with you two," Rhonalyn said.

Her words cut through Gage with a painful reminder of Lord Henry's words the night of Allard's death. Air locked in his chest.

"Wick's the one who let her come," Manton snapped back.

"That's n—"

A whistle from down the road interrupted Rhonalyn.

"There they are!" Manton's voice held relief as he tugged Nigel around.

Gage exhaled in relief as well, then evaluated Sir Wick and Aisley with confusion.

Rhonalyn asked exactly what was on his mind, "Why are you both soaking wet?"

"I'll explain later," Wick answered. "Right now we need to depart

Burnel as quickly as possible. Manton, is there a way out of here that doesn't involve main roads?"

Manton's features smoothed back into the calm and composed smuggler Gage was beginning to grudgingly appreciate. "I know just the path."

❧

Rhonalyn hiked along the trail behind Manton. She was breathing heavily and sweating from the effort of the climb. When they had started out hours before, she'd ridden with Aisley, who had been shaking so badly she could scarcely walk straight. Wrapped in a cloak, the child still rode, but the trees were now thick and too low for anyone higher than the child to stay on horseback.

According to Manton they were cutting northeast over hills between Burnel and Koth, and they would swing back west as they came down the far side. Initially, before the morning's events, Manton had said they would reach Koth by end of day and lodge there for the night. But due to their late start and the rough terrain of the hills, that was now unlikely.

Where they ended up for the night, though, was hardly the first or biggest concern on Rhonalyn's mind.

Wick and Aisley had explained what had happened in Burnel, everything from Aisley spotting Sir Nolan across the square to them jumping into the river to evade the soldiers.

Rhonalyn could see Sir Nolan as Aisley had described him. Fury raged through her. How was it her guardsman was being treated so. Her body quivered, and she clenched her hand around the coin in her skirt.

No longer could she deceive herself into believing her men were still off somewhere in Delkara, looking for her. They weren't safe.

Her guardsmen were prisoners, and they were being used against her.

And this time it wasn't just Unavowed soldiers involved. The trap had included Burnel soldiers. Was Burnel's lord with the Unavowed? Or was it, as Gabe suggested, that the Unavowed had probably promised payment to the Burnel soldiers if they took into custody anyone who came for Sir Nolan and delivered them to the Unavowed? But if that were the case, what lies had the Unavowed told the lord and soldiers of Burnel about Sir Nolan, her, and Lady Aisley to convince them to set such a trap? She clenched her fists. And where were the rest of her men? What had the Unavowed done with them? Were they alive? She wanted to believe they were, but fear that they might not be crept through her regardless.

Like many of her guardsmen, Sir Nolan had a wife and children awaiting his return. No doubt his family and all the rest of those in Keric expecting their loved ones back were beginning to wonder why their fathers, husbands, and sons had not yet returned from their duties as her royal retinue. And her father, King Bryant, would have no answers for them or himself as to their absence.

Swallowing hard and feeling the sting of grief, Rhonalyn swiped her hand at her face. More tears came. She whisked them away as she walked. Tears were pointless. Her men, or at the very least, Sir Nolan, needed her to stay focused and get to King Strephon to deal with the Unavowed.

Initially, she had argued with Wick about turning around in order to not leave Sir Nolan behind.

"Your knight's duty is to protect you," Wick said. "Staying away and staying safe is the best way you can help him, and it's the only way you can protect him."

"He's right," Manton said. "Free, you still have the chance to rescue him, which is why you should return to Keric and rally your army. Don't go to King Strephon, begging for his help. Bring your own strength from Keric. Return with enough soldiers to deal with the Unavowed's treachery."

She couldn't deny the appeal to Manton's words, but she still doubted if her father would agree to such an action, even with the loss of her retinue. Risking war and violating their peace treaty with Delkara by marching an army across the border was not something she could see her father doing. And if he refused to take such an action, not only would her returning to Keric do her men no good, she would be dooming herself to inaction and disgrace. No, the only way she was going to convince her father to send an army would be if King Strephon himself requested Keric's aid. So, the only person she could go to was King Strephon, not that she was about to tell Manton that. "I've come this far," she said, "yet you'd have me turn back?"

"No, I'd have you only alter your course to the west." Manton replied. "If you let me, I can see you to the Delkaran coastline in three days. I know a man who can ferry you out and get you onto a ship heading into Nikor Harbor. The Unavowed will be watching the bridge north of the harbor. They won't anticipate you arriving by merchant vessel. Once docked, it's not far from the harbor to Keric's border. Once you cross, you can call forth your army and return to conquer the Unavowed."

"That's one choice," Gabe said, a concerned look on his face. "Or you could go east to Edelmar for aid. From here it's about a two-and-a-half-day journey to Edelmar's border, less time than it'd take to reach the coastline of Delkara and Manton's acquaintance who may or may not get you onto a ship actually headed for Nikor Harbor."

Gabe's point about trusting Manton and his smuggler friend wasn't lost on her, but she knew even less about Edelmar than she did about Delkara. She had no guarantee that, even as a Keric royal,

Edelmar would help her, especially when it came to military action.

"To get into Edelmar, you'd have to swim the Apse River or find someone with a boat," Manton said. "Asplin, Maneo, and Duvall have all closed their eastern gates to Edelmar. I heard it this morning. No one is being allowed to enter or leave Delkara."

"What? That can't be!" Wick's startled tone and clear suspicion made his word sharp. "Why would all three cities close their gates? Hundreds of people cross the border between Edelmar and Delkara every day, transporting goods and services to both sides of the Apse."

"My guess?" Manton answered. "For exactly the reason Gabe just suggested. They don't want Keric's princess fleeing into Edelmar to share her story of what's taken place. The account they want spread is that she was killed by my people—rebel commoners whose leaders can be found in the cliffs of Nikor. That way King Bryant might even help King Strephon invade the cliffs to locate and kill my people, those who have sacrificed everything to stand against the greed, injustice, and corruption of the Delkaran lords."

Rhonalyn narrowed her gaze at Manton. His lies intermingled with his truths so flawlessly it was impossible to tell them apart. She shook her head. "My decision remains unchanged. We go to Ithera and King Strephon."

"You're a fool if you think he'll help you," Manton snapped.

She gave him a blithe smile. "Yes, but according to you, I'm a fool that you need alive to protect your precious rebellion. So, as agreed, you'll see me to King Strephon." She held his gaze, her heart beat loud in her ear. She and Manton remained locked in silent battle.

Finally, Manton dropped his gaze. "So be it."

For a moment, Rhonalyn felt the elation of victory, then she descended into the frightening reality of what she faced. More than ever, she felt alone and horribly vulnerable.

41

With Athalos trailing him, Gage trudged after the others. Were the gates to Edelmar really closed? Even if they weren't, only the others could have gotten across. With his mark and without Sir Wick's uniform, he had no means to escape. So, perhaps it was better that Rhonalyn had chosen to continue on in Delkara.

But with all Gage had seen and heard, he was no longer so certain about her plan of approaching King Strephon. With corruption so far spread in Delkara, there was no guarantee they could safely reach King Strephon, even at Ithera. All it would take was one wrong soldier or lord between them and Strephon, and they would end up in the Unavowed's hands. Or it would be Manton betraying them to the rebels and using Rhonalyn to manipulate the balance of power in Delkara.

Gage shuddered. No matter which path he considered as an option, his soul despaired. Adequate forces were needed, but who should and could be the source of those forces? Rhonalyn believed uniting with King Strephon would provide them what was needed. But Gage doubted not only their ability to reach Delkara's king but also if King Strephon actually had the power to respond to what was taking place in his kingdom. What if too many of Strephon's lords had already turned against him? It could be that Strephon would actually need Rhonalyn's forces to tip the scale against the Unavowed and combat the undermining taking place among Delkara's lords and people.

On the other hand it could be Rhonalyn's determination to journey to Ithera was perhaps because Keric's princess needed Strephon's power. Rhonalyn was in line to rule Keric, but she did not yet sit on that throne. What if Rhonalyn and Strephon were both leaders in name only with not enough power between them to stop this? Gage's body quaked at the thought.

Every strand of support around him felt like it was snapping beneath him. In anger and fear, he turned his mind toward the one he had become accustomed to blaming in such moments. "God, why have You allowed all of this to happen?" Aisley's comment about people's wickedness leapt to mind, and he thought about Adam and Eve standing fearfully before God. They did not ask God why corruption and evil now existed. They knew why.

Haaken's comment back at Awnquera returned to Gage's mind: *"If God put an end to evil here and now like you want, not one of us would still be breathing."*

Gabe hiked after the others, his mind churning. God had helped Adam and Eve when what they deserved was to be destroyed. God had also instructed Noah to build an ark to allow people a chance to choose His rescue instead of staying in their evil and perishing in God's judgement against it. Gage swallowed and ducked a tree branch. He had blamed God for everything that he saw wrong with the world. And after Novia had drowned, he had demanded God give him an assurance of His care and protection before he would risk trusting Him again.

He had demanded that the God of the Universe answer him, and in God's silence he had felt betrayed and abandoned. But now he cringed at the reality. It had not been God who had abandoned him, but he who had walked away from God. Fear and self-protection had been his choice of companions, and in denying God's authority, he had attempted to take on keeping himself and others safe—a weighty burden that he had carried with determination and resentment. He had been as prideful as Adam and Eve, believing that he was better off ruling himself.

In his mind, he saw himself, like those in Noah's day, disregarding his Creator's authority and walking his own path far from the ark.

Words, that Prior Joseph had spoken to Manton during their first visit to Brunel's monastery, surfaced in Gage's mind: *"It is a spiritual war, not a physical battle. Every man, both common and noble alike, is a slave to darkness until he surrenders to God."*

Gage took a deep breath. He considered God, and this time what he encountered was not a distant God who refused to show up for him but a God who had always been there. The world's chaos surrounded him, and God's grace offered a different way. Haaken's written words rang through him: *"When the Creator's judgment comes upon all sin, what a fool I would be to not be standing within His grace."*

A tremor of fear traveled through Gage's body, knocking him off balance. He caught himself against a tree. For a moment, breathing hard, he watched the others continue on, while his mind raced.

Dishonorable or not to ask, shameful or not to need it, he didn't care anymore. He had to know. He stumbled back into motion and cried out in his mind. "God, there's no reason You should forgive me or help me. I've rejected You. I've hated You. I've walked my own paths and defied You. I've spoken against You and been Your enemy. I'm unworthy and sinful, a person who doesn't deserve to demand anything of You, least of all Your kindness. But please, tell me, God, is there any chance that, despite what I am, You might still help me? Will You let me enter your ark?"

"All are welcome here." Prior Joseph's words, spoken over Eliab, filled Gage's mind.

"God, is that true?" he asked. "Am I really welcome too? Do You truly care enough about me to rescue me?" He was so afraid of the answer that for a moment Gage wished he could take back the question.

"Seek, and you will find. Knock, and the door will be opened to you." The words entered his mind and were accompanied with such a resounding presence and powerful beckoning that Gage inhaled a sharp breath.

Despite God's clear affirming answer, something kept Gage in place, impeding him from being welcomed. His breathing quickened. "God, I don't understand. Help me! Why can't I receive Your rescue?"

One word settled over Gage's soul, and he saw what held him captive. He swallowed hard. "I understand. All are welcome, but it isn't enough for me to want to be rescued. I have to step through that open door. I have to enter the ark." He exhaled slowly.

He had to surrender.

He had to depart the path he was walking, relinquishing his control, and accept that God's way was the solution to setting all things right. In the battle to keep himself safe, he had to concede his own inability and accept his defeat. He had to hand himself over to the One who could kill both his body and his soul. He had to submit himself to God, Creator of the world and King of kings.

In a fight between trepidation and longing, Gage grappled with the two choices before him. Then, in what felt like reckless abandonment, he made his decision. "God, I need You, and I know You hold all authority and power and are worthy of it. You are my Creator and my God. I want You as my King, thus I surrender myself to You."

A bold, rich presence of strength and exaltation rushed through Gage, carrying such a resounding and undeniable feeling of favor toward him that Gage responded with jubilation. He had thought he would feel like a prisoner, spared from death but a captive. Instead it was as if chains he didn't even know he had been carrying were falling off him.

The coiled pressure in his chest and his fears and doubts that had felt so insurmountable just moments before were silenced by the conquering power of a vast presence of calm.

Gage blinked and breathed deeply. His whole body felt lighter, and his mind felt as if it were coming alive for the first time. He trekked along the trail, overflowing with an abundance of gratitude and a fear-filled awe. The God of the Universe—supreme in power, righteous in all conduct, and perfect in judgment—had set him free.

Gage's eyes burned. He was rescued, and he was safe. He walked forward freely in an audacious liberty. The acknowledgement of that felt almost insane to him since physically nothing had changed around him. He was still hiking the same trail with no knowledge of what the future held, but strangely, amazingly, he was no longer afraid of that future.

Gage tipped his face skyward, and with his senses vibrantly alive, he closed his eyes to absorb the sunlight flickering through the trees and the warmth of its beams.

When he opened his eyes, he noticed Rhonalyn in front of him wiping a hand at her face. Liquid beneath her fingers smeared a patch of dirt on her cheek. She was crying.

Compassion so strong it hurt rose within Gage, and for the first time he recognized just how callous he had been toward her.

42

Wick dropped into the grass to eat his portion of their midday meal. His legs shook, and his head ached. Figuring it was the aftereffects of the morning's chase, he chewed a mouthful of bread and glanced over at Lady Aisley. The girl was seated on a downed tree four strides from him. She raised a weary smile when Princess Rhonalyn joined her.

Prince Gage approached the two and held out a waterskin to Princess Rhonalyn. "I thought the two of you might be thirsty."

Looking taken aback, Princess Rhonalyn accepted it from him.

"I see you finished your cheese," Prince Gage added. "Would you like more?"

Wick sat forward. Had he missed something? Why was His Highness suddenly going out of his way for her?

Apparently, Princess Rhonalyn was also curious about Prince Gage's sudden transformation, for she turned to Lady Aisley and asked in the noblemen's tongue, "Why is he acting so strange?"

Lady Aisley shrugged.

Squinting at the girl, Princess Rhonalyn's voice became strident. "Tell me you did not say anything to his friend this morning about me ranting about him."

Lady Aisley shook her head. "Nay, I did not."

"Then why is he behaving this way?"

Lady Aisley looked ready to melt under Princess Rhonalyn's interrogation and blurted out, "Mayhap he hath decided he likes you!"

Wick choked on the bread in his mouth and pressed a fist to his lips to stop the coughing laugh that threatened to follow.

Prince Gage did not appear amused. Mortified was more like it.

Thankfully, Princess Rhonalyn was still turned toward Lady Aisley. "He is a peasant," she sounded offended and appalled, "and I am a princess. For him to even consider me in such a manner would be absolutely unacceptable, and he would be a complete fool to act on it."

Wick watched a flush rise up Prince Gage's neck and his ears turn red. "Should I take it you don't want more cheese," he said in the commoners' tongue.

As if just remembering he was still standing there, Princess Rhonalyn looked up at him. Pink spread into her cheeks too, though her voice remained strident. "No. I don't."

"Fine. You could've just said so." Spinning around, His Highness stocked off toward his horse.

Lady Aisley shrank beside Princess Rhonalyn. "Verily, you did not have to be rude to him," she murmured in the noblemen's tongue.

Princess Rhonalyn turned on her. "Excuse me?"

The girl cringed further and shook her head. "Nothing."

"If you have something to say, Lady Aisley, say it!"

In sympathy, Wick flinched with the girl. He wanted to intervene on poor Lady Aisley's behalf, but he reminded himself he couldn't unless he wanted to explain more than just how he and Gabe had met.

"It…it is simply that I do not want him to be right about you."

Chagrined, Wick drew in a breath. She was talking about him. He drove his gaze into the ground.

The pitch of Princess Rhonalyn's voice heightened. "Him! Him who? And what exactly did he say about me that you do not wish to be true?"

The pressure in Wick's head increased, making his eyes throb and his ears buzz.

"He said that…that in a leader, kindness and compassion are as important as being bold and fierce."

"Did he indeed? And who is this person who thinks he knows what a leader ought to be, hmm?"

Wick braced himself.

Lady Aisley shook her head. "No one of consequence."

Feeling insulted but grateful she hadn't given him up, Wick breathed a little easier.

Princess Rhonalyn eyed the girl. "Really? Then how do you know him?"

Amazingly, Lady Aisley did not even glance his way. "He is a friend. That is all."

Wick blinked, flattered by her label since earlier she had indicated he'd have been considered unqualified to hold such a title.

Princess Rhonalyn huffed. "An ill-begotten one, no doubt." She stirred angrily and added with growing vehemence. "And how dare the two of you discuss me, as if—"

"Hey, would you stop speaking in the noblemen's tongue and keep your voice down?" Manton glanced off into the trees, then back at Princess Rhonalyn. "We're not far from a small manor, it isn't wise to be careless."

Her Royal Highness leveled a glare at him and answered in the commoner's tongue, "If we're that close, perhaps you shouldn't have chosen this s—" She paused as if realizing something. Her gaze flicked to Lady Aisley, and a tinge of pink rose again in her cheeks. She huffed and finished in a less harsh tone. "Well, it doesn't matter now anyway."

Looking befuddled but satisfied, Manton went back to eating.

Rising, Wick strode on slightly unsteady legs past the two girls to join Prince Gage by the horses. He paused at His Highness's elbow and said, "Not to sound like her, but you are acting a bit strange. Is everything alright?"

Prince Gage scoffed. "Politely offering her something to eat and drink is me acting strange?" He met Wick's gaze with a frown and questioned in a remorseful tone, "Have I really been so terrible toward her?"

Wincing, Wick sought a diplomatic answer.

At his hesitation, Prince Gage sighed. "Never mind. I've got my answer."

"Now, hold on, you've not been that bad," Wick countered.

Prince Gage groaned and scrubbed his hands down his face. "Perhaps not, but clearly I've failed in what I should've been and what I want to be. With God's help, I want to change that. I want to be different. I want to do better."

Wick blinked, taken aback by His Highness's confession and his remorse but even more so by his comment about seeking God's help. The last time he had heard Prince Gage speak of God, His Highness's opinions and attitude had leaned far more toward the resentful than the deferential. Curious and grateful, Wick wished he could inquire into what had changed and why, but it was not his place. Feeling an awkwardness abruptly drift into the silence between them, Wick shuffled his feet and, ignoring his headache, teased. "So, you and Princess Rhonalyn, hmm?"

"Oh, don't you start too." Suppressed amusement and a tinge of annoyance filled Prince Gage's face as he shook his head. His eyes flashed, and red spread to his ears. "I wouldn't be interested in her if she were the last woman alive."

Wick chuckled at His Highness's response, then turned serious. "Little does she know, though, that rightfully you could be."

Prince Gage gave him an appreciative nod. Then his lips twisted. "So could you."

Wick opened his mouth, then closed it. He had never even considered the possibility of marrying royalty. Edelmar had no princesses, Delkara's one princess was already married, and he never thought he'd spend time with anyone from Keric, let alone the kingdom's princess.

Prince Gage laughed and leaned closer. "And I do believe she likes you far better than she likes me."

Wick scoffed. "Only because I cater to her and don't dare ask her directly to do anything since that"—he tipped his head—"is the result."

Prince Gage's eyebrows rose. "So you say."

Wick felt heat rise up his own neck. "That is *not* what's happening here," he hissed. "I swear."

"I know." His Highness laughed. "But now we're even."

Smirking, Wick nodded. "Yes, I believe we are."

43

RHONALYN FOUND HERSELF clenching her fingers as she walked. Aisley's words had continued to roll around her mind long after they had resumed their journey, and Rhonalyn questioned herself because of them. Was she truly unkind?

She knew she could be formidable and sharp at times to those around her, but wasn't that to be expected? She was the future ruler of Keric, being commanding was necessary. She could not let people walk all over her or second-guess her. She had to speak with authority, or no one would show her deference.

Her thoughts churned through memories as she angled around a tree and leaned backward to balance herself as she followed Manton and his mule downhill. Her mother had always been gracious, kind, and compassionate. But what good had that done her? A few people who actually knew her mother had seen those qualities and appreciated them. But because of her quiet, peaceful nature, her mother's ideas to improve her people's way of life were always ignored.

Never bold or fierce enough to require that her husband heed her, her mother had always awaited someone else to be the force behind her. Therefore, so much of what Keric's former queen had to offer never transitioned from thought to reality. Few people other than Rhonalyn herself had seen her mother for who she could have been and truly was—a brilliant, caring woman who would have improved the lives of her people. Her mother's voice, her thoughts, and her ideas had been too hushed, too passive to be heard.

Watching her mother be ignored over and over, Rhonalyn had promised herself that that would never happen to her. To honor the diminutive flames of passion her mother had carried, she had determined to do everything in her power to burn bold enough to be seen, acknowledged, and heeded, so that her goals would be accomplished.

And unlike her mother, she had blazed brightly, wielding her power without apology. Now, though, doubts she had never experienced before crept through her. Had she sought so fiercely to be different from her mother, that she was no longer like her at all?

Uncertainty spiraled through her. She had wanted to be a version of her mother who actually succeeded, but was being like her mother even possible any more?

She considered Gabe's comments at the beach about her actions and attitude toward Lady Aisley. She evaluated as well her interactions with Gabe, Wick, and Manton and felt shame trickle through her.

She debated between accepting the uncomfortable conclusion she had just reached or shoving it away for now. After all, she was not yet queen, and the journey and goals ahead would require of her not kindness but resolve. She would worry about whether or not she was kind once her men were found safe.

Behind her, someone burst into a fit of coughing. She glanced over her shoulder. A few strides above her, Wick caught himself against one of the sharply angled trees and leaned over, coughing hard.

Frowning over his struggle to catch his breath and hoping he would not slow them down, Rhonalyn flicked her gaze back around to Manton's mule and wound after the animal through the trees. At each step she planted her heels and leaned carefully backward to keep herself from launching headfirst down the increasingly steep slope.

Midway down a particularly sharp part of the incline with fewer trees, more coughing burst from Wick. His hacking above her was followed by a startled exclamation and a swooshing sound. Before Rhonalyn could turn to investigate, something slammed into the back of her legs, knocking her over. With a cry, she toppled onto Wick.

His moving body carried them both downhill in a rush of dirt and debris. They swept past Manton's mule, then Manton, and were headed toward tree trunks. Rhonalyn closed her eyes. Wick's arm wrapped around her, and a moment later, they both jerked to an stop.

Rhonalyn cautiously opened her eyes. They had halted three strides from the tree trunks below them. Feeling the pressure of Wick's arm keeping her from sliding further, she looked up. He was gripping a small tree above them, holding them in place on the hill.

"Are you alright?" he asked, his voice quivering. He loosened his grasp on her but did not let go entirely.

Twisting around, Rhonalyn dug her hands into the hill to keep herself in place and forcefully disentangled herself from him. "I'm fine," she snapped angrily.

Wick used the small tree to draw himself into a sitting position. "A thousand apologies. If I'd known I'd lose my footing I'd have made sure I wasn't above you."

"Well perhaps you should have thought to take such a precaution regardless." She glared at him.

He tried to say something, but his teeth chattered while sweat trailed down his face.

Realizing there was something far more wrong with him than just a cough, Rhonalyn worked her way sideways before shoving herself back upright.

Manton descended to her. "Are you both alright?"

A rush of dirt accompanied Gabe also joining them. "What happened?"

Rhonalyn jutted her chin at Wick, who had yet to gain his feet. "Wick is unwell."

"I'll be fine. I just l-l-l-lost—"

"You're definitely not fine," Gabe said. "You're trembling from head to toe!" Stepping forward, Gabriel grasped Wick's arm and wrapped it over his shoulder. "Come on, up you come. It's no wonder you fell."

"No, you d-d-d-don't have to help. I c-c-can manage on m—"

"Stop. You once did similar for me. Let me return the favor." Gabe's tone did not allow for a refusal.

"But the h-h-horses," Wick said. "Who will bring th-th-th-them?"

Rhonalyn peered back up the hill to find Aisley descending toward them.

"I've got Clover," the girl called out. "And Athalos is coming on his own."

"Thank you." Gabriel adjusted Wick's weight beside him and commented with a smirk. "It would seem she's named your horse."

"So it would." Wick smiled, then burst into another fit of coughing.

Stepping farther away from the pair, Rhonalyn ground her teeth. Whatever was wrong with Wick was definitely going to slow them down.

44

THE FOLLOWING DAY, Gage watched Sir Wick with concern. Despite their night's rest in a shepherd's hut, the knight's condition had not improved. In fact, Sir Wick's cough was worse, and though he claimed he could walk, he wouldn't have made it far. Even riding Clover and wearing a cloak, his body convulsed with shivers. To make matters worse, halfway through the night Aisley had begun coughing as well and now rode Nigel because she too struggled to keep up and spoke of a headache.

The day before, after coming upon a newly cut road that ran southwest to northeast, they traveled southwest for a short time then turned north on a shepherd's path where goats and sheep had cleared a trail wide enough to allow for riding. That path eventually blended into a manor trail. They had circumvented the small village that morning, stopped for a midday meal once they were a good ways beyond it, and were now on a rutted road again, cutting northwest across Delkara.

No one spoke much. Sir Wick and Aisley both coughed on and off, shivering or sweating in turn, but it was when Aisley leaned to the side and threw up that Gage started to worry that whatever illness the two of them had might not be something they would simply weather through.

Tossing the lead line over Athalos's neck and leaving the horse to keep its own pace at the back of the group, he quickened his stride to catch up with Manton. "How much farther to Koth?"

"I'm not actually sure," Manton's tone lacked it's normal

confidence as he added, "because I'm not certain where we are."

"You what?" Gage thought for a moment that perhaps Manton was lying, but since Manton's lies were usually bolder than his truth, he concluded that was unlikely. "I thought you knew this path."

"I've only taken the trail over the hills," Manton explained, keeping his voice low. "I've never come this way going to Koth before. When I took the trail I was headed to Lapidus. I thought if we stayed on trails between villages and went in the general direction of Koth, we'd come upon the road leading to Koth."

Gage glanced along the road they were on. "This isn't that road?"

"If my memory serves me right, I don't think so. It's not wide enough or heavily enough used. And with how far we've traveled down it, we should have already reached Koth."

Frustration spread through Gage. He glanced back at Aisley and Sir Wick, who both looked miserably exhausted. He glared at Manton. "So, you're saying you have no idea where we are or where we're headed?"

"We're on a road." Manton gestured forward. "Sooner or later we'll either end up somewhere or cross paths with someone who can tell us where they came from and where they're going. Then I'll know where we are."

"Great," Gage muttered. "Let's just hope it isn't dark by then and that those we cross paths with aren't soldiers."

The sun was nearly down when the road led them into a village. Upon asking a local peasant, they learned they had come upon Verfeld Manor, located north and quite a ways west of Koth.

Somehow they had passed by Koth. That meant they were nearer Ithera, but it also meant they had no place to stay since the village of Verfeld was not on a trade route and had no inn.

The five of them tarried in the evening's shadows beside the village's well, quenching their thirst and refilling their waterskins while trying to decide what to do. The village was active but not overly busy and those who came and went greeted each other by name. Their small group was noted as strangers and for the most part acknowledged with kind regard.

"And where do you propose we take shelter?" Rhonalyn asked, her tone implying that Manton had better come up with a solution that didn't involve them sleeping outdoors again.

"I'll ask around and see what I can find," Manton said. "Perhaps for the price of an inn someone will be willing to host us for the night."

"Check about a healer as well. Gabe mentioned that a village like this should have one," Rhonalyn said with more than a little annoyance in her voice.

Weary and anxious about the coming night, Gage was thankful when Manton returned in short order and announced, "I've found us a place to stay and food, for a good price. Come." Manton led them west through the village, up a side lane to the south, and past several houses and curious villagers. He stopped in front of a mudded and thatched home, tucked against a hillside. Its left side guarded a fenced croft full to bursting with a vegetable garden, and its right side sat against a low barn outside of which roamed four clucking chickens.

A middle-aged woman emerged from the home's door, wiping her hands on her apron and then adjusting the cloth that was wrapped over her light-brown hair. Spotting them, her face lit up with a smile. "Ah, come, come. Look at you all. What a day you've no doubt had. Meant for Koth but landed here in our village instead." She waved them forward. "I have food cooked and more on the fire."

Gage wanted so badly to troop inside and eat without saying a word, but he doubted Manton had mentioned to her that they had sick companions. Aisley just then burst into a fit of coughing, announcing the fact. Gage nodded to their potential hostess. "We're grateful for your hospitality." He gestured to Sir Wick and Aisley. "But two of our number are unwell. Are you sure you wish us to enter your home, or would you prefer we settled in your barn?"

Rhonalyn sent him a glare.

Ignoring her, Gage awaited their hostess's response.

The woman tisked and shook her head. "What, and make those who are unwell settle with the animals? Nonsense. You will all come inside. My husband will be along shortly. For now you can tie your animals in the barn. After you've eaten, they can be taken to the common pasture to graze."

Once they had taken care of the animals, they all trooped inside. The scent of vegetables and meat drifted though the air as they made their way past the woman's fire and settled closely on worn wooden benches around her table. Within reach of where Gage sat, baskets of spun linen surrounded a floor-to-ceiling loom strung with cream threads being woven into a complex pattern.

Rattling through jars and dinging her wooden spoon on the edge of a pot hanging on a hook over her fire, the woman bustled around, gathering this and that from a nearby shelf and adding them to what she was cooking.

Gage shifted on the bench and glanced at Sir Wick and Aisley. Her face pale, Aisley blinked wearily and leaned against Sir Wick, who sat with his head propped in one hand and his side braced against the table's edge.

Their hostess a moment later placed full cups in front of each of them. Then she set upon the table a loaf of bread, a round of cheese, and a roast bird. She drew her pot from the fire. It held vegetables that had been spiced and stewed in a broth. Gage's mouth watered as the heavenly smell became even stronger, and his stomach rumbled.

"Eat," their hostess instructed. "I'll join you when my Lanswith arrives."

While Wick barely ate and Aisley only nibbled on some bread, the rest of them consumed the food eagerly. They were more than halfway through the meal when a man's voice called out from the door. "Mags of the Rags, I'm back from the day's hunt." The woman's husband propped a longbow and quiver of arrows against the wall and, turning around, stopped short.

The woman chuckled from where she stood by the fire. "Yes, I can see that."

The man's gaze swept from them to his wife. "We've got company!"

"That we do, husband."

Lanswith's brow furrowed and his voice took on consternation. "Did I forget you mentioning that we'd have guests tonight?"

Mags laughed. "No, they're unexpected visitors."

"Oh, thank goodness. Here I thought I'd forgotten something important." With a sigh, Lanswith tugged his hat off and sent it sailing toward his wife.

She snatched it out of midair and placed it on a hook near the fire. The action appeared so effortless on her part that it was clear it had been performed countless times before. "These travelers," she explained, "were headed for Koth, but ended up here in Verfeld. Fredric sent them our way, knowing we'd have space for them."

"Koth you say." Lanswith nodded to them. "Well, I dare say you did much better ending up here. A quiet village, good company, and excellent food." He settled at the head of the table and snagged his wife's hand as she sat down next to him. He pressed her fingers to his lips. "My love, thank you. Looks like a grand ol' feast."

Mags blushed and swatted at him. "Oh, don't be silly."

"Never. Now, introduce me, my dear, to those we've the privilege of hosting."

"I'd tell you their names, Lan, if I knew them," she said, "but we've not yet been properly introduced. They looked so weary and faint with hunger, I thought it better to feed them before peppering them with questions."

Lanswith laughed and said to them, "That's how we do it around here, you know. Feed you first, then season you with questions and conversation."

Gage smiled. He couldn't help but like the couple. Their mannerisms were so genuine and their kindness so congenial that he felt immediately at ease with them. "You can call me Gabe." He pointed around the table. "Her Rose and Amy. Then there is Wick and Manton."

Sir Wick nodded and then mumbled an apology and slumped over to lay his head on his arms. Aisley resettled against Wick's back, her eyes drifting closed.

Cringing, Gage pulled the couple's attention back to him. "We're very grateful for your hospitality. Our road has been long, and we are all pleased to make your acquaintance."

"Well, I'm Lanswith or Lan, and of course, you've met my Mags. Maggie is her given name, but Mags the Weaver, she's called round these parts so as not to be confused with Maggie, the plowman's wife. I've lived my whole life in this village, and Mags has been here more than half of hers. We've four children." Lanswith's interlaced his fingers with his wife's, and they exchanged a look of shared happiness and mutual sadness. "Our eldest is married to a local girl an' lives just down the lane with two children and a third on the way. Our two middle children are both at rest in the cemetery at the village church. And our youngest," Lan said with pride in his voice, "she's workin' at the manor house as a maidservant to our lady."

"And you're a huntsman for your lord?" Manton asked with the hint of an edge in his voice.

"I am that," Lanswith said. "Hunted for and with my lord for over twenty years now. His generosity toward his tenants is how you're eating meat tonight." Lanswith glanced around the table. "And you all, where do you call home?"

An awkward silence followed his question. It was a simple enough inquiry, but Gage knew the answers could easily lead to connections potentially dangerous for them all.

Manton spoke, as usual quicker than the rest of them to craft a lie. "We're not any of us from the same city. Rather, through travel and troubled times we've fallen in with one another."

Gage blinked. Not a lie. He relaxed, grateful that for once he could own what Manton said without having it twist in his stomach.

Lanswith nodded. "Here you'll find less trouble than many places. In these parts most people look out for each other, and our lord is a good man. Strict and not to be defied, but if you mind the law and keep the peace, he'll not trouble you or treat you wrong. To be sure, it's not been easy with taxes so high and people starting to feel desperate, but he's done what he can to make sure none go hungry, and everyone's looked after."

"High praise," Manton said.

Mags gaze and tone filled with sympathy. "I take it where you've come from, you've not experienced the same from your lord?"

"No." The hard pain in Manton's answer caused Gage to pause. Out of anyone there, he knew the most about Manton, but at that moment he was reminded how little he actually knew about Manton. Why had Manton actually joined the commoners' rebellion?

"I'm sorry," Mags said. "That's not as it should be." Her simple words carried compassion and understanding, and Manton nodded with a look of appreciation.

Rhonalyn leaned forward, joining the conversation. "You're right, of course, Maggie. And perhaps someday soon things will change for the better across Delkara. But until then, we must all continue on our paths. For us to continue on, we require a healer to help our companions. Do either of you know of one hereabouts?"

"A healer?" Lanswith cleared his throat. "Well now, that depends on who you ask. Used to be when anyone here had an ailment they went to the butcher's wife, Barta. She was a right good healer years ago, but in the last bit now she's been lucky to remember her own name, let alone what herbs do what. So, folks stopped going to her. Many go to Koth when they've got ailments and sickness. But there's another individual closer to here that a few folks go to when they're in need of such help. But she's—"

Mags paused her husband with a hand on his arm, then added. "It's said she's of superior skill and that her herbs and poultices are some of the best people've ever encountered."

Lanswith grunted. "Aye, some say she's blessed by the saints with skills from heaven, a voice like an angel, and beauty to match. But others who've gone to her claim she's a witch whose airy voice creaks like the trees in the wind. They say she dabbles in the dark arts for her poultices and is as ugly as a hag. They warn others not to seek her out unless they're willing to accept the consequences of dealing with the likes of her."

Gage saw Rhonalyn shudder and couldn't deny that he too felt concerned. At the same time the couple's contradictory descriptions struck him as odd, and he noted that even now Mags shook her head at her husband's words. Gage questioned, "Have either of you two ever had dealings with this individual?"

Lanswith shook his head. "Never had a reason to."

Gage looked at Mags, who remained conspicuously silent. "And you?"

She met his gaze, her eyes evaluating him. "I have."

"And who do you think she is? A healer? Or a witch?"

"This I'll tell you," Mags answered. "Your friends could not ask for anyone better skilled. As for who and what she is, if you seek her out, you must determine that for yourselves."

"Where can we find her?"

Mags pointed over her shoulder. "Past us here, go through the trees, across the village fields, and climb the hill to the north. When you get to the top, look west and search for a tall pine with a dead top. Head through the woods toward it. If you keep true to that course, you'll come across a batch of pines. In their center hangs a lantern. If the lantern is lit, look for a second one. When you reach the second, follow it to a third and so on. If lit, the lanterns will lead you to her. But if the first lantern in the pines isn't lit, turn back and seek help elsewhere."

"Why? What happens if someone follows the unlit lanterns?" Rhonalyn asked.

Lanswith leaned forward, lowering his voice. "If you do and you come upon her, she'll curse you instead of help you."

Mags rolled her eyes at her husband. "Don't go starting more lies. You won't find her, is what'll happen. The lantern tells you if she's there. It's often lit, but sometimes it remains unlit for days. Now, you could go tonight, but it's already late. I suggest you go in the morning once you've rested and can afford a return trip if the lantern's not lit."

45

The next morning, Rhonalyn shivered as they wove into the shadows of the patch of pines. The prickly green branches stretched out above their heads and grew thick and interwoven, creating a canopy that blocked the little sunlight the morning's gray clouds let through. Pine needles coated the ground around them, stifling the growth of other plants, muffling sounds, and crunching like eggshells beneath boots and hooves alike.

Rhonalyn rubbed at her arms and glanced about in frustration. She could already feel precious time slipping away. "Of course the person we need has to live way out here in a creepy forest," she muttered.

She had so hoped they would wake to find Aisley and Wick better and could nix seeking out the healer or witch or whatever she was and press on to Ithera. As it was, Gabe led the way bringing along the mount on which Wick and Aisley were barely managing to stay astride. Wick's body wavered with each step, and his eyes were glazed with fever. In front of him, Aisley, in between coughing, nodded off against his chest, beads of sweat upon her pale brow.

Rhonalyn heaved a breath. From her perspective, it was possible the two of them needed intervention beyond medicine. And considering what had been said about the person they sought, it may either be they were headed for a person who could help or someone who might contribute to the problem. But they'd come too far and needed help too badly to turn back now.

"I see the lit lantern." The relief that filled Gabe's voice held a tinge of uncertainty to it, as if he too questioned their current path. "Does anyone see the second lantern?" he asked.

They approached where the first lantern hung, and Rhonalyn peered through the trees around them.

"There." Manton pointed to another flame in the distance, flickering amid the forest's shadows.

♾

Upon reaching the fifth lit lantern in the trail, Gage was beginning to wonder how many more there would be. At the sixth, he lifted his gaze to search for the next and saw a worn path ahead. He followed it with his eyes, and there in the depth of the forest was an opening to a well-disguised shelter tucked amid two huge trees and a mound of rocks.

Twigs stuck out from under a lumpy roof of moss and grass that made the structure almost indistinguishable from the forest around it. Had it not been for the worn ground and the opening of its low doorway, he may have passed by the mound completely. They'd come to the right spot, but he hesitated to enter.

"Well," Rhonalyn said, "are we going to just stare at it? Or is someone going inside?"

One of them had to investigate, and Manton made no move to do so. Gage took a breath. "Right." He handed Clover's lead to Rhonalyn, glanced at Sir Wick and Aisley, and headed for the shelter's entrance.

Ducking low, he stepped inside. The ground past the doorway dropped away in four earthen steps that led to a smooth-packed floor. The scent of dirt and moss filled Gage's nose. He angled around a low branch in the ceiling and stepped between a set of huge rocks bulging from either side of the entrance tunnel that curved along a wall of boulders amid the structure's center.

He came around the boulders to find himself in an enclosed space, roughly five paces across and eight paces long and partially lit by natural light. The light came from two trapdoor-like sections of the ceiling that were propped open. Opposite the boulders he had passed on his way in, a section of the shelter's far wall was constructed of shadowy, uneven, and mismatched smaller rocks. Between the rocks were dark hollows holding ceramic jars, dried plants, and who knew what else.

The two other sides of the structure were half dug from the dirt and then finished at the top with sticks lashed and woven around tree trunks and then mudded to form a solid barrier. On the ground in the corner to his right was a heap of reeds with a pile of neatly folded wool blankets atop it. Nearby, a lit lantern hung on a support post, two paces beyond which was a fireplace tucked into a recess in the shelter's side. Left of the fireplace, close by a large flat stone situated at the base of the rocky wall, was a bucket full of liquid, and from a protruding rock above it hung a basket holding rolled strips of cloth. Gage wasn't sure what he'd expected to find when he entered the shelter, but the vacant, neatly kept space wasn't it.

"Is anyone here?" he called out. The lanterns had been lit, so where was she?

A scuffing sound came from the end of the rocky portion of wall, and out of the wall's shadows a person emerged, making Gage realize there had to be more space amid or behind the rocks on that side of the shelter than he would have assumed. The figure before him was shorter than him and definitely female, but her features were impossible to determine, for she was shrouded in a dark garb, like a nun's habit.

Instead of a wimple, though, she wore a dark hood. Within it, a wrap covered not only her neck and face but also her hair and forehead, leaving only slits for her eyes. Even her hands were tucked within her dark sleeves, and with the dim light, all he could truly see of her was the glint of her eyes. When she spoke, her voice sounded exactly as Lanswith had described it, like the creaking of trees in the wind. "What has brought you here to me?"

"We have two sick companions who need help. They are both coughing, feverish, and fatigued." Gabe tried to make his voice sound more confident than he felt. "We were told you could help them."

"If you desire my help, you must bring them here."

Her creaky voice made Gage's skin crawl. He gestured over his shoulder. "They're just outside."

"Then bring them within." She moved toward her lantern and, opening it, used a small twig to transfer some of its flame to wood already stacked in the fireplace. It crackled to life, and the glow of firelight filled the space. She turned toward the heap of reeds, then paused and eyed him. With one of the raised portions of roof nearby, Gage could just make out her chestnut-colored eyes taking him in. She squinted. "Why do you remain?" Her tone sounded suspicious and angry. "If your companions are truly ill, you shouldn't leave them waiting."

Blinking, Gage opened his mouth, then closed it. He had no desire to explain his hesitation, and could think of no other response to give her. Turning on his heel, he headed outside, hoping they hadn't made a mistake coming here.

It took a lot of effort and a fair bit of maneuvering, but he managed to return supporting Sir Wick beside him. While he was gone, the woman had spread the reeds into two spots on the floor with a space to move between them and had covered each with a blanket. Gage eased Sir Wick's clammy arm off his shoulder and lowered him onto the closest makeshift bed.

Manton entered behind him carrying Aisley, followed by Rhonalyn. Manton laid the girl on the second blanket, then said something about not taking up space and retreated outside.

Unwilling to leave, Gage placed himself against a wall out of the way and stayed to watch and intervene if need be.

Aisley stirred and looked around. "Where are we?" she murmured.

"It's alright." Rhonalyn knelt beside the girl. Her gaze shifted toward the approaching dark-garbed figure. "We've brought you to a healer." There was a note of hesitancy in her voice.

Thankfully, the woman did not seem to take offense, but crouched next to Aisley. She laid the back of her fingers against Aisley's forehead. Then she moved her hand to the girl's cheek. Aisley twisted sideways and burst into a fit of coughing.

When Aisley stopped coughing, the woman turned and evaluated Sir Wick. The knight shuddered at her touch, and his eyes flickered open. "Please help Aisley first." Air caught in his words, and he too began to cough. Once his body ceased contorting with each hacking breath, he groaned and pressed a hand to his side.

The healer pointed over her shoulder, her voice creaking. "Fetch that lantern."

Knowing Rhonalyn wouldn't respond, Gage retrieved the lantern and held it out to the healer.

"Hold it here." She directed him to suspend it over where Sir Wick lay. Gage complied and watched her hands—clean, with unwrinkled skin and neatly kept fingernails— pry Sir Wick's broad hand away from his side. There beneath was a hole in the knight's tunic, surrounded by a dark stain.

Gage leaned forward, concern racing through him. "What is that?"

The healer ignored him as she undid Sir Wick's belt and drew up his tunic. When she uncovered the skin beneath the stain, Gage flinched at the sight. A circle of fierce red surrounded a narrow wound that was ringed with purple and weeping pus.

The healer placed her fingers at the upper, outer edge of the reddened skin and pressed. Then she moved her fingers closer, working her way toward the wound. A finger's-width from the injury, the pressure she applied made Sir Wick moan and stir. She adjusted her hand to an equal distance on the lower side of the wound and pressed there. The knight cried out and drew up his hand in an effort to push her away.

Gage curled his toes, remembering all too clearly the pain he'd experienced while half-conscious and being treated by the monks of Saint Jerome's Abbey. His stomach twisted. He understood better now the hands that had held him down and commanded him to lie still.

The healer rose and glanced briefly at Rhonalyn but then directed her words at Gage in her horrible voice. "The girl I can help. She isn't in danger. Him, I'll do what I can, but his wound is concerning."

Gage nodded stiffly, telling himself Sir Wick would be fine. But the reassurance found no place to reside in the hollowness that her words created inside him. He needed to breathe, but all he could see were the commoners killed in the meadow, the bodies he'd crawled through after the rebel ambush on the Unavowed, Bardon struck by the arrow from the Blue Crow's archer, Allard falling off his horse, and Novia's limp body. His lungs burned. Death swirled around him in a growing darkness, taunting him and suffocating him with its power to take away those he cared about.

Like a landslide, all the grief and fear he had known previously swept through him, and he wavered on his feet. He knew there was solid, safe ground somewhere, if only he could remember how to reach it, but everything around him was moving. All the debris from his past was taking him with it.

On his arm five sharp points of pain pierced through to his senses and snapped his awareness to where he stood on solid ground in the shelter.

The healer was standing in front of him, her brown eyes locked with his. Gage broke his gaze from her intense stare and looked down to where her fingernails were dug into his arm just above his vambrace. He jerked away from her and gasped. "What are you doing?"

She shook her hooded head at him and turned away. Walking to the fire, she pulled a ceramic pot out from between two rocks, dipped it into her bucket, and then placed it into the fire, which sizzled upon contact with the wet pot. Next, she began gathering dried plants from this and that crevice in the rock wall.

Shuddering, Gage rubbed his right hand over the fingernail marks she had left in his arm and glared at her back as she worked. His insides swirled in anger at her violation of his space, but he also felt relieved that her actions had anchored him once again.

The healer crumbled pieces of two plants into a mug. The rest of the plants she'd collected she set on the large flat rock alongside a bowl she seemed to make appear out of nowhere. She mixed into it ingredients from two small jars stored in the rocks. Once she'd finished, she drew a knife from between two other rocks and began cutting or crushing the plants, which she added to the bowl. A moment later she hooked the pot out of the fire and poured a small portion of its contents into her bowl. Then she dumped the herbs she'd gathered in the mug into the pot and set it aside.

Amid the aromas suddenly coming from her combined tasks, Gage was sure he could smell the cloying scent of licorice root, then his nose tickled with the strong, bitter smell of what he thought might be feverfew. Since his knowledge of the medicinal properties of the plants was mostly limited to what he'd learned while weeding Brother Sholan's herb garden, he shifted uneasily, hoping the healer knew what she was doing.

A while later, she strained into the mug what she had brewed in the ceramic pot and handed it to Rhonalyn. She instructed in her creaky voice, "Have her sip this slowly till it's gone."

To Gage's surprise, Rhonalyn set herself to the task without complaint or reluctance and soon had Aisley sipping the mug's contents. Meanwhile, the healer filled a second mug from the pot and approached Sir Wick.

She crouching beside him. "Wake and drink. What I have will help your body fight what is ailing you."

Wick remained still, though his chest rose and fell in ragged breaths.

Setting aside the lantern, Gage knelt and jostled the knight's shoulder. "Wick. She says you need to drink."

The knight's eyes fluttered open. "Please, just let me rest. I just want to rest."

"Drink first," the healer commanded in her horrible creak, "then you will be able to rest well."

The knight's eyes drifted back closed.

"Wick!" Gage shook the knight hard, fear coursing through him at Sir Wick' clammy skin and fatigue. At this point, regardless of whether he trusted the healer or not, Sir Wick needed help, and she was all they had. "Wick, you must stay awake long enough to drink. Wick! Do you hear me?"

The knight's eyes popped open, and he stirred, trying to shove himself up on an elbow. "Yes. I'll drink."

Catching hold of his shoulder, Gage supported Sir Wick's weight, so the knight could drink from the mug. A grimace in response to the contents, followed by a bout of coughing, then actual drinking eventually resulted in Sir Wick managing to empty the mug.

Gage was about to lower the knight back down when the healer instructed. "Wait, keep him there." She swapped the mug for her bowl and several rolls of cloth. Unrolling one strip of cloth, she worked it under Wick's back. "There. Now let him down."

Gage did so, then watched as the healer used the other cloth she held to soak up the contents of her bowl. Drawing up Sir Wick's tunic, she pressed the poultice-soaked cloth against the knight's wound.

A wince wrinkled Sir Wick's face, then disappeared. Using a third cloth and tying it to that which she'd already wrapped under him, the healer secured the poultice in place. She rose then and returned to her fire.

Rising to his feet, Gage glanced at Rhonalyn and Aisley. The young girl already seemed to be resting more peacefully than she had the last two nights. He sighed and scrubbed a hand down his face.

"If you've not got food for yourselves," the healer said, "you should go now to the village and get some. These two are likely to sleep on and off for a day or more."

"A day or more?" Rhonalyn sounded dismayed.

The creak in the healer's voice intensified. "Healing takes time."

Rhonalyn rose and headed straight toward Gage. Not sure why she was coming to him, he cringed.

"We can't wait that long," she whispered, standing within a hand's length of him.

He understood her angst, but he didn't know what she wanted him to do about it. "They can't travel like this," he said, "and we're not leaving them behind. We have no better option than to stay and pray they recover quickly."

She huffed and spoke angrily. "I warned him not to make light of that superstition. He should have listened."

Gage stiffened. "You think this is because of the baby from the refuse pile?" At the edge of his vision, he saw the healer go still. He cringed. She had to be listening. He just hoped she didn't share Rhonalyn's concerns.

"I think it would explain this," Rhonalyn said. "And shouldn't it be considered when it comes to treatments?"

"Eliab didn't cause this," he replied. "Besides, if touching that baby was to blame for them being ill, I'd be sick too. I held him just as much as either of those two did."

Rhonalyn paused and frowned, considering his words. "That's true. It should be all three of you." She inhaled a breath. "So, maybe he's not to blame, but regardless of why…" Her voice wavered with restrained emotions that bordered on tears. "There isn't time for this. Nolan and the others—" She shook her head. "They need me to get where we're headed."

"I understand that." Gage felt her predicament of being responsible for multiple lives more keenly than she could possibly know, but her getting where she was going was not the only priority to be considered. "I know you want to be doing something to help them, but also realize that you not getting there, may actually keep Nolan and the others in better stead." He intended the comment as reassurance, but the moment he said the words, the full truth they carried registered in his mind. Her men *were* more likely to be kept alive if the Unavowed thought them still useful to lure her to them. The moment the Unavowed realized she had eluded their traps and reached King Strephon, her men's presence would change from valuable bait to condemning evidence. Evidence the Unavowed would no doubt seek to rid themselves of as quickly as possible.

Rhonalyn stared at him, her expression aghast. She too had clearly followed his words to their conclusion. She shook her head, her voice fracturing. "I can't believe that. I won't believe it."

Gage reach out. "I didn't mean—"

"Don't say it!"

"I was just going to—"

"Just stop! I don't want to hear it." She turned and fled from the shelter.

Gage groaned. He had said the worst possible thing he could have said. Her men were being held as prisoners, and he'd basically just told her "better that than dead." He was surprised she hadn't hit him or burst into tears. Weapons and combat he knew how to deal with, but he had never been good at talking to people. He glanced at Sir Wick, who always knew what to say, and noted that the healer was still frozen in place.

She instantly stirred back into motion, refilling her pot with water and gathering herbs. Watching her, Gage had the distinct impression she was avoiding his gaze. He couldn't blame her, but her presence and listening ear put him on edge. It was too easy to treat her like she wasn't there, and he had a feeling that was exactly how she wanted it.

<h1 style="text-align:center">46</h1>

THE UNEASE THAT Gage felt toward the healer grew over the next hour. It wasn't anything specific about her that unsettled him but rather the secrecy with which she chose to surround herself.

While Rhonalyn remained absent, he had tried asking the healer questions. Was she from the village? How long had she been a healer? Who had trained her? Each time she acted as if she hadn't heard him, but he knew she had.

He was thankful, though, that in reverse she was not some nosy old woman attempting to glean every tidbit she could from them. Not that there had been much to glean after his and Rhonalyn's conversation. Manton remained outside, whittling, foraging, and keeping track of their mounts. And when Rhonalyn returned, the only exchange she and Gage had was about retrieving food and drink from their packs.

Gage continued thinking about Rhonalyn's men and a way for her to reach King Strephon in secret. With their options limited, he dismissed idea after idea until he landed on a plan that was risky but possible.

Lanswith had spoken well of Verfeld's lord, and they'd seen no evidence in the village of the Unavowed. The local lord could be safe to approach and might possibly be willing to reach out to King Strephon on Princess Rhonalyn's behalf. A lesser lord requesting the honor of his king's presence at his manor would be abnormal but far less suspicious than anything else Gage had come up with to get King Strephon and Princess Rhonalyn in the same place.

With Sir Wick so unwell and Manton being who he was, Gage knew the task of approaching the local lord would fall to him. He would need to be sure before starting down such a path, because there was no room for error. If he was wrong, his assertions in response to Manton's doubts about his loyalty to Rhonalyn's safety would likely be put to the test, especially where his mark was concerned.

He glanced at the healer again, wondering about the strange woman's allegiances. Was she a safe person or not? Could he leave the girls and Sir Wick in her care while he investigated the local lord? He frowned. Perhaps he should wait until Sir Wick was better, so that at least someone he trusted would be on guard while he was gone. But what if Sir Wick didn't get better?

The thought sent a spike of fear through him, and the mere idea of losing Sir Wick undid him. His heartbeat quickened, and the land-slide of angst came rushing at him. He knew he couldn't control the chaos, nor could he save himself from it. But at the last moment, he was reminded that he didn't have to save himself. He had a place to go opened to him by a God who was bigger than all the chaos surrounding him. He breathed slowly, absorbing anew the knowledge that no longer did he have to try to carry and solve his own fears. He didn't have to be enough. He was within God's protection and rescue. He swallowed and closed his eyes. Was Sir Wick though? Did the knight also stand within God's mercy?

Not since he was a boy had Gage considered the eternal state of anyone else's soul. In one regard it felt odd to make such a mental inquiry, yet when he looked at Sir Wick, stripped of strength and possibly facing death, what seemed strange resounded as not just reasonable but essential. For when else did the future and safety of anyone's soul become any more relevant?

Gage took solace in what he did know of Sir Wick, for evidence strongly indicated that the knight walked in surrender and submission to God. After all, it had been God's urging upon Sir Wick's soul that had led them to assist Aisley and Princess Rhonalyn.

Sir Wick, it seemed, was under God's authority, and regardless God held the power of life and death. Gage marveled over how that thought no longer caused a stir of angst and resentment in him. Instead, it brought peace.

Movement across the shelter snapped his attention to the healer. She rose from beside the fire and spoke in her creaky voice. "I've left a mixture of leaves for more tea if either of them stir and are in need of it. What's there should last till I return."

Gage frowned. Return? Why was she leaving? And where was she going? Obviously she did not live in the shelter. But was she departing for her home or somewhere else?

Before he had a chance to ask, the healer moved across the shelter to the same section of rocky wall from which she'd first emerged. Circling around a slight curve in the wall and pressing into the uneven rocks, she vanished from sight. Gage assumed she would reemerge from the nook or hole and depart out the same entrance they had been using, but she remained absent.

He strode to the uneven end of the rocks to investigate. He found a dark crevice-like opening, too narrow for him to squeeze through. He peered into the blackness, wondering where it led.

Turning, he pointed at Rhonalyn. "Stay here with them."

"What? No. What are you doing? Get back here!"

He ignored Rhonalyn's protests and hurried out the entrance. Circling the shelter, he found a woodpile and ax but no opening near the structure's far side. He glanced farther abroad and spotted the healer's dark form moving through the forest.

As he debated whether or not to follow her, he noticed about twelve strides behind the woman something arise and begin to trail her. It was a large gray creature.

Gage's heart skipped a beat. He stepped forward and opened his mouth to yell a warning to the woman but then thought better of it. If he caused her to run, it may only increase the likelihood of the animal attacking her. The creature currently maintained its distance, but that might not last long. It was big enough to be a small boar, but it was too thin to be one. More than likely it was a lone wolf. At least, Gage hoped it was alone.

He sprinted after the healer and the creature, praying that two humans together could scare it off. He reached for his knife regardless.

He slowed as his sprint brought him near to her and the creature. What he was observing didn't make sense. Wolves were rarely seen in daylight, and this animal was trotting behind the woman, not slinking or moving with stealth. Its tail did not have the bushy thickness of a wolf's tail, and its body was thin and scraggly.

Gage realized then what it was and almost laughed in relief. He shook his head, feeling silly now for his concern. The animal wasn't a wolf but a wolfhound. The large dog no doubt served as her protector while she traveled through the woods. But where had it been while she was in the shelter? Perhaps in the tunnel that she had apparently departed through, or maybe it had been lying somewhere out of sight in the woods, awaiting her.

Gage squinted at the two of them, even more curious now. The healer wasn't headed toward the village, so where was she going? He continued to follow her. Using his knife to nick the bark of trees as he passed to guide him on his return, he kept her and her huge dog in sight.

He was afraid the dog would pick up his scent and turn on him, but whether it smelled him or not, it gave no indication of noticing or caring that Gage was following.

After a fair distance, the healer paused at a massive oak tree. She seemed to be searching around it for something. The dog sat down near her, its red tongue lolling out of its mouth.

Gage searched for a tree to conceal himself behind. He eased sideways and behind a large tree's trunk, then looked back toward the healer.

The dog remained by the oak, but the healer had disappeared. The dog stood, shook itself, then tore off with the speed of a charger at full tilt. Gage knew he had no chance of catching up with the dog. Nor did he care to, since he was far more interested in where the healer had gone. He ran toward where he had last seen her at the tree.

Nearing the massive oak, he spotted the woman's dark form a bow's-shot ahead to his right. She was working her way over a stretch of rocky ground. Gage came even with the oak she had stood beside before and was contemplating the oddity that she and her dog would go different directions when he gasped and jerked to a stop.

The rocky ground in front of him dropped off into a chasm. The fall he had narrowly avoided taking rivaled the drop from Einhart's tallest tower and made his heart lurch even though he still stood on solid ground. Water coiled around boulders at the bottom of the ravine, the sound of its movement muted by the distance.

Feeling lightheaded, Gage backed away from the edge, his heart pounding.

He took in the area, blinking at the sheer cliff edges of the rift that continued as far as he could see in both directions and at the distance of three horse lengths between where he stood and its opposite rim. He glanced after the healer in astonishment. How had she gotten to the far side? No log was wedged in the chasm, and there was no rope bridge strung across it.

Opposite the oak was an equally massive elm with branches stretching out over the chasm. He searched it. High up, intermingled in the void between the dual trees, he spotted two ropes. One was secured to a branch of the oak and the other to the top of the elm. He traced them downward and noted they both were swung to the chasm's opposite side.

Gage marveled at the reckless daring required to launch oneself over such a drop, supported by only a rope and hoping it conveyed you all the way to the far side. He touched his unmarked wrist shuddering at memories the view stirred in him of having dangled by a chain over a similar drop.

Picturing the healer swinging across the chasm on the rope, his perspective of who she was and his list of questions about her grew exponentially. It wasn't lost on him either that her chosen route prevented anyone from following her. Though if her dog was any indication, there was a path around, not that anyone would have had any luck finding it on the rocky ground.

Gage took one last glance over the ravine's edge and then across to the far side. Scoffing, he turned back. No wonder people called her a witch. From what he'd seen so far, one might easily conclude she could vanish through walls and fly. The question that bothered him, though, was why. Why would she take such risks and precautions to keep people from knowing anything about her?

47

Gage spent what remained of the day in restless indecision about when to attempt what he now felt certain was their best path forward. Since he didn't trust the healer and feared Manton would try to stop him from going to the local lord, he waited for some indication of the right timing.

As the sunlight faded, Manton volunteered to take the animals back to the village's communal grazing land. He said he would spend the night at Mags and Lanswith's and return the following morning with food, which he'd pay for by selling Clover. Gage accepted Manton's plan. It needed to be done, and food was the one area in which he did trust Manton.

Throughout the day, Aisley had slept soundly in between bouts of coughing and being given more tea. Sir Wick on the other hand rested fitfully in a feverish haze. Flushed, coughing, and stirring often in agitation, the knight was clearly in distress. Gage wished there was more he could do for him, but other than giving him the tea, cooling his forehead with a damp cloth, and soothing him with quiet words, there was nothing else he knew to do.

When he and Rhonalyn began to spread their blankets for the night, Aisley woke fully for a bit. She drank some water, ate what little food they had left, then fell back asleep. As they settled to sleep as well, Gage was relieved to hear Sir Wick's ragged breathing remained steady and uninterrupted by coughing. Soon Rhonalyn's own breathing joined the two in slumber. Gage, however, remained awake far into the night.

Staring into the darkness, he prayed for Sir Wick's healing and for God's direction, but he received the same frustrating silence he had back on the beach.

He fell asleep fearful and hungry and was startled awake sometime later by something brushing over his arm.

A dark form stood above him. Gage gasped and jerked upright.

The healer turned around. Liquid splashed at her feet. In lantern light, her startled brown eyes met his. As Gage took in the rest of her, his concern drained away. She was simply doing chores, not trying to sneak up and murder them in their sleep.

He dragged his hands through his hair, then rose. Scooping up his blanket, he rolled and tied it, then tossed it onto his pack.

Across the shelter, the healer put down her bucket. She then crouched to add fuel to the fire from a fresh stack of wood piled against the wall.

Seeing how much work she had done, Gage was surprised and disturbed that he had slept through so much of her comings and goings. His stomach growled. He dug out his waterskin, hoping a drink would stave off his hunger. He tipped the skin up but found there was only a swallow left in it. Frowning, he tossed it back on his pack.

The healer approached him, holding out a mug that dripped liquid.

Realizing she must have just filled it from her bucket, Gage felt both grateful and unnerved by her observation of him. He nodded anyway and took the mug.

By the time he emptied it, she was again gathering plants from the nooks and crannies of her rock wall.

Crossing the shelter, Gage set the empty mug on her flat stone. Rhonalyn stirred awake at his movements. She drew aside her blanket and rose to her feet, while questioning him about their food supplies.

Gage was in the middle of telling her that Manton would bring food from the village when Aisley pushed herself up on an elbow and yawned.

Gage smiled and nodded. "Look who's awake." He was relieved Aisley looked much more herself. The color in her face had returned, and her eyes were bright and inquisitive once more.

"Are you talking about food?" Aisley asked. "Cause I think I could eat a whole loaf of bread all by myself."

The healer's creaky voice made Gage shiver. "Then you must be feeling better?"

"Yes, I am." Aisley glanced over her shoulder. "Is Wick any better?"

"His breathing sounds easier," the healer answered. "But it's how his wound looks this morning that will tell me the most."

Gage was listening for the difference in Sir Wick's breathing when the scuffing of someone coming through the shelter's entrance caused him to glance that way. He expected to see Manton. Instead a young, energetic voice filled the shelter. "Healer, it worked! It worked!"

A boy burst into the center of the shelter. Barefoot and wearing a tunic that was too big for him, he slowed just long enough to locate the healer. Rushing to her, the boy threw his arms around her. "What you gave me to help my mum worked. She's getting better!"

The healer's dark-garbed form, which had stiffened at the boy's abrupt entrance and embrace, relaxed. She touched his head. "I'm glad to hear it," she said in her horrid voice. She reached down then, peeled his arms from around her waist, and turned him around. "But, as you can see, I've others here to attend to. So, be off with you." She shooed him with her hands.

The boy giggled and looked up at Gage. "I like it when she uses her scary voice."

"Tobias!" The healer's tone held a warning and a hint of exasperation.

"I know, I know. I heard you." Tobias mimicked the healer's creak in his next words. "Be off with me." With a grin, the boy held up a finger and turned back. "But before I go, I've got a great stor—"

"No stories. Not today," the healer said, "Get home with you, and make sure your mother continues to rest. That means you doin' all the chores until she's been well for at least two full days. You hear me? Now, off with you."

"Oh alright. But it was such a good story." The boy glanced at Gage and then Rhonalyn and frowned. "Wait, they aren't from the village." His eyes lit up. "Are they travelers?"

"Tobias." The healer's warning tone returned.

Tobias huffed. "Oh, I know. Be gone." He threw up his hands and grumbled, "I never get to meet new people or ask them any questions. No, just mind your own business. How boring is that?" Tobias continued to complain as he left the shelter.

The healer turned back to her fire and resumed what she'd been doing as if everything was exactly as it had been before. But the boy's unexpected arrival, lively presence, and undaunted responses to the healer had shattered Gage's perspective of her. He had thought perhaps she was hiding something sinister, but now he wondered if it was actually quite the opposite.

He watched her move around the shelter like a phantom who wished to stay invisible. She changed the poultice covering Sir Wick's wound and spoke quiet reassurance to Aisley, who had crawled over to sit beside the knight. Sir Wick's eyes flickered open, and this time it was Aisley who helped him sit up to drink.

Sir Wick's gaze held exhaustion and pain but no longer the haze of confusion that had gripped him the pervious day, and the healer's report of his wound sounded hopeful. Gage smiled and felt his soul fill with relief and gratitude.

"I brought food." Manton's quiet voice behind him made Gage jump.

He turned around, wondering how long Manton had been there.

Manton tipped his head. "Come help me with the packs." Manton's concerned tone indicated there was more to his request than just needing an extra hand.

Gage glanced at the others, then followed Manton outside.

As soon as they reached Athalos and Nigel, Manton spoke. "We have a problem. We were followed, maybe from Burnel or Lyster."

"What?" Gage's mind raced. "How? And who?"

"I don't know. But last night when I reached Lanswith and Mags's place, they told me three men came to the village yesterday morning asking if anyone had seen two girls matching Rose's and Amy's descriptions and if they had any information about their whereabouts. A villager apparently directed the men to Lanswith and Mags. The men arrived at their door less than an hour after we left. They wanted to know where we'd gone. Even offered money for everything Mags could tell them. She said she didn't like their looks, so she told them we were headed for Koth."

Gage's stomach twisted. "Did she say if she thought they believed her or not?"

"I didn't dare ask. The men's questions had Lanswith suspicious. He asked why they were looking for Rose and Amy. I told him I didn't know, but I don't think he believed me. Right now we owe our safety to the fact that Mags didn't like their looks. But if they tracked us this far, it won't be hard for them to set a watch on the road and any routes we might take out of here. There's no one I know in Verfeld to help smuggle us out of here either."

"No," Gage said, "but there's someone here I can perhaps call on for help."

"You?"

Gage wasn't sure whether to feel offended at Manton's questioning tone or pleased that for once he had managed to surprise and unsettle him. "I have a few connections of my own, that in this situation I might be able to utilize to help us."

"You? Here in Delkara?"

"Yes."

"Well, at this point I'll take whatever help we can get," Manton muttered.

Gage hoped that was true because he had a feeling Manton would be not at all happy the moment he realized Gage's choice of help.

48

Gage departed from the shelter on Athalos, eating as he rode for the local lord's manor. He kept to the woods for as long as possible, then skirted the fields and village to avoid being seen. When he could keep out of sight no longer, he trotted Athalos toward the manor's open gate. Its small gatehouse was covered with vines and flowers. The stone walls on either side of the entrance were not high, built it would seem more as a barrier for keeping wild animals out and farm animals in than for protection against human foes. Above the walls in the rising sun were two chimneys and the rooflines of Verfeld's small but neatly kept manor.

An older porter in a worn yellow-and-white livery stepped out of the gatehouse as Gage drew even with it. Drawing Athalos to a stop, Gage nodded at the man and addressed him in the commoners' tongue. "Good day to you. I seek an audience with your lord."

The porter viewed him with a keen eye. "His lordship's not here. He's out with his sons, checking on his tenants and riding his fields. His steward, Sir Ogden, is present. Do you wish to speak with him instead? Or perhaps her ladyship?"

Swallowing, Gage shifted on Athalos. "Thank you but no. My business is with your lord." He turned Athalos away from the gate and headed toward the village. He didn't like the idea of wandering about, looking for the manor's lord, but at the same time he wasn't about to trust just anyone with what he had to say.

Neither the village nor the fields were large, but it took him longer than he would have thought to locate the lord and his sons. He finally spotted the three nobles on foot. Their small retinue of men-at-arms were walking the far side of a barley field being harvested with scythes by a group of serfs. Gage sat on Athalos in the trees off the edge of the village, observing the lord and his sons.

The three nobles were distinguishable by their dyed tunics, leather jerkins, and swords, and walked with five men-at-arms wearing minimal armor and tabards of yellow and white. The lord's two sons followed their father, jostling and laughing with each other. The elder looked to be on the verge of knighthood, while the younger was yet a youth of probably no more than fourteen.

The lord paused to speak with the serf directing the barley harvest. His lordship then checked the grain that had already been cut, made a few gestures, and continued on.

Departing that field, the party trekked to the edge of another where an ox driver had just brought along a wagon into which field-workers were beginning to load harvested melons that were piled along the field's edge. One of the workers struggled to get a particularly large melon up over the wagon's side. The lord hurried forward and assisted him. Together, lord and serf hefted the large fruit the rest of the way into the wagon. The peasant nodded his thanks. Then, to Gage's surprise and admiration, all eight men, nobles and men-at-arms alike, began to help load the melons.

With the additional hands, it didn't take long for them to finish the task, and when it was done, the lord and his retinue headed toward the village. As they did, Gage noticed the roving gazes of the lord's men-at-arms and knew if he stayed where he was, he was bound to be noticed before he had a chance to approach the lord on his own terms.

Turning Athalos, he withdrew and headed for the village well. Once there, he used the bucket to retrieve water for himself and

Athalos. He watched the lane, keeping an eye out for anyone watching him, and waited for a way to approach the lord where their conversation would attract the least amount of attention.

The lord and his sons entered the village west of Gage but turned toward him. While coming along the lane, they passed an open-sided shelter where a man worked the foot treadle of a lathe, turning a piece of wood into what looked like a tool handle.

"Good day, Jenkins," the youngest of the lord's two sons called out.

"And to you, Master Paten," The woodworker replied with a smile and a deep nod. "Lord Braxton. Master Charles."

"Is your hand better?" Paten asked, his voice jumping in pitch.

"It is."

"Ah, good." Charles said, "Then we can attempt the task this evening."

The woodworker laughed. "This evening it is."

Others in the lane made way and warmly greeted the nobles. Even a metalsmith, with the windows of his shop propped open, paused with his metal tongs hovering in the wavy heat of his forge to dip his head. It reminded Gage of the way people responded to his family when he, his father, and Haaken journeyed together.

Feeling confident in his decision to approach the lord, he tied Athalos in the trees opposite the well and intended to slip out of the village on foot to petition Lord Braxton as the lord made his way back to his manor.

The pounding of many hooves approaching from the direction of the lord's manor interrupted Gage's plan. He delayed near Athalos, and like everyone else in the village, he observed the arrival of a large company of horsemen that swept up the lane.

A handful of the riders were fully armored knights while the rest were soldiers in partial armor. All of them except the noble they were escorting wore face-concealing helmets and displayed in some fashion a livery of yellow upon which was a green downturned chevron.

At the company's approach, Verfeld's five men-at-arms shifted their hands to their swords and encircled Lord Braxton and his sons. The arriving force passed Gage and came to a stop in front of Lord Braxton's small group, paused at the heart of the village. The noble maneuvered his horse to the front of his company. He looked to be no older than Lord Braxton's eldest son, Charles, and wore an ostentatious tunic of tan and red with a plush hat and a gold chain of office draped from shoulder to shoulder over a trim of dark fur.

Lord Braxton, in his much simpler attire, addressed the man in the noblemen's tongue. "Baron Fitch, to what do I owe such an unexpected visit?"

"I have come hither to witness the end to your meddlesome and irksome ways," the younger baron replied with contempt.

"Verily! My meddlesome and irksome ways? Do you mean because I refuse to aid or judge anyone—peasant or noble—without first hearing all sides, or do you mean because I insist on participating in justice and not tyranny?"

Baron Fitch sneered. "Your actions violate your sworn duty as my vassal and as a noble of Delkara. Not the least action of which is your habit of providing for and aiding only the needs of your own village while giving less than satisfactory heed to the requirements of the kingdom as a whole."

Lord Braxton stiffened. "As lord of Verfeld, I have obeyed every law of the kingdom and paid every tax you have demanded of me, all while seeing to the needs of my village. How is there any violation or defiance in that toward my sworn duty?"

"I am not finished. You art also harboring wanted criminals."

"I have done no such thing!"

"Have you not? Is not a lord responsible for all those in his village?"

"Of course." Lord Braxton's voice tightened as a hint of anger and concern seeped through it. "But no lord can be held accountable for every person who passes through his village, only for his own actions or inactions based on the knowledge he possesses. I have harbored no one. Nor have I known of any criminals toward whom I should have taken action. Had I, I certainly would have apprehend them and brought them to justice. Thus"— Lord Braxton's voice turned accusatory—"mayhap next time when you send men seeking five strangers in my village you wilt have your men report to me as to why they have come and what criminals they seek. Then I can act accordingly."

Gage sucked in his breath. He had assumed until then that the two noblemen were discussing actual criminals, not him and his four companions. And though he'd been called a criminal before, hearing the title applied to Rhonalyn as well as him was disturbing. Why would a Delkaran baron be searching for Keric's princess by calling her a criminal? Was Baron Fitch seeking to conceal why he was looking for Rhonalyn, or was he trying to conceal Princess Rhonalyn's identity to protect her? Or had the baron been told that she was a criminal? Was the baron part of the Unavowed, working against them, or working for them?

"You admit, then, you knew of their presence in your village?"

"I admit," Lord Braxton answered, "that I was told yesterday that five strangers passed through my village and that three men came afterward looking for them—men whom I assume now to be yours, though they wore no livery. But how I was to know that the strangers your men sought were criminals, I am at a loss to understand."

"At a loss? Are you indeed, Lord Braxton?" Baron Fitch scoffed.

"Tell me, if you personally have had no contact with her, then where is she?"

"Where is who?" Lord Braxton said.

"You know who I mean! Why else would you conceal her?"

Gage tensed.

"I assure you I have no knowledge of who or what you mean." Lord Braxton sounded genuinely confused, thankfully so.

"You art lying." Fitch shouted.

Braxton's younger son, Paten, stepped forward, indignation rising in his youthful voice. "My father does not lie!"

"Verily? Does he not? Your father knows full well there is more to sworn fealty than just paying taxes. And yet for months now he has chosen not to fully align himself with that loyalty."

Months? Confusion swept through Gage. Baron Fitch was definitely looking for Princess Rhonalyn, but there was also far more going on between this liege lord and his vassal.

"Baron Fitch, my loyalty is—"

"Your loyalty is divided at best and at worst, subversive."

"How dare you speak so!" Charles, Lord Braxton's eldest son, snapped. "Our father is no traitor."

"A traitor is exactly what he is." Fitch lifted his hand, and a dozen of his men-at-arms dismounted and unsheathed their weapons. The baron announced in the commoners' tongue, "Lord Braxton, you're under arrest. All your properties and belongings are hereby forfeited until such a time as your case can be judged by King Strephon and a subsequent manager of these lands determined."

"You can't do that!" Paten shouted. "My father's done nothing wrong."

Gage, too, was startled by the baron's proclamation. Why would the baron march into Verfeld seeking Rhonalyn and instead arrest the manor lord? He swallowed hard. Was Fitch attempting to trap and draw Rhonalyn out, or was the baron using her as an excuse to come after the local lord?

"Take his lordship into custody," Baron Fitch commanded.

The baron's soldiers advanced toward Verfeld's lord.

Villagers stirred and murmured angrily, and the lord's two sons and all five men-at-arms drew their weapons. Lord Braxton did so as well but slower as if reluctant to make such a choice. "Don't do this, Fitch," he pleaded. "This is wrong, and you know it. Call off your men."

"It's already done." Baron Fitch nodded at his men. "Take him, and then burn this village to the ground."

"No!" Lord Braxton's cry was lost in the clash of weapons.

49

Horrified, Gage watched Baron Fitch's soldiers attack and Lord Braxton's five men-at-arms attempt to block the onslaught. The village lane turned into the grounds of a melee.

Meanwhile, two soldiers split from the baron's main force and entered the metalsmith's shop. The smith swung his tongs at them and hollered something about his lord. The first of the baron's men knocked the smith's makeshift weapon aside and, with a thrust of his blade, ran the smith through.

Gage gasped. The soldier withdrew his sword, and the smith's body crumpled. The second soldier took a shovel of coals from the smith's forge and tossed them in a cascade of sparks out a window. Before vacating the shop, he sent a second scoop of coals across the shop, igniting its far wall.

Using the embers outside, the baron's men lit anything that would hold a flame. Within moments fire was consuming the smith's shop and being dispersed across the village.

Thatched roofs burst into flames. Craftsmen, mothers, children, and the elderly fled their homes, screaming, coughing, and crying. The able-bodied from the fields yelled as they saw what was happening in the village and came running.

A butcher burst from his home, bellowing and swinging a chopping knife at two of the baron's men who were about to light his neighbor's house ablaze. The butcher's short blade was no match for the reach and slash of a sword. He was dead before his body hit the ground.

Fury filled every fiber of Gage's body. He stepped forward but then halted. What could he do? Without armor or a proper weapon, he was as vulnerable as the villagers. And even those better equipped for the fight were massively outnumbered. Already four of Lord Braxton's men-at-arms were dead, their bodies sprawled in the lane amid an increasing number of dead or injured villagers.

A handful of Baron Fitch's knights had Lord Braxton surrounded. The manor lord's earlier hesitance to draw his weapon was gone. Now he fought with a vengeance, wielding his sword with an adeptness and fierceness that kept at bay his many assailants.

Farther up the lane, pushed beyond Lord Braxton by the overwhelming assault, Charles fought back to back with the manor's one remaining man-at-arms. The young noble and his man handled their swords with skill, attacking those coming at them with bold cries and fierce clashes of metal. But, facing multiple opponents each, they were hard pressed and losing ground.

Charles's sword bound with one of his attacker's blades. With his weapon occupied, a second soldier lunged and sliced Charles's unprotected arm. Charles cried out. The soldier attempted a second sweep at Charles's head. The lord's son parried the first man's blade and thrust forward, catching the tip of the second man's weapon just in time to divert it away from his head. Charles warded off two more attacks and made a swift counterstrike that caught a soldier under the edge of his armor, injuring him enough that the soldier disengaged from the fight.

Paten, however, was clearly not as experienced with his sword. A knight had driven the youth against one of the burning homes only a lance's throw from Gage. Flaming pieces of thatch fell around Paten while he hacked and swung with his blade, trying to counter his assailant's strikes. Blood saturated Paten's tunic from a slash to his side and a cut on his forehead.

The youth's arms were shaking and already falling lower at each swing. He wasn't going to last much longer.

A year prior, Gage would have assumed the baron's men would fight only until they could force those they faced to surrender. But there was no honor in these men. They had already killed villagers and men-at-arms. Thus, he had every reason to fear the knight would kill Paten too.

Anger and determination filled Gage. He couldn't stand by and let the boy die. He sprinted toward the back of Paten's attacker, drawing the only weapon he had. His knife was little more than a hand's length long and would have done him no good had he been coming at the knight head on, but thankfully he wasn't, and Paten had him distracted. Darting forward and ducking behind Paten's attacker, he stabbed his blade into the back of the knight's knee where there was a gap in his armor. A howl of pain filled Gage's ears as he yanked the knife out. He flipped it around and rose with it fisted like a spike.

In front of him, the knight shifted to swing around at him. Knowing he had only one chance before his short blade became useless, Gage threw himself against the knight. He seized hold of the man's helmeted head, wrenched it sideways to expose an opening between the helmet and chest plate, and drove his knife into the gap.

The knight stumbled a step, then collapsed under him. For a moment, Gage stood over him, staring into Paten's shocked yet grateful gaze.

Then the youth's eyes widened. "Behind you!"

Snatching up the fallen knight's sword, Gage swept the weapon around. Its blade clashed against the blade of another of the baron's knights. Their weapons bound against each other, halting the knight's sword from slicing into Gage's shoulder.

His heart pounding, Gage turned his blade in a swift arc over his enemy's weapon, driving it down and outward. He felt the resistance against his blade give way as the knight twisted his sword free, then swung at Gage's side. Gage parried the blow but at the wrong angle and gritted his teeth as his wrist took the full force of the hit.

He had no time to adjust his grip before deflecting three more of the knight's swift, vigorous strikes. With a surge of strength and desperation, Gage made a counterstrike of his own and stabbed at the knight's groin. The knight blocked him and answered with a lunge and thrust at Gage's chest that Gage avoided by a finger's breadth. Breathing hard, Gage swept his weapon around, making two strikes at gaps in the knight's armor and putting him on the defensive.

A large chunk of smoldering roof thatch hit the ground to Gage's left, filling the air with smoke and heat. The knight used the distraction to feint a strike toward Gage's head, then redirected his blade toward Gage's hip.

With his eyes stinging and a cough bursting from his chest, Gage attempted to bring his weapon down fast enough to block the blow but wasn't able to ward it off completely. The man's sword sliced his skin just above his knee. Pain rushed through Gage's senses. Gritting his teeth, he turned a bellow of pain into a war cry and slashed at the under edge of the man's helmet.

The knight dodged his attack but in so doing stepped within Paten's reach. The youth swung at the knight's armored side like he was taking an ax to a mighty oak. The ringing blow of Paten's blade dented the knight's plate armor but didn't cut through it.

Turning, the knight thrust back at Paten, which left his right side open to Gage. Paten met the man's blade and drove it up with his sword, and Gage used the opportunity to sweep his own blade against the knight's exposed inner arm. He felt the catch as it passed through fabric and sliced deep.

The knight hissed and slashed back at him. Gage blocked the hard blow. The clang of metal rang in his ears and made his hands prickle. He parried another blow, then another. Driven backward by the fury of the knight's strikes, he felt the increasing heat of the fire behind and above him. Paten attempted to intervene, but the knight pulled a small blade from his armor and sent it flying at the youth.

"No!" Gage's heart and body lurched. Paten tried to duck the blade but lost his footing. The youth crashed sideways through the open door of the burning home. He must have hit a support post as he fell because the burning roof shifted. Half of its thatch collapsed inside, and the other half fell forward in charred and flaming chunks between Gage and the knight.

50

GAGE RECOILED BACKWARD as the house's thatch blazed between himself and his attacker. Heat and sparks flew up in his face, pressing him against the building's wall. Smoke and fire spread around him, making him cough and squint against its heat. Holding up his arm to protect his face, he shuffled along the wall to reach the doorway, then ducked into the building. Inside, flames licked at piles of unburnt thatch, but in other places the fire had already consumed the roofing, leaving smoldering, blackened strands of dried plant stocks coiled into ash.

His eyes stinging, Gage spotted Paten crawling out from under a table. Relieved to find the youth alive, Gage rushed to him. "Are you alright?" He brushed pieces of burning thatch off the youth's tunic and helped him up. He feared he would see a knife impaled in the youth's chest, but all he found were the previous wounds to the boy's side and forehead. "Thank God he missed," Gage said.

In the next moment, renewed heat enveloped them. A pile of unburnt thatch and a blanket had burst into flames to their right.

"This way!" Gage drew Paten away from the heat and toward a section of the home where the thatch had already burned and the structure's wall had not taken up the flames. The blackened curls crunched under their boots, and soot, heat, and smoke filled the air. Coughing, they huddled together against the wall, feeling the heat on their skin. They turned their backs to the flames and used their arms to protect their faces.

The fury of the remaining thatch's blaze did not last long, and yet as the crackling hiss of the dying flames quieted, they heard the pounding of hooves departing the village.

Paten stirred. "Father! Charles!" The youth ran for the house's charred doorway, dodging smoldering chunks of thatch as he went.

Gage raced after him. "Wait!" He lunged out the door, sword in hand. The sight before him made Gage's stomach twist.

The baron's force had departed, leaving the village lane littered with bodies. Among them several soot-covered villagers ran back and forth from the well, attempting to douse the flames of houses still burning, while others knelt weeping over the dead or clutching the wounded. A number of mothers and the elderly stood in huddled groups, sheltering their children. Two horses with empty saddles bearing Baron Fitch's colors wandered among the dead. Multiple homes still burned while others had collapsed, and a few stood as charred shells.

Paten wove among the casualties as if in a daze, then cried out and ran forward. He collapsed beside a form sprawled next to one of the baron's fallen soldiers. A sword was still clutched in Charles's bloody fingers.

Gage pressed the back of his hand to his mouth as Paten pulled Charles's head and shoulders into his lap against his own blood-soaked tunic. "Charles? Charles! Open your eyes. Please. Please open your eyes!"

Gage knew all too well the pain the youth was experiencing. His own chest tightened with it, causing each thudding beat of his heart to echo with grief. He wanted to turn away, to escape the scene and all the memories it ignited inside him. But the sight of Paten held Gage rooted to the spot. Pain pulsed inside him. He remembered wanting nothing more than to cease to exist at the moment he'd known Allard was dead. He thought of Old Tobin and the way the man had come and sat beside him, letting him grieve and then helping him not drown in it. But no old man came to Paten's aid.

Swallowing, Gage dragged air into his lungs and pushed himself forward. He walked to where Paten was and knelt beside the youth. He had no idea what to say, but he knew he couldn't leave the boy alone.

Paten jostled his brother's shoulders once more. "Please, Charles. Please. Wake up!" Tears choked out Paten's last word and rolled through the blood on the boy's face.

Gage felt hot trails of tears cascade down his own face, and he gripped Paten's arm in silent acknowledgement of his anguish. With a heart-rending cry, Paten bent over his brother's body and sobbed. Gage stayed beside him, unable to move or speak. Their tears intermingled in the blood and dirt of the senseless violence and loss.

A pleading female voice drifted to them. "Someone help me, please!"

Gage glanced about and spotted a woman kneeling beside a man who had a head injury that was bleeding profusely. The woman pressed her skirt against the man's wound and looked around for anyone willing to assist her. A few villagers were tending to those injured, but others stood too shocked to do anything. Many clutched their own wounds or sobbed over the bodies of the dead.

Gage stirred. Someone needed to restore order so that grief did not steal even more lives from them, like it had Bardon's. He opened his mouth but then paused. He glanced at Paten. Charles was dead, and Lord Braxton was nowhere in sight, thus Paten was the next leader of these people.

Some would have said the youth was in no condition to help, but from Gage's own experience he believed that being seen in grief and trusted with a purpose might actually be the best way to keep the youth from disappearing into his misery. He knelt and touched the youth's arm. "Master Paten, your people need you."

Paten lifted his head. His eyes were red, and fresh tears streaked through the soot and blood on his face. He voice held nothing but anguish. "My brother's gone."

Tears pooled again in Gage's eyes and rolled unbidden down his cheeks. "I know, and you are not alone in your loss. Your village has been devastated, and all here will grieve this day with you far into the future. But right now, those injured and yet alive need help. Your people, your village, they need you to rise even in your grief and lead them in helping each other so that people do not perish who could have been saved."

"I'm not a leader." Paten's voice trembled. "I'm not even a knight yet."

"Listen to me, leading only takes putting your mind to the task. Look around you, see what needs doing, and set someone to do it. You know these people. You can do this. Identify who can do what, then appoint them to it. I'll help you. Start with that woman over there. Who is she and the injured man she's tending?"

Paten glanced where he pointed. The youth's eyes widened, and he stumbled to his feet. "Nathan! Ebba!" Paten started toward them but then stumbled to a stop. Turning in a circle, the boy seemed to take in his village. He glanced back at Gage, and with a look of resolve, raised his voice and started calling out people by name and asking them to take on specific tasks.

"Micah, aid Ebba with Nathan's wound."

"You six, help with the other wounded."

"Andre and Wilkin, help put out the remaining fires."

"Odel, tie the loose horses out of the way."

"You two and Hollis, carry the dead to the churchyard, so that they do not remain laying in the lane."

Each request was made as a strong yet earnest plea.

Gage admired the villagers. Every person, even those who had been weeping over their own dead, answered Paten's call and set about helping their neighbors.

Paten drew back close to Gage. "We need the other healer." The youth's frightened words echoed Gage's own thoughts as he observed the sheer number of wounded. Paten shook his head. "But how are we to get so many people to her?"

"Have her come here," Gage replied.

"She won't come. She never leaves the woods."

"What?" Gage blinked. "Why not?"

"None know, but she's adamant about it. People must come to her. She won't come to them."

Gage frowned. "Well, today she'll have to make an exception."

"Who's to persuade her?" Paten looked at Gage as if hoping he might.

Gage had a better idea. He searched the area for someone he had recognized earlier. He found the boy helping a thin, tired-looking woman who cast a grateful smile at the lad as he sat her on a charred bench. Gage called out. "Tobias."

The boy glanced up, said something to the woman, then trotted to him.

Gage turned back to Paten. "Send Tobias. He knows her well and can perhaps persuade her where someone else couldn't."

"Persuade whom?" Tobias asked.

"The healer," Paten answered. "She must come and help the injured."

Tobias shook his head. "She won't leave the woods."

"Well she must," Gage said. "Tell her what's happened here and that her help is urgently needed to tend to sword wounds and burns. Inform her people's lives depend upon her coming to help."

"Do as he says, Tobias."

Wide-eyed, Tobias nodded to Paten, then sprinted away.

51

GAGE WAS HELPING Paten settle a wounded man in the shade of a large tree near the church when the sound of hooves charging up the lane caused them both to stiffen. Gage cast about for the sword he had set aside and saw Paten's hand close around the hilt of his own weapon. Then Paten released his grip and called out. "Mother!"

Gage looked toward the approaching riders. A bronze-skinned woman with copper-colored hair galloped up the lane astride a saddle-less horse. Her fierce gaze swept over the village with a look of distress and alarm. She had clearly faced her own troubles, for her face and fine dress were smudged with soot, her sleeves were shoved up past her elbows, and her shoes were coated in mud.

Behind her, sliding to a stop on a charger, was a man wearing a silver-embroidered tunic also soiled with soot, and on a third mount was a maidservant in an equally dirty dress seated in front of a young man wearing a singed livery of the yellow and white of Lord Braxton's manor.

"Paten!" The lady of the manor's dropped off her horse and ran to her son.

"Mother! Are you alright?"

As the mother and son embraced, the squire and maidservant both went looking for their own people.

Meanwhile the man with her ladyship held back his sword as he dismounted and spoke. "Baron Fitch came to the manor looking for your father and someone else apparently of great interest to him."

"Never mind that now, Sir Ogden," Paten's mother said. "Can you not see my son is injured?" She gripped Paten's arms and glanced at his side and head. "How badly are you hurt? And where are your father and Charles?"

Paten's voice trembled. "Father was arrested and taken by Baron Fitch, and Charles…Charles is…is…" Fresh tears cascaded down Paten's face.

"No. Not Charles." Tears filled the woman's eyes. "No."

Paten turned and led her to where Charles had been laid in the churchyard. The youth sank with his mother beside his older brother's body, his tears turning back into sobs. His mother placed a hand on Charles's motionless chest and wrapped her other arm around Paten's head, her body shaking in her own silent grief.

Stepping away from them, Sir Ogden caught hold of one of the passing villagers. "Hollis, tell me what happened here."

Hollis glanced toward Lord Braxton's wife and son and, in a quiet voice, relayed to Sir Ogden all that had taken place but without the context of Baron Fitch and Lord Braxton's exchange since it had been made in the noblemen's tongue.

Sniffing and lifting his head, Paten picked up the tale where Hollis had left off, telling Sir Ogden and his mother in the noblemen's tongue what else had been said.

Her ladyship swiped at tears trailing down her cheeks. "Aye, I should have guessed when Fitch left the manor house that he was not finished." A hard edge entered her voice. "Long has he waited for such an excuse to take action against us." Her face twisted in grief. "But never did I expect him to do something such as this. So many times Braxton and I discussed whether to train more men-at-arms, but always it seemed ill advised to take men out of the field, especially with food the more pressing need. But now…"

"You could not have prevented this, Lady Ellen," Sir Ogden said. "Baron Fitch's soldiers would have outnumbered and decimated no matter how many Verfeld men were trained."

"Did he burn and kill at the manor house as well?" Paten asked.

Lady Ellen inhaled. "Nay. They shoved people around and thoroughly searched the house for whomever they were seeking. But they did not kill anyone or set the house ablaze. Though they did burn a barn and some outbuildings. I had thought that was the end of it until we were putting out the fires and noticed smoke from the village." She looked around, and her voice caught. "So much loss and pain caused in so short a time. What a hateful, evil man." She choked on more tears. "And he has your father." She gripped Paten and tipped her head against her son's. "I thank God though that he did not take you too."

"Verily, I think Baron Fitch's men thought they had killed me," Paten said. "And were it not for this stranger"—Paten gestured toward Gage—"they would have succeeded. The moment I thought I would be struck down, he came to my aid, wielding a weapon like a trained swordsman. Mother, he saved my life, twice."

"Did he indeed?" Sir Ogden said, his voice piqued with interest.

Lady Ellen's gaze fell upon Gage with a look of curiosity and appreciation. She switched to the commoners' tongue. "My son says you saved his life."

Gage responded with a respectful dip of his head. "I simply helped where I could, Your Ladyship. I'm glad I could make a difference and grieved that I couldn't do more."

"Mother, he is being humble," Paten said in the noblemen's tongue. "He risked his life to protect me and has been helping here in the village ever since. It was even by his suggestion that I sent Tobias to appeal to the healer in the woods to come aid us. Barta is doing what she can, but the poor thing can hardly recall what to do with a poultice let alone what she once put in one."

Sir Ogden stirred. "This man knows and is associated with the witch from the woods?"

"Sir Ogden," Lady Ellen snapped, "are there not matters far more paramount in nature today than one's associations with her? Wounded must be looked after." Lady Ellen glanced at Gage and switched back to the commoners' tongue. "If things were different, I'd honor you with more than words for your protection of my son. But as it is…"

Gage dipped his head. "You've no need to explain, Your Ladyship. Please just tell me how else I can help."

Busy assisting wherever he was needed in the village, Gage helped the people of Verfeld and prayed the healer would come.

He had nearly given up hope that she would when he spotted her dark form shuffling through the line of trees into the village. The healer held a blanket gathered in a bundle, and her hood was pulled so low that only her fabric-covered chin showed. She hunched in a way that made her appear short, even a little hunchbacked, and moved like every step took significant effort.

Had it been Gage's first encounter with her, he would have been more susceptible to thinking of her by the title Lanswith and Sir Ogden used for her. Certainly, she didn't attempt to make herself amiable, and once again he wondered why.

He approached her from the side. "Thank you for coming."

She flinched away from him, then shuddered, and said in her creaky voice. "Show me to the injured."

"Of course. This way." Gage wondered if the edge in her voice was fear or anger but doubted she would oblige him with a clarification. Noting her struggling to keep the blanket aloft, he carefully took it from her and led her to where the injured had been gathered. Moans, weeping, and cries of pain rose from men, women, and children alike.

A dozen or so uninjured villagers were among the wounded attempting to tend to them. Many of them paused and straightened to stare at the healer as she approached. Their gazes followed her path with wary and even angry expressions.

The healer crouched to look at one man's deep sword wound. As she did, the uninjured villagers clumped together, murmuring to one another. Gage cringed and hoped no one would do anything stupid in response to her presence.

The healer rose and spoke to him in her horrible creaky voice. "Put my blanket of plants and oils there. Then find me pots, water, and vinegar. I'll need a fire close at hand as well."

Gage set down her blanket then searched the villagers for someone who looked the least like they wanted to run from the healer or burn her at the stake. He spotted Mags bent over a little girl. He approached her and noted that the girl she was with had burns on her arms and hands. He swallowed hard. "Mags, can you find pots for the healer to use, along with some vinegar?"

Mags glanced up at him. "The healer? She's here?" She turned around before Gage could answer, and her weary expression transformed into a smile. "She came. Oh, God bless her. Yes, of course I've pots she can use." Mags touched the little girl's shoulder. "I'll be back, Linden. And don't you worry. She may appear frightening, but you'll find that the healer's a beautiful person."

Gage spent a good part of the next hour observing that exact paradox. People would recoil at the healer's voice, enshrouded form, and hunched movements, but as they received her kind words and gentle actions, they accepted her help with nods of thanks. The healer's fortitude in dealing with wounds that made Gage's own stomach queasy amazed him, and he admired her knowledge and steady confidence in choosing treatments as well as how honoring she was in implementing them no matter how gruesome the task.

The majority of those who were healthy put as much distance between themselves and the healer as they could. As for Gage, he went back and forth from assisting her in treating wounds to fetching plants or ointments from her blanket.

Upon returning from one such run, he heard soft singing as she was treating Linden's hands. When he came close enough to see Linden's face, Gage stopped short. It wasn't the little girl singing but the healer. The lyrics were in a tongue he did not know, but the beauty of the melody enthralled him. The song was mournful and yet hopeful, filled with an intensity and sincerity that tugged at him.

The healer turned to gather more salve onto her fingers, and her eyes flicked to him. She instantly fell silent. She turned back to Linden and spread the salve over the girl's hands.

"Please"— Gage stepped toward her— "don't stop on my account."

The healer pointed to the bottle he had brought and spoke in her creaky voice. "Put that over there."

Gage flinched, then blinked back a rush of grief. For it was as if something too precious to lose had just vanished in front of him. His heart aching at what was already a fading memory, he set the bottle down and watched her work. Every moment he spent with her, he discovered something new about her, and yet he understood her even less.

The healer glanced over at him. "Has Tobias come yet with the plants I asked him to find?"

Gage shook his head. "I haven't seen him."

She grunted. "He must've had trouble finding them." She gestured at him. "Sit."

"What?"

"Sit." She pointed at his leg where he'd been cut. "The ointment is for you."

Gage sat and extended his injured leg to her, his mind trying to make sene of her. She set about cleaning and tending his wound. He flinched more than once despite her gentleness and found himself curling his toes and digging his fingers into the ground against the pain. When she spoke, her creak was less pronounced, even carrying a hint of amusement. "As I've told others, it's important to keep breathing."

Gage chuckled. "Right." He took a few breaths and said, "You know, I think I liked it better on your side of this tending business. Even if I did almost vomit on that one man."

She laughed. It was a rich, vibrant sound that caught him completely by surprise. The voice that followed grated so badly with the sound that Gage wished all the more he could hear her real voice. Instead she spoke in her creaky voice, "I did think you turned a bit green." Her tone softened. "Though, you managed well enough."

"Glad to hear it." Gage gritted his teeth, then relaxed. "Because, believe it or not, I'm not normally a healer's apprentice." He hoped his words would solicit another laugh from her, but instead she closed the jar, rose, and headed to the next injured individual, leaving him to wrap a cloth over his own wound. Gage shook his head, got to his feet, and continued assisting her.

52

WICK EASED HIMSELF backward to lean his shoulders against the shelter's wall. His arms trembled at the effort it took just to move that much. He felt through his tunic to check that the poultice was still in place on his side, then let his hand drop into his lap and heaved a sigh. He couldn't help but replay Tobias's words about what had taken place in the village and his desperate plea for the healer's help.

The healer and boy had left while Wick was stuck there, too weak to rise and go with them. Prince Gage was in the village, and he couldn't watch over him, let alone render aid. Frustrated, he glanced at Princess Rhonalyn. "Do you think it is as bad as the boy said?"

She shrugged with annoyance. "You're guess is as good as mine."

Wick grunted. At least he knew Prince Gage was safe. Tobias had told him that much before dragging the healer out the door.

"Why would a baron order a village burned?" Lady Aisley asked. "There can't be justice or reason in such an action, can there?"

Wick shook his head. "No, I doubt it."

"Maybe we shouldn't discuss it," Princess Rhonalyn said, her tone suggesting he drop the topic.

Wick took the hint and shifted to talking about what they had seen of other villages on their journey. As they spoke, he noted how astute Lady Aisley was in her observations of each place. When it seemed the topic had run dry, he was about to ask something about Keric but then heard what sounded like disgruntled voices outside.

From what Wick knew, Manton was alone beyond the shelter's door. Surely, the rebel wasn't talking to himself. A cry burst out and was cut off. The warning it represented sent a rush of fear up Wick's spine.

He shoved away the blanket that covered him, and despite the fatigue that made his body sluggish to respond to his commands, he reached out for his belt beside the makeshift bed. It wasn't much, but he wanted his knife.

His fingers closed around the leather just as a man with a sword entered the shelter. Even in the dim light, Wick noted the fine fabric of the man's mud-spattered tunic. The nobleman's gaze swept over the three of them and brightened with a look of success when his gaze fell on the girls.

Wick hesitated, unsure whether the man was friend or foe.

A large, brawny peasant stepped into the space behind the nobleman, his expression hard and his hands also gripping a sword. Wick's heartbeat sped into a pounding rush. Peasants in Delkara weren't allowed to bear swords.

A third man, also in peasant's attire, entered the shelter backward, cursing and struggling as he fought to contain a small, flailing form that he held clutched against him. He turned with his quarry.

Heat rushed through Wick's body. The man was holding Tobias, one hand clamped over the boy's mouth and his other wrapped around his waist. Tobias's wide eyes were full of anger and fear.

Lady Aisley gasped, and Princess Rhonalyn stepped forward, demanding sharply, "What's the meaning of this?"

Nothing good, Wick was certain. Casting his gaze down, he pulled his belt to himself and seized his knife. The tip of a sword swept above his fingers. "Don't be a fool."

Wick looked up, straight into the nobleman's hard gaze.

The man tapped the sharp edge of his blade against the inside of Wick's arm. "Take your hand off the weapon."

Swallowing, Wick withdrew his hands from his knife.

The nobleman thrust his sword tip down, piercing the leather of Wick's belt and lifting it skewered on the end of his blade like a conquered insignia. The man swung it toward his brawny companion. "Corbett, see that this knife remains out of his reach. If he's anything like his sword-wielding companion in the village, he'll be trouble even with just a knife."

Sword-wielding companion? The man had to be talking about Prince Gage. The hair on Wick's arms rose. "What've you done with Gabe?"

"Your friend from the village? Nothing. He's at the witch's side in the middle of far too many villagers. But I do believe the four of you'll do for my purpose."

"What purpose?" Princess Rhonalyn demanded, a tremor running through her voice.

The nobleman glanced her way, his eyes narrowing. "You must be the one Baron Fitch was so interested in finding. Or is it her?" His gaze flicked to Lady Aisley.

Princess Rhonalyn shifted. "I don't know what you mean."

The man laughed. "Oh, I think you do. And I think Baron Fitch will be quite pleased when I offer you and your three companions to him."

Princess Rhonalyn's body quaked, but her voice remained firm. "I can get you money if that's what you seek."

"Money?" The man snorted. "I'm not so small-minded. I've bided my time as the respectable steward to the intolerable Lord Braxton and his high-and-mighty wife too long to take in exchange a purse of coin that'll run empty. No, I want something far more significant. And what better chance than this? With Lord Braxton arrested and you four to barter with, I believe Baron Fitch will grant me what I desire."

"You speak of bartering." Rhonalyn's voice strengthened. "Do you even know who I am or what I'm worth?"

Wick had to admire Princess Rhonalyn's audacity in trying to regain control over the situation, but he flinched at where she was headed with it.

The man shook his head. "It doesn't matter to me who you are, only that Baron Fitch finds you valuable."

"You can say that knowing nothing," Princess Rhonalyn said, "but I assure you regardless of what you want from this Baron Fitch, I'd be worth far more to you ransomed back to my father—King Bryant of Keric."

Wick held his breath.

A flicker of surprise registered on the nobleman's face. "You're a princess of Keric." He scoffed. "Well, that explains Baron Fitch's determination to have you in his grasp. All the better for me."

Princess Rhonalyn looked mortified. "He will kill me. It's your duty as a nobleman to protect me."

The man leaned forward. "What he wants with you is his business, not mine."

"You can't be serious."

"Sir Ogden, are you sure about this?" the brawny peasant, whom the steward had called Corbett, questioned. "What if she's right? What if her father would be a better choice? If we hold onto her instead and offer—"

"Think, fool!" Ogden snarled. "Do you want them coming after us to find her?"

Fear flickered across Corbett's face. "No. You're right. Better we take her to the baron."

"Exactly. So, stir your stumps, and secure the lot of them."

Panic tightened in Wick's chest. He cast his gaze around for anything that could serve as a weapon.

"And, Corbett," Sir Ogden said, "tie him up first, for he clearly plans on ignoring my warning."

Wick jerked up his gaze. The nobleman's eyes held his for a moment, then flicked back to Princess Rhonalyn.

Angered that he'd given himself away, Wick drew a breath as Corbett deposited his weapons out of reach and approached him. The man's large frame bent over him, and his hands closed over Wick's forearms.

Wick's heartbeat spiked. He pulled his arms down as hard as he could and at the same time tried to sweep Corbett's legs with his own. His intention was to topple the man and perhaps get an arm around his neck. But his limited strength failed him. Corbett barely even wobbled.

Looking vexed by his attempt, Corbett yanked forward on Wick's arms and thrust his knee into Wick's face. The contact was so hard it snapped Wick's mouth shut, chipping a tooth and causing a popping in his jaw. He vaguely heard someone cry out but couldn't identify who through a buzzing that rang in his ears. Grunting, he shook his head, trying to rid himself of the noise and disorientation, but the effort only made him dizzy.

Corbett twisted his grip on Wick's wrist and, stepping around him, dragged Wick's arms behind his back. Every bit of Wick's body trembled under the man's hold. Too weak to battle further, he accepted his defeat. As Corbett bound his wrists together, Wick closed his eyes, unwilling to look at Princess Rhonalyn or Lady Aisley. So much for protecting them.

"Bind Tobias next," Sir Ogden said, his voice grating over

Wick as the ringing faded from his ears, "then the girls."

A cry of pain burst from someone, and Wick lifted his head. The peasant holding Tobias exclaimed angrily, "He bit me!"

"Oh, give him here," Corbett said, heading across the shelter. "I'll tie him up."

"Be my guest." The man shoved Tobias toward Corbett.

Flinging his hands out, Tobias stumbled into the shelter's uneven rock wall.

"Come here, boy," Corbett said, reaching for him.

Tobias turned toward Corbett, a bowl in his hands. He threw it at Corbett's face and screamed, "You'll not take me!"

Corbett ducked the bowl, which flew past his head, but its powdery orange contents dusted his face and shoulders. The bowl shattered against the wall, and Corbett, covered in the powder, straightened with a wrathful look. He headed for the boy, then he stopped and began pawing at his eyes. "Ow! It burns! Get it out! Get it off!"

The man who had been holding Tobias ran for the water bucket. Standing free, Tobias grabbed Lady Aisley's hand and yanked her toward the uneven rock wall.

"You little rat! Where do you think you're going?" Sir Ogden lunged at the two of them.

"Quick! Come on!" Tobias pulled Lady Aisley with him and disappeared from sight, as if they'd walked through the wall.

Sir Ogden thrust after them, leaning his body against the rocks. There was a cry from within the rocks, then Sir Ogden growled in anger and shoved away from the wall.

"Get outside and find them!" Sir Ogden yelled over Corbett's bellowing.

The other man thrust the water bucket into Corbett's hands and ran out of the shelter.

Corbett poured the water over his face and stood blinking and groaning. Princess Rhonalyn stood against another portion of the rock wall, her eyes wide. Wick saw her hands behind her back, searching for anything useful in the hollows of the rocks, even as her gaze traveled to the shelter's exit.

"Don't even…" Sir Ogden extended his sword and touched Princess Rhonalyn's cheek with it. "Show me your hands."

Her fingers paused their desperate search into the crevices, and her chin trembled.

"Now!" Sir Ogden barked.

Flinching, Her Royal Highness extended her empty hands before her.

Sir Ogden grabbed her right wrist and yanked her to him. The force of his pull spun her all the way around so that her back hit his chest. He wrapped his arm around her and pressed his sword across her body and again against her cheek. "I won't repeat myself, so listen well. If there's any more trouble"—Sir Ogden glanced Wick's direction as he spoke in Princess Rhonalyn's ear—"it will be you, Princess, who I'll punish for it. Do I make myself clear?"

Wick remained perfectly still, his lungs refusing to draw air.

Her Royal Highness's face drained of color and her chest rose and fell with swift breaths. "Yes," she breathed. "I understand."

"Good." Sir Ogden shoved her toward the door. "Now, both of you, get outside."

Wick swallowed and exhaled. But then panicked. As weak as he was, even with his hands free, getting up would have been a challenge. Bound, he had no idea how he was supposed to do as the man said. He glanced at Princess Rhonalyn, afraid Sir Ogden would interpret his struggle to comply as his intentionally causing trouble.

Princess Rhonalyn apparently understood his look of alarm for she appealed to Sir Ogden. "Wick's unwell. He'll need help to do as you ask."

The man gestured with his sword. "Then help him."

Stiffening, she walked past Corbett, who was still rubbing his eyes. She reached down and, hooking her arm through Wick's, attempted to pull him up.

Wick cringed as he tried to draw his legs beneath himself. "I'm sorry, Your Royal Highness," he murmured.

"This isn't your fault," she said, anger smoldering in her voice, "but I need you to help me get you up. On the count of three. One, two, three…" She heaved upward with surprising strength.

Wick drew his trembling legs together and managed to gain his footing. The moment he was upright, though, he tipped toward the wall. Without the use of his arms, he had no way to catch himself. Princess Rhonalyn shifted her grasp to stabilize him. Mortified that she was having to keep him on his feet, he tried hard to gain his own balance, but it was like the ground wouldn't stop shifting.

"Get outside." Sir Ogden ordered.

"We're trying." Princess Rhonalyn pulled Wick with her one step at a time toward the exit. Wick's skin prickled with the disgrace and humiliation of being a prisoner and in need of a woman's help, but at the same time he was grateful for Princess Rhonalyn keeping him upright. Painstakingly, they stumbled their way out of the shelter with Sir Ogden swishing them onward with his sword.

Outside, Manton sat in front of a third sword-bearing peasant. Manton's arms were tied behind his back, a doubled rope was bound through his mouth, and a nasty looking bruise was forming on the side of his face. His eyes locked on Sir Ogden with a look of livid fury.

Wick swallowed and murmured to Princes Rhonalyn. "I think I can keep my feet now." His legs trembled under him, but his head was clear. She let go, and he maintained his balance.

The man who had been sent after Tobias, returned, shaking his head. "There's no sign of the other two anywhere."

Sir Ogden growled and grabbed Princess Rhonalyn's arm. "We don't have time for this." He snarled at Corbett as if blaming him for Tobias's escape, "You're just lucky she's the one Baron Fitch wants and not the younger one." He jerked Princess Rhonalyn toward the other man. "Bind her and put her on the mule. The other two can walk."

Princess Rhonalyn spoke. "I can walk. Put Wick on the mule instead. Weak as he is, he'll never keep up."

Wick winced. He appreciated her wishing to spare him the struggle, but he also regretted her suggestion because it meant they would reach their destination faster.

53

GAGE TARRIED A few steps behind the healer as she explained to a village woman how to tend to her burns. When the healer was finished, she headed toward the last few villagers she had not yet tended.

Gage trailed behind her, wishing he could make sense of her.

Suddenly, she stopped and lifted her head toward the descending sun. Urgency filled her creaky voice. "I've stayed too long! I must go!"

"What? Why?" Gage threw out his hand. "You're helping heal people. Isn't that what you do?"

"Yes, and no." Her brown eyes swept to his for the briefest moment, and she murmured in her creaky voice, "You may be the answer, but I've no time now." Shaking her head, she moved away from him. "Someone else must see to the last of the injured." She set off toward the village fields.

"Wait!" Gage hurried after her. "What is it? What's wrong? Let me help, please?" Since he'd been the one responsible for pushing her into coming to the village, he felt responsible for whatever trouble had arisen for her as a result.

Ignoring him, she burst into a run in front of him. No longer the hunched, shuffling woman who had entered the village, she flew across the ground in her dark garb as if her feet had gained wings.

Following after her across the fields and into the trees, Gage tried to catch up. He realized after trailing her deep into the forest that she wasn't heading back to the shelter. She turned that direction, though, when she reached the chasm. Breathing hard, Gage pursued her along its rim. Seeing the same oak tree he'd lost her at before, he put on a burst of speed, hoping to get to her before she eluded him again.

He opened his mouth to plead with her to wait and explain herself, but before he could call out, she grasped the ropes and swung out over the ravine. Gage closed his mouth and came to a halt at the oak.

Clinging to the ropes, the healer swept up and over the edge on the far side of the chasm. The moment that her feet hit the ground, she hooked her ropes onto the tree's closest branch and rushed on.

Gage felt relief that she was safely on the other side but also frustrated that she had evaded him yet again.

The fear and urgency in her voice echoed in his head, and he couldn't shake the feeling that her coming to the village was somehow going to cost her. If he could find a way to follow her, could he perhaps prevent that from happening? Or would he just make matters worse? After all, she might be going home to a jealous husband. In which case, him showing up would not help.

He stood at the ravine's edge, wondering if it were even possible to find the path that her dog took around to the far side. His curiosity and concern tugged at him, but already he had been absent from the others far longer than he had anticipated.

He turned back toward the shelter, but then he paused. Her dog. Where was her dog? He considered the day's events and how the healer had traveled from the village to the oak, skipping the shelter. Was the animal still waiting for her somewhere on her normal route from the shelter? He cringed, hoping he didn't encounter the wolfhound himself on his way through the woods.

Following the nicks he'd previously left in the trees, he made his way back to the shelter. Thankfully, he didn't come across her dog. He circled the shelter and frowned. Neither Manton nor Nigel were anywhere to be seen.

Panic gripped Gage. Had Manton taken Rhonalyn and Aisley and departed without him and Sir Wick? Gage entered the shelter. He came up short. The makeshift beds were a mess and Wick's saddlebags lay along the wall, but no one was there.

Even more concerned and confused, Gage headed back outside. As he emerged, he spotted Nigel's packs heaped between two rocks. He breathed easier. Manton wouldn't have departed without his packs. Feeling uncertainty though over why Manton and the others would have gone anywhere at all, especially with Sir Wick still so unwell, he glanced toward the village. Might they have trekked there to find him? Other explanations swept through him, but Gage refused to let his mind wade their murky waters until he'd checked the village first.

He started toward the village at a walk but was soon running. He entered the charred remains of the main lane and began a swift, thorough search among the villagers. It didn't take long for him to realize none of his companions had come there. He returned to the trees opposite the well. Athalos nickered at him and tugged against his tie. Relieved to find that at least his horse was still where he'd left him, Gage approached the animal.

Athalos tossed his head, then pushed at Gage with his nose as if urging him to get moving. Gage untied Athalos's reins but then just stood there, gripping the leather with no idea what to do next.

Where were the others? Had Baron Fitch's men somehow learned where they were? It was the only thought that made any sense. But when and how? And how had the baron known where to find them?

Had the healer revealed their location to Baron Fitch? If she had, wouldn't the baron have gone straight to the shelter? Gage's heart sank. Or had he given them away himself, when he—a stranger to the village—had suggested sending Tobias to get the healer? He swallowed, but there was no moisture left in his mouth. Any villager could have surmised that he hadn't been alone at the healer's shelter.

Horror and fear rushed through him. He steadied himself with at least the knowledge that there had been no bodies at the shelter. They hadn't been killed on the spot. But if they'd truly been found by the Unavowed, how long would that last? What if it was already too late to save them? Panic twisted in Gage like a living thing. Athalos snorted and sidestepped away. Gage kept his grip on the horse's reins, feeling powerless and at a hopeless loss.

His fear thickened, constricting him with each beat of his heart. His vision began to tunnel, and numbness crept into his limbs. He couldn't pull himself out. Ashamed of his fear and yet incapable of stopping it, he felt his knees buckle. He lurched as he hit the ground. The pain jarred his senses, and in that brief moment, a reminder enveloped him that God knew everything and was bigger than the chaos. Lightheaded, Gage grasped at that truth, speaking it in his mind. "He is bigger than all of this. Nothing is beyond His control. Everything is known by Him. I can't overcome this, but He already did."

Startlingly, fear's grip suddenly released him, and air rushed into his lungs. Gage's heartbeat eased, and he turned his words into a prayer. "God, You know where they are. You know what will happen if the Unavowed lay their hands on Rhonalyn. Have mercy, I beg You, God. Rescue them all from whatever and whoever they face. And, God, please show me what to do. Even if I must go to Strephon myself, marked as I am, I will. Just tell me what to do, and I will obey."

A thought filled his mind. *Ask her for help.*

"Her who?" Gage glanced around. His gaze fell on Lady Ellen, who in her soot-stained dress stood, directing villagers to gather whatever they had left and make their way to the manor house. She was the one person he didn't want to ask.

Yet in uncomfortable and trembling obedience, he stepped

forward trailing Athalos. As he approached the woman, Gage dipped his head. "Lady Ellen"—his heartbeat speed up— "forgive the interruption, but if I may, I need your help."

She smiled wearily. "What can I do for the stranger who saved my son's life?"

Gage swallowed. "Do you know of those the commoners call the Unavowed?"

"No, why do you ask?"

"They are soldiers who ride without colors or coat-of-arms and who've committed acts of treason in Edelmar and Delkara. There are lords who assist them and allow these traitors access to their manors. Thus, the Unavowed remain unstopped and their master unknown."

Lady Ellen stiffened. "Are you suggesting my husband is one of these lords?"

"No," Gage replied. "I mention them because over the last few days the Unavowed have been seeking a particular woman, the same woman Baron Fitch came looking for today."

Emotions churned across Lady Ellen's face. "You think Baron Fitch is assisting these traitorous, these 'Unavowed' soldiers?"

Gage nodded. "That or he commands them."

He expected his words to bring fear or surprise to her face, but instead hope filled Lady Ellen's features. "If you're right about that and Fitch is a traitor to Delkara's crown, that'd give recourse against him. My husband may not be lost to me. If King Strephon could be shown the truth, he would strip away Baron Fitch's barony. We would be free of his tyranny." She recoiled from her own words. "But with what evidence? Such a case must be presented carefully." She glanced at Gage. "Fitch is a powerful baron. King Strephon won't listen to just a claim. There must be indisputable proof of what you say."

"If I'm right, " Gage said, "Fitch is holding captive friends of mine who are allies of King Strephon. I just need to find out where, then I'll have proof."

Lady Ellen eyed him and nodded. "Nissdin's keep is where you'll most likely find anyone detained by Fitch, but you'll need a way to get inside." She tapped a finger to her lips. "I've an idea." She set off, beckoning him to follow. "Come. I'll explain as we collect what you'll need."

54

RHONALYN FELT SIR Ogden's hand tighten on her arm as his man rode back toward them, a dark silhouette against the setting sun.

"I did as you said," the man called out. "I told 'em only that you'd found the location of those Baron Fitch sought." The man pulled in his horse. "His instructions were for you to meet him at the edge of the forest."

Sir Ogden nodded. "Good. Saves us trekking into Nissdin."

With fear rolling through her stomach, Rhonalyn glanced over her shoulder and caught Manton's gaze. Even gagged and with his hands bound behind his back, determination glinted in his eyes.

Rhonalyn's heartbeat quickened. Would Manton make the first move to try to escape or should she? She looked up at Wick. He was barely managing to keep his seat on Manton's mule and wouldn't be able to utilize any of the advantage of being mounted. If she and Manton succeeded, they would likely be leaving him behind.

She cringed at the thought, but it couldn't be helped. They needed to take their chance before it was too late. With a plan forming in her mind, she twisted her head around to glance over her shoulder at Manton. Sir Ogden jerked her forward so hard that the cord binding her wrists cut into her skin. She cried out in anger and pain and watched in shock as blood trailed down her arm.

"I suggest, Princess," Sir Ogden said, his voice cold, "that you keep your eyes on the road so that you don't hurt yourself again."

Her body flushed with fury.

His fingers tightened even harder. "Don't you mean, 'Thank you for the warning'?"

Inhaling, she answered breathlessly, "Yes. Thank you."

"That's better." He quickened his pace, pulling her forward until they were out in front of the others.

Rhonalyn clenched her jaw to keep a whimper from escaping her lips at his grip and breathed through the pain as she kept pace with him. She tried to come up with a different way to fight him, but nothing she thought to say could touch a man who didn't care who she was. There was no way out of this. Trembling, she blessed Tobias for taking Aisley with him in his escape and hoped he would keep the girl safe.

They soon reached the edge of the forest. Dragged off the road into trampled grass by Sir Ogden, Rhonalyn flinched as he drew his sword and squinted into the setting sun. She glanced at the sinking ball of fiery orange herself and wondered if it would be the last sunset she'd ever see.

She could feel behind her the others join them but dared not glance over her shoulder. Instead, she narrowed her gaze and saw a city surrounded by fields in the direction Sir Ogden stared. It was not from the city though but rather from an encampment of tents and pavilions to its north that riders came. Eight armored knights wearing yellow and green surcoats rode surrounding a single unarmored rider.

As they approached at a gallop, foreboding spread through Rhonalyn's body. The knights in their face-concealing helmets slid to a swift stop and separated to allow the nobleman to ride forward. Barely older than Manton or Wick, the young baron wore a collar of gold draped across the dark fur and red weave of his tunic. His hard eyes fell upon her and flickered with a look of surprise. She swallowed hard, wincing at her state and at the same time feeling outraged to be presented thus—bound and striped of her power.

Still holding her by the arm, Sir Ogden bowed and said in the noblemen's tongue, "Baron Fitch, I believe this is the one you were seeking."

"Verily." Baron Fitch gestured, and his men-at-arms dismounted. "And you have my gratitude for bringing her to me, Sir…?"

Rhonalyn felt Sir Ogden's stiffen, though his voice remained steady. "Sir Ogden, Steward of Verfeld. And mayhap to express your gratitude for my loyal service of providing someone of such significant value to you, perchance you would name me the next lord of Verfeld. I assure you my devotion to you would be absolute." Sir Ogden bowed again.

The baron's gaze moved from Sir Ogden to evaluate Rhonalyn. "I supposed it would be a fair reward."

Her skin crawling, Rhonalyn held the baron's gaze, refusing to show submission. He gave her a twisted smile and flicked his fingers. His men advanced. Angst and outrage filled Rhonalyn at their approach. One of the baron's knights reached out for her, and just as she wished she could pull back, Sir Ogden retreated with her, raising his blade. "If my request is indeed fair, Baron Fitch, then it seems to me fitting that I should receive from you a token in pledge of that reward. Would you not agree?"

"I would"—Baron Fitch shifted his horse's reins and kicked the animal forward—"if I were certain you had not simply withheld her in order to come hither now to barter with me."

The pitch of Sir Ogden's voice rose. "I did not, I assure you. I learned of her whereabouts only after your departure from Verfeld."

"Then tell me, who else now knows her whereabouts and your intention to bring her to me?"

"None, Your Lordship! Only these men with me."

"And her young companion? Where is she?"

"Dead," Sir Ogden said. "There was a bit of a skirmish when we came upon them. The girl and their other companion regrettably did not survive."

"Pity you were unable to bring them all, but"—the baron pulled a ring from his finger and handed it to one of his knights—"as a token of your service and the agreed reward, I give you what you have earned."

The knight dismounted and strode toward Sir Ogden, holding out the ring, a thick band of silver surrounding a green stone.

Lowering his sword, Sir Ogden released his merciless grip on Rhonalyn's arm and reached to take the ring.

The moment he did, the knight's opposite hand, moving so fast that Rhonalyn saw it only as a flash, thrust at Sir Ogden's chest.

Sir Ogden grunted. Rhonalyn glanced over and gasped. A thin blade protruded from Sir Ogden's chest. The steward's eyes rolled, and he toppled backward. Rhonalyn stumbled away from him and the knight, her heart pounding in shock.

Cries of alarm behind her and a scuffle brought three other thuds.

Horror knotted in Rhonalyn's chest. A knight strode past the mule upon which Wick still sat, slumped. Three other knights drew Manton forward and heaved him up behind Wick. Then they took hold of her and lifted her onto Sir Ogden's charger. A knife cut through the cords around her wrists, and for a split second Rhonalyn's mind stirred with the knowledge that she was no longer bound. But then the horse was yanked into motion.

The baron's men closed ranks around her. She gripped the animal's mane and was reminded of the night the rebels had first taken her. The abrasion and purple lines left on her wrists from the cords throbbed. With no one close enough to lay their hands on her, she risked glancing back. She spotted, sprawled in the trodden grass at the edge of the forest, the bodies of Corbett, Sir Ogden, and their two other companions.

Rhonalyn's breath shuddered, and her body wavered as she faced forward again. She swallowed against the bile that rose into her throat and wondered how many more horrors, afflictions, and treacheries the day would hold. With her chin trembling, she bit her cheek and commanded herself to shed no tears in front of anyone, no matter what happened.

Blinking, she looked toward the horizon and realized they were riding to the encampment. Before she could sort out why the camp and not the city, they were passing through the camp's outer perimeter. The moment they were within its border of white tents, the baron turned in his saddle and issued orders. "You four, see to those two. Sir Auberon, with me. The rest of you, deliver her to the pavilion next to mine."

Rhonalyn could do nothing but watch as the knights drew her away from Manton and Wick.

55

WITHIN THE SIZABLE pavilion next to Baron Fitch's, Rhonalyn paced between a set of fur-draped chairs and a table with benches. She determined if she stood on one of the chairs, she could reach an unlit lamp hung upon a ceiling support, but without any flame it offered little use as a weapon. She turned to face the table. The fur of the closest chair brushed her bare ankles below her commoner's dress, and she shuddered at the sensation.

She rubbed her wrists. The throbbing purple lines where the cord had dug into her skin were fading, but the cut still stung. She glanced toward the pavilion's door. On either side of it, observing her every move, stood two of the faceless knights who had escorted her there. She had no doubt that if her actions were deemed capable of providing her a defense or an escape, the guards would intervene. As it was, they let her pace, and she didn't attempt to slip under the tent's tightly stretched walls. Nor did she try again to step out the pavilion's door.

When they first released her, she had marched for the door, but one of the guards had stepped in her way. "Baron Fitch requests you stay inside."

"Does he indeed?" she spat. "Well I am Princess Rhonalyn of Keric. He has no right to keep me here. Get out of my way!"

The knight held his position and remained silent behind the mask of his helmet. Twice she tried to go around him. Each time he blocked her way. Eventually, she paced away, and he returned to his post beside the doorway.

"The two men who were brought here with me, where were they taken?" she demanded.

Neither guard answered.

"To detain me is an act of war against Keric. You could be hanged for this."

Neither man shifted.

"What does your baron want with me? Why did he bring me here? Answer me!"

They might as well have been deaf and mute.

She had ceased at that point trying to get any responses from them and paced instead without speaking.

Due to the tent's flaps being closed, the air was muggy and stifling. Sweat dampened her dress and mixed with the dirt and grime on her skin, filling her nose with her own stench. Everything she had ever held as personal strengths were gone.

All the experience of the days since she had stood in royal regalia congratulating herself for her skill in negotiating the harbor toll with King Strephon, accumulated in an undeniable truth—the power that she had thought she possessed was not just fragile but fleeting, and the previous protection and authority of her title was now that which made her valuable only as a commodity in trade to someone who she was pretty sure wanted her dead.

Her breath caught, and her stride faltered. Death loomed before her as a black abyss, and every bit of her was terrified by it. Despite all she had been, done, and planned to do, she had nothing to cling to now, no hope or certainty of any ability or power capable of transcending death. Everything she had once thought mattered now felt so tremendously and horrifyingly irrelevant.

She turned away from the knights and clamped a hand over her mouth, suppressing a scream of panic that filled her lungs. She was nothing, and she was going to die as nothing.

☙❧

The two knights released their hold, and Wick fell to the ground with a groan. Having been hauled from the mule's back by the guards, he and Manton had been dragged through a tent to an open field that was being walled in by tents. Two huge trees stood in the space, and he and Manton had been deposited near the eastern most of the two trees.

With his hands still bound and his face against the ground, Wick's body trembled, and his arms ached from the unnatural angle of having his wrists tied behind his back. Having struggled the whole journey just to stay atop the mule, he was exhausted and glad to just lie still.

At the rattle of chain links, he tipped back his head. One of the knights was gathering a set of iron shackles from the base of the tree. Two other knights pulled Wick up by his arms and placed him on his knees. Meanwhile, Manton was seized and drawn past him. The knight with the shackles sliced the rope binding Manton's hands and another cut off his rope gag. They then yanked Manton's arms in front of him and latched the shackles around his wrists. A rope was thrown over one of the tree's branches. Its one end was tied through the chain linking Manton's hands. Two knights heaved down on the rope's opposite end, hoisting Manton until his arms were stretched above his head, and he was balanced on his toes. The knights tied off the rope and kept their distance as their fourth member approached Manton.

Wick's throat went dry, and his skin prickled at what he knew was coming.

Manton's face was a hard mask, but his chest rose and fell with rapid breaths.

The knight spoke to Manton in the commoners' tongue, his voice carrying contempt and amusement. "You and your little commoner rebels like to believe you're a bane to us, but you're only the nuisance of flies biting at our horses' ankles." The knight unsheathed his dagger. "Still, there's a good deal of satisfaction in killing flies." He made a slash toward Manton's chest.

Manton flinched, his body rocking on his toes.

The knight—who had halted his blade just before Manton's body—laughed. "That's right, fear me. By the time I'm done with you, you won't just flinch. No, you'll tell me everything you've ever known about every rebel you've crossed paths with, and still you'll be begging for mercy."

His heart racing and stomach twisting in knots, Wick mustered as much zeal as he could force into his voice and used the one move he had left, praying it would work. "Knight," he called out in the noblemen's tongue, "you art mistaken in your assumption. You think us commoners, but we art part of Her Royal Highness's retinue."

The knight swept around, staring at Wick with a look of surprise and uncertainty. "You art knights of her guard?" he said in the noblemen's tongue. "It is not possible."

Wick scoffed, even as his body wavered with lack of strength. He put as much boldness into his voice as his exhaustion and pounding heart would allow. "And how perchance would you know what is and is not possible when it comes to the retinue of Her Royal Highness, Princess Rhonalyn of Keric? I tell you, we have traveled with her in disguise and have protected her in Delkara from commoners and lord's men alike. So ask whatever way you will, but you wilt find that inquiring about these commoner flies of yours is of little use."

The knight growled, then turned to his fellow knights. "Let him down."

56

"Your Royal Highness."

Rhonalyn glared at Baron Fitch, standing in the tent's doorway between his two knights. Her slew of angry comments and questions all stuck in her throat. His soldiers hadn't been given an order to kill her, but a word from him could change that in an instant.

The young baron's expression became a half-grimace, half-smile. "Forgive me for my response earlier. I was taken aback by your unexpected presence and did a poor job welcoming you as my guest."

She blinked. His guest? Was he playing with her or being genuine?

He continued as if truly trying to explain. "Then there were other matters to which I had to attend, but I hope now to make amends for my earlier negligence. Prithee, let me show you to the accommodations that have been made ready for a guest of your station." He held back the tent's flap.

Curiosity warred with unease within Rhonalyn. Why was he now offering her respect? Had there truly been a misunderstanding?

"Unless you would prefer to stay here?" he added with a hint of either confusion or annoyance.

Figuring that she would end up wherever he wanted her regardless, she accepted his offer and chose to follow him.

The cooler outdoor air greeted her with blessed relief after the smothering heat of the closed tent. She was tempted to breathe easier, but Baron Fitch's presence beside her and the two guards—so close behind her they needed only to reach out to lay hands on her—left plenty of doubt as to her actual standing as the baron's so-called guest.

The baron led her past a second large pavilion of yellow and green. Banners fluttered in the breeze on either side of its open doorway, and inside, furs and ornate furnishings had transformed the space into a lord's chamber. She noted a full set of armor displayed on a rack near the back of the tent, a dark, lion's-foot table holding parchments, and a hooded peregrine falcon perched on a stand. A jess and leash tethered the swift, fierce bird to the spot.

Beyond the tent was enough open ground for a dozen more pavilions. Across a lane, other tents and pavilions of yellow and green had been pitched in formation inside a large area bordered by plain linen tents pitched so closely together they formed a wall around the colored pavilions. She knew from her journey into the camp that there was a second section and outer wall to the encampment beyond the inner layer and that somewhere out there were Wick and Manton.

Baron Fitch led her between two large yellow-and-green tents. Both had their doors tied open to let in the breeze and were furnished with rugs, furs, and four-poster beds. A lack of personal items within each suggested neither was yet occupied. Fitch brought her to a third such pavilion, this one with its door closed. He motioned for her to enter it.

Having no idea what awaited her inside, Rhonalyn hesitated.

"Everything needed should be present within," Fitch said. "The maids wilt assist you. If something is missing, send one of them to me. I wilt see it provided. As for Sir Faran and Sir Knox"—he gestured to his two knights—"they wilt remain outside to see you are not disturbed."

Rhonalyn frowned in confusion. "Everything needed for what exactly?"

Fitch's eyebrows rose, but his tone remained unchanged. "For you to restore your proper appearance, of course. Including water to bathe in and a clean dress."

Rhonalyn blinked in surprise and uncertainty, but at the same time she couldn't help but imagine what it would be like to be clean and clothed in a dress that did not have mud, dust, and sweat dried into it.

Fitch gave her a flat smile. "I assumed you would wish to look yourself before attending this evening's feast."

"A feast? This evening? That I'm to attend?" She wasn't sure whether to feel hopeful or frightened by the news.

"Aye," Fitch said, "though until then, there wilt be many comings and goings as groups arrive, wagons are unloaded, and pavilions are pitched. So, prithee remain safely within until I come for you."

Assenting to what she was no longer sure was a veiled command, Rhonalyn entered the pavilion.

It was a good while later in the light of lamps hanging about the pavilion that Rhonalyn glanced in a looking glass that one of the four maidservants held for her.

"Is it to your likin', or should I give it another try?" the maid asked.

Rhonalyn tilted her chin and evaluated the way the woman had pinned up her damp hair. She pointed to a section. "If you could smooth that spot there, I think it will be adequate." She still didn't even know any of the maids' names. Every time she asked anything personal about them or anything beyond the task at hand, they ignored her. She had stopped inquiring, but it was disconcerting.

"You're certain you don't wish the skirt re-hemmed?" the youngest maid asked.

"I'm certain." Having already taken the dress on and off multiple times to allow them to fit it, Rhonalyn had little patience left for the difference of two finger's width of dragging skirt. "I'll manage it as it is." Just like she had managed to rescue her mother's gold coin and tuck it inside her new underclothes and like she managed to keep a calm expression despite the day's events.

Beyond the tent's walls, she heard the increasing bustle of activity in the camp. By the sound of it, groups of riders and wagons were arriving, and voices called out orders about locations and supplies, directing people to sites inside the inner encampment.

"Now, the jewelry," the oldest maid said.

Rhonalyn looked up in surprise. "Baron Fitch provided jewelry too?" She had placed on her fingers her own two rings but had not expected to wear anything more.

The maid nodded and handed her a small silver-inlaid box. Rhonalyn unlatched its lid. Inside lay a necklace, bracelets, earrings, and a hairpiece, all of them matching and exquisitely crafted. The hairpiece was no crown, but it was far superior to nothing.

"Shall I put 'em on you?"

Rhonalyn trailed her hands over the pieces with their gleaming metal and numerous gemstones. "Yes."

Once the jewelry was in place, Rhonalyn moved to the center of the pavilion's rug and swept herself in a circle. She had forgotten how much delight she felt in the rich flow of expensive fabrics, the weight of an ornate hairstyle, the cool touch of precious metals, and the brush of earrings swinging against her skin. She halted her spin. The fabric of her skirt swirled into curves around her, then unfurled into a smooth cascade. Rhonalyn brushed her hands down the material, straightened her shoulders, and filled her lungs, basking for a moment in the feeling of being herself once again.

The maids, having finished with their task, gathered her commoner's dress and the items used to transform her, then left the tent.

After their departure, Rhonalyn went to the doorway and pulled aside the tent's flap. Sir Knox stepped in front of her. "Your Royal Highness, do you need something?"

She took a step back, but her gaze traveled past him to the hustle and bustle of the encampment. A banner bearing a pallet shield of blue and yellow flapped in front of a matching vertical-striped pavilion. Wagons rolled by, and riders in orange tabards trotted through her line of sight. She could just make out a set of black battle-axes crossed on the orange before the riders disappeared behind the pavilions. Another group followed them wearing halved colors of green and black with a dark-red standing phoenix upon their shield's center. She didn't know who they served, but the fact that other lords men were present felt reassuring but also confounding.

"How long until the evening feast?" she asked Sir Knox in the noblemen's tongue.

"It wilt start once the last lord's entourage has arrived."

Surprised to receive an answer, she dared to inquire further. "How many lords are already here, and how many are left to come?"

"Since I am unaware of how many lords are present currently, I cannot tell you."

"Very well." Rhonalyn turned back into the pavilion and let the flap fall back into place. Questions swirled within her. Why would Fitch host lords at an encampment and not in his manor's great hall? And why bring her there if his intention was to kill her? Or had her assumption about why he had been seeking her been wrong? Was Fitch an enemy or an ally?

As she stood there within the finery of the pavilion and the rich layers of her dress, she realized she felt more caged than free and was pretty sure that if she were Fitch's guest, she didn't want to find out what it was like to be his prisoner. Fear wound its way back through her, and she searched the pavilion for anything she might use as a weapon. Other than the lamps, there was nothing of any use.

She told herself at least at the feast she might be able to snag a knife. That is, if Baron Fitch truly intended for her to attend the feast and not just be a spectacle at it. Agitation twisted in her stomach. Her fingers sought the edges of her mother's coin in her skirt, only to be reminded that the coin was no longer where she had kept it since leaving Keric. Finding it at her waist instead, she swallowed hard and sank down on the edge of the bed, her breathing shaky.

57

THE FLAMES OF the pavilion's lamps around Rhonalyn flickered as someone drew back the door flap. Rhonalyn lurched to her feet. The fabric of her dress rustled, and her jewelry swung, clinking her earrings against her neck.

Baron Fitch evaluated her with his gaze, then gave a satisfied nod. "Verily, my efforts were not in vain, I see. Doors!" He stepped aside.

Hands pulled back both tent flaps, revealing six knights in dark-red surcoats embroidered with crowned golden lions with one paw on a shield and the other on a sword. Rhonalyn drew a breath. Could it really be Delkara's royal guard? The red knights split apart, and there stood their king.

At sight of Strephon in all his royal regalia with a sword at his side and at the sides of every one of his men, Rhonalyn felt such a flood of relief she nearly spoke informally. "Str—Your Majesty."

Strephon let out a burst of air. "Princess Rhonalyn!" He moved toward her, stepping closer than was proper. "I cannot tell you how thankful I am to see you." His fathomless eyes searched hers. "When Baron Fitch told me he had found you, I scarcely believed him." The muscles in Strephon's angular jaw tensed beneath his closely trimmed beard. "The last news I heard of you was from your guard when they sent word your retinue had been attacked in Dinslage and you had been stolen away by armed commoners. I dispatched men to assist your retinue, but upon arriving in Dinslage, they could find no trace of you or your men. I have been beside myself ever since trying to discover your whereabouts. Prithee, tell me how have you come to be so far north?" He opened his mouth as if to ask more but then paused, awaiting her response.

His regard and outstretched hand of compassion filled Rhonalyn with an abundance of appreciation and for a moment she teetered on the brink of wanting to melt against him and in tears letting his power encompass and comfort her. But the moment she envisioned doing so, she stopped herself. By no means would she take any action that would hand herself and her power over to him. He was a fellow royal, not her king nor her rescuer. She glanced toward Baron Fitch but refused to give him that title. He had not rescued her. She clamped down on her convoluted feelings and reminded herself that there was work yet to be done. Her men were still missing, and she needed Strephon's help to locate and rescue them.

Strephon had asked for an explanation of her travels, and she would give him what he asked, for there was much he needed to hear. He knew about the commoners, but it was the threat of the Unavowed that he needed to understand. She glanced once more at Baron Fitch. He had facilitated her reunion with Strephon, but still she felt uncertain about him.

"Will you not speak to me?" Strephon asked, his voice holding concern.

She returned her gaze to him. "May we not speak privately?"

Strephon's eyebrows rose, but he waved away his knights. "Leave us." Then he turned to Baron Fitch. "You no doubt have other matters to attend to, particularly with this evening's feast fast approaching."

Fitch's gaze shifted between the two of them, then he lowered his head in a brief bow. "I do indeed, Your Majesty." He straightened and departed with his knights who let the pavilion's door fall closed.

Suddenly alone inside the pavilion with Strephon, Rhonalyn was even more unsettled. In the past, always one of her maids, lady-in-waiting, or guard stood with her or within sight at such a meeting. She knew Strephon's knights were barely out of sight and could be called at a moment's notice, but still it felt different since they were his people, not hers. Unsure if she was afraid or just uncomfortable, she inhaled a slow breath and reminded herself that they were two royals about to discuss matters of treachery. Fear and awkwardness were bound to be part of the equation.

"Well?" Strephon said. "We art alone. Will you not now tell me what you hesitated to say before?"

She decided it was best to give him the worst of it first and quickly. She spoke in a hushed but firm voice, "You have traitors in your midst, lord's men who seek to undermine you."

Strephon's eyebrows shot up, but then he seemed to take the information in stride. "Prithee, go on."

She did, telling him what had happened outside of Dinslage in the meadow. "Their plan was to kill me and blame my death on the commoners."

"Yet you escaped, thank goodness."

"Aye, and after two days hiding from them, I sought to return to my guard. But by then those of my guard who had been searching for me were missing. I believe this was by the hands of those same treacherous soldiers. My two guardsmen, who remained at the inn, served unwittingly as bait in a trap to bring me out of hiding—a trap that was thwarted due to the quick thinking and"—the words caught in her throat—"self-sacrifice of my men."

Strephon's forehead furrowed, and he shook his head. "This is distressing news indeed. Tell me, have you had any further encounters with these soldiers? Can you tell me anything more about them that could be useful in apprehending them?"

"Aye, I have learned more. It is they, not rebel commoners, who are crossing the border between our two kingdom's and attacking us both. They are disguising themselves in whatever way benefits them in redirecting blame and sowing discord and distrust among us and our people. Your authority and leadership especially are being thrown into question among your people by these treasonous lord's men."

"It seems I was right then," Strephon said. "It is high time to deal with them." He smiled. "I tell you the hour of your arrival and this information could not have come at a better time. It is in great part for this very purpose—to deal with the treason taking place among my lords—that this gathering has been called."

Astonished, Rhonalyn spoke. "Then you already knew you had traitors in your midst?"

"Aye. I have been trying to root them out for months. As to who specifically leads them, that I have not yet discovered."

"What of Baron Fitch?" Rhonalyn asked, lowering her voice even further.

"Fitch?" Strephon sounded confused. "You suspect him of being against me?"

When he said it aloud, she found herself far less confident of her speculation. "Well, his actions have been of a questionable nature. He injured and killed commoners and noblemen, set fire to a village, and murdered three commoners and the steward of Verfeld right in front of me."

Strephon's voice took on an understanding tone. "You art concerned Baron Fitch's actions were unjustified and thus, that he is acting in a treasonous manner. I assure you, neither is the case.

"Fitch's men tracked you to Verfeld, and like me, he believed you were taken by rebel commoners and was concerned about the lies they may have told you and that you may from their grasp fall into the hands of traitorous soldiers and lords. He no doubt hoped to recover you before anyone could succeed in making you vanish again. Fortunately, the traitor who did find you was more interested in currying favors with Fitch than turning you over to those who very well may have made you disappear."

So Verfeld's lord had been part of the Unavowed. Cold ran up Rhonalyn's spine, making her shudder. "Aye, it was fortunate."

"And surely you recognize that Fitch was justified in striking down Verfeld's steward, the man thought he could use a princess to barter with a baron." Strephon added. "As for the lord and village, lords claim they art holding to law and justice, but they subvert justice by concealing and protecting those aligned against me, noble and common alike. So you see, it is a hard and messy business trying to determine who I can trust and who I cannot."

"I understand." The complexity of what he faced was by no means lost on Rhonalyn. Especially since in Keric they too had been deceived into believing commoners had risen up against them, when in reality it was lords' men. "I have other information about who might be involved with the traitors here in Delkara. A few days ago, we encountered in Burnel one of my men held prisoner in the city square. He was left as another trap for me. The lord there—"

"The lord there was a traitor. He hath been arrested, and replaced."

Rhonalyn sighed in relief. "And my man, Sir Nolan?"

Strephon's forehead furrowed. "I am afraid no one from Keric was found in Burnel. A thorough search was made, since it was hoped you would be discovered, but your knight must have been moved. I promise you, though, we will keep looking for your men."

Rhonalyn swallowed to conceal her distress. She hated the thought of her men facing who knew what abuses. They were currently beyond her reach, but she comforted herself that they would not remain so much longer.

She felt grateful that Strephon was aware of the treason in his kingdom and that he was already hard at work addressing it. She had feared more than she realized that she would come to him with the state of Delkara and discover him oblivious at best and at worst incapable of dealing with those in his own kingdom who were on the move against him. Finding him not just able but already deeply committed to the task restored her admiration for him.

She embraced the new hope that perhaps the Unavowed were nearer to being defeated than she had thought possible. She lifted her chin. "Prithee tell me how I can help you end this treachery in Delkara." She could have sworn she saw amazement in Strephon's gaze, that mingled with amusement, then approval.

"I would very much value your help and counsel to determine the next moves that ought to be made. But first," Strephon said, "attend this evening's feast with me and meet the lords who art loyal to me." Strephon smiled. "You art, after all, already dressed for the occasion. And mayhap this time even hungry enough to eat before doing business?"

She laughed and felt layers of stress and fear fall from her shoulders. "Aye," she said, "I wilt not this time insist upon business before food, I promise. Though with that in mind, I believe it would be beneficial for you to seek the insights of the two men who were brought here with me."

Strephon's smile faltered. "Ah, I should have, but I was informed just a few moments ago that your two men have already departed the encampment."

"What do you mean departed? Wh—"

Strephon held up a hand. "I was told one of my lords commissioned their assistance. A baron of mine had information about a possible location of one of your other guardsmen but needed confirmation before taking action. Your two men eagerly volunteered to help."

Rhonalyn blinked. She couldn't picture Manton being eager to help find her guard, but she could definitely picture him eager to get out of the encampment and away from lord's men. Wick, on the other hand, truly could have been eager to help, though with his injury she hoped the location was close and that he was traveling by wagon.

"You seem concerned?" Strephon questioned.

"Nay." She shook her head and deflected. "I just would have expected them to speak with me first before departing."

"Well, they no doubt understood the urgency in the request."

"Verily." She pasted on a smile, hoping that Manton was looking to disappear and not planning anything involving his rebel friends.

58

LATER THAT EVENING, Rhonalyn smelled the feast before she saw it. Her stomach rumbled hungrily at the tantalizing scent of roasted meat and cooked fruit mingled with the sweet smell of what she was pretty sure was caramel. In place of Baron Fitch's men, she was escorted by four of Strephon's own guardsmen. She rounded a last tent and faced the strip of ground where the feast was being held between Baron Fitch's personal pavilion and a large red pavilion bearing Delkara's royal crest. A dais had been constructed at the end of the strip nearest King Strephon's pavilion. The raised platform held a table covered with a golden cloth, candelabras, and dishes, backed by ornate chairs.

Log fires crackled in at least twenty braziers surrounding the area, and flames and sparks rose from a huge fire pit at the feast's center. Firelight and shadows danced across the guests who took their places amongst the feast's trestle tables. It was not a large company, maybe a hundred people at most, the majority being lords and knights, though a few ladies could be seen in their midst.

While still in the darkness beyond the braziers, Rhonalyn was directed by one of the guardsmen. "King Strephon hath requested you await hither for his announcement of you."

Annoyance trailed through Rhonalyn at being asked to tarry in the dark. But considering the feast was not a merry party but nobles gathered to address treason in the ranks of those not present, she understood the need and benefit of Strephon's hand extended in welcome. Still, she wondered how long she would have to wait.

With her stomach growling, she folded her arms, only to flinch when her fingers landed on the deep bruises left by Sir Ogden's grip. Letting her arms fall back to her sides, she took a slow breath and smoothed her skirt.

A resounding clang from a gong made her start and brought the feast's guests to silent order. Two guardsmen outside Strephon's red tent drew aside its flaps. King Strephon strode forth from the pavilion, followed by several nobles. Upon Strephon's brow rested a much grander band of gold and jewels than he'd worn earlier. It had an impressive red jewel at its center, and draped around his shoulders and trailing to the ground behind him was an ermine-trimmed cape of silver and gold.

The guests pounded the tables in a thunderous greeting. Strephon ascended to the dais and lifted his hands, bringing the group back to silence. Strephon's voice rose over the crowd with such calm confidence that Rhonalyn felt the tension in her body easing as she listened to him. "Deep is my appreciation tonight for you all—those who art loyal and true to me, who have willingly come hither—answering my call to join in restoring peace and prosperity to Delkara. Long have you all endured resistance, offenses, and acts of treason and been only in part free to respond. But my preparations and plans are now complete to turn the tide against those who have continued to oppose me and who have attempted since the very day of my crowning to undermine my authority. It is time to put an end to their treachery. We will reclaim what hath been lost over the years and restore Delkara to her former strength and glory."

A cheer burst from the crowd.

Strephon lifted his hands once more, shushing the crowd. "Also, I am pleased to announce…" He delayed his next words while walking across the platform. "That in this fight with us is Princess Rhonalyn of Keric."

A surprised murmur spread through the nobles and knights present.

Taking her cue from Strephon and his guardsman, Rhonalyn moved toward the dais.

Strephon dipped his head to her. "And tonight she joins us at this feast, at my bidding."

With her heartbeat quickening, Rhonalyn gripped her lengthy skirt and ascended the two steps to the dais. She felt dozens of eyes within the encircling flames come to rest on her. She inhaled slowly and strode toward King Strephon. Perhaps due to the setting or something she saw in his gaze, she felt she ought to bow to him. In a flicker of resistance, she questioned doing so. But they were allies, and she was lower in status than him, so she dipped her head and bent a knee. It was a brief acknowledgment, yet when she lifted her gaze, she could see his pleasure.

In the next moment, the feast's guests thundered their approval.

Thankful to have gotten off on the right foot but also feeling her cheeks warm, Rhonalyn was grateful Strephon turned toward the table that was being occupied by those who had come from his tent. They each bowed as Strephon introduced them to her. "This is Baron Rayburn and Baroness Murielle of Deubor. Carys. And of course, you know Baron Fitch of Nissdin and Baron Selwin of Nikeldon."

Rhonalyn's gaze skimmed over the two lords and the rising couple and slowed in curiosity on the untitled woman whom Strephon had introduced as simply Carys. The woman was still in the midst of bowing. Her long golden hair fell in waves in front of her and cascaded over the shoulders of her regal scarlet dress. Then Carys lifted her head, and Rhonalyn jolted. The skin across the left side of the young woman's face, from her hairline all the way around one eye and down her chin past her lips, was a dark reddish-purple. The horrifying dark hue trailed into Carys's normal skin in a ragged edge that made it clear the color was by no means bruising. More patches of the accursed coloring were on her neck and upper arms. Making it appear as if that which had touched and marked her face was spreading outward across her body. Had the young woman been any closer to her, Rhonalyn would have backed away from her.

As it was, Rhonalyn was stunned when Strephon offered the young woman the chair directly to his left. Shuddering at the mere thought of accidentally brushing arms with the woman, Rhonalyn felt stunned that someone like Carys was allowed within the camp, let alone how or why a touched and untitled woman was seated at the king's high table. She felt disturbed and yet also relieved when Strephon motioned her to his opposite side rather than next to Carys.

In the next moment, food was placed upon the table, and the feasting began. A female voice murmured near Rhonalyn's right ear. "I find her as repulsive as you do, but if you desire to stay in Strephon's good graces, you should really stop staring so severely at her."

Rhonalyn yanked her gaze away from Carys and turned toward the noble lady beside her who Strephon had introduced as Baroness Murielle. "I did not realize I—"

"Oh, prithee," the dark-haired woman said in a hushed, dismissive tone. "At first encounter it can hardly be helped. I mean, who would not stare at the likes of her? But my brother can be quite protective of his disturbing little pet, so as I said, you may wish to curb your gaze."

"Your brother! You art Strephon's sister?" Rhonalyn studied Murielle with more interest. The baroness's dark hair looked nothing like Strephon's nor did her blue-gray eyes, but her facial features bore some resemblance to his.

"Verily, though as you may have witnessed he prefers to introduce me as the baroness of Deubor." Murielle scooped a bite of custard, then paused with it held midair. "As a royal of Delkara, however, who hath long heard the history of Keric and Delkara, I have to say, I am surprised you and my brother are, well, shall we say 'amiable' toward one another?" The custard disappeared into her mouth, and she took a moment to swallow. "Personally, I would never have expected you to enter Delkara at all, let alone travel hither and join in such a goal." Murielle gazed at Rhonalyn with an air of expectancy.

Strephon's voice cut into their conversation. "I do so hope you art making Princess Rhonalyn feel welcome, Murielle."

At his strident warning tone, Murielle smiled past Rhonalyn. "Indeed, Sire."

Rhonalyn felt certain Murielle had in fact meant to be quite unwelcoming, but whether that was due to the history of division between Delkara and Keric or something more personal, she had no idea.

She had no time to figure it out either, for Strephon himself engaged her in conversation then. He asked her about Keric and what sort of changes she wished to make to improve her kingdom. She ate and talked, appreciating his interest in her perspective and opinions and finding his insightful questions refreshing. He shifted the conversation eventually and asked what number of men-at-arms her father kept at the ready to deal with threats and if she thought them adequate. His question caught her unprepared and reminded her of her missing retinue. Distress gripped her, and she lost her focus on the conversation. Her gaze drifted past Strephon and to Carys. Rhonalyn flinched for the young woman's eyes were pinned upon her, and it was as if Carys were seeing straight into her and finding her wanting. But more than that, something in Carys's hard expression told Rhonalyn that she best tread carefully.

Jerking her gaze away and feeling hemmed in by two women who clearly did not want her there, Rhonalyn shuddered. The wooden chair beneath her suddenly felt too hard, the air too thick with smoke and scents, and her churning mind too overwhelmed and wearied by the day's events. A dull, aching pain spread through her head, and she pressed her fingers to her temples.

"Are you well?" Strephon asked, his voice filled with concern.

"Nay," she replied. "I am afraid I have a sudden headache."

"After such a day, it is not hard to understand why. Mayhap you would prefer to return to your pavilion to rest? We can talk more in the morning." Strephon rose and offered her his hand.

Feeling grateful for his understanding and choosing not to look at Murielle or Carys, she placed her hand in his and allowed him to help her rise. He passed her off to the same four of his guardsmen who had accompanied her to the feast and murmured something to his closest man.

The guard dipped his head. "Aye, Your Majesty." The knight extended his armored arm to Rhonalyn. "Your Royal Highness, prithee allow me to help you to your pavilion."

She took his offer and glanced over her shoulder. Strephon had already retaken his spot at the high table and was talking with Baron Fitch. Glad her exit had not disrupted the feast, Rhonalyn was grateful to be escorted back to the solitude of her pavilion.

She hoped sleep would rid her of the headache and unravel the confusion and unease she felt. She needed Strephon's aid to find and rescue her men, and she wanted justice toward whoever commanded the Unavowed, but meanwhile the look Carys had sent her haunted her. There was something amiss in the encampment, and she felt sure the devilish young woman was a part of it.

59

Sitting in a dark tent with his back to Manton and his arms suspended outward, Wick groaned. "Would you stop pulling already? You're only making the chafing worse."

Stretched sideways, Manton continued to strain against the shackles linking their wrists. "If I just had a little more slack, I might be able to reach it with my foot."

Fires outside the tent cast just enough light through the fabric walls for Wick to see the iron loop Manton was attempting to reach. It was one of two the soldiers had screwed into the ground in opposite corners of the tent. Chains ran from both loops to the shackles fettering their wrists and restrained them back to back in the center of the tent. Wick heaved an exhausted sigh. "You're not going to be able to work loose with your toes what two men twisted into the ground using a pole."

"Never underestimate persistence," Manton growled.

With hunger gnawing at his stomach and a dull ache in his side, Wick responded angrily. "Persistence won't make these chains longer. They knew what they were doing, Manton. Give it up."

The pressure on his shackles finally relented, and the rattle of metal was followed by a bump against his back as Manton shifted straight.

They sat in silence then while beyond the tent's walls was the crackle of fires, the clank of chains, the murmur of voices, the distant whinny of a horse, and the thunk of tankards. With his awareness pushed outward, Wick flinched when Manton's hard voice broke the silence.

"What did you tell them?"

"Tell who?"

"You know who," Manton said in an angry whisper. "Out there at the tree when you spoke in the noblemen's tongue to the knights. What did you tell them?"

"Oh, that." With all that had happened, Wick had forgotten about his use of the noblemen's tongue in front of Manton. "I told them they were mistaken, that we weren't rebel commoners but protectors of Her Royal Highness and part of her retinue."

His revelation was met with silence. Wick scoffed. "You're welcome for keeping them from torturing you." He had been afraid at first the knights would challenge his assertion and do as they had threatened regardless, but they didn't. In fact they had accepted what he had said so completely that for a moment, he had even hoped they might set him and Manton free. Instead though, three of the knights had kept them detained in the field while the fourth went to inquire of Baron Fitch.

While waiting, one of their guards gestured. "The others are starting to arrive."

Twisting to see across the area, Wick watched a double line of soldiers with prisoners march through an open tent into the field. The soldiers wore split colors displaying a stag's head on brown and a tower on white. As for the prisoners in their midst, three wore nobleman's clothes, another a monk's robes, and the fifth a surcoat of maroon with a silver badger on it.

Alarmed by the sight of such prisoners, Wick glanced at Manton, hoping to see understanding on his face, but instead he was met by an expression of bewilderment and dismay.

The soldiers steered their captives toward the other tree and fettered them each through links in a long chain that had been fastened between the two trees.

The soldiers were just completing their task when another company of soldiers arrived. The distinct blue and green colors of Nikledon made Wick's heart skip a beat, then lurch into double-time. He turned his head away, knowing that if anyone in Nikledon's ranks recognized him from his and Prince Gage's fight and ensuing escape from Nikledon, his claim of being a nobleman would be countered with assertions of his aid of a rebel thief.

With his face angled down and his heart pounding, Wick stared at the grass, wondering why multiple lords' soldiers would be gathering prisoners of noble rank in an encampment outside a Delkaran city. Were it not for the prominently displayed colors and coats-of-arms of the soldiers, he would have assumed, as he had until then, that it was a gathering of the Unavowed, but now he wasn't so sure.

The fourth knight of his and Manton's guard returned and spoke to the others. "We have new orders. For now we are to secure these two in a tent here in the encampment. At least until things are settled."

"And those in the carts?"

"Sir Treyson and his group will see to them. Duties will then be assigned once every group has arrived. Each party has been instructed to provide at least a knight and two soldiers to take part in guard rotation."

"Right then let's get this done before we have more company."

Two of the knights seized Wick's arms and hauled him to his feet. Wick's mind raced with questions while his legs struggled to hold his weight. What were the things that needed settling? Why were they being held? And where was Princess Rhonalyn?

Now chained with Manton in a tent, he could only conclude that

Baron Fitch was indeed part of the Unavowed or at least an enemy of Keric. Because no lord ordered the guardsmen of another kingdom's royalty unlawfully held prisoner without knowing the statement he was making. Though considering they were being kept out of sight and separate from the other prisoners, that statement was perhaps not yet intended to be public, which created its own collection of concerns as to why the baron was keeping them alive.

"You expect me to thank you?" Manton scoffed and jerked the chains that linked them. "You told them I was a guardsman of Keric and turned me into a lord's man. Which means I'll die as a mockable statement against Keric's crown rather than with the honor due a Delkaran rebel commoner, who's been fighting against tyranny." Manton spat bitterly, "But what would that matter to you? You're one of them—a noble."

Indignant, Wick bawled his fists and growled back. "Yes, I'm a nobleman who disagrees with your actions, but that doesn't mean I align with what other nobles are doing. If I did, do you think I'd be chained here with you? And for that matter, why would I intervene to protect you, a rebel commoner?"

"Perhaps because, though effective, torture is an unreliable means of information gathering. Maybe you told them to chain us up together so you can get what they want from me another way."

Wick blinked, startled by the depths of Manton's distrust and paranoia and at the same time offended that his own past actions and honorable character could be wiped away so easily. "Seriously? You think me desirous and capable of plotting such a manipulative and devious scheme with Baron Fitch's knights and at a moment's notice? We've traveled together for days. Don't you know me better than that by now?"

"Know you? As a nobleman you mean?"

Wick's indignation turned into an embarrassed flush. "I see your point. I lied at the start about who I was. So how can you believe anything I've said or done since or what I'm saying now?"

"Exactly."

Wick gritted his teeth, resenting anew Prince Gage's choices and his own orders that had led to him being a liar. "It seems, then, since we've both deceived each other, that neither your words nor mine will be of any use for us to convince each other of anything."

"So it would seem," Manton said, then fell silent.

Wick found himself looking for something to say. He silently sighed. But why did he care? It wasn't like it mattered what Manton thought or whether or not they trusted each other now. Manton was the only one of them who would suffer if either of them chose to reveal the truth. There was no gain or loss for Wick in what he'd said and done. Though regardless of what Manton thought, Wick was thankful to have been spared watching the soldiers torture him. Considering Manton's choices, a clean judicial death may have been just, but torture was never that.

"Are you titled?"

Manton's question surprised Wick. He was suspicious of Manton's motive for asking but decided to risk giving him part of the truth. "I'm the seventh son of a lord, thus I'm just a knight."

Manton scoffed. "Just a knight, which means in your position you've had the ability to carry a sword and the right to use it to defend yourself and your family. Me, I'm the firstborn of a man who watched as his wife was bludgeoned to death by a lord's son who disliked the way she responded when he struck her three-year-old son for not showing him sufficient deference."

Wick swallowed. A hundred thoughts ran through his head but only one question came out of his mouth. "Who was the nobleman?"

"It doesn't matter anymore," Manton said, "he died of an illness before I was old enough to kill him for what he did to my mother."

Wick couldn't think of anything to say, and silence filled the space.

"You're a lord's man," Manton said, "you're required by law to turn in marked individuals. You knew about Gabe's mark, why didn't you turn him in?"

"Because he was marked falsely and unlawfully. He's not a thief and shouldn't be punished for something he didn't do. And I'll have you know, due to my choice to protect him, there are those now in Delkara who would consider me as much a rebel as you. I don't approve of your methods, Manton, but I do care about justice and the well being of commoners as well as nobles. You've observed my actions over the last several days, you must know by now that I'm not like the nobles that you despise."

Manton snorted and bumped against his back. "What I know, knight, is that a person's actions when they know others are watching them can be just as misleading as their words."

Wick sighed and asked wearily, "Then how do you, Manton, judge if a person is trustworthy or not?"

"By observing what they do when they think no one's around them. That's what shows the truth of who someone is. What loyalty they'll keep and whom they'll betray is made evident by what they do in the dark." Manton's shoulder bumped against his. "And, you were right to distrust me. I was never going to take you all to Ithera. I chose to show Her Royal Highness Delkara, hoping that her seeing what was happening here would change her mind. And it did, but not enough to steer her away from King Strephon. Had we reached Koth, companions of mine would've detained you all to prevent exactly this—her ending up in the hands of the Unavowed."

Wick wasn't surprised by Manton's confession, but still fury burned in his chest. "Here you accuse me of being like the nobles. I saved you from torture because I believe no one should be treated so. Meanwhile, you'd have made prisoners of the four of us."

"Yes, because this is a war." Manton's hushed voice took on a new level of intensity. "And now the Unavowed have Keric's princess. You saw the other prisoners out there. They're not commoners. They're moving against their fellow lords, which means the Unavowed are no longer hiding. Delkara is lost."

Wick found himself twisting his wrists in the shackles, even as he rejected Manton's suggestion that the Unavowed's conquest of Delkara was inevitable. "They haven't won yet," he grunted. "Others are still out there. Gabe is still out there. Your people are still fighting back."

"Except that the knight spoke the truth," Manton admitted in a tone of defeat. "My people have only the resources to harass, not to win. As for Gabe, what can he do? No one of rank will listen to him, and marked as he is, he won't get far. The borders are closed. And considering who's being held prisoner out there, he'd be hard pressed to find anyone left in Delkara with enough power and means to change the course of this. No, the scythe of the Unavowed has done its reaping, and the field is left bare."

"You know who their prisoners are?" Wick asked.

"I know three by appearance, others by insignia or reputation. Among those the soldiers of Phenes brought, I recognized the lord of Ivett. From the insignia of the silver badger on the knight, I would guess that the noble with him is Koth's lord. The monk is Abbot Micah of Burnel's monastery."

Wick stiffened. "You mean from the same monastery we just left El—"

"One and the same." Manton added. "And if I'm not mistaken, the thin, pale lord fettered beside the abbot is Burnel's lord. As for those in the custody of the Nikledon soldiers, I recognized Lord Hadrian of Delipp and the lord of Legan." He scoffed. "Fools, the lot of them. They could have rallied together and used their power to stop the Unavowed while they had the chance, but they didn't. And now because of their spineless efforts and half-applied principles, even what little they bothered to protect will suffer and probably at a higher price, just like those in Verfeld."

A shudder ran through Wick's weary, abused body. He didn't know how much of Manton's suppositions were true, but he feared Manton was right about at least one thing: the Unavowed were on the move.

60

With a cloud-covered sun rising behind him, Gage cantered toward Nissdin. Athalos fussed beneath him about the noise of Gage's armor. Him disguising himself in the mended and cleaned uniform of one of the soldiers left behind by Baron Fitch, had been Lady Ellen's idea for how he could enter and search Nissdin's keep. He hadn't fit the one knight's armor so he rode as a soldier, whose armor was lighter and less substantial than that knights but still more complete than most soldiers.

Gage had wanted to depart for Nissdin the night before, but Lady Ellen had pointed out that the gates would be closed and that arriving in the morning would mean fewer questions asked and provide him more time to search. It also meant once he found the others, he could locate and use a Nissdin carrier pigeon to send word to Ithera, requesting that King Strephon ride to Nissdin where he could see for himself the proof of Baron Fitch's treachery.

The plan hinged on a number of suppositions: that Rhonalyn and the others had actually been taken by Fitch, that they were in fact in Nissdin, that King Strephon was actually at Ithera, and so on. Yet as flawed as the plan was, it was all Gage had.

Putting on the pilfered uniform, he had hoped the chainmail, plate armor, helmet, and sword would make him feel like he once had as a jouster—confident and invincible. But the armor felt less like an assurance and more like the hot, cumbersome weight of a burden he was uncertain he was capable of carrying.

The gauntlets made his fingers clumsy, the straps of the plate armor rumpled the padding and pinched his skin, and the helmet's face shield restricted his sight. He longed to be able to move freely, but despite the aggravations of the armor, having metal between himself and any enemy's weapon did hold at least some sense of added protection.

He just hoped he made a convincing enough Nissdin soldier that he didn't need to put the armor to the test. He also hoped he didn't need the additional knives he'd concealed about his person.

Crossing through the extended shadows of tree branches, Gage spotted two moving forms ahead. One was human. The other appeared to be an animal. He kept his gaze on the pair and, drawing closer, recognized them both. Surprise and hope burst through him. It was Tobias and the healer's wolfhound. He urged Athalos toward them.

Tobias looked up, and his expression filled with panic. The boy veered toward the woods, trying to pull the huge dog with him. For a moment Gage didn't understand his actions, then the reason dawned on him. Stopping Athalos, Gage tugged off his helmet. "Tobias! It's alright. It's me, Gabe."

The boy let out his breath and released his grip on the wolfhound's collar.

Gage urged Athalos closer but with the dog present refrained from dismounting. "Tobias, how'd you come to be all the way out here? And, my companions from the healer's shelter, do you know where they are?"

With fear in his eyes, the boy nodded. "Aisley insisted we follow 'em. So we did, hoping somehow we could help 'em get away. But then Baron Fitch came with his knights. Without even so much as a warning, they killed Sir Ogden, Corbett, Mortsen, and his brother.

Then they took Keric's princess and your two other companions back to an encampment."

"A camp? Where?"

Tobias shuddered and pointed over his shoulder. "Northwest of Nissdin. A whole bunch of lords arrived there last night. I didn't recognize all their colors, but I told Aisley that sneaking in was a bad idea. Once it was dark, she said no one would notice her in the shadows, and she went. I waited for hours, but she didn't come back."

Gage's stomach twisted. An encampment of lords of which Baron Fitch was a part. Was Aisley more at risk or safer because other lords were present? He had no way of knowing.

"I tried hard to convince her not to go." Tobias's young voice was filled with mournful distress. "But she wouldn't listen."

Gage shook his head. "It's not your fault. You did what you could and were wise not to follow her. Thank you for your help, Tobias. Return to Verfeld. I know where they are now. I'll ride to Ithera and seek an audience with King Strephon to—"

"King Strephon's not at Ithera," Tobais said. "He's at the encampment."

"King Strephon's at the encampment?" Gage gripped Athalos's saddle, trying to recalibrate his understanding of the situation with Tobias's additional information. "You're sure?"

"I'm sure," Tobias replied in a defensive tone. "His was the third party to arrive. I mayn't know all of which colors belong to which lords, but I know the royal coat-of-arms of Delkara. And I saw with my own eyes His Majesty in his king's helmet."

Gage stared down the road. How could that be? Why would Baron Fitch search out Princess Rhonalyn, calling her a criminal, then take her to King Strephon? The Unavowed had wanted her dead, not as their prisoner. And as Rhonalyn herself had pointed out when Manton claimed King Strephon was head of the Unavowed, if Strephon had wanted her dead or as his prisoner it would have been pointless for him to negotiate with her first and then let her leave Nikledon.

Gage took a breath and stared down the road. Had he gotten the situation wrong then? Was Fitch not part of the Unavowed? Could it be instead that the young baron had been aware of Sir Ogden and his men and come to Verfeld knowing that Rhonalyn wasn't safe there but had also not wanted to give her away? Had Baron Fitch's intentions been to rescue Rhonalyn? It was possible.

Yet from all Gage had witnessed of Fitch's actions at Verfeld, it seemed unlikely. Fitch's men had killed villagers and the lord's son when they could have just taken them into custody. Whatever his allegiances, Baron Fitch was not an honorable man, so what did he want with Keric's Princess?

Could it be King Strephon was at the encampment but unaware of Princess Rhonalyn's presence there? What if Fitch had sought out Rhonalyn to use her against Strephon? Possibilities ran through Gage's mind. He questioned Tobias. "Did King Strephon arrive before or after Baron Fitch took Princess Rhonalyn and the others to the encampment as prisoners?"

"After," Tobias replied. "And only the two men were taken as prisoners. Keric's princess was cut free before they rode to the camp."

Gage blinked. Rhonalyn had been freed but not Sir Wick and Manton. That didn't make any sense unless…could Rhonalyn have denounced Manton as one of her kidnappers? But why would she not tell them that Sir Wick wasn't involved? Or had she, and no one had cared? Or had Sir Wick been recognized as having fled Nikeldon with him, a marked rebel? Or was Tobias wrong and Rhonalyn was still a prisoner? What if Fitch had cut her loose only for appearance sake?

Unsure what to believe or think, Gage knew he needed to find Sir Wick and the others and learn the truth about Baron Fitch's allegiances. To do so, he would have to venture into the encampment not knowing what he might encounter there, but it didn't matter, he was determined to rescue Sir Wick, and if need be, the other three as well.

61

With his helmet on and his sweat-moistened gauntlets tight on his reins, Gage nodded to the three Nissdin soldiers stationed at a gap in the encampment's outer tent wall. He expected them to question him about his previous whereabouts and his late arrival, but the soldiers simply waved him past. His heart pounding, he rode into the camp, grateful for their lack of curiosity but also astonished they would trust his uniform so implicitly.

The moment he saw the camp's grid-like layout of tents, though, he realized why they weren't concerned about his identity or about securing the camp. In every direction were lanes upon lanes of tents occupied by lords' men-at-arms, each capable of defending their own with deadly force.

Among the colors, flags, and insignias represented, Gage recognized the coats-of-arms of Nissdin, Maneo, Phenes, Burnel, Dinslage, Duvall, Lyster, and Nikledon. He also saw three other lords' colors he had seen at Nikledon's fair, though he did not know to which Delkaran lords or lands they belonged. The soldiers present were busy and active but in a way that lacked direction or urgency. It seemed they were awaiting something or someone and simply keeping themselves occupied until such a time as action was required of them.

Ahead was a second wall of tents with an entrance that led through into an area in the center of the encampment. Through the opening, Gage spotted the top of a red pavilion and a red flag. As he watched, it flipped about twice then unfurled in the wind, displaying Delkara's royal crest.

Gage paused Athalos and considered what to do. He could approach King Strephon and ask about Princess Rhonalyn's whereabouts, but then what? He may learn that Strephon knew about Rhonalyn's presence in the camp, and everyone was safe, and Fitch was not part of the Unavowed. But if Fitch had Rhonalyn hidden away and had disguised his plans as a member—or as head—of the Unavowed, then him approaching King Strephon could put them all at risk. It could also be that Rhonalyn and Aisley were safe among the lords, but Sir Wick and Manton were being held as rebels. And if Gage revealed himself, he would more than likely be held too, unable to take action or advocate on anyone's behalf.

He had no desire to be in a position where it would be his word against any of the Unavowed. He needed proof, which meant finding the others without being discovered himself or giving Fitch a reason to kill them.

Gage considered the encampment's layout. Where would Baron Fitch keep his prisoners, especially if he wanted them kept a secret? Would it be somewhere close to the baron's own tent in the inner layer of the camp, or would Fitch put them in the outer layer, distant enough to allow him deniability?

Guessing the latter, Gage turned Athalos down a lane that ran beside tents occupied by Nissdin soldiers and began his search in the outer camp. Fitch's soldiers hung around their yellow-and-green tents in groups of two to five, doing everything from sparring to tossing dice and playing cards while eating and drinking. Despite the soldiers being at leisure, all activities were done in a constrained manner, confirming to Gage that they were indeed awaiting something. For nowhere was the mindless debauchery and drunkenness of men free to indulge themselves.

Steering around soldiers in the lane and glancing in tents as he rode, Gage flinched at every crack and smack of the wooden wasters echoing around him from multiple sparring matches. A soldier leaving one of the matches lifted a hand at him in greeting. Panicking for a moment, Gage hesitated, then lifted his hand back. The soldier tipped his helmeted head and turned toward another soldier. Hoping he had not just given himself away, Gage gritted his teeth. He urged Athalos a little faster, his rapid breathing filling his own helmet.

Athalos snorted and shifted beneath him.

Gage forced himself to decrease his breathing and tried to slow his heart rate. He was relieved when no soldiers called out and Athalos carried him onward with only snorts and head tossing and didn't try to dump him.

Tent after Nissdin tent was either empty or occupied only by soldiers.

He reached the end of shelters of yellow-and-green and found himself facing a line of horses and mules and a wall of open-faced tents forming the encampment's whole southern side. Picketed the length of that edge of the camp were the mounts and cart mules from it seemed every company there. The tents held the animals' tack and feed, and to the east down the line of animals, parked in a clump, were supply carts. Most were half-sided carts with no tops, but a handful of other wagons were tall, squarish, and cloth-covered.

Gage steered Athalos to these wagons and pulled back a corner of one of the cloth covers. Beneath was a portcullis-like metal lattice. His stomach clenched. They weren't wagons for moving things. They were cages. He glanced about. Nowhere was any sign of who or what had been transported in them. In the trodden grass behind the carts though were ruts telling where they'd been. Gage laid his reins across Athalos's neck to follow the tracks backward to where they'd been unloaded, but Athalos resisted his direction. Gage shifted his hands to pull Athalos around. Athalos shook his head, sidestepped, and nickered.

Down the picketed line, a mule brayed back.

Gage knew of only one mule his horse had ever greeted. He gave Athalos his head and let his horse trot that direction. He spotted Nigel a moment later. The mule tugged at his tether and brayed at them.

"You're here," Gage murmured, "so where's your master and the others?" He glanced back at the cages. "Hopefully, wherever those have been. Otherwise, I may have to search this whole camp."

To draw less attention and be better able to track the carts, Gage slid off Athalos and tied him beside Nigel. He then followed the wheel ruts across the camp, speeding up or slowing down to avoid or let pass this or that soldier or group of lord's men. Keeping one eye on those around him and the other on the ruts, he tracked the wagons' route north.

The ruts eventually turned west and drove through a tent that made up part of a wall of the encampment. Occupying the open-faced tent were two chatting soldiers, one wearing Lyster's chevron of blue on red and the other a tabard with blue and yellow stripes.

Above the tent Gage could see the tops of two large trees. Since it would have been strange not to utilize the trees' shade, he guessed the tent that the two men guarded was not an exit from the camp but rather an entrance to another portion of it. Would the guards let him walk through into the area like those at the main entrance had? There was only one way to find out.

His heart speeding up, Gage strode into the tent, trying to look like he knew what he was doing. The Lyster soldiers stepped toward him, and panic squeezed the air from Gage's lungs.

"Hey, any news yet from the morning's meeting?"

Swallowing to moisten his mouth, Gage shook his head at the Lyster soldiers. "No, not that I've heard." He pointed toward the back flaps of the tent. "I have orders to…" He trailed off, not sure how to finish his sentence.

"Yeah, yeah." The Lyster soldier waved dismissively at him.

Taking that as permission, Gage proceeded, pushing through the back flaps of the tent and into the area beyond. As the fabric settled behind him, his stomach dropped.

Shackled along a chain running between the two trees were noblemen. Some were dirty and bruised. Others were clean and unharmed as if they'd anticipated a feast but were greeted instead with chains.

Gage swept his gaze over those along the line, searching for Manton and Sir Wick. He spotted Lord Braxton instead. The man's tunic was singed and torn, and his face was still bloody from the battle he had lost the day before. Farther down the line, Gage recognized Lord Hadrian of Delipp. Hatless, with his metal-gray hair tangled and his beard scruffy, the older lord looked exhausted but uninjured. In the middle of other nobles Gage didn't know, he noted with a sharp intake of breath the abbot from Prior Joseph's monastery in Burnel.

He stared at the line of prisoners. Why would nobles and an abbot be brought to the camp? He tried to make sense of the situation. Could it be King Strephon was holding royal court in the encampment instead of at Ithera? That would explain the prisoners. Disputes and accusations among lords and high-ranking individuals were judged in royal court. So, it was possible the lords and other prisoners had been brought there for their cases to be presented before King Strephon. The thought provided Gage hope that perhaps despite what Manton said, justice may still exist in Delkara. Then he frowned. But how was

King Strephon supposed to judge rightly when someone like Baron Fitch could tell any which way he wished the story of how and why a nobleman like Lord Braxton was arrested?

"You next on guard duty?"

The voice made Gage jump and turn. With his helmet blocking his view, he hadn't noticed a Nikledon soldier come up beside him. He swallowed hard. The soldier's chainmail hood rested around his shoulders rather than under his lightweight helmet, and he eyed Gage questioningly.

Trying to find an answer, Gage glanced from the soldier's blue-and-green tabard to the mix of colors represented among the dozen or more lords' men stationed around the outer edge of the area. "No, I…um, was just sent to ask one of the, um,"—he motioned out toward the trees—"prisoners a question. I was trying to locate him. I've found him now." He took a step forward.

"Wait!" the guard snapped.

Gage jerked to a stop. With his heart reverberating in his ears, he turned back to the soldier, fearing he was about to be revealed as an imposter.

The soldier jutted his chin at him. "Aren't you forgetting something?"

Having no idea what he meant, Gage stood frozen in place.

"Your weapons," the soldier said. "We're supposed to leave them here when you approach the prisoners."

"Right. Of course." Gage took a breath. Relieved yet uneasy about leaving his weapons behind, he stripped off his belt holding his looted sword and dagger and deposited it near the tent wall before trudging toward the chained men. Nowhere could he see Sir Wick or Manton, but he continued regardless, his mind scrambling for a plan.

He angled toward Lord Braxton, noting the two noblemen

shackled on either side of him. All three men watched his approach with a mix of fear and fury. Braxton's fists coiled in the metal cuffs holding him. Straining against his shackles, the lord spat at Gage, "You're murderers, all of you!"

Convinced Lord Braxton was right about the Nissdin soldiers's actions at Verfeld and having lost Allard to the Unavowed and been himself accused and chained by the Unavowed, Gage understood all too well Lord Braxton's response. He crouched in front of the man, close enough to be heard at a whisper but not reached. "They are murderers. They unjustly killed your son, Charles, and many of your villagers. But hear me, your youngest son, Paten, and your wife Ellen are both alive and well."

For a moment Braxton's face filled with relief, then anger consumed his voice once again. "And to keep them that way, what do you want from me?"

Gage winced. So much for building trust. He'd hoped his words would help convince the lord that he was on his side. He swallowed. Actions spoke louder than words. At least that's what Baron Roger always said, but dare he take such an action? He needed information, and the only way he was going to get it was if Lord Braxton trusted him.

Gage glanced up and down the line of prisoners to confirm no guards were in line of sight to see what he was about to do. Then he withdrew one of his concealed knives and slid it, hilt first, across the grass into Lord Braxton's reach. "I'm not here to threaten you. I believe you were arrested unjustly, and I want to prove it. In return, if you're willing, I need your help."

The noblemen on either side of the lord murmured to one another. Taking the knife, Lord Braxton made it disappear into his tunic, then squinted at Gage. "My help with what?"

"Baron Fitch is holding three friends of mine prisoner. Two men and a young woman. They would've been dressed as commoners. One man has dark hair and the other light. Have you seen them?"

Braxton shook his head. "The only prisoners I've seen are the ones here, and there're no commoners among us."

Gage considered for a moment. "What about the princess of Keric? Have you heard anything of her?"

The nobleman left of Braxton shifted and spoke quietly. "Two guards earlier were talking about Keric's princess being at last night's feast."

Gage's breath caught. "Was she there as a prisoner or as a guest?"

The nobleman shook his head. "By the way they spoke, it could have been either."

Gage's mind grappled with the information. Rhonalyn being alive and at the feast implied King Strephon knew of her presence in the camp, but what about Sir Wick and Manton? "Do you know if—"

His question was cut off by the nobleman's sharp, quiet warning. "Incoming." The man ducked his head.

Lord Braxton recoiled as well, his chains clanking as he diverted his gaze.

Realizing another guard must be approaching and then hearing the rattle of armor behind him, Gage stood up and whirled around, hoping to intimidate whoever it was into leaving them alone. "Back off! I'm handling this!"

62

As the words left his mouth, Gage found himself staring at a knight's surcoat of blue and yellow stripes. He lifted his gaze to an open-faced helmet and instantly recognized the high cheekbones and deep-set eyes of a man he'd last seen on a manor outside Nikledon. Panic smashed through Gage, and the mark on his wrist pulsed with phantom pain.

"It would seem my reputation precedes me." Sir Jarret leaned forward, his eyebrows lifting. "You were saying something about handling things?"

Desperately hoping the face-concealing Nissdin helmet would keep the knight from identifying him, Gage sidestepped out of Jarret's line of sight. "Yes, and, I um, was just finished." Forcing his trembling legs not to lurch into a run or buckle beneath him, Gage turned and headed toward his weapons. If nothing else, he would go down fighting this time.

He expected Sir Jarret to catch hold of him and yank him around or else yell for other guards to stop him. But, without interception, he reached where he'd left his belt. Snatching up the weapons, Gage attempted to strap on the belt as he kept walking, but his fingers wouldn't cooperate. With his heart pounding and heat filling his chest, he desperately wanted to turn to see if Sir Jarret was coming after him, but he didn't dare look back.

Finally succeeding in buckling his belt, Gage reached the entrance tent. His limbs were cold and his fingers tingled. He reached out to grab the tent flap to pull it aside. He couldn't grasp the fabric, his hand was shaking so badly. Shoving through the fabric instead, he hurried onward.

The two soldiers in the tent glanced his way but made no attempt to stop him. Gage kept moving. Within five strides he reached the lane. Ten more strides and he was mingling with the encampment. He hastened south, his heart racing and his body quacking. Memories of the beating he had taken at Sir Jarret's hands, the shackles, the knight pinning him against the wall of the smithy, the searing pain of the branding, Jarret's threat of further abuses all of it bled fear into every fiber of his being. He had no doubt if the knight saw through his disguise, Sir Jarret would shackle him and then take pleasure in causing him pain.

His mind consumed with that though, Gage fled across the camp. He was all the way back among the Nissdin soldiers' tents, before his mind could think beyond getting out of the knight's sight and reach. Positive no one had followed him, he slowed to breathe and found himself having to grip the guy line of a tent to keep himself upright.

He had no more doubts. There were members of the Unavowed in the camp. But were they there simply because they were lords' men or were they present for their own reasons? And was Baron Fitch one of them?

Gage shook his head. He couldn't spend time worrying about why right now. He needed to find the others as fast as possible and get them out of the camp. But if not with the other prisoners, where were Sir Wick and Manton? Since Rhonalyn had been at the feast, she was likely to be somewhere in the camp's center. But nothing in Gage wanted to venture there.

He was alone. If caught, he would be at the full mercy of whoever laid hands on him. No matter what, he would be shackled for his mark and either be facing a member of the Unavowed or be stuck trying to convince King Strephon to believe him over whatever lies the Unavowed told.

Fear of what that could mean for him along with the unlikelihood of success compared to the significant consequences of failure spiraled together inside him, growing and converging into an all-too-familiar consuming anxious panic. Gage let go the guy line and quickened his steps, wanting nothing more in that moment than to be on the move.

Realizing after more than a few strides that he was heading straight for Athalos, Gage heard Haaken's accusing voice in his head. *"You are running scared."*

He shoved the thought aside. He didn't care. He needed to get out of here.

"Fear will always tell you that any risk is not worth doing what is right."

Gage slowed between two tents, his heart pounding. What was he doing? Was he really going to just leave without Sir Wick? And what about Manton, and Aisley and Rhonalyn? His breath caught. "Oh, God, help me! I want to run."

He saw in his mind, God as King of the Universe directing him toward a task and himself backing away and running toward what he thought was safety. Gage swallowed hard. He knew where true safety was and it wasn't in walking away. He'd been welcomed into rescue by the One who possesses absolute power and control over all things. Why was he still running and why was he still afraid?

Almighty, all-knowing, and all-seeing, his God reigned over every circumstance, every ruler, every person great or small. Creator of it all, able to speak the world into existence and a storm into silence. "LORD God," he prayed, "nothing exists outside Your reach or beyond Your control. I know You have brought me here for a purpose. Please, don't let me run." At the declaration and request, Gage felt the anxiety swirling through him yield before something not of himself. Swallowing and exhaling slowly, he dipped his head. "God, I am Yours. Tell me what You would have me do."

An urge filled him to enter the encampment's center. Gage stirred to obey but then hesitated. He was safe facing death, but he had no guarantees that he wouldn't suffer loss or pain. Obedience could still cost him dearly. He clenched his gauntleted fingers around his sword's hilt as his mind raced. If he didn't go after Sir Wick and the others, he and they may face that cost regardless.

He needed to find them. The certainty of that knowledge pulsed within him like a second heartbeat. Yet a choice still lay before him. Go forward trusting that God knew what He was doing, no matter the cost, or turn away and seek a different path to find the others? Gage considered the ramifications of the choices. He disregard what God was telling him, but He'd already lived in regret long enough. He didn't want to return there.

With fear clenched around his throat, Gage turned around and walked to the center of the camp, only half seeing the soldiers around him. He faced the entrance in the second wall of tents, beyond which flew the red-and-gold royal crest of Delkara, and he trekked forward.

The two Nissdin guards standing on either side of the opening extended spear shafts into his path. "There's no entrance to this area for soldiers," the guard to his left said, "not unless you've been summoned by a lord."

With a burst of audacity, Gage answered, "Our Lord has summoned me."

"Oh." Sounding taken aback, the soldier withdrew his spear. "Well, then...you may continue." He tipped his helmeted head at his fellow guardsman, and the other second soldier also removed his spear, clearing Gage's path.

Feeling exhilarated and terrified, Gage strode forward into the core of the camp.

Large pavilions in different lords' colors filled the area. Some were closed. Others were opened to the air. Knights and lords conversed in the shade, strode the area, or stood in the sunlight, speaking with each other.

Gage made his way to gain a line of sight inside the two prominent Nissdin pavilions. Judging by their colors, banners, and furnishings, he assumed they were Baron Fitch's tents. Both were empty. Noting the mix of guards outside King Strephon's royal pavilion, he trekked onward until he could see within it. Past the guards, he spotted Baron Fitch, two other barons, and a third man with a commanding presence wearing a crown and royal attire. Strephon had changed a great deal from the childhood memory Gage had of him, but the man was definitely the Delkaran royal Gage had met as a boy.

Looking at ease with the three barons, Strephon called one of his knights forward and spoke something that sent the knight striding out of the pavilion and across the encampment.

Since Gage wasn't about to approach Delkara's king with Fitch present, he followed King Strephon's knight, hoping to perhaps learn something from whatever mission Strephon had sent him on or perhaps pass a message through the knight back to Strephon.

The royal knight wove through pavilions and approached four other royal guards posted outside a Nissdin pavilion. The knight said something, and one of his fellow guardsmen entered the tent. Having apparently completed his mission, the sent knight departed. Gage was about to turn after him when the tent flaps opened, and in glistening jewelry and a lavish blue-green dress Her Royal Highness, Princess Rhonalyn of Keric emerged.

Seeing her, Gage clenched his fingers. He was tempted to march up to her and demand answers, but the four Delkaran guards falling into step around her made him question his initial judgment of her. Was she free, or was her commanding appearance deceiving? And where were Manton and Sir Wick?

63

RHONALYN SOAKED UP the morning's sunlight as she walked toward King Strephon's tent. She had slept fitfully, but with food and a fresh dress she felt restored. And now King Strephon sought her council.

Eager to assist in finding her men and taking on the Unavowed, she headed toward Strephon's large tent. One side was drawn back, and she saw Baron Selwin, Baron Rayburn, and Baron Fitch within. She strode forward and felt the confidence once more of her restored power as all three barons made way for her.

She approached Strephon. "You requested my help."

A boyish smirk crossed Strephon's face. "Verily, I did." He flicked a dismissive hand at his barons. "Leave us."

Baron Selwin took Strephon's command in stride, and Baron Rayburn stiffened at the order but obeyed it. Meanwhile a flicker of anger and then annoyance crossed Baron Fitch's face before he too complied. Wondering anew if Strephon was too trusting of Fitch, Rhonalyn gratefully watched Strephon's royal guardsmen settle into their protective stance around the pavilion.

Strephon's voice pulled her attention back to him. "If we are to deal with the traitors in our kingdoms, there are challenges that must be anticipated and overcome." Strephon walked to a map hanging on the side wall of his pavilion. It displayed all three king-doms, from the seaside harbors in Edelmar of Ivenyhan and Opes to those in Delkara of Nauta and Nikor, all the way to the mountains surrounding the high villages of Keric. Strephon tapped a finger on Arcis. "How many men can Keric muster if it comes to a battle?"

His question paused Rhonalyn. The night before he had made it sound like he had the matter of the Unavowed well in hand, but now his question made her fear he had only begun to chip away at something quite large. Feeling the way she had back in Arcis's solar when her father had revealed the state of Keric's coffers, she clamped down on her uncertainty and fear and spoke calmly. "Do you really think it might come to that? A battle?"

Strephon's eyes remained on the map. "I believe it is possible and something that should be planned for and considered." He turned to face her, his eyes finding hers. "If our two kingdoms come together in a united force, I believe mayhap the traitors wilt choose not to fight and wilt surrender instead, which would save time and lives. Thus, I ask you, how many men could Keric bring?"

Rhonalyn considered the men-at-arms each Keric's manor trained for defense and whom Keric's crown could call on in times of need. She did not want to admit it to Strephon, but she had no idea the number of knights and soldiers quartered at each manor. Never had she needed such information. The issues arising over the years requiring men-at-arms had never been dependent on overall numbers, just on what number of men with which skills were needed to resolve a specific problem.

Strephon's expression devolved into a mixture of frustration and concern. "You hesitate to answer. Do you doubt me?"

His expression looked so much like that of a hurt little boy that Rhonalyn shook her head. "Nay, it is not that. I just…I do not wish to give you an answer that may be inaccurate."

"You have not been trusted with such information, have you?" he asked. "Your own father, your commanders, they have left you on the outside of such matters of troops and your kingdom's defenses."

Feeling exposed and found wanting, Rhonalyn floundered. "I…I am trusted. It is simply that…well, I am not yet queen. Thus, I am not the caretaker of such information."

"I see." Strephon's voice shifted from pity to a challenge. "Here you are fighting for your people, but would the forces of Keric answer and fight for you if you commanded them? Or do they answer only to a king and not their future queen?"

Rhonalyn bristled, her own doubts goading her.

Strephon's voice softened. "You are Keric's princess and future ruler. You have every right to require respect from them. You should not have to wait for your people or your father to bequeath to you your own position."

"You think I do not know that?"

Despite her outburst, Strephon's gaze and voice remained steady. "Nay, I think only that mayhap you need someone to give you permission to stop doubting yourself and to claim your title for what it should be."

Rhonalyn inhaled. Her wounded pride wanted to tell him off, but her heart rang with an echo of his words so forcefully that she could not deny desiring exactly that.

Strephon turned and walked away from her. "Unlike your father and your commanders, you see your kingdom for what it is and what it could be, and I have witnessed you take bold steps to establish a new course for Keric. You desire to profit and protect your kingdom." He turned back toward her, his gaze pleading. "Do not permit them to do to you what too many of my own lords have done to me. Do not allow their voices to tell you that you are incapable of being what you have known all your life you were meant to be."

Rhonalyn's heartbeat quickened. Not since her mother had anyone spoken to her in such a manner. Strephon's words rose within her like a lost anthem of dreams of achievement she had let fade, and she willingly joined herself to the power of it. She *was* Keric's future ruler. She did not have to answer to or appease her kingdom's lords or seek their permission to use her authority. She was Keric's queen. She had every right and responsibility to defend and determine her kingdom's future. Her commands were to be followed, not questioned. And the garrisons of every manor should be known by her and answer to her.

Strephon stepped toward her, his fingers curling into a fist. "Verily! Protect your authority from the naysayers in your court. For if you do not, believe me, their voices of dissension will grow. Years ago, newly crowned King of Delkara, I thought that if I was patient with my lords and people, they would all come to see what I sought to accomplish and have faith in me. But they saw my kindness and lenience as weakness, and what started as doubts in some lords grew into treasonous actions. And now they defy me at every turn and fight against me."

His gaze rose to hers, "You yourself have experienced how far their treachery hath spread. No longer can I stand by. I must take action to save my kingdom. The lords who art loyal to me understand, alas, the need to draw swords against those of their own who art complicit in this treason. And such I granted them just days ago in anticipation of this gathering. It is a start but by no means the end of removing these traitors. A pity it is, though, that such resistance is made when what I seek could have been to the advantage of all."

His eyes searched hers as he continued. "You, Princess Rhonalyn, unlike anyone else, understand this struggle. For you too have desired more for your kingdom than what is and hath been. You too have faced barriers to helping your people and had to override those who would hold to traditions that have no place nor benefit anymore. Is that not so?"

Rhonalyn nodded in acknowledgement of the hardships of the road they had both walked. "Aye, it is so."

He smiled at her, and she felt in that moment that they weren't just fellow royals anymore, but also friends. "Then both you and I have the responsibility not to step aside or relinquish our visions of what could be. We must hold to our authority." Strephon stepped toward her, his gaze eager. "Let us rise together and triumph, showing all who have doubted us that we art rulers who wilt accomplish more than any thought possible."

Feeling breathless at the power of his words, Rhonalyn's heart swelled, and she answered, "Let us, indeed."

64

Gage abandoned his line of sight of Princess Rhonalyn and King Strephon. He couldn't hear what they were saying anyway, and he didn't want to risk an encounter with anyone else before speaking with Rhonalyn alone. He thought of her pavilion. Could he slip inside it before she and her Delkaran guard returned and wait there to gain a private word with her?

He headed for her pavilion, or at least what he hoped was her pavilion. He delayed to let a blonde woman leave the area the opposite direction, then strode to the pavilion's door. More than a little worried the tent wouldn't be empty, he devised an excuse in case someone was inside.

He slipped within and exhaled. It was empty. He took in the pavilion's layout and furnishings. There was no second room or curtain to conceal himself behind in case Rhonalyn's Delkaran guard escorted her inside. The only spot to hide was under the four-poster bed.

He trudged around the bed and considered the height of its frame. He would fit but just barely. Unstrapping his sword, he tugged off his helmet. He would have to pull the two items in after him.

There was no easy or quiet way to get to the ground in full armor. He knelt, then dropped sideways with a clank. Lying on his back for a moment, he waited. When he heard nothing from outside, he began to squirm sideways. Dragging his sword and helmet with him, he wriggled under the bed, watching the edge of the frame to make sure his chest cleared it and that he didn't catch on the board or ropes.

He was nearly to the center of the bed when a scuffling sound beside him was accompanied by a small voice. "Is there gonna be room enough for us both?"

Lurching, Gage tried to both bring up his head and draw his sword, but all he managed to do was smash his face into the mattress and tangle his arm in the grid-work of ropes. He fought to free himself but couldn't get himself unhooked.

"Stop moving!" the female voice said in fright. "You're going to break something or alert someone that we're in here."

Recognizing her voice, Gage released his sword and twisted his head around enough to see a wide-eyed Aisley, lying like a post beside him. With his heart still racing, he demanded, "What're you doing under here?"

"I thought you knew I was here."

"Obviously not." Gage heaved a breath. "You nearly scared the life out of me."

"Well, you gave me just as much of a fright. When you entered, I thought you were one of them. You marched around the bed, and when I saw you kneel, I thought for sure you intended to grab hold of me and drag me out. But then I saw your face and knew I was safe."

"Safe?" Gage asked in a frustrated whisper. "How is this safe? Who else knows you're in here?"

"Only one other person."

"Princess Rhonalyn?"

"No," Aisley answered hesitantly. "A woman. A lady, I think. The knight was scared of her."

"A lady? What lady?" Gage restrained his impatience. "Start at the beginning."

"Well, last night I snuck in and around the outer camp but couldn't find Princess Rhonalyn or Wick and Manton. I slipped under a tent this morning into this section of the camp but got caught by a knight. He wasn't happy and was taking me to the biggest of the yellow-and-green pavilions when a woman intercepted us. She was unusual looking. One whole side of her face and parts of her neck were colored purple the way the spot on Eliab's stomach was. The knight showed her deference, but he kept his distance from her like Princess Rhonalyn did with Eliab, like he was scared of her. The lady thanked him for finding me and told him to give me to her so that she could deliver me back to my mistress. He shoved me at her, then backed away, saying he was happy to let her deal with me.

"Once he left, the lady instructed me to follow her. She took me to a different tent for a while, gave me some food to eat and commanded me not to leave. Then she brought me here and instructed me to hide until Princess Rhonalyn returned and then pass along a message to Her Royal Highness."

"What message?" Gage asked.

"Wick and Manton are still in the encampment."

"That was her message" Gage asked. "She didn't say where they were, just to tell Rhonalyn they're here in the camp?"

"Yes, and before I could ask her anything else she left."

Gage frowned. Had Rhonalyn inquired about the two men? Was that why someone was using Aisley to secretly pass a message to her about them? He squinted at Aisley. "What else did you learn while sneaking around this camp?"

Aisley opened her mouth to answer, but a clunk and rattle as someone entered the tent, snapped her mouth closed and widened her eyes.

65

Shoulder to shoulder with Aisley, Gage held his breath. From the skirt hem he could see and the sound, he guessed the person who had entered the pavilion was a maidservant. The woman hummed to herself as she set something down and rattled this item and that. She departed a few moment later. Almost immediately after, boots and then a blue-green skirt pushed through the pavilion's door. The boots paused just inside, but the hem of the dress floated past where Gage and Aisley lay.

"Good. Food has been laid for you," a male voice said. "You have a bit more than an hour before His Majesty requests you rejoin him."

"Very well." Rhonalyn sounded calm but not exactly at ease.

The boots left, and Gage breathed normally again. Still, he waited a good thirty or more beats before nudging Aisley. "Go—carefully and quietly."

"Me?" she whispered

"Yes, you. And tell her I'm under here, so she doesn't scream and bring the guards."

Aisley nodded, then squirmed out from under the bed.

Gage winced when he heard Rhonalyn's questioning voice. "Where did…? How…?" Then silence.

He watched the pavilion's door. The cloth remained still.

A rustle of fabric much nearer to him made Gage shift his gaze. He found himself staring into Rhonalyn's glaring face as she peered under the bed. She gestured forcefully for him to come out.

Rolling his eyes, he scooted toward the side of the bed farthest from the door. With help from Aisley, he got himself, his helmet, and his sword out without too much clunking. Sitting on the rug with his back against the bed, he pulled Aisley down with him, out of sight of the door.

Rhonalyn knelt in front of them. "What are you doing here?" she asked in a tense whisper. "You're going to get yourself caught, sneaking around like a soldier and hiding in my tent!"

"I came to find the four of you and keep the Unavowed from finishing what they started back at Dinslage," Gage hissed.

Rhonalyn shook her head. "I'm safe here. King Strephon's guards and lords are loyal to him, and a number of the nobles connected to the Unavowed have already been arrested."

"And I'm telling you," Gage spoke forcefully, "I know for certain a member of the Unavowed is here in this camp walking around free right now."

A look of alarm flashed across Rhonalyn's face. "Then King Strephon should be informed about him at once." She shifted as if to stand, but Gage seized her arm.

"You're not listening to me! Stop and think! Who's to say there aren't other members of the Unavowed among King Strephon's lords or even his own guard? Just because he believes his people are loyal doesn't mean they are. We don't know how many more of the Unavowed might be present or what they're planning."

Rhonalyn's face and tone became fierce. "Well, they aren't the only ones with plans. King Strephon has been preparing to move against the Unavowed for months. That's the purpose of this encampment. This afternoon he will judge those arrested among his lords who have cooperated and allied with the Unavowed, and then he will move against any others who are uncovered. So you see, it's not us who should be afraid but the Unavowed. Together, Strephon and I will root out the Unavowed's leader, find and rescue my men, and restore and rebuild our kingdoms."

"Find and rescue *your* men?" Anger surged through Gage. "What about Wick and Manton? Or have you not given them a second thought since you were handed that dress?"

Stiffening, Rhonalyn spouted, "Of course I've thought about them!" She glared at him. "And for your information, yesterday evening they went to go help rescue one of my men."

Gage sat forward. "Went? As in, they aren't in the camp? You're certain?"

Rhonalyn frowned. "Yes, Strephon told me so himself."

"So you saw them leave?"

"No, I didn't see them depart, but—"

"Then they could still be here?"

Rhonalyn sounded flustered. "I don't understand. Why're you questioning what Strephon told me?"

"He's questioning it," Aisley said, "because I was instructed to tell you Wick and Manton are still in the encampment."

Rhonalyn glared at the girl. "Instructed by who?"

"Keep your voice down," Gage said.

Rhonalyn flinched and questioned in a lower tone, "Who told you to tell me that?"

"A blonde woman with a half purple face."

"Carys." Rhonalyn's expression darkened. "What is she up to?"

"Who's Carys?" Gage asked.

"She's someone who shouldn't even be allowed near a noble's feast, let alone welcomed at a king's table, yet despite being touched as she is and having no title, she sat directly to Strephon's left. She's significant to him, though as far as I can tell she's no one of significance."

Ignoring the prejudice in her vehement comments, Gage focused on matters at hand. "So, is Carys lying or is Strephon?"

"It makes sense that Carys would be the one lying," Rhonalyn answered. "She doesn't like me and could easily be trying to stir up trouble." She frowned across the pavilion. "Though it could also be that Baron Fitch lied to Strephon, and for whatever reason Carys is taking it upon herself to inform me."

"If that's the case," Gage asked, "why pass the information to you through Aisley? Why not tell Strephon herself and let him tell you?"

Rhonalyn snorted. "Perhaps because Carys does not wish herself to take the risk of revealing such news to Strephon about his friend. Or is she trying to have me accuse Baron Fitch of lying in order to turn Strephon against me?" Rhonalyn rose and paced the length of the bed, her expression furious. "Which one of them is lying to me?" Her fingers knotted into fists. "I hate this. One of them is my enemy, but how do I know which one?

Gage gritted his teeth. "They may both be, The Unavowed seem to specialize in sowing discord."

Rhonalyn's face hardened into a look of grim determination. "Well I'll not stand by and let that happen. There has to be a way to reveal who is lying, starting with figuring out whether or not Wick and Manton are truly still in this camp."

"I agree," Gage said, "but we need to tread carefully. Because regardless of who is revealed, you and Strephon are both standing within the Unavowed's reach."

66

RHONALYN SWEPT HER gaze over the crowd of lords and knights already gathered at the location of the previous night's feast. The warning Gabe had issued that there could be any number of members of the Unavowed in the camp made everyone around her suspect. She hated the agitation the speculations created within her.

Strephon was not yet present, but she was escorted by his guardsmen to the dais regardless. In place of the feast's table, a canopy had been raised over the platform to shade the chairs and throne.

Rhonalyn pressed her hands into her skirt. Baron Fitch stood on the far side of the canopy, talking with two of his knights and Baroness Murielle's husband.

Holding her smile in place, Rhonalyn drifted to the edge of the line of chairs and noted that the guardsmen who had accompanied her were taking up positions in front of the platform. They completed a loop of red uniforms standing at intervals around a rope fence encircling a large empty oval at the center of the crowd.

Rhonalyn looked toward Strephon's tent, wondering if she should try to intercept and speak to him before the event began. She wanted to ask him about Wick and Manton, tell him what Carys had passed along to her, and implore him to have the camp searched. But Gabe's warning rang through her. With Gabe in mind, she glanced toward her pavilion and noted the lone Nissdin soldier entering the back of the crowd. Those present were knights and lords, which made Gabe stick out in the crowd, but he had insisted on following her to the event. At the same time he had also insisted Aisley stay in the pavilion.

A pounding of metal and a rush of cheers burst across the crowd. Rhonalyn swept her gaze back toward Strephon's tent. He was already on the dais, with Carys close behind him. Rhonalyn forced herself to maintain a neutral expression. She wanted to warn him about the woman, but she knew it would be stupid to do so now. All she had against Carys was the word of a ten-year-old whom no one else knew was present, except for Carys herself.

The woman glanced her way. Carys's discolored face held no emotion, but as their eyes met, Rhonalyn could have sworn there was a challenge of fear and force in Carys's gaze.

King Strephon gestured for Rhonalyn and the rest of those who had been at his table the night before to take their seats with him. They did so, with the exception of Baron Fitch who remained standing to address the crowd in the noblemen's tongue. "Hear me now. Who among you wilt be the first to present to His Majesty his contribution of loyalty?"

"I shall!" a lord called out, then motioned to a knight beside him. The knight, in a surcoat of brown and white with a stag and a tower on it, nodded and departed the crowd. Rhonalyn assumed the knight was leaving to retrieve whatever his lord's contribution was.

"Who wilt be second?" Baron Fitch asked.

"I," another lord called out, and a second knight was sent from the crowd.

The process continued until at least six knights had departed.

By then the first knight returned, marching into the rope oval. Behind him came four soldiers, also in brown and white, encircling someone.

The soldiers parted rank, releasing into the center of the oval a shackled man, who appeared maybe ten years older than Rhonalyn's own father. His nobleman's attire was rumpled and dirty, and anger was evident in everything from his fierce expression to his clenched fists. Clanking his shackles, he spat at Strephon and spoke in the noblemen's tongue. "So this is my reward, is it? Years of faithfully serving your father and trying to counsel you to not destroy your own kingdom, and this is how I am treated?"

"Nay," Strephon replied. "This is what you art due for ignoring my orders and undermining my authority. Had you, instead of defiance, shown me loyalty like you did my father, you would not stand in chains before me."

"Defiance?" the nobleman scoffed. "It was not defiance but common sense that halted me from aligning with you. A wisdom that others here should have heeded. You art not fit to lead Delkara nor to wear that crown."

The nobleman's spiteful fury made Rhonalyn press back against her chair. She now understood better Strephon's words about being doubted and questioned by his own lords. She glanced in his direction, but Strephon rose to his feet, causing her gaze to land on Carys instead. As the woman stared at the accused nobleman, her discolored face showed little emotion, but cords of tension were visible on Carys's neck. Whether her angst, though, was on Strephon's behalf or on behalf of the nobleman it was impossible to tell.

"Your own words art witness enough against you," Strephon announced. "I judge you guilty." He turned to the watching crowd. "Who wilt show their loyalty to me by executing him?"

"Allow me, Your Majesty." Baron Selwin rose from his seat down the dais, dropped into the roped-off area, and drew his sword. The soldiers withdrew, leaving the shackled nobleman and Nikledon's baron alone within the circle of King Strephon's red knights.

The treasonous nobleman jutted his chin at his executioner.

"Barely five years ago, Selwin, I would have said you had not the guts for this kind of thing." The lord spit at the dais. "But it seems Strephon hath had quite the influence on you and your young friends."

"Unlike you," Baron Selwin said as he flourished his sword, "I serve my king and follow his orders." Selwin swung his blade.

The nobleman dodged the weapon with a quick sidestep. "Nay, you serve a murderer who hath no right to sit upon Delkara's throne."

Facing each other, the two men moved in a circle, their eyes locked.

Rhonalyn gripped her chair. She had not expected Strephon's judgment of the Unavowed to involve trial by combat.

"No longer wilt you spout your treachery. You art finished!" Selwin thrust at the nobleman, who threw up his arms. Metal chimed on metal as the sword clashed against the lord's shackles. Shoving the young baron's blade away with his fettered wrists, the nobleman roared and rushed at Selwin. The nobleman's hands reached for the young baron's neck. Selwin's eyes widened, but even as the nobleman's fingers touched his throat, Selwin swept his sword at the man's side.

Rhonalyn jerked her face away. The crowd's response told her Selwin had succeeded in his cut but she did not wish to see what that meant.

Shifting her gaze to the baroness of Dubour seated beside her, Rhonalyn noted satisfaction on lady Murielle's face. The woman's eyes then widened, and the crowd gasped. Then a collective whoop followed. When the crowd fell to aimless chatter a moment later, Rhonalyn knew it was over. She glanced back at the field. Selwin stood with his bloody sword over the nobleman's sprawled body.

All sound faded around Rhonalyn as soldiers ducked under the rope to collect the nobleman's body. In her mind, she traveled back to the meadow when the mounted soldier had rushed at her with his drawn sword. If Manton hadn't intervened and Gabe and Wick hadn't gotten her out of there, she would have been killed in a similar fashion. She pulled herself out of the memory and hardened herself against the sight before her. All those who aided or were part of the Unavowed should pay for their crimes. Justice had been served.

The nobleman's body was carried off the field, and a group of soldiers wearing Selwin's blue and green made their way forward with another prisoner, a thin, ill-kept man who fell to his knees when shoved forward. His filthy nobleman's clothes had seen better days. His hair was greasy, and his yellow fingernails were long and twisted.

"Your Majesty, I present the previous Lord of Burnel for your judgment," Baron Selwin said.

Burnel! Rhonalyn stiffened. She pictured Sir Nolan in Burnel as Wick and Aisley had accounted him to her. Her heartbeat quickened. Where had this nobleman taken Sir Nolan so that he had not been found when Strephon's men searched Burnel?

"I myself," King Strephon said, "can bear witness, Lord Channing, to your crimes of treason against me and against Delkaran law. Thus, I find you guilty." Strephon raised his voice. "Who wilt execute him?"

"I, Your Majesty." A knight wearing the red and blue of Lyster stepped forward.

"Wait!" Rhonalyn called out, rising to her feet. She climbed off the dais between two of Strephon's guardsmen and snapped her fingers at one of them. "Your dagger. Now!"

The guard looked startled but obeyed and handed her his shorter blade.

She seized the weapon. With her fingers clenched about its hilt, she marched toward the kneeling lord. The Nikledon soldiers backed away from him.

The lord looked resigned, his eyes holding nothing but dull acceptance. Rhonalyn pressed the edge of the dagger to his throat, feeling only hatred for him. "Tell me, where is my knight?"

Confusion entered the man's expression. "Your knight?" he asked in a wobbly voice. "I am unsure who you mean, Your Ladyship, but… but mayhap if you tell me his name?"

Your Ladyship! Fresh anger coursed through Rhonalyn. He didn't even know who she was. "His name is Sir Nolan. He is part of the royal guard of Keric! And he was your prisoner." A stench like that of Lyster's refuse pile, hit her nose. Rhonalyn gagged and shifted back a step. She flicked her gaze down the nobleman, concluding that his filthy clothes were the source of the smell.

Something akin to understanding churned on the lord's pale, gaunt face. "Sir Nolan, aye." His expression became a mix of recognition and sad reflection. "I remember him. He was kind."

Rhonalyn flinched. "What do you mean *was* kind?"

Someone strode up behind her, at the same time the Nikledon soldiers laid their hands on the nobleman's arms. The lord flinched and hissed in a breath. Baron Fitch was suddenly at Rhonalyn's elbow, his voice tight. "He was already questioned, Princess Rhonalyn. You are not going to learn anything new that we have not. Now step aside"—he took hold of her arm— "and let someone capable of wielding a weapon carry out his sentence."

Furious, Rhonalyn flicked her gaze from Fitch's grip to his face. "Baron Fitch, take your hand off of me."

"Do as she says and remove your hand," King Strephon ordered, striding up beside Fitch.

Letting go of her and stepping back, Fitch lowered his gaze before Strephon.

Rhonalyn gritted her teeth. Fitch could feign submission, but she knew who he really was, and there was no way she would be deterred by him. Whatever reason he had to prevent her from talking to the previous lord of Burnel, she would find it.

She turned back to the nobleman, but Strephon stepped up to her and whispered in her ear. "This is not helpful, Princess Rhonalyn. Come back to the dais. Fitch is right, he hath already been questioned."

Trying to determine if Strephon was right and her hopes were futile or if he'd been lied to, Rhonalyn turned her gaze back to the chained nobleman before her. She noted in that moment details about him she had failed to take into account before. The man's eyes, which darted between her and Strephon, were bloodshot. His bruised and damaged skin was sunken upon his bones, like he had either suffered a lengthy illness or prolonged hunger. His greasy hair was not only dirty and tangled but matted. And his filthy nobleman's clothes were threadbare, with frayed holes beneath which could be seen the scars of healed wounds.

Rhonalyn's blood ran cold. There was no way this man had been ruling over Burnel just four days ago when her knight had been held prisoner there, yet he knew Sir Nolan.

Strephon cupped his hand under her elbow and tried to turn her. "Come away, Princess Rhonalyn. I promise you, we wilt find your men another way."

The nobleman's bloodshot eyes met hers, and with a look of rekindled strength he called out to her. "Do not believe him! He wilt not help you find your men."

Rhonalyn froze in place. Was he speaking about Strephon or Baron Fitch? The soldiers yanked the nobleman backward. The action shifted the shackles on his wrists, revealing something branded beneath. It was a mark of a flail and crossbow with their handles crossed.

Rhonalyn inhaled a sharp breath. The nobleman wasn't a member of the Unavowed. He had been their prisoner, along with her own knight. She turned to Strephon. "The brand on his wrist, to which lord does it belong?"

Trying once more to turn her away from the man, Strephon answered with an edge of annoyance in his voice. "It is not a lord's brand. It is how my men mark my enemies. Now, come away, and let justice be done here."

"Justice," Rhonalyn whispered. She looked at the lord of Burnel and in that moment knew his words had been meant about Strephon. Every presumption she had made in the last months collided with Strephon's declaration that the Unavowed's brand was how *his* men marked *his* enemies. The ramifications of his words rewrote event after event in her mind, everything from the moment she had heard that her mother's gold had been taken by well-armed commoners, who she now realized had been in possession of knowledge no commoner should have known, all the way to negotiating with Strephon to pay a second time for a toll he had, in fact, stolen, to the staggering realization that for the last two days he had been asking her for information about Keric's defenses.

Strephon was head of the Unavowed. Manton had been right. Delkara's king was responsible for attacking her people, for stealing from her, for the attempt on her life, for her missing guard, for the traps set for her, for all of it. Strephon had said that he and Fitch were concerned about the lies that the rebel commoners may have told her. Lies? Rhonalyn shook her head. It was not the lies Strephon had feared her knowing but the truth that the rebel commoners could tell her about who he really was. Fury like Rhonalyn had never known before erupted inside her.

Strephon was her enemy. And she found him guilty.

67

GAGE HAD BEEN far enough forward in the crowd to see Baron Fitch come up behind Rhonalyn. He had begun pushing forward through the crowd when Strephon intervened. Gage could not hear the exchange that followed between Strephon and Rhonalyn, but it appeared for a moment like Rhonalyn was going to return to the dais. Then she asked something. Strephon answered her, and Rhonalyn stiffened. Emotions flicked over her face—shock, horror, fury, then fierce outrage, followed by a rage-filled scream.

For a split second, confusion filled Strephon's face, a feeling Gage shared. Then Rhonalyn yanked up the dagger she clutched and brought it down at Strephon's chest.

Panic flashed over Strephon's face. He grabbed for Rhonalyn's arm and caught her wrist just as the weapon sank into his royal tunic. Forcing her hand backward, Strephon withdrew the dagger's bloody tip from his chest.

Gage stared stunned by what Rhonalyn had just done, while a look of terror crossed Rhonalyn's face.

With a snarl, Strephon twisted Rhonalyn's wrist. She screamed and dropped the blade. Strephon released her arm, then backhanded her across the face. The blow was loud and so hard it knocked Rhonalyn off her feet. Gage's insides lurched, and he pushed forward.

The agitated and confused crowd around him surged forward as well, all trying to see what had just happened. Smashed from every side, Gage couldn't make headway.

Jostled, he could scarcely catch sight of Rhonalyn let alone get any closer. The next glimpse he got of her, she was being hauled to her feet between two of Strephon's knights. She looked dazed and fearful.

Pressing a hand to his bleeding chest, Strephon growled at her, "You really would have done better, Princess Rhonalyn, to have stayed my friend."

"You sent soldiers to kill me!" Rhonalyn screamed.

Strephon stepped closer, his words seething with anger. "I would not have had to intervene if your royal guard had done their job and not let those wretched commoners kidnap you to fill your head with their lies about me. I had no choice at that point. I had to make sure you did not return to Keric and disrupt my plans."

Gage blinked. Strephon commanded the Unavowed soldiers. No wonder Rhonalyn had tried to kill him.

"Plans! What plans?" Rhonalyn strained against the knights holding her. "And where are my men?"

Ignoring her, Strephon strode back to the dais. Only once he was standing before his throne did he again face those present. The crowd immediately hushed. With his hand still pressed to his wound, Strephon addressed his knights. "Bring me her guardsmen."

Anger and fear surged through Gage. Her guardsmen were there at the camp!

A cry went up, and the crowd pressed backward, making way for four of Strephon's knights to depart. Gage's stomach twisted. He had little doubt as to what Strephon would do to Rhonalyn's men.

A space closer to the rope opened in front of him. He shoved forward stepping behind two knights. His mind raced in spiraling dread. Even if he could elbow his way into the ring, he had no way to stop what was about to happen. Anything he could do would only momentarily delay the inevitable and add himself to the casualties. He stood there, his heartbeat rocking his body. There had to be some way to prevent what was coming.

Strephon's knights returned. Gage's heart skipped a beat at what he expected to see, then pounded at what he saw. Strephon's red guards dragged the unbound Sir Wick and Manton forward into the rope oval and threw them to their knees in front of Rhonalyn. Gage could see her confused and terrified expressions.

"Which one shall pay with his life for her actions?" Strephon asked. Lifting his bloody hand, he pointed at Wick, then Manton. "The first? Or the second?"

Calls burst from all around Gage, voting on one or the other. Gage grabbed the arm of a Maneo knight beside him, who was yelling for Sir Wick to die. "What are you doing?" Gage screamed. "This isn't justice. He's innocent!"

The Maneo knight shook him off, then eyed him and yelled over the clamor of the crowd. "What're you even doing here? You shouldn't be here in the inner camp."

"He's right." A hand seized Gage's arm. "What're you doing here?" The Nissdin knight's grip tightened on Gage's partially armored arm. "Answer me!"

Silence sliced across the whole crowd, pausing the knight's inquiry and drawing everyone's attention back to Strephon. "The first it is then!" Strephon yelled.

Gage's cry of dismay blended with a scream from Rhonalyn and the crowd's roar of approval. Gage twisted his arm, trying to jerk away from the knight holding him, but the knight yanked him close and opened his mouth to say something.

"Who wilt execute him for me?" Strephon's bellowed question again silenced the crowd.

"Allow me, Your Majesty!" a fury-filled voice replied.

Gage's chest tightened fiercely, and he felt sick as he spotted the lord who entered the ring. The man volunteering to execute Sir Wick was none other than Baron Hewitt of Duvall, the eldest son of the Delkaran nobleman Gage's own uncle had once befriended. Gage himself had interacted with Hewitt more than once as a youth, but that was before Hewitt had become the baron of Duvall and apparently one of Strephon's Unavowed.

Hewitt ducked into the rope fence. With his right hand gripping the hilt of his sheathed dagger, the baron strode straight for Sir Wick.

Gage's body quaked with the pound of his heartbeat.

Hewitt placed his left hand on Sir Wick's shoulder and bent over him. The baron appeared to say something in Sir Wick's ear. Then Hewitt straightened and thrust his dagger into the center of Sir Wick's chest.

Gage felt the impact of Hewitt's blade as if it had been driven into his own body. Air left his lungs, and he stared in horror at the scene before him.

Sir Wick collapsed backward, his hands gripping the dagger embedded in his chest. The knight's back hit the ground, and his head rolled sideways. Sir Wick's eyes drifted backward, then went still. The crowd cheered. Rhonalyn screamed. Gage froze. It was as if all feeling had left his body. He was no longer aware of the knight's hand on his arm, the ground beneath his feet, or even his own heartbeat. He couldn't move or speak, and yet he could hear and see with livid clarity.

"Shall I kill her second guardsman as well, Your Majesty?" Baron Hewitt asked.

"Nay. Leave him alive, for now." Strephon jutted his chin at his red knights. "Shackle Princess Rhonalyn, and chain her and her last guardsmen with the others. My celebratory mood hath been spoiled for the day. I wilt judge her and the rest of these traitors tomorrow." With that, Strephon marched off the dais.

The crowd stirred as Strephon's guardsmen dragged Manton and Rhonalyn away. Meanwhile, the Nissdin knight still grasping Gage's arm, released him with a shove that sent Gage sprawling. "Get back to the outer camp where you belong. And don't let me catch you in here again, or his fate will be yours."

Ignoring the knight, Gage looked toward where Sir Wick's body lay. Several of Baron Hewitt's men in their green-and-black surcoats with its red phoenix took hold of Sir Wick's body and lifted it. As they carried off the knight's body, Gage stumbled to his feet. He shoved his way through the dispersing crowd, following after Hewitt's men, unable to think past his compulsion to keep Sir Wick in sight. There was no wisdom or planning to his actions. He just had to keep Sir Wick's body from being taken from him. He had to be there. He had to…what? There was nothing left to do. Wick was gone. Excruciating pain twisted in Gage's chest. He staggered sideways, then righted himself. He couldn't help Sir Wick, not anymore, but he wasn't going to leave him either like he had Allard, not without saying goodbye.

With his vision blurring, Gage pushed himself after Hewitt's men.

He trailed the group to a large green-and-black pavilion of Duvall. Two of the six knights helping carry Sir Wick's body turned around at the pavilion's door to take up guard posts while those still bearing the body entered the pavilion. Gage caught sight of Hewitt inside the tent just before the flap closed.

One of the newly posted guards noticed Gage and stepped toward him. "What're you doing here?"

Gage halted. With his mind too numb to form words but somehow screaming at him in alarm, he shook his head and backed away.

The two knights exchanged a look, then moved toward him.

Gage turned and tried to run, but his feet snagged on each other. He lurched sideways, rebalanced himself in a lumbering step, and burst into a run. Something impacted the back of his legs, slamming him to the ground.

Gage gasped and fought his way forward trying to regain his feet and flee, but the guards seized his arms and, yanking his hands out from under him. Someone pulled off his helmet, and a hand clamped over his mouth.

Detained by the two Duvall guards, Gage didn't bother fighting further. What was the point? Even if he could escape them, he had nowhere to go. Once the alarm was raised, he would never make it out of the encampment.

He was marched toward the very pavilion that he had wished he could enter.

Pushed face first through its fabric, he caught sight of Hewitt and his knights before he was kicked in the back of his legs. He landed on his knees on a rug beside a table in the pavilion's sparsely furnished interior. With his head pushed downward, he stared through the supports of two benches and at a pile of furs in the tent's corner, then glanced to his left. Wick's body lay sprawled on the ground surrounded by Baron Hewitt's knights.

Fury and pain washed through Gage, igniting every numb part of him with rage. Drawing air in through his nose, he thrust his chin against the hand clenched over his mouth to lift his head, locked his gaze with Hewitt's, and screamed in the back of his throat.

The hand across his mouth tightened and it's owner spoke. "Apologies, My Lord. He followed us back here. I had no choice but to bring him inside."

Hewitt's fear-filled gaze flicked over Gage. "Was he the only one to take interest?"

"It seems so. But what shall we do with him?"

Hewitt's eyes landed on Gage's face, studying him. A furrow creased the baron's forehead. "Wait, I know you." Hewitt's eyes narrowed as he stepped closer. "Why do I—" His eyes widened. "No. It can't be! Prince Gage...of Edelmar?"

"Prince Gage? Where?" Sir Wick sat up amid the circle of knights, his fingers still clutching the hilt of the dagger in his chest.

68

WICK BIT HIS tongue. Seeing Prince Gage's ashen face, he realized he probably should have announced himself in a less shocking manner. Wide-eyed, His Highness wavered on his knees. Had it not been for the two knights gripping Prince Gage, he likely would have toppled. His Highness murmured something against the hand still clenched over his mouth.

"Let him go," the baron ordered, "and return to your posts."

Abruptly released, Prince Gage pulled forward his arms to catch himself, and with his eyes locked with Wick's, spoke in an airy whisper, "You're alive. How are you alive?"

With mortifying clarity, Wick realized that His Highness must have been watching when the baron had stabbed him. He offered an apologetic smile. "Yes, I'm alive."

Prince Gage's eyes dropped to the dagger's hilt that Wick still held against his chest.

"Oh, right." Chuckling awkwardly, Wick shook his head. "It's not what it looks like." He drew the dagger's hilt away from his chest, forcing himself not to wince as the rough edge of its snapped-off blade pulled free. Blood trailed from the shallow wound and soaked into his tunic. He would have a bruise around the gash, but that mattered little. "See?" Wick said. "It wasn't a full blade. The wound isn't deep."

"I don't understand. How is this possible?" Prince Gage asked.

Not entirely sure of the answer himself, Wicked nodded toward the baron, who was staring at them both, looking bewildered. "His lordship approached and said in my ear, 'If you want to live, grip the blade and die convincingly.' So I did, and here I am."

"But why?" Prince Gage's perplexed and concerned gaze sought out the baron. "Why did you spare him? Are you not loyal to Strephon?"

The question seemed to startle the baron out of his surprise, and he shook his head. "Nay, I am not. Nor have I ever been."

"If that is true," Prince Gage said, struggling to his feet, and also switching to the noblemen's tongue, "then how are you here as a member of this encampment and not as a prisoner in it?"

The baron scrubbed a hand over his mouth, while his neck and face reddened. "I am here because my father died a year after King Maurice." For a moment the strange comment seemed all the baron would say. Then he continued. "A fever killed my father, but that is not what King Strephon thinks happened."

"Go on." Prince Gage said.

The baron heaved a breath. "Right. How to explain. Roughly six months after King Maurice's death and Prince Strephon's ascent to the throne, King Strephon invited a handful of the firstborn sons of Delkara's lords to Ithera Castle. I thought it an honor to be included but strange that our fathers were not." The baron shook his head. "Then I learned why. Late one evening, a handful of us were gathered near a hearth in the hall. King Strephon joined us and began to speak about using his rise to power to bring significant changes to Delkara. His plans sounded good, and I thought he was telling us because he wished us to take word back to our fathers and convince them of his intentions. But nay. King Strephon went on to say that we should not have to wait to have our own power. He told us then that he had taken his own power by seeding caltrops at the top of a hill on King Maurice's riding trail."

Wick sucked in a breath. He imagined the small, spiked weapons of war—used to lame people and horses—sprinkled across a riding trail.

Prince Gage's voice held dismay. "Are you saying Strephon killed his own father?"

"I am saying that King Strephon not only made it clear to us what he had done to gain Delkara's throne, but that if we made the same choice and removed our own fathers, he would protect us and guarantee us our positions, along with significant advantages in the years to come."

"He offered this." Prince Gage exhaled. "And then your father died."

"Exactly. King Strephon assumed that I had done what he suggested. I told myself it was better for me, my family, and my city if I kept my mouth shut and stayed in Strephon's favor. In that way I could use what power I gained to help protect the people of Duvall. But in order to maintain the illusion of my alliance with Strephon, I had to push away anyone who might compromise what King Strephon thought true of me—including your uncle, Baron of Awnquera."

The baron's forehead furrowed, and grief and regret filled his voice. "Ever since my father's death, I have thus been trapped and isolated, maintaining the deception of my loyalty to King Strephon. And every compromise I have made since to keep my secret hath sunk me deeper into his clutches and made me a shameful collaborator in his treachery. At first I served his plans ignorantly, but I have since learned what he shared back then was only the tip of a spear meant for war not peace. King Strephon's ambitions go far beyond changing Delkara. This morning, he revealed to his barons that he means to use what he hath done in Delkara to conquer Keric and Edelmar and reunite all three kingdoms under one ruler."

"All three kingdoms under one ruler—as in, his?" Wick shook his head in contempt. "Does he think he can just march over our border and demand we surrender? We art not as defenseless as we appear."

"He assumes nothing," the baron replied. "Apparently, King Strephon has long invested in determining Keric and Edelmar's strengths and weaknesses. I know not exactly how he hath gained this knowledge, but he hath been using those he calls his crows to do so. The cracks Strephon hath found in your kingdoms' defenses, he will exploit, and he will remove any impediments in his way by whatever means and cost necessary.

"When I left King Strephon's tent this morning, I cried out to God, something I have not done in years. I begged that He would have mercy on all of us in Delkara and that He would provide a means to warn Keric and Edelmar of what is coming." The baron looked between the two of them, his expression filled with wonder. "And God answered my prayer, bringing into my path not just a Keric knight but a prince of Edelmar."

Flinching, Wick opened his mouth to answer.

Prince Gage beat him to it. "God hath answered your prayer but not quite the way you think. Baron Hewitt, this is Sir Wick of Edelmar, son of Lord Jacob of Clement, previous knight of the White Fortress and guardsman to myself."

"A guardsman to Your Highness? Yet he was called one of Princess Rhonalyn's guard. How could he have been assumed to be one of her guards? Unless…" Baron Hewitt eyed Prince Gage. "Unless you were with Princess Rhonalyn and your guardsmen were not in uniform, thus mistaken as part of her retinue. But why would—"

"Halt!" The commanding voice outside the door of the tent continued sharply. "Stay where you are. State your business."

Wick and every person around him in the tent froze, listening.

Outside, a feminine voice answer the guard, her words too quiet to be distinguished.

"Verily, I understand your request," the guard replied, "but the baron does not wish to be disturbed. You wilt have to return later to speak with him."

More indistinguishable words followed, then the same guardsman called out. "Nay, I said halt. Baron! She is coming within."

Baron Hewitt snatched Prince Gage's face-concealing helmet from the ground and thrust it into His Highness's hands, then gestured his knights toward Wick.

Prince Gage yanked on the helmet, but Wick frowned, unsure what he was supposed to do. Two of Baron Hewitt's knights grabbed a fur from the corner, while another shoved Wick flat. The weight of the fur dropped over him, covering Wick in a hot, smothering darkness.

Four heart beats later, Baron Hewitt spoke. "Carys! To what do I owe such an unexpected visit?"

"Where is he?" The woman's quiet voice was tight with urgency.

"Where is who?" Baron Hewitt responded tersely.

Anger spread into Carys's tone. "The knight that you offered to kill. When your men took him from the field, he was still breathing. Where is he?"

Baron Hewitt's voice rose in pitch. "Still breathing? Well, considering his wound, I can not imagine that he wilt last much longer."

"Then tell me where he is," Carys demanded, the imperativeness in her tone increasing.

Sweating, Wick held perfectly still under the fur.

"Why do you care about finding a man that King Strephon sentenced to death?" Prince Gage asked, his voice steady yet curious.

There was a pause before Carys answered in a far calmer tone, "Because I seek to help him."

There was a moment's silence, then Prince Gage instructed. "Show him to her."

"You are sure?" Baron Hewitt asked.

More silence followed. Having no idea what was transpiring, Wick dared not move. Were they leaving with her, pretending to take her where he was? Or was everyone staring at one another, trying to figure out what to do next?

The fur pulled off him. Wick blinked and stared at a young woman with honey-gold hair and a startlingly duel-colored face. Her brown eyes, holding surprise and then relief, dropped to his wounded chest. Drawing forth a dark leather satchel slung over her beautiful dress, she nodded to the baron's knights. "Prithee, help him take off his tunic, so I can better see his injury."

Prince Gage nodded in his helmet. "Do so."

Baron Hewitt motioned, and two of his knights assisted Wick in sitting up and removing his tunic.

As Wick lowered his arms, he watched Carys note the broken dagger beside him before she crouched to evaluate its impact point. She eyed where the blade's ragged edge had lacerated his chest. She also glanced at the dressing still covering the puncture wound on his side. "Untie that, and I wilt replace it too." She drew two cloths and a corked bottle from her bag. Dousing both pieces of fabric in liquid from the bottle, she held them out to him. "Put these on your wounds, then tie them in place." She held out the rolls of cloth.

Nodding his thanks, Wick took them from her, his fingers brushing hers. She pulled her hand back, and several of the knights hissed and muttered.

The baron stepped toward Gage and spoke in a low growl. "Are you sure about this. She is King Strephon's witch."

"I know who she is." Prince Gage pulled off his helmet and

stepped toward Carys, his voice eager as he addressed her. "You have helped us before. That is how you identified and rescued Aisley this morning, how you knew Wick's and Manton's names when you passed along your warning to Rhonalyn, and how just a moment ago you recognized my voice. You art the healer from Verfeld."

69

Gage waited for the healer to acknowledge his words from where she had frozen in front of Sir Wick. Her brown eyes and the urgency in them when she entered the pavilion had been what gave her away. The sight had instantly flashed him back to the moment in Verfeld when she turned toward him, panicking about it being so late.

"Carys?" He spoke her name gently. "Prithee, I know I am right." He touched her arm, hoping to convince her to respond.

She flinched away, then stood, but refused to meet his gaze.

Gage couldn't stop his eyes from traveling over her countenance to the darker skin around her lips, nose, and left eye. It was as if someone had thrown a cup of wine at one side of her face, and that its color had dripped down her neck and over her arms. Gage pulled his gaze back to her face. He had seen her on the dais from a distance but hadn't recognized her. And in Verfeld, he had worked beside her but not really seen her. Now he absorbed all of who she was, and he realized and grieved the truth. No matter which way she chose to live, with her skin concealed or revealed, someone would always accuse her of being a witch. And yet she had risked helping those burned and injured in Verfeld, and she had risked coming here. He spoke with quiet appreciation. "I know you art the healer who helped in Verfeld."

Carys's expression held rigid, while a shadow passed though her downcast gaze. When she replied, her soft, feminine voice carried a graceful strength that spoke of someone who knew what it was to endure through hardship. "Sir, if there is a healer who helped in

Verfeld, surely she is not the same woman as she who stands beside King Strephon of Delkara."

Gage caught his breath. "I agree. So, why is she here?"

Carys's eyes flicked to his, then to Sir Wick. "To try to save a man's life." Her gaze then sought out Hewitt. "And to learn if Baron Hewitt of Duvall accidentally or intentionally failed to kill an enemy of King Strephon."

"And now that you have your answer?" Hewitt said. "What wilt you do with it?"

Carys's lips, edged by her wine-colored skin, lifted in a brief smile. "Rejoice that I have discovered here, of all places, a baron willing to defy Strephon and risk his life to save someone else's. And others willing to do the same." She dipped her head to those around the tent.

Her brown eyes settled back on Gage as she continued. "Long hath help been unobtainable. And now, I find it before me, at the last possible hour. Countless days have I secretly spent in the woods outside Verfeld, seeking someone I could trust for a task that could disrupt Strephon's power, change Delkara's course, and protect all three kingdoms." She hesitated. "And mayhap I am being a fool now to reveal to near strangers a secret I have for so long stewarded, but no longer is there time for certainty or caution. King Strephon intends to execute every prisoner he hath gathered here, because, though not of powerful names or titles, they are men who have respect and influence. If they chose to rise against Strephon, they could use their leadership to rally and unite others against him. They represent almost all of the last holdouts of Delkaran power not controlled by Strephon. Without them, taking away Stephon's authority will mean nothing. The task, once it is accomplished, needs those in Delkara who can arise and stand against Strephon."

"What task are you talking about?" Hewitt asked. "And, verily, if it holds such significance, why have you not accomplished it before now yourself?"

Gage cringed at Hewitt's accusing tone but was aligned with his question.

"I have not accomplished it, because I cannot," Carys answered calmly. "It requires a clandestine journey of several days, and"—she turned up her arms— "I am not someone who can travel anywhere unnoticed. Even if I slipped away from King Strephon, others along the journey would give me away and put the task at risk."

Listening to Carys, Gage was even more curious about who she really was. Her presence in an Unavowed encampment standing beside Strephon explained her caution and her fear in speaking and taking action against Strephon, but why and how had she come to stand beside Delkara's king in the first place?

"You still have not answered my question." Hewitt's voice held both concern and curiosity. "What is this task that you claim can take away Strephon's authority?"

Carys looked toward Sir Wick. Her eyes slid from the knight's wounded chest to the broken dagger beside him. Her gaze lingered upon the snapped blade, then rose to Hewitt's face. "The task is to deliver the last orders written and sealed by King Maurice. These orders Queen Marjorie, Delkara's Queen Mother, tasked me to smuggle from Ithera Castle and get to the one baron who holds the ability to open the orders and thus the one baron able to implement them."

"Last orders from King Maurice?" Hewitt stepped closer to Carys. "What orders?"

Carys shifted backward. Her gaze swept over all present who waited expectantly for her answer. Trepidation edged into her features and words seemed to fail her.

Gage reached for her arm. "Carys."

The mere brush of his fingers made her jerk away. Her whole body tensed, and her panic-rimmed eyes snapped to his.

Wincing at her reaction, Gage tried to reassure her. "Carys, all of us in this tent are already traitors to Strephon. You have ventured this far, prithee, tell us the rest."

She shuddered and closed her eyes. When she opened them, it was as if she had donned the dark garb of the healer. All emotion had been swept from her face. Gage half expected her voice to creak as well. "I wilt tell you what Queen Marjorie told me. King Maurice, recognizing the danger of Strephon's ambitions, took measures to provide a means to protect Delkara's crown and legally depose Strephon if he seized Delkara's throne."

"How is it possible that his orders could legally depose Strephon?" Hewitt asked.

"I know not the particulars, only that what King Maurice put in his orders makes it possible. King Maurice commissioned Baron Renaud, his most loyal baron and a skilled military leader, to train a group of elite soldiers in secret. Baron Renaud did. And after the last feast before King Maurice's death, Baron Renaud was sent to join his soldiers in hiding and was instructed to keep them at the ready until he received King Maurice's next orders."

"Baron Renaud, you say?" Hewitt sighed and shook his head. "The man is dead. He was murdered at that very feast. Stabbed and pushed from the parapet of Ithera Castle. His body was carried away by the Valens River, never to be recovered."

Carys's lips twisted into a smile, and amusement entered her voice. "Aye, Baron Hewitt, you are not the first to deceive Strephon by faking a man's death. King Maurice's intention was to use Baron Renaud's supposed murder to protect Delkara's throne and to test the loyalty of his other lords. But he never got the chance. Just days later, King Maurice was killed, and Strephon took the throne as his successor.

"King Maurice's orders, written but not yet sent to Baron Renaud, were kept concealed by The Queen Mother, along with the truth about Baron Renaud and his location. Queen Marjorie anticipated having her own allies in the castle to entrust with the orders, but when Strephon took the throne, he replaced everyone serving within Ithera Castle. It was thus years into his reign before Queen Marjorie risked taking me into her confidence. Two months after that she entrusted the orders to me with the command to get them to Baron Renaud, so that he could use the orders to overthrow Strephon."

Sir Wick commented grimly. "It says a lot when a man's own mother wants him deposed."

"Well, she hath ample reason," Carys said. "Ever since King Maurice's death and Strephon's ascent to the throne, the Queen Mother hath been locked within the walls of her own chambers, not permitted to see or speak to anyone other than King Strephon, me, and her two keepers"

"He holds his own mother prisoner?" Baron Hewitt exclaimed.

Picturing his own mother put in such a position, Gage dug his fingernails into his palms. "So, it is not that Queen Marjorie of Delkara hath been ill and bed-ridden, as we were told?"

"Nay," Carys answered flatly, "neither illness nor grief hath been what kept her confined, though she hath been ill, which is how she and I became acquainted. King Strephon brought me to Ithera to tend to her. He wants her alive, so that she wilt see what he makes Delkara into." Carys's brown eyes drifted to stare at something only she could see. She swallowed and refocused her gaze on Gage. "And, in a similar way, he wilt keep Princess Rhonalyn alive to use against Keric. Already, Her Royal Highness hath told him too much about

Keric's defenses. And now, he hath no need to maintain an illusion of kindness toward her."

The implication of Carys's words spread like ice through Gage and twisted his stomach.

"Is there really any question then about what needs doing?" Sir Wick asked. "We must take action."

Hewitt grunted. "It is all well and good to say that we ought to rescue Keric's princess and the prisoners yonder, but this camp is comprised of men loyal to King Strephon. Even with the advantage of surprise, we would be slaughtered if we battled them, and my knights and I cannot feign the death of every prisoner Strephon plans to execute on the morrow. Short of attempting to poison the hundreds of pots of pottage in this camp, what possible victory can so few of us gain against so many? Really, Princess Rhonalyn had the right idea. It is a pity she was not successful."

"Nay, not a pity," Carys said, apprehension in her voice. "A mercy. Strephon hath no successor, and there is no other established legal heir. Thus, his power would fall to his three strongest barons. They would have killed Princess Rhonalyn on the spot, then finished executing all prisoners to extinguish the threat those men represent. For it is not who Strephon is that unites and motivates these lords and barons but rather what he hath promised them that consumes their minds and aligns their goals."

Gage felt ill thinking about what the future may look like for all three kingdoms if Strephon was allowed to pursue his plan. With anxiety swirling through him, he found himself silently pleading, "God, we need Your help. Show us how to stop Strephon, please. Tell us what to do."

A moment later in the tense silence of everyone's thoughts, an idea stirred in Gage's mind, expanding into the semblance of a plan.

Elated by the clear answer and yet also apprehensive of the risks involved, Gage spoke slowly. "We cannot win this fight here and now. We can, however, possibly steal away Strephon's victory and rescue allies who could help us win in the future." With his heartbeat quickening, he went on to explain the plan that had taken shape in his mind. When he had finished, he added. "Obviously the details will still need to be sorted out, but we have the next few hours to do that."

"Your plan has merit." Hewitt shook his head. "But I cannot participate in it. If I reveal myself as disloyal to King Strephon, it will not just be my death sentence but my family's as well, and all of Duvall will be taken from me and handed to a lord that is loyal to Strephon."

"Aye," Gage said, a fierceness filling his chest and spilling into his words, "but how long until you find yourself at that crossroad regardless? Right now, allies who could stand with you against Strephon are yet alive. On the morrow they will be executed if we do nothing. If you do nothing, perhaps you could remain hidden longer, but for what better purpose than this? Sooner or later, you will end up having to either fully submit yourself and your power to Strephon and be consumed by him or else be expose as the traitor that you are and lose everything. Hewitt, use your position now when it can still accomplish something good. Do not wait until there is nothing left to save!" Gage cringed at the severity of his own words. Never before had he dared challenge anyone in such a way, but there burned a fire inside him that was unlike any conviction he had ever known.

The Duvall knights shifted and murmured among themselves. There was anger in some of their voices but agreement in others.

"I would bear the risk myself," Hewitt replied, "but I cannot do what I know will get my family killed. And regardless of whether your plan succeeds or fails, if I have a hand in it King Strephon will send word and have my wife and children killed."

Gage nodded. "Then something must be done to protect them." He thought for a moment then asked, "Do you have any of your own messenger pigeons with you?"

"Aye, I do."

"Then send word before we take action. Tell your family to cross the border to Awnquera. My uncle will host them. It is not a guarantee of their safety considering Strephon's plans to eventually march on Edelmar, but your family can warn Edelmar, and my uncle will shelter them. That I know."

"I believe you," Hewitt nodded, "and I wish that were possible. But the bridge's gates are closed by King Strephon's orders, no exceptions. And among those on guard there are some of His Majesty's own knights." Hewitt's forehead furrowed. "But, there is mayhap another way. There is a boat moored along the city wall, kept in case of siege. If I send word, my family could take it across the Apse to Awnquera." Hewitt sighed. "But nay, King Strephon's men receive messages from him by the pigeons of my manor's dovecot. There is no way to ensure my message will not be intercepted by Strephon's knights."

A short broad shouldered knight with a square jaw and close-cut beard stepped forward. "My lord, I have with me one of my family's pigeons. Send word by it, my wife will deliver your message to your family."

Hewitt exhaled. "Sir Damian, that is a generous offer." The baron glanced around his knights. "But what then happens to all of your families?"

A bearded, blue-eyed knight met Hewitt's gaze. "It is your family, foremost, that King Strephon will seek to punish if we do this. Send your family in the boat. But let your message also instruct Sir Damian's wife to spread a warning that it is not safe to remain in Duvall. At least then our families will have a chance to defend themselves and flee."

Hewitt rubbed a hand over his mouth and again looked around his knights. "If this is done, Duvall will be lost to us all. We will have no homes to return to."

"Aye, for a time, my lord," Sir Damian replied, "but hath not the dishonor of what hath been allowed to take place under King Strephon's reign and what we have been asked to do for him already stolen our homes from us? Already we carry the stench of our deeds and struggle to look our families in the eye. And there are fathers, brothers, and sons chained yonder whose families no doubt fear them dead. We have the chance to change that and restore what hath been stolen. Prithee, allow us to take action to save others and to help depose the murderer who sits on Delkara's throne, so we might make peace with our own consciences. Let us become worthy again of our homes and families."

The knight's request hung in the air with both accusation and plea. Gage held his breath.

Silence stretched as if every one of Hewitt's knights were holding their breath, awaiting a response that would either forbid or permit them to restore their honor.

"I have asked much of you all since my father's death," Hewitt said. His face and voice filled with shame. "But I see now that the worst that I have asked hath been your obedience to my choice to sacrifice integrity for safety." Hewitt shook his head. "No longer. Today, we do what is right. I will send the message. And God help us, we will snatch away King Strephon's victory, escape to fight another day, and do what is necessary to rally together and fight with all those willing to oppose Strephon."

Murmurs of agreement flowed through the baron's men. Gage inhaled and watched others do the same. Shoulders squared, faces firmed in resolve, and a strength of unity flowed among them.

Hewitt crossed his arms over his chest. "To victory or in defeat—"

Every Duvall knight present thudded crossed arms to their chests upon the red phoenix standing upon the divide of Duvall's green-and-black shield and responded as one. "We rise from the ashes!"

70

THE DECLARATION ECHOED in Gage's mind hours later as he kept stride with Sir Damian and three other Duvall knights. They were crossing the outer encampment in the setting sun. Having changed into the green and black of Duvall to match the knights, Gage kept his head down since his helmet no longer concealed his face. They trekked toward the camp's southern edge where the companies' mounts were kept and where he had left Athalos.

After so much discussing and planning, it was a relief to finally be on the move. But launching into the plan also created its own mix of anxiety. The atmosphere of the camp had also shifted since that morning. Impatience stirred among the ranks. Conversations were hushed and tense.

One of Baron Hewitt's knights said rumors had flown through the camp about Princess Rhonalyn's attempt on Strephon's life, along with speculations about the severity of His Majesty's injury and his subsequent halt to the day's event. Add to that, the plans Strephon had made known to his barons that morning, and it was little wonder the encampment felt like a taut bowstring.

Gage hoped the tension worked in their favor.

Each of four groups were to accomplish a specific piece of the plan. Some of them needed more time than others. His group required the partial light and then the darkness before the camp lit fires, torches, and braziers. The later it became, the more soldiers in the camp would have their armor off for the night and their weapons laid aside.

He and the Duvall knights with him approached the line of mounts, which seemed to stretch on and on.

"Each of you, look to your sections and finish your tasks as quickly as possible," Sir Damian said. "Sir Archibald wilt keep watch. Godspeed."

They split up, and Gage slipped through the horses to reach his section of the tents making up the encampment's outer wall. Thankfully, with the mounts picketed in front of the tents, he and the others would be decently concealed as they worked.

His hands shaking, Gage grabbed a set of saddlebags, threw them over his shoulder, and set to his task. Every bridle he could find he unfastened, then bagged whatever piece he could strip from the headstall to make it unusable. Any he couldn't dismantle he cut through instead. He then removed the girth strap from every saddle and pushed it out the underside of the back of the tent to be collected and removed by one of Hewitt's knights.

At first it was slow going, his heart pounding and his hands trembling as he worked. But eventually, the fear of being noticed and caught settled to a more steady pound, and he made his way more quickly down the line of tents. He knew each time he changed whose tack he was dismantling or sabotaging due to the insignias and colors. Light faded around him, and the saddlebags on his shoulder grew heavy from the stolen pieces placed in them.

Down the line from him, every few moments a mount was taken out of the row by Sir Damian and made to disappear out the back of the tent wall. Gage knew a handful of Baron Hewitt's soldiers were outside the encampment, gathering the mounts sent through.

While discussing this part of the plan, the question had been asked of whether or not the encampment had an outside patrol. Carys had informed them that the city of Nissdin served as the encampment's distant guard and would signal if a threat approached. No one departing the camp would be considered a threat.

Gage felt astounded by Strephon's faith in the loyalty of his lords and at the same time thankful Hewitt's own knights were not so blindly trusting. While planning, they'd informed Hewitt of soldiers among Duvall's own ranks that should not be included in the baron's plans for the night. Hewitt accepted their judgement and without hesitation sent orders that would keep those soldiers far removed from their plans.

Gage unbuckled the last few pieces of tack and finished off his portion of the tents. Passing off the full saddlebags to Sir Damian, he headed for Nigel and Athalos. He put a saddle on Nigel and added a front harness and leather barding he had saved to Athalos's tack. When he was done, he nodded at Sir Damian, who held aside the tent wall for him to lead the two mounts through into the night.

❧

In the loosely fitting yellow-and-green Nissdin uniform with its face-concealing helmet, Wick strode through the firelight of a brazier and into the entrance tent to where he and Manton had first been taken as prisoners. He addressed the Lyster and Nissdin soldiers on duty in the tent with the sort of expectant tone his White Fortress commander would have used. "I'm seeking Sir Treyson. Is he within?"

According to Carys, the keys to the prisoners' shackles were kept by whichever of the lord's knights were on duty in the area, while the keys to Nissdin's prisoners and the padlocks on the chain running between the two trees were held by Sir Treyson, Baron Fitch's constable.

Prince Gage had stiffened at the name, muttering something about him and Felix, and when Carys had described the man's thick neck and chiseled face, Wick realized he too had met Sir Treyson. The knight had unlocked his and Manton's shackles before they had been hauled before Strephon.

"Sir Treyson? He entered a bit ago," the Nissdin guard replied. "I haven't seen him leave, so you should find him within."

Nodding, Wick marched forward, thankful food and drink had restored his strength enough to allow him to spearhead this part of their plan. He shoved through the loose flaps into the area beyond and avoided looking toward the tent where he had been chained or out into the darkness by the trees where he knew he'd see Princess Rhonalyn. Instead, he focused on searching the area's edges for Sir Treyson. He spotted the Nissdin knight walking away from another guard who was using the area's braziers to heat a tankard of something.

Heading for Sir Treyson, Wick fell into stride beside the constable and spoke in a clipped manner. "Sir Treyson, something's come to my attention that I believe you'll want to address."

Sir Treyson's loud, commanding response made Wick flinch. "Well, out with it. What is it?"

Wick kept his voice low. "Sir, better if I show you. We can go through here." He led the constable to the tent where he and Manton had been chained. Ducking inside the dimly lit interior, Wick stepped aside.

Sir Treyson marched in after him and stopped short, staring at two Duvall soldiers, standing on either side of Lady Aisley who held a lantern. "What is—"

Sir Treyson's voice was cut off as one of the two Duvall soldiers stepped forward and slammed a fist into his face. A Duvall knight who'd been waiting at the opposite end of the tent fell upon Sir Treyson from behind, clamping a hand over his mouth. As the four scuffled, Wick drew forth his sword and put himself in front of Lady Aisley.

The Duvall knight managed to force a gag into the constable's mouth while he and the Duval soldiers struggled to wrestle the constable into submission. The only sounds that followed were grunts and the scuffling of leather on metal as the three of them attempted to keep Sir Treyson in the center of the tent and bring him to the ground.

The Duvall knight, with one hand still clamped over Sir Treyson's mouth and the other gripping the constable's shoulder, tripped on the chains running from the metal loops in the corners of the tent. The knight lost his footing but kept his grip on Sir Treyson, dragging Nissdin's constable backward with him. The other two Duvall soldiers added their weight to the imbalance, and they all toppled over, pinning Sir Treyson in place.

"Get the shackles," the Duvall knight said with a grunt.

Handing Aisley his sword, Wick helped them chain Sir Treyson to the spot and felt a good bit of satisfaction at the justice of it. The Duvall knight secured the constable's gag with another cloth and then searched the growling Sir Treyson for the keys they needed. Wick held his breath, praying that they hadn't made a mistake trusting Carys's information.

71

"Let me go!" a young girl's frightened protest echoed to where Rhonalyn sat chained in the dark at the end of the line of nobles.

Lifting her aching head and blinking her eyelashes loose from the crustiness of dried tears, Rhonalyn squinted toward the sound. In the light cast by the fires of two braziers, she caught sight of a Nissdin soldier and a knight in green-and-black dragging a small figure between them. The girl twisted and fought as the soldier and knight pulled her out toward Rhonalyn.

Misery swelled within Rhonalyn. Not Aisley too.

The two men thrust the girl to the ground, three paces down from her. They moved around the girl, chains rattling, then shoved Aisley sideways and trekked away.

Staring at the girl's dark, huddled form, Rhonalyn wept fresh tears and spoke to her. "Aisley, I am so sorry. I have been such a fool. This is—"

"Shhh," Aisley hissed. "It is alright, Princess Rhonalyn. We have a plan."

Rhonalyn paused, not sure which one startled her more—Aisley's calm voice or the girl's assurance that getting chained beside her was part of some plan. "What do you mean? Where is Gabe?" Rhonalyn glanced toward the Nissdin soldier who had brought Aisley and was now on patrol. He wasn't the right build to be Gabe.

"He is a bit busy," Aisley replied as she crawled closer. "Here." She pushed something metal into Rhonalyn's hands. "See if it works.

If it does, stay quiet, and stay put. They will come to us. Now, if you will excuse me, I have a padlock to find."

With that, Aisley slipped back the way she'd come toward the base of the tree. In the darkness Rhonalyn could just make out her small form and hear the clink of metal on metal.

Bitting back the dozens of questions that rose on her tongue, Rhonalyn clenched the thin metal item Aisley had handed her. Recognizing it as a key, she twisted around one of her shackles to try it in the lock. It took several attempts to get it into the slot, but finally the key slid into the shackle. She pushed down. There was a quiet click, and the metal fetter around her wrist popped open. She inhaled a breath and unlocked her other hand. Once free of the metal, she looked for Aisley. Finally she spotted her dark form still crouched at the base of the tree.

Resisting the urge to crawl toward her, Rhonalyn tightened her hand around the key. She glanced down the line of other prisoners. Somewhere on the thick chain was Manton and the previous lord of Burnel, along with all the other men and lords that Strephon held prisoner and planned to execute. Would the key she held unlock any of them? And if it did, what then? She swung her gaze toward the armed guards patrolling the edge of the area in front of the braziers that cast their light like a moat in front of the surrounding tent walls. Beyond those tents she knew were dozens of additional soldiers and knights.

The hope inside her sank. What plan could Gabe and Aisley possibly have that would get them out of this?

A rustling noice came back toward her. She leaned forward, then jerked back as Aisley appeared in front of her. "Did your key work?" The girl asked.

"Aye, my hands are free."

"Thank goodness. Pass it to me then. I will get it to the others while I sneak to the other padlock."

Rhonalyn frowned. "What padlock?"

Aisley scooped the key out of her hand and crawled past her. "I will explain when I return."

❧

Wick slowed in a darker spot between two braziers where his eyes could adjust and peered out at the line of prisoners. Having heard nothing from Aisley for longer than he expected, he was beginning to fear something had gone wrong.

He was just about to march out to check on her when out by one of the trees he heard two owl hoots. Relief eased Wick back into the light of the braziers. The keys had worked, and the padlocks were open. He glanced toward Baron Hewitt's knight, who had also settled into the patrol awaiting confirmation.

The knight disappeared back into the tent where his fellow soldiers tarried. The Duvall knight returned a moment later with one of the soldiers. They both carried crossbows and took up patrol as if they were meant to be there. They were two of only five of the guard carrying crossbows.

Wick focused on his next task. Since currently he wasn't able to bear the weight or strain of using a crossbow and had only his sword to use, he would have to be much closer to his target. He chose a Phenes knight standing in a corner and began to work his way toward him.

Past the corner though, a knight of Nikledon broke off his conversation with a Maneo soldier and cut across the area on an intercept course with Wick.

His heart pounding, Wick resisted the urge to reach for his sword. It was too early for him to engage in a fight. They needed more time. Even if the knight somehow suspected him, he needed to find a way to delay any kind of confrontation.

"Soldier, where's your constable gotten off to?" the knight asked. "We're all wondering about those drinks he promised us."

Drinks. Was that all he was after? Wick exhaled. "If Sir Treyson promised drinks, I'm sure he'll get to it."

"Right, but when? Next month?" The knight snorted and fell into step beside him. "By now, we were supposed to be done with guard duty, now instead we're all stuck here another night."

Wick's stride faltered and heat flushed his body. He knew what the knight meant by "done with guard duty." Every prisoner there was supposed to have already been executed, including Wick himself. He wanted to draw his weapon and end the knight's patrol right then and there the same way the knight would have ended him. He clenched his fists, grateful for the helmet he wore since he knew his face displayed his fury.

Hatred twisted in Wick's chest. This was who Strephon's soldiers and crows were. Men who cared nothing for the lives of others, not for Allard's life or Bardon's, or his. They deserved to face vengeance for what they'd done, and Wick felt himself eagerly anticipating bringing it to them.

A quiet question filled his mind. *"Why are you here, to harm or to rescue? 'Vengeance is Mine,' says the Lord. Repay no one evil for evil."*

Wick's thought grated over the words, and his soul shuddered between his raging desire and the request for him to surrender it. He glanced at the Nikledon knight, loathing him and all the others so much and wanting to make them pay.

Were they not at war? Did that not justify the violence he wanted to do to them?

Questions again countered. *"Is that what you were sent here to do, to seek retribution in violence? Or were you sent to save captives? What is your mission? Is it revenge or rescue?"*

Wick balked at the choice. He wanted both. These people had voted for him to be executed. They had cheered when they thought him dead. And now they complained because others yet lived.

Yes, and in that, they, too, are captives, imprisoned in the darkness of their own sin. Death awaits them as surely as it awaited you. Would you now vote for them to die? Cheer when they perish? Complain that they yet live?

Feeling gutted by the questions and at a loss to know how to respond, Wick jerked when a distant cry of alarm yanked him from his thoughts.

It was time to move.

✂❧

"Fire! Fire in the tents!"

Rhonalyn tensed. The alarm—hollered from the eastern portion of the camp—was followed by another call of fire from the southwest side. Was this part of Aisley's and Gabe's plan?

An orange glow in both areas expanded above the tent wall. Shouts and cries in the outer camp grew louder. Those on guard duty drifted together in the mote of light, questioning each other. Usually water or sand was kept ready near fires to extinguish flames, but it didn't seem that was happening at either location.

"Lord Duvall's pavilions are on fire!" someone yelled from the southwest side of the camp. "Fetch water! Bring help!"

Aisley appeared out of the darkness, making Rhonalyn jump. "The main chain is free." Aisley murmured to her. "It will not be long now. I passed word to the others to keep quiet and, as soon as they can, to get to the horses."

"What horses?" Rhonalyn questioned.

Aisley didn't get the chance to answer for just then eight soldiers in green and black tabards spilled from a tent into the light of the braziers. The soldiers spread in every direction, heading for the guards already present. For a moment, their presence stirred even more questions among those on patrol, who moved toward them, asking what was happening. Then the first green-and-black soldier reached a Lyster knight. In a swift, fluid motion, he seized the knight's arm, twisted it behind his back, and sliced a dagger across the knight's throat.

Rhonalyn gasped.

All around the area, other Duvall soldiers killed, detained, or fought with the mix of lords' men. Swords were drawn and the guardsmen rushed at their attackers. Meanwhile, guards on two sides of the area raised their crossbows to shoot at the Duvall soldiers. Before they could get shots off though, they were dropped by bolts fired from crossbows held by the Duvall knight and soldier who had previously joined their ranks.

At that point, knights of Burnel and Dinslage raised the alarm. "Attack! Betrayal! Duvall is attacking!" Their calls, however, simply blended into the chaos raised by the fires.

A Nikledon knight lunged forward to strike at an approaching Duvall soldier. As he did, the Nissdin soldier beside him snagged hold of his chainmail coif, jerking him off his feet and crashing him to the ground. Furious, the knight attempted to rise, but the sword of the Nissdin soldier hovering over him convinced him to stay down and relinquish his weapons.

Snatching away his surrendered blade, a Duvall soldier rendered the guard unconscious while the Nissdin soldier searched him. Rising with a key in hand, the Nissdin soldier gripped his side and sprinted toward where Rhonalyn and the other prisoners were.

Defeating their Duvall attacker, soldiers in brown and white and red broke free and swiftly intercepted him.

Halted from his goal and facing the two guardsman, the Nissdin soldier raised his sword. Fending off their strikes and blows, he skillfully held his own against the two of them, but he was prevented from making any progress with the key. He parried his two attackers' strikes once again, and this time instead of trying to push forward, the Nissdin soldier stepped back. Flinging up his arm, he hurled the key over their heads. It flew into the semi-darkness and landed in the grass halfway between him and the line of prisoners.

Rhonalyn stiffened, unsure what to do.

Aisley bolted for the spot the key had landed.

At the same time the red-and-white soldier diverted from his fight with the Nissdin soldier and also ran for the key.

Aisley reached the spot first but only barely. She dug in the grass, snatched the key up, and with a scream darted back toward the line of prisoners.

Rhonalyn cried out as the approaching soldier pursued Aisley, his dark form gaining on the girl. The soldier raised his weapon and reached to grab Aisley's shoulder. Rhonalyn's heart leaped into her throat.

A large prisoner burst from the dark forms down the line from her. Apparently freed the same way she had been, he ran at Aisley and her pursuer. The soldier following Aisley slowed his stride momentarily, then continued onward despite the larger prisoner coming at him.

Watching the three of them about to converge, Rhonalyn held her breath.

Aisley veered from between the two just as the soldier swung his weapon at her. The blade swept toward the large prisoner instead. The man flung out a hand, halting the soldier's blade in midair. Had it not been for the chime of metal against metal, Rhonalyn would have sworn the prisoner had grabbed the sword with his bare hand. The man shoved the soldier's sword up and drove forward, slamming into the soldier's armored chest. Soldier and prisoner went down together, wrestling across the ground in a dark, writhing mass.

Other prisoners stirred forward, and the heavy chain Rhonalyn had been shackled to knocked against her ankles. More dark forms separated from the chain. Those who were free, including Manton, ran out to engage in the fight, using their unlocked shackles like flails against their enemies.

But the advantage of surprise was already gone. The Duvall soldiers were too few in number, and the prisoners, who were able to assist them, were barely enough to keep the Duvall soldiers from being overwhelmed.

Manton and the others fought on, but as Rhonalyn absorbed the clash of weapons, chains, and mayhem around her, despair crept through her. The moment the encampment realized what was happening, all of this would come to nothing.

A Duvall soldier with another key ran toward the line of prisoners, persisting in the effort to set other prisoners free, despite there being nowhere for them to go. Within moments more forms were released from their shackles and entered the battle, which Rhonalyn could see ending only one way. She inhaled a sharp breath. She supposed if nothing else, instead of being killed as bound prisoners, they could at least die fighting. Scooping up her own shackles, she gripped them in the darkness and rose. As she ran forward, she found herself wondering if the other side of death would be better or worse than being Strephon's prisoner.

72

Listening to the sounds of alarm, Gage clenched his borrowed sword and held Athalos in place beside Hewitt's four mounted knights. They had assembled in the dark, facing the encampment's west side but at a distance to avoid their accompanying small herd of saddled mounts from being heard by those inside the camp. Amid the mostly riderless mounts, a good handful of Hewitt's soldiers sat on horseback, each holding a half dozen or more lead lines. They all awaited a path to be opened into the encampment in order for them to deliver the animals to their intended riders.

Aisley's signal must have been received because Gage could see the glow of the fires that Baron Hewitt and half a dozen of his men had stayed to start and spread inside the camp.

"Come on," Sir Damian muttered beside Gage, "what is taking those two so long? Get it down."

Just as he finished speaking, a tent in the midst of the pale outer edge of the encampment wall buckled inward, no doubt due to its guy lines being cut.

"Now!" Sir Damian called out.

The riders around Gage burst forward, and he loosed Athalos's reins. The horse leaped into a run with the others toward the encampment. The air around Gage filled with the thunder of charging hooves and the rattle of armor. His heartbeat pulsed in his head, and his breathing came in gasps of fear and anticipation.

Their small company reached the encampment's edge. They tore over top of the collapsed tent, across a lane, past a brazier surrounded by confused soldiers of Deubor, and barreled toward a tent wall opposite the one they had just trampled.

That tent was already collapsing when the first knight in their company rode his horse straight into it. Ropes, fabric, and the main pole were all dragged forward with the horse's momentum, tearing a breach into the area around the two trees where Gage had last seen the encampment's prisoners.

He sucked in a breath. Around the trees, soldiers, knights, and prisoners were all engaged in a furious skirmish with swords, fists, knives, and shackles. Bursting into their midst with the other riders, Gage swung at the closest enemy he encountered. His sword clanged against the pauldron armor of a Maneo knight, sending him stumbling toward the Duvall soldier he had been fighting.

Swerving Athalos toward a new target, Gage angled the horse like a battering ram into soldiers from Lyster and Deubor, who had the sword-wielding Lord Braxton and shackle-swinging Lord Hadrian backing toward the western tent wall. At the blow from Athalos, the Lyster soldier smacked into the ground like a board. Meanwhile, the Deubor soldier spun like a top and was still stumbling in a circle when Gage left them behind.

Nowhere in the area did Gage see Hewitt, who was supposed to meet them there, nor did he see Rhonalyn or Sir Wick. He did, however, spot Manton and Aisley. Aisley was holding a short dagger and dodging around Manton to stab at a Burnel knight whom Manton was struggling to subdue. Aisley attacked the knight like a small mad dog, biting low and where least expected.

Gage couldn't reach the two of them but slowed Athalos to intercept a Burnel soldier heading toward them. He slashed the soldier's sword aside and turned Athalos's hindquarters into the guard, smashing the soldier to the ground. Three of Hewitt's mounted knights swept around him. The first of the riders swung his sword from side to side as he slammed through the fray of skirmishers. As he hacked at every enemy in his path, the two other knights steered wide to employ crossbows. Their bolts found their marks in soldiers from Dinslage and Maneo.

Urging Athalos back around toward the center of the area, Gage veered sharply to avoid a brazier and galloped for the closest enemy. He swung his sword, striking the helmet of a knight of Dinslage who had a hold of the abbot from Burnel. He then smashed into the side of a Phenes knight battling a Nissdin soldier, whom Gage assumed had to be Sir Wick, since he was fighting with them.

Rushing on, Gage cringed when Athalos leapt over the body of a dead lord to avoid trampling a Duvall soldier who was on his knees, clutching his side. The soldier was too far from his sword and too injured to defend himself.

Gage spun Athalos around, intending to circle back to help the soldier, but Sir Damian beat him to it.

Sliding his horse to a stop, the Duvall knight reached a hand down to the injured soldier, ordering him to grab hold. The soldier pushed himself to his feet and grasped the knight's arm. Sir Damian turned his horse in a circle, sweeping the soldier up behind him.

Twisting Athalos around, Gage swept his eyes over the area. The herd of saddled mounts were riding through the breach in the wall, which was now on the opposite side of the area from him. At sight of the horses, the majority of the Duvall soldiers broke from those they were still fighting and ran for the mounts, urging the prisoners to do the same, among which were Manton and Rhonalyn. But between the two trees, dark forms were still fettered to the main chain.

Gage kicked Athalos toward them as prisoners and soldiers

fled past him. He slid to a stop beside the five prisoners still chained and found Aisley with them. "What keys are still needed?" he asked. "Which lords?"

"Lemar."

"Deubor."

One of Hewitt's soldiers stumbled up, blood running down his neck and arm. "Lemar's. I've got it." He thrust a key into the nearest set of groping hands.

A shout burst from Gage's left. He swung his gaze to that portion of the tent wall. A Nissdin soldier held open the flap for Nikledon soldiers to surge through into the area.

Gage looked at Aisley and the four remaining prisoners. "There's no time to locate the other key. Drag the chain, get to the mounts, and find a way to ride out of here!"

The blue-and-green company of Nikeldon soldiers started toward them, weapons drawn.

Gage turned Athalos to face them. He, two of Hewitt's knights on horseback, a Duvall foot soldier, and Sir Wick were all that stood between the unarmed prisoners and the deadly assault that was coming. Behind him, Gage heard the clash of swords and the stir of mounts. He gripped his weapon and said a silent prayer that all they had done and were about to die for would not be in vain.

73

A TENT TO the west split open. Gage's heart sank, then leaped. Hewitt and the rest of his men poured through the opening on foot. The Nikeldon soldiers slowed and then stopped as if unsure if the baron's men in the area were defying him or under his orders. Their hesitation gave Hewitt enough time to seize control of the situation and direct his men. His soldiers spread across the area, using their swords and armored bodies to shield the retreating prisoners.

The Nikledon soldiers had their answer. Their faces fierce with anger, they ran at Hewitt's men.

Hooves pounded behind Gage, and in the next instant horses were among those on foot.

"My lord!" A knight released five horses' lead lines and tossed a sixth to Hewitt.

The baron flung himself into the saddle of his charger. His other men and Sir Wick endeavored to do the same, grasping reins and gaining the tops of their mounts while clutching their swords. The sea of spinning hooves and twisting hindquarters created its own defense against the approaching soldiers, but only for a moment.

Then the Nikeldon soldiers were among them.

With height and horseflesh on their side, Gage and the others trampled and pummeled their enemy, taking some damage and two losses in the process.

A whistle rent the air from the direction of the breach. Gage kicked at an enemy soldier, slammed the hilt of his sword into another's face, and glanced toward the sound.

A Duvall soldier with Aisley seated behind him rode through the breach behind the four chained prisoners riding on three closely held horses.

Inside the area, apart from the group Gage was with, no one else remained alive of Duvall or the prisoners. He and the others had accomplished their goal; they had no one left to safeguard.

With a shout to his men, Hewitt drove his horse toward the breach. Gage, Sir Wick, and the rest of the company also broke free from the battle and raced after him.

Their company thundered through the opening, smashed aside Deubor soldiers in the lane, and tore over the flattened outer tent, bursting into the darkness beyond.

Gage was on the back edge of the riders. Engulfed by the darkness, he had just sheathed his sword when Athalos's front legs buckled. The animal's head drove into the ground and his hindquarters vaulted forward in a somersault that threw Gage out of the saddle. He landed hard on dark ground and felt Athalos's body slam down beside him. The horse struggled over, bumping Gage's arm, then side. A hoof clipped his hip and another landed on his chest without any weight. Then Athalos was gone, pounding away into the night after the other riders.

Groaning in pain, Gage shoved himself to his hands and knees. Despite breathing hard, he could hear the chaos in the camp behind him. He glanced back and saw numerous tents aflame. The phoenix had indeed arisen in fire and flown. He winced. If only his own wings hadn't failed him.

Foot soldiers from the camp carrying torches poured from the breach toward him. Grunting, Gage thrust himself to his feet and stumbled into a ran. He searched for signs of the company he had been riding in just moments before. He spotted the diminishing silhouettes of their retreating forms ahead and could vaguely hear their mounts' fading hoofbeats.

With a burst of panic, Gage hastened after them. There was no way he would be able to catch up to the company on foot, but he wasn't going to stay where he was and be captured.

With urgency flooding him, he ran through the tall meadow grass. He wished he could unbuckle his armor and let it fall away, but he couldn't risk slowing to do so. Nor did he wish to leave his back defenseless. Instead, he ran over the pitted ground, squinting in the dark and trying to keep track of Hewitt's company. He knew they would divide into smaller groups as soon as they were far enough away, which meant his chance of finding those he was supposed to be with was decreasing by the moment.

Out of the darkness in front of him appeared a looming form. Silhouetted against the sky, he realized it was a horse with a small rider on it coming back at him.

"Gabriel! There you are!" Aisley spun the horse, then leaped out of the saddle, gripping it's reins. "Come on! Get on!"

Gage ran toward her. The animal snorted and threw its head at his approach. He seized its reins and saddle and heaved himself on the horse's back. As he did so, he discovered to his surprise that he sat upon Athalos.

With a dozen questions filling his head but no time to ask them, he grabbed Aisley's hand and hauled her back up behind him, hoping Athalos would permit her once more to ride him. Gage felt the pressure of Aisley's grasp upon the edge of his armor. Counting on the girl being able to keep her grip, he kicked Athalos into a gallop, tearing away from the camp and the approaching soldiers.

Athalos raced after the others. Gage breathed in relief to have the pounding of hooves again beneath him. Sooner than he expected, the company's fleeing forms came into sight on the horizon. He urged Athalos onward but need not have bothered. The horse seemed every bit as eager as he was to rejoin them. Despite Athalos's speed, though, they couldn't seem to close the distance to reach the company of riders. Gage comforted himself that at least each stride put them farther from their pursuers.

74

RHONALYN LEANED INTO her horse's galloping hoofbeats and steered firmly to keep it even with but not on top of the soldier riding beside her. She had no idea where they were headed, but it didn't matter. All she wanted was to put as much distance between herself and Strephon as possible. Every other concern could wait.

The riders around her slowed, causing all the mounts to bunch together. Rhonalyn pulled back her horse's reins to bring it to a trot along the outer edge of the group. The other mounts jostled closer around her, then they slowed even further, pressing together. The breathing of so many horses and the creak of saddles filled the darkness.

"Knights of Duvall," a strong, authoritative voice said from behind Rhonalyn, "locate those you were designated to travel with, then split off into your smaller groups. Previous prisoners, my knights have supplies and will explain the plan once you are fully away and confident of your surroundings."

"Not to find fault," a voice said, "since I'm extremely grateful to be alive and free, but in the dark we won't cover much ground. King Strephon won't sit back and ignore our escape. They'll come after us."

"They'll try," someone said, "but after what we did to their horses' tack, it'll take them time to do so. Unusable bridles and girth-less saddles aren't much good for speed or long-distance travel."

Chuckles followed the comment.

"Yes," the first voice said, "and by moving quickly and breaking into smaller groups, the hope is that we'll each avoid being discovered. We're now all traitors to Delkara's crown, and thus we have a common enemy in King Strephon and those loyal to him. Our homes are not safe for us to return to, but if we work together we've a chance to fight back and save our kingdom and those we love. So, I urge you, no matter the risk of the task my men pass along to you, see it accomplished. There's not time for me to explain more now, but I assure you that I hath pledged all of my resources and power to dethroning King Strephon and restoring peace to Delkara. Join me in doing what is necessary."

"Hear, hear!" riders called out.

"Now, men of Duvall, as quickly as you can, find those with whom you've been designated to travel."

Murmurs and a stir of movement followed as lords, knights, and soldiers identified each other. Rhonalyn wondered where and with whom she was supposed to go since she wasn't one of the men. A thought struck her then, and she called out, "Aisley?" Twisting in her saddle, she questioned frantically, "Is Lady Aisley present?"

Everyone fell silent, and her heart clenched.

"I'm here." Aisley called out, her voice breathless. The girl then added dolefully, "Stuck in the dark, fleeing soldiers, again."

A laugh burst out, and the voice of a dead man teased, "Says the girl who, in the dark, stole into a camp of enemy soldiers to find and help her friends."

Her mind reeling, Rhonalyn tried to make sense of the impossible. "Wick! Is that…is that really you?"

He laughed again. "Yes, Princess Rhonalyn. It's really me. Baron Hewitt did not kill me."

A lump formed in Rhonalyn's throat. "How?" Her mind's vivid image of him dying continued to contradict his words.

Nervous yet proud chuckles came from several riders, and some-one said, "Because he died convincingly. That's how."

"Though not convincingly enough for Carys." A deep voice com-mented, as horses and riders split off from their group.

"Thank goodness for that," the authoritative voice said. "Otherwise we may not have had her help."

Carys's help? Rhonalyn blinked. Was she hearing them right?

The riders resumed breaking into groups, and a horse pushed up beside hers. "Princess Rhonalyn," the authoritative voice said, "you are to ride with me. I am baron Hewitt of Duvall."

☙❧

Gage steered Athalos out of the way as mounts and riders stirred around them.

Aisley shifted behind him. "I'm to go with Baron Hewitt, and you to Verfeld, yes?"

"That's right." Gage twisted and spoke over his shoulder. "And before you depart, Lady Aisley. Thank you. If not for your help I wouldn't be here nor would many of these lords. You've shown remark-able courage today. And, truly, I still don't know how it is you came back for me."

"You were riding beside us one moment, and then Athalos was running without you. I knew that you must've fallen off. I just did what anyone would've done."

Gage shook his head. "No, Lady Aisley, you did what no one else could do. You rode Athalos back to me, and I still can't believe that he let you."

"Oh, that." Aisley added in a guilty tone, "Please, don't tell Princess Rhonalyn. In the mornings, before anyone else is awake, I've been making friends with Athalos and Nigel." She added more eagerly.

"I discovered that Athalos likes being scratched just below his ears."

"Is that so?" Gage laughed. He noted the riders around them were diminishing quickly. "Well, Lady Aisley, as happy as I'd be to continue sharing my horse with you, I believe you need a mount that can take you in the direction you're meant to go."

"Since Wick is accompanying us to the spot that Carys suggested we go, may I ride with him?" Since Aisley had listened in on the last of their planning after Carys had retrieved her from Rhonalyn's tent, the girl was better informed than any of the freed prisoners.

"I'd assume so," Gage replied. "Meanwhile, I must locate Sir Damian, Lord Braxton, and Manton. Nigel's packs are still at the healer's shelter. So, I have a feeling Manton'll go with us that far. As to what he'll do happens after that, that waits to be seen."

"I hope he stays." Aisley gripped Gage's arm, and before he could object to her actions she swung down from Athalos. "In Verfeld, if you happen to see Tobias, will you please tell him I'm alright."

"I will." Gage promised, then instructed. "Now, find Wick quickly, and don't get trampled down there."

Aisley responded with what sounded like a roll of her eyes. "Yes, Mother."

Gage snorted. Long gone was the demure girl Rhonalyn had been trying to craft into a proper lady-in-waiting. Little wonder it was, though, that Aisley disliked wearing shoes and doing needlework. The little firebrand preferred it seemed to be out befriending dangerous animals, hiding under beds, and volunteering to get fake captured. He chuckled at the image, then cringed, imagining the risks the girl had taken and how it would go at the lodge putting her and Rhonalyn back together again. It was too late though to change Aisley's destination. Besides, as things were, she would be safest at that location.

While planning, they had discussed at length who to put in

which group and where they would go. The hardest of choices was where to send the group with both Rhonalyn, due to her significance to Strephon, and Hewitt, because of the audacity of his betrayal. The two of them were likely to be Strephon's top priorities, and the farther Hewitt and Rhonalyn traveled, the more likely they were to be revealed to Strephon.

Carys had thus suggested Rhonalyn, Hewitt, and anyone unable to travel a significant distance take a shorter route and hide under Strephon's very nose. So their plan had been made. Rather than fleeing across Delkara, they would loop around and travel to a royal hunting lodge on the Valence River. According to Carys, it had been one of King Maurice's favorite retreats and a place Strephon hated. Sitting empty, the lodge was a spot Strephon was unlikely to search. There was also no village near it. No one would be put in harm's way by their taking refuge there, nor would there be any risk of anyone betraying them.

Safety and concealment were not their only goals, though. The lodge would, if everything went according to plan, also serve as a meeting place for a council of war, which they very much hoped would include Baron Renaud—if after four years the man could indeed be located at the place he had been commanded to await his next orders.

Carys had insisted she would not share Baron Renaud's location or the location of King Maurice's orders with anyone besides Gage and Sir Wick, therefore the task of retrieving the orders and delivering them to Baron Renaud fell to Gage. The orders were concealed, Carys had said, in her healer's shelter in a small chest, buried under the flat rock on which she gathered and crushed her herbs.

Gage thought back to his and Carys's conversation before she'd departed Hewitt's tent.

"You are not coming with us?" He had assumed that she would.

Carys's brown eyes met his questioning gaze, and she shook her head. "There is not time for me to explain all the reasons why, but I cannot leave my place beside Strephon. My presence would only hinder your escape, and if your plan tonight succeeds, you will need all the information and help you can get. I can better gain and give both if I stay. When you return, look for me at the healer's shelter. Until then I entrust you with my secret and my hope for a better future for us all. Retrieve the orders, and then travel to Salvas. Go to the shipwrights there. Tell them you need the Adviser. Ask if they can help you find him. That is how you are to make contact with Baron Renaud."

Gage hesitated before asking, "Do you truly believe he will still be there, awaiting orders from a dead king?"

Carys's duel colored forehead furrowed. "I hope and pray so, because according to Queen Marjorie, he is the only person able to open and implement the order to legally depose Strephon. Those orders could change all of this from a revolt to the legal dethroning of a false ruler. And that shift has the potential to transition the loyalty of a dozen or more Delkaran lords, all of whom currently serve Strephon only because they believe they are duty bound to keep their oaths to Delkara's crown. Thus, I believe Baron Renaud is our best chance to unite enough power to stop Strephon before he twists Delkara into a weapon against Keric and Edelmar and brings destruction upon all three kingdoms."

Gage could still see the absolute conviction in Carys's face of what she believed Strephon was capable of, and a shudder ran through his body. He had seen enough of the brutality and wanton disregard for life that Strephon and his men displayed that he didn't doubt Carys's or Hewitt's assertions about Strephon's abilities or his goals.

"Gabe." Sir Damian's voice pulled Gage from his thoughts. "I've gathered Lord Braxton and your companion. We should depart."

Thankful that Hewitt's knights were abiding by his request for them to conceal his identity, Gage glanced toward the two riders trailing Sir Damian and addressed the thinner of the two forms. "Manton."

"Gabriel," Manton said in a tone of both annoyance and appreciation.

"Well," Gage said, "you were right about Strephon and about this being a war. Though, I'm not sure exactly what footing that leaves you and I on going forward, considering our history."

"That mark, you've blamed me for," Manton said, "it proclaims you Strephon's enemy. You've now made that true three times over. And you know what they say, my enemy's enemy…"

Gage touched his right vambrace. For the first time ever he felt something other than anger for the brand beneath. He eyed Manton's dark form. "Are we allies then?"

"I hope so."

Sir Wick's voice cut between them. "If you violate his trust again, Manton, I promise you there'll be no where you can go." Sir Wick turned his horse, and Aisley, Gage was relieved to see, was tucked behind him. Sir Wick spoke to him, "Gabe, if not for my injuries, you know I'd—"

"You'd be riding with me, I know."

Sir Wick heaved a breath. "Stay safe."

"Don't fret about him," Sir Damian said. "I'll watch his back. You have my word."

"I'll hold you to that."

"I would expect no less. Godspeed."

"And to you all." Sir Wick turned his and Aisley's horse back toward their group of riders, which Gage knew was comprised of Princess Rhonalyn, Baron Hewitt, Lord Burnel, four of Hewitt's knight, and four of Hewitt's soldiers.

Gage called after them. "May God give us all success in our missions and grant that all of us might witness Strephon's power be stripped away."

"Amen!" Hewitt called back. "Until we meet again." The baron turned his horse and split away, followed by those traveling with him.

Gage pulled his gaze off their disappearing forms and commented. "Lord Braxton, I believe you know best the way to your manor. Will you lead us?"

"I will," Braxton replied with a grim earnestness. "And I anticipate that on the way you'll explain Baron Hewitt's plan, for I'm eager to hear how we can bring an end to King Strephon's murderous reign."

"For once I agree with a lord," Manton said.

"Explain I will," Gage said, "for there's much that needs accomplishing if we're to defeat Strephon."

Urging Athalos onward with the others, Gage headed for Verfeld and for where King Maurice's orders were buried beneath the healer's shelter.

1. Have you ever been in a situation where you had to trust your safety to someone you barely knew? In Rhonalyn's position, would you question the motives of strangers offering to help you? Why or why not?

2. Rhonalyn believes that loyalty is a commitment to carrying out certain actions for someone because of what that person has promise to do for you. What do you think? What is loyalty? Is it transactional? Or is it relational? Additionally, can someone be trustworthy without being loyal, and vice-versa?

3. Gage decided to go after Rhonalyn and Aisley, and he told himself it was to help them, but then he realizes later that that wasn't his only motivation. While making a decision have you ever told yourself and perhaps even convinced yourself that your reasons were selfless when in reality they were not?

4. How does Haaken's question about whether or not Gage can trust himself to do what's right challenged Gage when he realizes he deceived himself about his own motives? The Bible talks about this reality in Jeremiah 17:5-15 and gives the solution in Proverbs 3:5-7. How does this exhortation challenge you when it comes to your own decision making?

5. Have you ever felt like God has given you too much to handle? In the midsts of his own problems, Gage is handed

Rhonalyn and Aisley to help too, and he's angry at God for piling more on him. As the situation unfolds though, how does Gage actually begin to see God's provision and plan in what initially felt like God disregarding him?

6. Has there ever been a time when you asked God for help and were answered by what felt like silence? Gage wants to get to know God better and asks God for help to do so. Gage is answered by what feels like silence, but in what way had God actually already answered Gage's request?

7. Have you ever had in your life someone who felt like everything to you and when they were gone, their absence left a gaping hole? What did you do? Where did you turn? Both Gage and Haaken lost the people they had been turning to for support, how were their responses the same and how were they different?

8. Manton and Rhonalyn can't both be right about who they think Strephon is, and yet they are both convinced of what they believe. Proverbs 18:17 talks about this kind of situation. Have you ever thought you understood what was happening, then heard another side to the story, and suddenly were no longer sure what was true? How did you navigate this?

9. How do you determine what is true? Are you willing to change your mind when you are presented with a reality that counters what you thought was true?

10. Why do you think Gage got so angry at Rhonalyn for going through his saddlebags? Has a past experience ever altered and or intensified the way you responded to something?

Were you able to slow down to sort out why and then apologize to the person for your reaction?

11. Gage has a hard time being kind to Rhonalyn, why do you
     think he struggles so much in his interactions with her?
     What changes could he have made that might have helped
     their relationship be less antagonistic?

12. Have you ever had to make a decision that would impact
     other people's lives? Did you wish you didn't have to be the
     one to bear that responsibility? When Wick puts it on Gage
     to decide if they go to Ithera, what change happens that
     allows Gage to make that decision despite his fears?

13. At the potters and brickmakers, Manton offers their help
     around the place, and Rhonalyn is angry when Gage volun-
     teers her to help too. Why do you think she feels this way?
     Gage and Aisley both enjoy their experience helping, why
     do you think this is? How might your own mindset about
     yourself and your position impact your attitude about help-
     ing others?

14. Have you ever paused like Haaken to really consider the real-
     ity of what it means that God created everything?

15. When Gage reads Haaken's thoughts about the way that
     God deals with Adam and Eve, he wonders why God didn't
     just make humans compliant slaves. Have you ever consid-
     ered what God wants from humanity? How might what
     you believe about God's goal in creating you change how
     you see God?

16. Why does Wick dislike Manton so much? How did Manton's

and Gage's lies to each other while traveling together contribute to creating this situation? In what ways does the two of them finally telling the truth actually start to unravel the conflict between them and with those around them who have been drawn into their conflict?

17. Manton, Rhonalyn, and Gage are all afraid of helping the infant found on the refuse pile. What are the different reasons for their fears? Has fear ever kept you from trying to help someone? In what ways do Wick's actions change what could have unfolded had he not done what he did?

18. Have you ever wondered like Gage if God really wants you or cares about you? Have you ever thought about the fact that anyone else in Noah's time could have gotten on the ark had they wanted to? God left the door open until the very last moment. 2 Peter 3:9 says, "The Lord is not slack concerning His promise, as some count slackness, but is [patient] toward us, not willing that any should perish but that all should come to repentance." Check out 2 Corinthians 5:14-21, Romans 5:8-21, Romans 6:5-11, and 1 Timothy 2:3-7 to hear more about God's heart toward you and all those He has created.

19. How do you evaluate whether or not someone is trustworthy? Manton makes the comment that he evaluates a person not by what they do or say when they think people are watching, but what they do when they believe they are unobserved.

20. How did what Gage heard and saw of Lord Braxton and his sons while in Verfeld, first convince Gage to risk trusting them, and second convince him to risk helping them? Have

you ever figured out someone might make a good friend when you heard what their enemy had to say about them? Or vice versa, have you heard what a person's friend had to say about them and learned that you may not want to be connected to them?

21. When you learned who was behind the Unavowed, were you surprised? Have you ever been deceived by someone so thoroughly that you believed they were something they were not? Were there telltale signs of their deception that when you look back you can now see? How might the situation have unfolded differently had those signs been noted earlier?

22. Have you ever been afraid that something God was asking you to do might cost you everything? Gage almost flees the encampment rather than risking the possible consequences of seeking out and trying to help the others. In the end, Gage chooses to obey the One who knows the future, who holds his future, and who has dominion over all things. Are you choosing your own path or are you obeying the One who knows the best way forward?

23. Have you ever, like Baron Hewitt, chosen to not stand against someone because you felt like it was a safer choice for you and others? Did you consider other options? What did Hewitt's decision cost him and his men? What if Hewitt had gone to Edelmar to seek help? How many lives might have been saved?

24. Are there ways you have compromised on what you know is right because of something in your own life that you are afraid to deal with or because of someone you are afraid to

stand against? Have you prayed for God's help? Have you in faith taken the first steps to do what is right? God tends to reveal His provision once we're on the path He has asked us to walk.

25. What would you say are some of Gage's biggest heroic moments? Often we think of a heroic person as someone who rises up in some big moment and saves people, but sometimes the most heroic acts we do and the most significant decisions we make happen in moments inside us that no one else besides God will ever see.

"God has not given us a spirit of fear, but of power and of love and of a sound mind." 2 Timothy 1:7

Acknowledgments

THIS BOOK EXISTS only by God's will and grace. Years ago God put this story in my heart, and I embraced it, having no idea the perseverance it would take to write it. I have wished thousands of times, especially over the last three years, that I could give up and walk away, but always God has asked me to stay the course and keep writing. I have found myself with Gage struggling to choose to walk God's paths.

Writing this book was a mission of obedience that involved far more suffering than joy. Prayers and tears are woven into every part of this story, and many of the hardest sections to write were the parts that talked about God. Every time I had to make a decision about what to include or how to include it, I questioned and debated, not sure how to proceed with this or that topic, and each time God would reveal the way and then confirm it.

Even then, though, there were rounds and rounds still of editing needed to align the concepts throughout this story. Each time I worked through the book, God would bring to light new layers that needed solving. His hand of clear guidance was a steadying reassurance, and His consistent provision a challenge to my doubts, while His faithfulness and confirmation reminded me again and again that He had a purpose for this book.

I pray that He will use all He created in this story for His glory, and I am so abundantly thankful for who He is. He allowed me to partner with Him to create this story, and He has provided me so many amazing people who have supported me in so many ways as I worked on this book.

The foremost being my mother. Mom, I never would have been able to write this book without your generous and selfless support. You have been there for me in so many ways that there is no way I could list them all. I am so grateful for your voice of truth, encouragement, challenge, faith, compassion, endurance, and sanity as I have navigated this project. You have patiently endured my crazy ups and downs and sacrificed of your own time to listened as I talked for hours about plot issues and character troubles, letting me cry on your shoulder when it all felt like too much, processing with me everything from theological questions to website issues and speaking fears, cheering me on when I felt like quitting, trekking with me on so many of my author adventures, and editing and proofreading more random documents than any daughter has a right to ask of her mother. From the depths of my heart, thank you!

Rachael, my faithful friend and fellow writer, your prayers and faithful support have meant so much. You have walked with me through so many of my frustrations and fears involving this project and continually pointed me to Christ. Our lives are so very different and yet God has given us such sweet fellowship. I know our lengthy theological discussions and late night conversations have impacted this book, and I know that watching your obedience to God has encourage me to stay faithful and has made its way into this story.

Kate, my wonderful friend and inspirer, you have never ceased to encourage me in my writing and in my faith. Our deep worldview conversations over the years are a joy and challenge that have very much influenced my writing. You were with me at homeschool conferences years ago as I watched authors selling their books and I dreamed of doing what they were doing. And now years later, I am selling my books and you and I have gotten to present as co-speakers at conferences.

Meagan, my fellow Craftsman and INFJ friend, more than once you have helped me see this project from a different perspective and have inspired new pieces of this story. Thank you for letting me both celebrate and vent about my writing journey and for letting me be part of your writing journey.

Colton and Matthew, my incredible alpha readers, I cannot even begin to express how grateful I am for the two of you. I so desperately needed help, and you guys graciously endured reading a very rough draft of this story and spent the time to help me sort through what was and wasn't working and to give me your feedback. Your suggestions and comments were invaluable and made this story so much better. The two of you are the reason five-year-old Allard showed up to push Gage off his stump, and I'm so very grateful because that's now one of my favorite images of Allard.

Kevin, my editor, thank you for putting my commas and clauses in the right places.

Tara Mayberry from TeaBerry Creative, my interior designer, thank you for making this book's interior flow and look so professional.

Elena, my cover designer, thank you so much for your wonderful work bringing to life this book's cover. It has made such a huge difference getting to work with someone who wants to match my vision for the design.

Eileen, Betty, Pat, Kate, and Bri, my wonderful proofreaders, thank you for painstakingly working through this story and helping clean up this book. Your keen eyes and wordsmith skills are so very much appreciated. (The word that wins the most surprising spelling error caught in this manuscript is "chard." It is now correctly spelled "charred" like burnt wood, not chard like the plant.)

BriAnn, my audiobook narrator, thank you for all the work you have already done working on the audio version of this manuscript.

My siblings and all my friends who supported me, prayed for me, kept me sane, etc. during this writing project, thank you so much. You all have been a blessing to me, and I am so grateful for all of you.

C.J. Milacci, for all the questions you answered about Kickstarter, and Jeremiah Friedli, for the information you provided about Kickstarter, thank you both.

To all my Kickstarter backers, who helped get this project over the finish line, thank you. I could not have gotten here without all of you. Your support in pledges and presence on the Kickstarter was a huge blessing. Jessica Greyson, Annette Carpenter, Rachael Lofgren, Amy Russell, Russell Sprouts, Teagan and Laura Kime, The Lambert Family, Melanie Lehman, Bailey Chudek, Gabriel, Gerald Huebner, Kayla Chudek, Clementine Dagley, Mike Lehman, Trish, Zach Burnham, Jeremiah Friedli, Tim Tori VickiMiller Tilton, Emeri Wolff, Meagan Briggs, Aspen, Kristina, Katie Briggs, Matthew Medema, Asa Finkenbinder, Amy Ullrich, Jael, Heidi, Liberty Durmaz, Lydia Lobb, Priscilla Krahn, Ariel, Katrina, Glenn Mathot, Katrina, Lightraiders, Scott Vondrasek, Joy, Jayna Baas, Jessahlyn Bellovich, Schumacher Family, Artherholt Family, J.A. Webb, Janelle Trillo, Lee Anne Womack, Marina Carlton, Marcy, Kayleen, Nadiya A.J.A, Laurie Christine, Raymond Keith, Terry Adams, Hannah, and Lydia.

Thank you so much to all of you for being part of making this book a reality!

Books by Given Hoffman

Contemporary Suspense
The Eighth Ransom

Medieval Action/Adventure
The Tournament's Price
The Rebel's Mark
The Healer's Secret
The King's Orders

Nonfiction
The Voices of the Pioneers: Homeschooling in Minnesota

Visit GivenHoffman.com to learn more.